THE OBSESSIONS OF LORD GODFREY CAVANAUGH

STEPHANIE LAURENS

ABOUT THE OBSESSIONS OF LORD GODFREY CAVANAUGH

#1 New York Times *bestselling author Stephanie Laurens concludes the tales of the Cavanaugh siblings with the riveting story of the youngest brother and his search for a family of his own.*

The scion of a noble house who is caught in a storm and the lady who nurses him back to health strive to unravel a web of deception that threatens her family and ensnares them both, forcing them to fight for what they hold most dear—family, each other, and love.

Lord Godfrey Cavanaugh has no thoughts of marrying as he drives into North Yorkshire on a plum commission for the National Gallery to authenticate a Renaissance painting the gallery wishes to purchase. Then a snow storm sweeps in, and Godfrey barely manages to haul himself, his groom, and his horses to their destination.

Elinor Hinckley, eldest daughter of Hinckley Hall, stalwart defender of the family, right arm to her invalid father, and established spinster knows full well how much her family has riding on the sale of the painting and throws herself into nursing the initially delirious gentleman who holds her family's future in his hands.

But Godfrey proves to be a far from easy patient. Through Ellie's and her siblings' efforts to keep him entertained and abed, Godfrey grows to know the family, seeing and ultimately being drawn into family life of a sort he's never known.

Eventually, to everyone's relief, he recovers sufficiently to assess the painting—only to discover that nothing, but nothing, is as it seems.

Someone has plans, someone other than the Hinckleys, but who is pulling the strings is a mystery that Godfrey and Ellie find near-impossible to solve. Every suspect proves to have perfectly understandable, albeit concealed reasons for their behavior, and Godfrey and Ellie remain baffled.

Until the villain, panicked by their inquiries, strikes—directly at their hearts—and forces each of them to acknowledge what has grown to be the most important thing in their lives. Both are warriors, neither will give up—together they fight to save not just themselves, not just her family, but their futures. Hers, his, and theirs.

A classical historical romance set in North Yorkshire. Fourth novel in The Cavanaughs—a full-length historical romance of 90,000 words.

OTHER TITLES BY STEPHANIE LAURENS

Mastered by Love

Black Cobra Quartet
The Untamed Bride
The Elusive Bride
The Brazen Bride
The Reckless Bride

The Adventurers Quartet
The Lady's Command
A Buccaneer at Heart
The Daredevil Snared
Lord of the Privateers

The Cavanaughs
The Designs of Lord Randolph Cavanaugh
The Pursuits of Lord Kit Cavanaugh
The Beguilement of Lady Eustacia Cavanaugh
The Obsessions of Lord Godfrey Cavanaugh

Other Novels
The Lady Risks All
The Legend of Nimway Hall – 1750: Jacqueline

Medieval (As M.S.Laurens)
Desire's Prize

Novellas
Melting Ice – from the anthologies *Rough Around the Edges* and *Scandalous Brides*
Rose in Bloom – from the anthology *Scottish Brides*
Scandalous Lord Dere – from the anthology *Secrets of a Perfect Night*
Lost and Found – from the anthology *Hero, Come Back*
The Fall of Rogue Gerrard – from the anthology *It Happened One Night*
The Seduction of Sebastian Trantor – from the anthology *It Happened One*

Season

THE OBSESSIONS OF LORD GODFREY CAVANAUGH

THE OBSESSIONS OF LORD GODFREY CAVANAUGH

Copyright © 2020 by Savdek Management Proprietary Limited

ISBN: 978-1-925559-25-5

Cover design by Savdek Management Pty. Ltd.

Cover couple photography and photographic composition by Period Images © 2020

First print publication: July, 2020

Savdek Management Proprietary Limited, Melbourne, Australia.

www.stephanielaurens.com

Email: admin@stephanielaurens.com

The name Stephanie Laurens and the SL Logo are registered trademarks of Savdek Management Proprietary Ltd.

❀ Created with Vellum

CHAPTER 1

JANUARY 16, 1850. ON THE ROAD WEST OF RIPON, NORTH YORKSHIRE

*L*ord Godfrey Cavanaugh flicked his whip at his leader's ear, encouraging his matched bays to increase their pace. The road ahead was straight and adequately surfaced, while the wind strafing him and Wally, his groom, was howling like a banshee. Winter in North Yorkshire; he'd been warned it would be arctic, and the blast slicing through his greatcoat and worming icy fingers past the scarf around his neck was the definition of frigid. As they bowled west, deeper into the countryside, and the chill intensified, he was rethinking his decision not to halt at the Unicorn Hotel, which they'd passed on their way through Ripon's Market Square, but it was only midafternoon, and his hosts were expecting him.

Their directions replayed in his head. Apparently, if he followed this road, then about a mile and a half out of Ripon, he should come upon a lane on the right, signposted to Galphay. He scanned the line of hedgerows ahead and was pleased to see an opening on the right, with a weathered signpost pointing that way.

"Won't be long, now." He slowed his horses.

The signpost was, indeed, for Galphay. With relief, he turned his pair and set them briskly trotting. To either side, the fields, clutched tight in winter's grip, lay brown and sere. The land stretched close to flat in all directions, the monotony broken by low hedges and occasional stands of trees, all presently bare, their skeletal branches rattling in the wind.

Raising his voice to be heard over the din, he called, "We've around two miles to go. We should see the drive on the right, before we come to the River Laver. If we reach the river, we'll have gone too far."

Perched behind Godfrey, Wally grunted.

Godfrey grinned. He and Wally went back a long way. Throughout his childhood, Godfrey had done his best to avoid his parents' notice; with two older brothers, an older sister, and an even older half brother, he hadn't found it difficult to play least in sight and slip away to explore. On such clandestine excursions, Wally—although five years older—had been Godfrey's shadow. An abiding trust and unstated friendship had developed between the young lordling son-of-the-house and the gangling stable boy tasked with keeping said lordling from harm. The connection had survived Godfrey's years of tutors and university so that when it had come time for him to choose a manservant, he hadn't hesitated by so much as a second in installing Wally in the role.

Other lords of the haut ton might prefer gentlemen's gentlemen who could turn them out in sartorial style, but Godfrey preferred to have someone he could trust at his back. As his chosen occupation of authenticating artworks involved significant travel, including on the Continent, having a man who could deal with almost any situation left Godfrey free to concentrate on his passion—the art.

He'd grown up running along corridors lined with paintings by various masters. At some point, he'd halted and looked, and a flash of insight into the construction of the painting—the brush strokes, the canvas, the paints, and more—had piqued his interest. Subsequently, he'd started examining all the paintings and sculptures he came upon; given his birth and social connections, their number had been legion. Once he'd come of age, he'd gone traveling on the Continent, looking and studying and learning.

He'd stumbled on his first forged sculpture in Florence. Months later, he'd exposed a fraudulent Da Vinci sketch the Conte de Milan had been about to buy for a considerable sum.

The art world wasn't that large, and word had got around. Subsequently, others—collectors and museum curators alike—had invited Godfrey to pass judgment on this acquisition or that.

Over time, his reputation had grown.

A month ago, he'd been contacted by the recently knighted Sir Charles Eastlake, president of the Birmingham Society of Artists, newly elected president of the Royal Academy, and erstwhile Keeper of the Paintings and longtime advisor to the National Gallery.

To Godfrey, Eastlake was something of a legend, a man whose status Godfrey aspired to and whose goodwill he knew he would be wise to court—indeed, it would not be overstating the case to say he craved it. Earning Eastlake's imprimatur would be a milestone in Godfrey's life. On behalf of the National Gallery, Eastlake had commissioned Godfrey to examine the painting a Mr. Hinckley of Hinckley Hall, North Yorkshire, had offered to sell to the gallery. The painting was purportedly by Mariotto Albertinelli, a master painter of the High Renaissance, the period of artworks on which the gallery focused.

Eastlake and the gallery directors were eager to finalize the acquisition before the end of February; Godfrey assumed they hoped to include the painting as a drawcard in their spring exhibition. Consequently, he'd set out to brave the gauntlet of Yorkshire in the height of winter. He'd debated driving his curricle north from London or taking the train to York and hiring a conveyance there. After consulting with Wally, he'd elected to drive; they'd made decent time along the Great North Road, halting at Stilton the first night and spending the second at Doncaster before setting out early this morning and traveling through Boroughbridge to Ripon and out along the lanes toward Hinckley Hall.

Although the skies had been overcast throughout the journey, the clouds hadn't thickened to ominous until the turnoff to York.

A vicious gust of wind caused the bays to skitter; Godfrey steadied them, then urged them on with a flick of the reins.

"Guv, I really don't like the looks of them clouds."

Godfrey raised his gaze to the gray and cloudy but otherwise unthreatening horizon. He frowned. "Which clouds?"

"The ones racing up behind us."

"What?" Swiveling on the seat, Godfrey looked back—at the roiling mass of charcoal gray swallowing the sky and bearing down on them. He knew the worst storms in the area came from the east, racing in off the North Sea. "Damn!" He faced forward, but given the uncertain surface of the minor lane, the horses were going as fast as he dared run them. Having one break a leg wouldn't help. "We'll just have to hope we make it in time."

A minute later, Wally said, "There's snow, and the storm's bowling straight for us."

Second by second, the light dimmed, fading to a portentous gloom. Godfrey felt the curricle shift as Wally resettled his scarf and coat, no doubt hauling the collar high and buttoning it all the way up.

"Here." Wally reached over, mittened hands gesturing. "Gimme the reins and get yourself buttoned up. There's no escaping it."

Grim-faced, Godfrey complied. As he buttoned the collar of his greatcoat, the first snowflakes whirled about them.

Ten seconds later, the blizzard struck in full force.

Within two minutes, the road ahead was blanketed in white, and the surrounding fields had vanished behind a veil of driven flakes. The air turned freezing, sharp and biting against any exposed skin, while the wind raged, gusting and roaring; it wasn't hard to imagine the storm as a ravening wolf that saw them as its prey.

Squinting ahead, Godfrey held his team steady, but despite his best efforts, the horses shook their heads, then hung them and slowed.

Wally leaned forward and shouted over the unholy din, "We'll have to get down and lead them. Should we turn back?"

Lips setting, Godfrey let the horses slow to a trudging walk while he calculated, then yelled in reply, "We're closer to our destination than to Ripon, and we haven't passed any inns or even a farmhouse along the way. Safe haven will be closer and more certain if we forge on."

Features pinched, Wally nodded. He leapt down from his perch and strode to grip the leader's harness and urge the beast on.

Godfrey stepped down on the other side of the curricle and went to the other horse's head. With him and Wally out of the carriage, it was much lighter, and between them, they persuaded the horses to come up to a brisk walk.

He'd never known snow to fall so quickly; they'd barely gone a hundred yards before the curricle's wheels started to catch, drag, and slide. Minutes later, the horses were having to lift each hoof free. Soon, Godfrey and Wally had to exert themselves to gain each forward step as well.

Heads down, they plowed on, engulfed in white and cold.

Time ceased to have meaning. Rationally, Godfrey knew they had to be nearing Hinckley Hall, but with the landscape transformed into a haze of white, he could only pray that he spotted the opening to the drive. At the rate the storm was dumping snow, the drive itself might be blocked. Worse, if the house was any distance from the road, unless they had lights blazing in every window, he would never see it.

"Oomph!"

Godfrey's ears only just caught the sound, which emanated from the other side of the horses. He raised his head and peered through the hazy gloom. He couldn't see Wally.

He halted the horses. Calming them, he rounded their heads and saw Wally lying facedown in the snow. Godfrey rushed to Wally's side as he groaned and tried to push upright.

Gripping Wally's arm, Godfrey helped the heavier man to his knees, then hauled him to his feet.

Wally staggered and ineffectually wiped snow from his chin. "Sorry, guv. Didn't see the hole under the snow."

"Are you all right?" Godfrey glanced at Wally's feet.

Wally took a step, and his ankle buckled. "Bugger—I've wrenched it."

Godfrey quashed his rising alarm. "Here." He looped one arm in one of Wally's and reached for the leader's bridle with his free hand. "Come on. Use me as a crutch." *We have to keep moving.* He bit the words back; neither he nor Wally needed reminding.

Getting the horses walking again took a degree of persuasion, and even then, the beasts would only consent to plod along. Not that it mattered; with Wally's gait hitching with every step, it was all he and Godfrey could do to keep up.

About them, the storm showed no sign of abating. Godfrey tried not to dwell on the stories he'd heard of storms in these parts that raged for days.

Heads down, he and Wally struggled along beside the horses, each step a battle against the thickening snow, the howling wind, and the ever-deepening cold. Picking out the lane ahead grew even more difficult as the hedges disappeared beneath drifts of disorientating white.

With frigid air sawing in and out of his lungs and Wally an increasingly heavy burden dragging on his arm, Godfrey had reached the point of wondering if they would ever reach safety—rather detachedly imagining news reports of a marquess's brother being found frozen to death beside a lane in North Yorkshire—when an odd shape standing on the bank on the other side of the road caught his eye. He halted and muscled Wally around so that the groom was leaning against the nearer horse. "Wait there."

Ducking against the wind, Godfrey rounded the horses and staggered and scrambled up the short bank to what looked to be some sort of sign. Using his greatcoat sleeve, already crusted with frozen snow, he brushed clear the face of the board mounted between two uprights—enough to read "Hinckley Hall."

They'd made it. Or at least, Godfrey amended, as he squinted up what he took to be the drive and saw no sign of any house, they'd reached the mouth of the drive.

He clambered and slid down, his boots sinking into snow nearly a foot deep. He trudged across and a few yards along what he thought must be the drive, confirming there was a solid surface beneath the snow.

The certainty gave him the energy to hurry back to Wally and the horses.

He found Wally almost unconscious, slumped against the leader's side.

"Come on! Almost there." Although Godfrey was taller than his henchman by several inches, Wally had always been significantly heavier. It took considerable effort for Godfrey to haul Wally up and around and get him and the horses moving again. They managed the turn into the drive in a shuffle, then Godfrey leaned forward and urged both horses and Wally on.

They'd gone only a few yards when the curtain of falling snow behind them parted, and a horseman as limned in snow and ice as they loomed out of the white.

Greatcoated and booted as was Godfrey, the man saw them, drew rein, and swung down from the saddle. Leading his horse, he hurried to Godfrey and Wally and, without being asked, lent Wally his shoulder, easing the drag on Godfrey. "Terrible storm," the man offered in greeting.

Godfrey managed a nod, then peeled apart his frozen lips to say, "We're making for Hinckley Hall." He tipped his head toward where he thought the drive went. "I saw the sign by the road, and I'm hoping we're on the right track."

"You are." The man joined Godfrey in steering Wally and the horses and curricle up the drive. "I'm heading for the Hall myself."

The man's horse was trotting along eagerly. The man nodded at the beast. "He knows where he's going and that it'll be warm and dry there."

Thankfully, Godfrey's pair appeared to take their cue from the newcomer and lifted their feet with greater enthusiasm.

Their expanded company forged on.

More or less following the lead of the man's mount, they rounded a bend. Godfrey raised his head and squinted through the if-anything-thickening wind-whipped snow. Through the bare branches of intervening trees, he saw a light glimmering a hundred or so yards ahead.

"That's it." The man nodded toward the light. "All we have to do is make it that far, but we'll need to stick to the drive."

Godfrey made no reply. The icy cold had seeped through his clothes and was sinking through his skin all the way to his bones. As he drew in a harsh and labored breath, that last one hundred yards might as well have been a mile.

~

Standing at Hinckley Hall's drawing room bow window, Eleanor Hinckley narrowed her eyes in an effort to pierce the impenetrable white screen obscuring the drive. Midafternoon, and the light had all but gone. Unable to make out anything at all, she sighed and reluctantly drew the curtain over the icy pane.

Swallowing her disappointment, Ellie faced the three older gentlemen gathered about the drawing room fireplace. "The blizzard's set in. Mr. Cavanaugh must have stopped in Ripon."

Her father, Matthew Hinckley, nodded in resignation. "Aye. Not a day for man or beast to be out braving that tempest."

Seated to the left of her father's bath chair, Walter Pyne grimaced. "Pity. I would have liked to make the fellow's acquaintance. I'm curious to see what this business of being an authenticator is all about."

"Aye, but," Edward Morris, seated on her father's other side, observed, "what with us likely stuck here now, courtesy of the storm, if the fellow rides from Ripon as soon as the thaw sets in, likely we'll still be here when he arrives."

Pyne arched his brows. "That's true."

Ellie bit her tongue on the information that Mr. Cavanaugh had written that he would bring a manservant. A London toff with a gentleman's gentleman would be more likely to sit snug at the Unicorn in Ripon and wait for the roads to clear sufficiently so he could drive or be driven to the Hall.

Pyne and Morris were her father's oldest friends and, as usual, had arrived midmorning to take Wednesday luncheon with her father and the family; given her father could no longer walk beyond a few steps and didn't venture out beyond attending church on Sundays, it was kind of both men to so indefatigably turn up every Wednesday to spend the day with him.

Her father fixed her with a sapient eye. "How deep's the snow?"

"Too deep for a carriage." Ellie glanced back at the curtained window. "I doubt even a rider would make much headway out there now."

"That means"—her father looked at his friends—"that, indeed, you'll need to stay on until it clears. You both know you're very welcome."

Pyne and Morris murmured their thanks and acceptances of the offer. Like her father, both were locals born and bred and suffered the inconveniences of winter storms with the stoic resignation of those who have long ago learned the futility of railing against Nature's unpredictable furies.

All three men looked at Ellie, and she summoned a smile. "I'll let Kemp and Mrs. Kemp know, but I'm sure they'll have already made arrangements." Both butler and housekeeper had served the family for most of Ellie's twenty-eight years; she felt sure Mrs. Kemp would already have sent the maids upstairs to prepare the rooms Pyne and Morris habitually used when they remained overnight at the Hall.

As the three men returned to their conversation, Ellie cynically observed that neither Pyne nor Morris were reluctant to stay, nor did they show any sign of concern over being trapped by the storm. Pyne's wife was widely recognized as an unmitigated shrew, and he tended to seize any excuse to absent himself from his own hearth, while Morris was a widower of many years, and his home, Malton Farm, was a cold, lonely, stone mausoleum presided over by a crotchety housekeeper who believed in frugality above all else.

Neither man would regard a forced sojourn at the Hall as a hardship, and with the roads almost certainly blocked throughout the area, there would be no activity on Morris's farm or at Pyne's business in Ripon. Better for both men to be trapped at the Hall than under their own roofs.

For her part, Ellie viewed the prospect of having Pyne and Morris as houseguests for at least the next few days with equanimity. They would chat with her father and keep him entertained, and that would be a blessing.

She glanced at the curtained window; even through the Hall's thick walls, she could hear the wind lashing and howling outside. The possibility loomed of the snow delaying Cavanaugh's arrival for weeks, but after a second considering the notion, she resolutely pushed it aside; there was no telling how bad the impact of a storm such as the one raging outside might be. As her mother used to say, there was no sense in borrowing trouble.

She returned her attention to the men to discover all three looking her way.

"I just hope this storm doesn't chase the blighter all the way back to London," Pyne remarked.

Don't even suggest it. "According to Mr. Cavanaugh's expectations, he should have reached Ripon before the storm, and they'll have been hit as hard as us here and rather earlier—no real wonder if he took shelter there. Regardless"—she reminded herself as well as her listeners—"he'll have to wait for the thaw before he can go anywhere, and given he's acting for the National Gallery, I can't see any reason he would retreat rather than come on."

Her father dipped his head in agreement. "True, but the delay will set the sale back by several weeks, if not a month or more."

Ellie pressed her lips tight. Despite fully supporting her father's decision to sell the painting that had been her late mother's favorite to the gallery, she hated discussing the reason for the sale, especially before his friends.

Pyne cleared his throat. "If you need any assistance—just to bridge the gap, you know—I'm sure I could help to some degree."

"I might not be able to manage much," Morris gruffly said, "but I'd consider it an honor to help as much as I can."

Her father's expression cleared, and he gently waved aside the comments. "No, no—thank you, my friends, but it's not a case of needing the money, at least not so desperately." Her father met Ellie's eyes, a soft, rather sad smile in his. "It's more a case of having screwed up my resolution over selling that painting to the sticking point—having to wait, possibly for weeks, for this authentication to take place before any sale can go forward is...not a prospect I relish."

Ellie returned her father's smile with a sad yet understanding smile of her own; she felt much the same way. But regardless of their attachment to the painting, the Albertinelli had to be sold, and for as much as possible, to provide the funds of which the Hall and the estate were so sorely in need.

By exercising due care, they would have enough to last them through the winter and into the first months of spring, but after that, the Hinckley coffers would be empty. She and her father had assumed any sale to the National Gallery would take months to finalize, but an additional delay such as the one now facing them might see them skating close to the wind.

Determined not to dwell on what was beyond her control, she found a smile and swept it over the men. "I'll go and speak with the Kemps." She turned to the door, just as the muted thunder of footsteps rushing down the main stairs reached her.

She inwardly braced. *What now?*

The drawing room door burst open, revealing Ellie's younger sister, Maggie, dancing with excitement. Before Ellie could ask, Maggie blurted, "There's horses and a carriage and I think three men coming up the drive. They're nearly here!"

"Good Lord!" Ellie rushed for the door, swamped by sympathy for anyone caught out in the storm. She hurried into the front hall. "Kemp?"

"Here, miss." The redoubtable butler was swiftly lighting several lamps and had already summoned the two footmen to assist. "Just let me get the lamps going before we open the door."

The thud of boots on the stairs heralded Ellie's brother, Harry. "What's afoot?"

"Strangers coming up the drive, seeking shelter." Ellie joined Maggie in peering out of the narrow window alongside the front door. Through the unnatural darkness that had closed in, she searched what she could see of the drive.

"There!" Maggie pointed to the left. "See that lump? It's moving."

Staggering and barely that. Ellie finally realized what she was looking at. "There are horses—a pair in harness and a single mount. Get the grooms as well." She squinted through the whirling snow. "And Johnson—there's a carriage that's too fine to be left outside."

It was the carriage that confirmed the thought that, despite all incredulity, had popped into her head. "My God—it's Cavanaugh!"

He'd come and had fought his way through the snow.

"Really?" Harry was incredulous—as incredulous as Ellie. "It's been storming fit to freeze Hades for nearly an hour."

"Exactly." Ellie rushed to the heavy door, lifted the latch, and hauled the door open. Wind rushed in, gleefully swirling snowflakes across the threshold. Kemp and the footmen came to stand at her back; the flames in the lanterns they held aloft wavered, then steadied, casting a semicircle of light over the narrow porch and across the forecourt.

Three figures, all in heavy coats, heads ducked against the storm's fury, weaved drunkenly into the light. All three clung together, as if supporting each other in their Herculean struggle to take another step.

One man held the reins of a pair of carriage horses, instantly recognizable as superior beasts even in the poor light. Ellie didn't recognize that man or the heavier man in the middle of the trio, but her eyes widened as she scanned the third man—the one leading a saddled horse. "It's Masterton."

The sound of more running footsteps reached her, and she whirled. "Here—give me that." She took the lantern from the nearest footman, Henry. "Harry, take Mike's. You two"—she pointed at the footmen—"get those men inside."

Mike and Henry turned up their collars and hurried out and down the steps, making for the weaving figures.

"Tommy and Hugh." Ellie waved the grooms forward. "Take the horses to the stable and see them cared for. Billy and James—ah, here's Johnson." She grabbed the stableman by the sleeve and dragged him past Kemp and Harry to the threshold. She pointed into the night. "That carriage needs to be out of the snow."

Johnson squinted, then nodded. "You're right about that." He glanced at the two stable lads, who had fallen in at his heels. "Come along, you two—Tommy and Hugh can lead the nags, but we'd best push the carriage, or they'll all freeze before they reach the stable."

The comment wasn't that much of an exaggeration. With the onset of darkness, the temperature was plummeting. Ice already liberally coated all three visitors.

If left to themselves, the three would never have made it up the shallow steps to the porch, but Henry and Mike were burly sorts; the pair insinuated themselves between the three men and all but rushed them onto the porch and inside.

Ellie checked that Johnson and his helpers had the horses and carriage in hand, then nodded to Kemp, and he swung the heavy door closed; he had to throw his weight against the panel to overcome the still-howling wind.

Mrs. Kemp and two of the maids came running, bearing blankets. "Cook is preparing some hot possets," Mrs. Kemp reported, then tutted at the sight of the three men drooping and dripping on the hall tiles.

Masterton staggered back a step and slumped against the front door. He coughed and managed to lift his head. Eyes closed, he grated, "We made it, thank God."

"What were you doing out in that?" Ellie asked. Masterton was a local or, at least, local enough to have known better.

He waved weakly. "I had a meeting earlier at Kirkby Malzeard. I was riding back to Ripon when the storm swept in." His gaze cut to the other two men, who were leaning against each other, barely managing to keep themselves upright. "I spotted them turning in to the drive. By their state, they'd been caught in the storm far longer than I. I assumed they'd come from Ripon, and I remembered Matthew was expecting that authenticator from London." Masterton raised a frosty brow. "Given the carriage and horses, it seems likely the gentleman is he."

The word "gentleman" appeared to register with the taller of the unknown pair. He drew in a shuddering breath, slowly raised his head, and bracing the other man—shorter and of heavier build—with one hand, endeavored to straighten to his full height.

Henry stepped in to help support the shorter man, who was wearing the sort of heavy coat favored by coachmen.

Relieved of that task, the gentleman—and despite the ice coating his dark hair and clinging to his chin, eyebrows, and lashes, the chiseled planes of his face and the way, even under such strain, he held himself left no doubt whatever of his station—glanced briefly about, then his gaze settled on Ellie.

Godfrey fought to straighten his limbs and attain an acceptable posture, but his wits weren't cooperating, and his senses seemed not to be anchored to his body. While he was grateful to be out of the hellish cold, the sudden warmth had him reeling, oddly disconnected from himself. On top of that, every muscle seemed stiff and unresponsive, and his vision wasn't all that clear. But he knew what good manners demanded. Focusing, however hazily, on the woman he assumed was the mistress of the house, he attempted a winning smile. "From the bottom of my heart, I thank you for your rescue, ma'am."

Long-ingrained habit had him sweeping her an elegant bow.

A mistake. He felt his senses tip, then slide away as oblivion opened her arms and embraced him.

Aghast, Ellie stared at the man she'd mentally viewed as her family's knight on a white charger—the bringer of hope for their future—as he crumpled to the wet tiles in a greatcoated heap at her feet.

For a second, shock held her immobile, then she crouched and brushed back the fall of dark hair that obscured his eyes; he didn't react.

"He's unconscious." *That can't be good.* She glanced at Mrs. Kemp. "Is the best guest bedroom ready?"

"Yes, miss." Mrs. Kemp turned toward the kitchen. "I'll set the girls to filling hot-water bottles and preparing a bed-warmer."

"Please." Ellie looked at Kemp and Harry. "We need to get him upstairs and warm as quickly as we can." She glanced at Henry, still supporting the second man—presumably Cavanaugh's manservant—who, while still conscious, looked dazed and barely aware.

"I'll take this one up and see to him, miss," Henry volunteered.

She nodded, rose, and waved for Kemp and Harry to pick up the fallen man.

They heaved him up between them, then staggered toward the stairs. She started to follow, then remembered Masterton. She swung around, but with a faint smile, her father's cousin waved her on. "I'll manage. You should see to him."

She didn't always agree with Masterton, but with that, she had no argument. With a nod of acknowledgment, she turned and, lifting her skirts, hurried up the stairs.

CHAPTER 2

*G*odfrey opened his eyes and realized he was dreaming. A golden-haired angel—a glorious figment of his imagination—hovered over him, concern, curiosity, and interest lighting her woodland eyes as they slowly traced his features. Her heart-shaped face had been sculpted by a master, with a wide forehead, high cheekbones, straight nose, and tapered chin, and her coloring—porcelain complexion, blush-tinted lips, delicately arched brown brows, and long brown lashes—accentuated the divine vision.

He was reminded of a Botticelli angel; no doubt that was from where his ever-ready imagination had drawn its inspiration.

Her eyes rose and met his, and he smiled and allowed himself to fall into the green, hazel, and gold-flecked depths.

She blinked and tilted her head, as if uncertain whether to speak.

Did angels speak to mere mortals? Could they?

Smiling his most charming and reassuring smile, he raised one hand and, oh-so-delicately, ran the pads of his fingertips admiringly down the curve of her face, from temple to chin. He felt her startle and, turning his hand to slide his fingers beneath her chin, murmured, "You're beautiful. Utterly perfect. I must have glimpsed you—or parts of you—countless times over the years, but I've never seen your features in toto before."

His gaze sharpened as his critical faculties swam to the fore, and his attention fastened on her lips. Using the leverage of his fingers beneath her chin, he drew her closer, and she leaned nearer, allowing him to examine the absolute perfection of the lines of her lips. "Flawless." He shifted his hand to cruise his thumb over the plump swell of her lower lip. "Almost," he breathed, "beyond my imagination."

Because this was a dream and it seemed churlish not to pay due homage to a manifestation of such utter perfection, he raised his head and, lowering his lids, touched his lips to hers in a kiss of devotion—an appropriate tithe to such exquisite beauty.

Her lips were warm and soft under his—another level of perfection. Unable to resist, he explored the contours, lush and full and so very enticing.

She didn't respond, but he hadn't expected her to; she was only a figment of his rambling mind, after all.

Satisfied with the outcome of the dream, eyes now closed, he drew back from the kiss. He let his hand fall to the bed and, still smiling, allowed the waiting arms of Morpheus to envelop him again.

Ellie stepped back from the bed and stared at the sleeping man. Her heart was tripping, and she felt a blush steal into her cheeks. Instinctively, she raised her fingers to her lips, following the path he'd traced, feeling the tingling that still lingered in the wake of that wholly unexpected kiss.

"He was asleep," she muttered. Speaking and flattering and kissing, yet nevertheless asleep.

She stood and stared at him and replayed his words. "He thought I was a figment of his imagination."

And he thought I was perfect. Her heart gave a little kick.

She frowned and stepped away from the bed, then crossed to the washstand and straightened the towels folded on the shelf beneath the bowl. She moved on to the large, lead-paned window, paused to glance out at the skeletal trees, half buried under snow and slowly disappearing into the encroaching gloom of a winter twilight, then briskly drew the curtains closed.

She turned and looked again at the bed—at the long figure stretched out beneath the mounded covers, his dark-auburn hair contrasting starkly with the white linen of the pillows—and her heart, silly thing, thumped again.

Sternly, she told herself she was behaving in an utterly missish way. Yes, Cavanaugh was handsome—in her view, handsomeness personified —but she'd seen handsome men before. Yes, he'd kissed her, but she'd been kissed any number of times before, and had there really been anything special about that barely-there kiss?

He'd thought she was perfect.

Swallowing a humph of self-derision, she crossed to the fireplace and inspected his clothes, which had been hung on a rack before the fire. It was nearly twenty-four hours since he'd collapsed in the front hall, and the recent interlude had been the first time he'd opened his eyes since then.

Concern for him—for his recovery and his health—remained very high in her mind.

She set about shaking out and folding the now-dry clothes. The feel of the fabrics beneath her fingers testified to their quality. The cut of his coat and trousers, let alone the quality of his boots, suggested he was a wealthy man.

She was laying aside his coat when a tap fell on the door, and it opened to admit Mrs. Kemp.

The matronly woman nodded a greeting and bustled to the bed to lay a hand on Cavanaugh's forehead. "Hmm. Still cool, but I'll be surprised if that lasts." The housekeeper straightened and frowned at her patient. "Has he stirred at all?"

"Yes." Ellie approached the other side of the bed. "He spoke— rambled—but slid back to sleep again. I don't think he truly woke."

Mrs. Kemp waggled her head. "Still, that's a good sign. Well, a better sign than him lying there unmoving."

Ellie forced herself to say, "He got very cold—he was almost frozen. Do you think he'll recover?"

Mrs. Kemp screwed up her face. "Seems like he was out in that bliz- zard for an hour or so. And he's not got a lot of fat on him—all long, lean muscle, he is—so not so much protection."

Ellie hadn't been in the room when Kemp, Mike, and Mrs. Kemp had stripped Cavanaugh of his sodden and partially frozen clothes and decently gowned him in one of her father's nightshirts; she tried not to allow Mrs. Kemp's description to raise any picture in her mind.

"But you're right—chilled to the bone, he was." Mrs. Kemp clucked. "I've heard of men who, after less than what he's been through, took to their beds and never rose again."

Her gaze on Cavanaugh's still and silent form, Ellie said, "I don't suppose there's any chance of sending for the doctor?"

Mrs. Kemp shook her head. "Not until the thaw, and with more snow still coming down, Johnson reckons it'll be a week or more this time, before it clears enough for riders to get through."

Johnson, the stableman, was their oldest resident and the most knowledgeable when it came to the local weather. As he spoke from experience and long memory, his pronouncements were rarely wrong.

Ellie frowned at Cavanaugh. "He has to recover." She wouldn't allow herself to imagine any other outcome.

"Well, he's youngish and looks to be in excellent health otherwise, and I daresay he's strong enough." Mrs. Kemp neatened the covers and tucked them in, then straightened and studied her patient. "Once he wakes, we'll get some of my honey balsam on his chest and, depending on how he does, perhaps a mustard plaster or two, and likely he'll be on his feet soon enough."

Ellie sincerely hoped so.

Mrs. Kemp noticed the folded clothes. She bustled across and gathered them up. "I'll get Meg to iron these. Excellent quality, they are. And Johnson and his lads are raving over the gentleman's horses and his carriage as well. High-steppers, the nags, and the curricle bang up to the mark, to hear them tell it."

Ellie studied the sleeping man as her imagined vision of Mr. Godfrey Cavanaugh, artwork authenticator, adjusted yet again; she hadn't expected such a person to be notably wealthy.

A tap on the door was followed by it opening, and Harry stuck his head around the edge. He grinned at Ellie and Mrs. Kemp. "The other man—Cavanaugh's groom—is awake and asking after his master. He's wanting to get up and come and see for himself."

Mrs. Kemp tutted. "Not until I give him leave." She hurried to the door, turning at the last to ask Ellie, "Will you be staying and keeping an eye on the gentleman, miss?"

She nodded. "I'll watch over him."

Harry stood back to let Mrs. Kemp past, then tipped a salute Ellie's way and followed the housekeeper from the room, closing the door behind him. Ellie wasn't surprised that he'd gone; at twenty years old, Harry harbored more interest in grooms and horses and carriages than in their masters.

Left on her own with the sleeping Cavanaugh, Ellie folded her arms and allowed her gaze to rest on his face. With his dark hair and pale skin, dark slanting brows, patrician nose, sharp cheekbones, the long, rather austere lines of his cheeks, his squarish chin, and thin but finely drawn lips, his face called to mind that of the classic fallen angel, but was saved from such cold perfection by the shallow lines bracketing his mouth. She was willing to wager that when he smiled, he would sport distracting dimples.

She scanned his unresponsive features, then watched the rise and fall of the covers over his chest. He was alive. "And at least he's not truly comatose," she muttered.

Seeing him lying there, so still and quiet, and with an insistent intuitive sense that he was normally a vital, active man, Ellie felt—and acknowledged—the guilt that now rode her shoulders.

He'd been on the road to be caught by the storm and reduced to this only because he'd been sent to assess their painting. Him being caught in the storm wasn't their fault, yet it wouldn't have happened if they—she—hadn't written to the gallery and offered to sell the Albertinelli.

Regardless of the family's need of the funds from the sale, their need wasn't worth any man's life. It definitely wasn't worth Cavanaugh's life.

She knew such thoughts weren't entirely logical, yet the incipient guilt, the weight that hovered over her, was real nonetheless.

Cavanaugh had to recover. That was all there was to it.

How long she stood and studied him, she couldn't have said, but a knock on the door preceded it opening cautiously, then Pyne looked in, saw her, and smiled. He opened the door fully and walked in, followed by Morris and Masterton.

"Came to see how the gentleman was doing," Pyne offered.

Morris added, "We thought he might like some company."

Ellie lowered her arms and waved at the bed. "As you can see, he's yet to regain consciousness."

Pyne frowned at the still figure beneath the covers. "He's still out to it? That's odd, isn't it?"

Masterton, who had hung back by the door, blandly observed, "He and his groom caught the worst of it. I ran into the storm not far from here, but they must have battled on for quite some time." He glanced at Ellie. "I heard the groom is awake."

She nodded. "Mrs. Kemp is seeing to him, but I gather he's got his wits about him enough to ask after his master."

"He"—Masterton indicated the sleeping figure with a tip of his head—"was all but carrying the groom when I came upon them. He wouldn't have had much in reserve."

That, Ellie thought, explained his collapse. "Mrs. Kemp believes he'll come around in time."

Morris had approached the bed and had been studying its occupant. "He's not that old, is he? I would have expected the National Gallery to send someone more...well, scholarly. More experienced."

"Hmm." Pyne joined Morris in considering the sleeping man. "One has to wonder how much authority the opinion of a man as youthful as he will carry." He glanced at Masterton. "You saw most of him. How old would you say he is?"

Masterton slid his hands into his trouser pockets. "He's in his early thirties, I would say."

Morris humphed. "Older than I thought, then."

"But still hardly august or impressive in experience." Pyne glanced at Ellie. "Hardly comforting, given how important his opinion on this painting will be to the Hinckleys."

Until then, Ellie had bitten her tongue and resisted the urge to leap to Cavanaugh's defense. "He was the National Gallery's choice. They wouldn't have sent him if they didn't have faith in his assessment. No matter how relatively youthful he might be, the gallery clearly respects his opinion."

Masterton added, "And ultimately, it's the gallery's acceptance of what he says that counts." He nodded at Ellie. "You're right. They chose him, so he must be up to the task."

She dipped her head Masterton's way. He and she didn't always see eye to eye, but he was in his thirties, too, younger than Morris and Pyne, who were contemporaries of her father.

Pyne grunted. "Yes, well." He looked at Ellie. "If you like, I would be happy to sit with him in case he awakes."

Ellie had any number of household tasks begging for her attention, yet... "Thank you, but there's no need at this time." Sensing Pyne's inclination to argue, she added, "Mrs. Kemp believes he might start a fever, so we need to keep a close eye on him for now."

The hint of an unknown, unpredictable, and possibly contagious illness was enough to dissuade Pyne from pressing his case. He and Morris exchanged looks, then with mumbled assurances that they would keep her father company instead, the pair retreated through the door, and after one last look at Cavanaugh's unmoving figure, Masterton followed.

The door clicked shut, and Ellie breathed more freely.

She'd seen the hard, assessing quality in Masterton's gaze. Six months ago, Masterton, a distant cousin on her father's side, had made an offer for her hand, which she'd declined. Firmly and resolutely. Despite that, she got the impression that Masterton was simply biding his time and was intent on renewing his offer. Regardless, offering for her and being refused did not afford Masterton any rights over her—over how she behaved or whose sickbed she tended.

Yet there'd definitely been an element of that sort of thinking in Masterton's last long look.

She knew that Morris and Pyne, with their long-standing friendship with her father, had nothing but her family's best interests at heart, yet they could be meddling and were rather stuffy, and their points of view often ran contrary to hers. As for Masterton...in her view, he kept his own goals, his own reasons for supporting her father in this or that, uppermost in his mind, yet as to exactly what those goals were, she'd never got so much as a hint.

She was glad the three had gone; to her mind, their connections to her family did not afford them any right to stick their noses into the family's business with Cavanaugh.

After another look at the sleeping man, she walked to the fireplace and settled in one of the pair of wing chairs before the hearth. From there, she could keep an eye on Cavanaugh while making inroads into the mending.

She was rehemming one of Harry's shirts when the door opened and Maggie peeked in. Her bright brown eyes scanned the room and found Ellie. Maggie grinned and slipped inside. After closing the door, she pattered across on light feet to claim the other wing chair. Leaning closer to Ellie, Maggie whispered, "How is he?"

Ellie smiled. "Sleeping. Earlier, he stirred and rambled a bit, so I don't think he's unconscious anymore—just asleep."

"Well, that's good, isn't it?" Without waiting for any reply, Maggie forged on, "He's not at all like how we envisioned him, is he? Not old and scholarly with a white beard and a cane, or a fusty old university don puffed up in his own conceit." She glanced at the bed and, after a moment, conceded, "He might be a painter, but he's certainly not an *old* painter."

Muting a grin, Ellie admitted, "No, he's not anywhere near as old as we expected." After a second, she added, "Masterton thinks Mr. Cavanaugh is in his early thirties."

Tipping her head in a birdlike way, Maggie allowed, "That seems about right." She transferred her keen gaze to Ellie. "It was so dramatic, the way he fell in a heap at your feet."

"It was a shock."

"Yes, but he was trying to do the pretty by you, even in extremis as he was."

Ellie glanced up from her stitching and saw that Maggie—eighteen years old yet still a free spirit—had stars in her eyes.

"He's so very handsome, Ellie. And his voice! It's so deep and smooth."

You're beautiful. Ellie heard the words in her head, in that deep, smooth voice, and fought to quell a shiver. She looked back at her needle. "He is very well-spoken."

Maggie all but bounced in her chair. "I can't wait until he wakes up, and we can speak with him and learn what sort of man he is." Maggie caught Ellie's admonishing eye. "Aren't you curious?"

Intensely. "Apparently, his groom is compos mentis, so even if Cavanaugh continues to sleep, his man should be able to tell us more. Enough, at least, to sate our curiosity."

Ellie told herself that given the dearth of personable gentlemen in and around Hinckley Hall, hers and Maggie's rampant curiosity—indeed, the curiosity of the whole household—was understandable. It wouldn't have mattered who had turned up at their door; simply being a personable gentleman would have been enough to spark their interest.

After another minute of gazing longingly at Cavanaugh's still figure —as if willing him to wake up—Maggie wriggled, then rose. "I only stopped by to see if he'd woken. Do you need me to do anything?"

Ellie tied off her thread. "You might check that someone has told Cook that the groom is awake, but the gentleman is still sleeping—just so she knows."

Maggie nodded and headed for the door. "She'll want to know to get her chicken broth ready." She waggled her fingers in a wave, then slipped out of the door.

Ellie remained by the fire, industriously depleting her basket of mending. While her hands were busy, her mind dwelled on Cavanaugh, her hopes centering on him waking soon, at least sufficiently to afford them greater assurance that he would, indeed, recover.

She was already tired of feeling weighed down by irrational guilt.

Admittedly, in light of his most recent utterances, once he recovered

and was on his feet again, managing him might be rather more complicated and, possibly, more fraught than she'd anticipated.

She glanced at the bed, then, lips firming, snipped a thread. "One
hurdle at a time."

~

Godfrey awoke to the sensation of being watched. Cautiously, he raised
his lids and saw Wally, seated in a chair beside the bed, staring fixedly at
his face.

His old friend's eyes lit. "You're awake!"

Godfrey blinked. "So it seems." He glanced around. "How long have
I slept?" His gaze reached the lady standing on the other side of the bed,
and his thoughts promptly scattered.

The angel.

My angel.

She's real?

Memories of his dream—which, on present evidence, might not have
been a dream—tumbled through his head.

"Ah." His gaze remained locked, immovably, on her.

On she who clearly was not a figment of his overstimulated imagination.

She returned his look with a steady gaze. "Hello. I'm Miss Hinckley."

"You have me at a disadvantage, Miss Hinckley. I vaguely recall that,
when we first met, I meant to bow to you, and I regret I appear to be in no
case to rectify my failure."

Her lips tightened as if she was holding back a grin.

Just how bad had his attempted bow been?

He sought refuge in a smile he'd been told was charming and held out
a hand. "Godfrey Cavanaugh, Miss Hinckley. I'm pleased to make your
acquaintance."

Just how pleased, he was careful to keep hidden; courtesy of his
upbringing in his mother's house, he was a past master at concealing his
emotions. But his angel was exactly as he remembered from his dream
that had been no dream, and he couldn't stop his gaze from roving her
face, recataloguing her features.

Under his scrutiny, she hesitated for a second, but then her head rose a
fraction, and she confidently stepped nearer and placed her fingers in his.
"I'm delighted to meet you, sir, and I speak for all at Hinckley Hall in

saying how pleased we are to see you awake and in full possession of your senses."

Was that an allusion to their earlier exchange? Looking into her eyes, Godfrey suspected it was.

Hazel eyes were often difficult to read, but not hers. Her meaning— that she expected him to forget that earlier exchange entirely, to wipe it from his mind—reached him clearly.

He couldn't stop his smile from deepening as he closed his fingers about hers and felt the slender digits flutter, then still within his grasp. The temptation to carry her fingers to his lips surged, but he manfully resisted. Not yet, or she might draw back.

Wally cleared his throat. "As to your question, you've been asleep for over a day. We arrived two days ago, and it's midmorning again."

Reluctantly, Godfrey released Miss Hinckley's hand and turned to his henchman. "The horses?"

"They're fine." Wally nodded at Miss Hinckley. "The people here took good care of them and the curricle, too."

Smoothly, Godfrey returned his gaze to Miss Hinckley. "It appears I'm indebted to the staff here, Miss Hinckley. Please convey my gratitude to all, at least until I can tender my thanks in person."

"Of course." She spread her hands. "But I assure you it is we at the Hall who consider ourselves in your debt, sir. You made the effort to reach us through the blizzard, after all."

Godfrey resumed his charming smile. "I have to admit I'm keen to see your family's painting—the Albertinelli." His mind supplied another memory, and he sobered. "There was another man out in the snow. He helped us get here—without his aid, we might not have made it." He met her eyes. "Is he still here?"

She nodded. "That was Michael Masterton. And yes, he's stranded here as well. The snow's still coming down, and it's already so deep, we're snowed in."

"Oh." Tales of snowstorms in Yorkshire flitted through his brain. "How long is that situation likely to last?"

"In these parts, a week or even more is not unheard of."

"I see." So he was going to have time at Hinckley Hall to get better acquainted with the intriguing Miss Hinckley.

"I had thought to ask," Wally said, "about whether you think we should notify your family, but with being snowed in…"

Godfrey met Wally's eyes and understood what his friend was actually asking: Should he use Godfrey's title or not? "I don't think that's necessary." Godfrey returned his attention to Miss Hinckley. "You said Mr. Masterton is stranded 'as well.' Are there others here?"

"As well as the household and Mr. Masterton, two friends of my father's—Mr. Morris and Mr. Pyne, local gentlemen—had called, and they also will have to remain until the thaw."

So there was no one in the house who would recognize him. Godfrey looked across the room to where his clothes sat stacked on a dresser. "In that case"—he shifted his legs and started to sit up—"I expect I had better get dressed and come downstairs."

"Oh no." Agitation bloomed in Miss Hinckley's fine eyes, and concern invested her expression. "You're already running a fever. It's only slight at this point, but we can't allow you to risk your chill transforming into a fever of the lungs."

The words "fever of the lungs" sent a very real chill through him.

Before he saw the threat, Wally—also exercised—gabbled, "You know you've been susceptible since you were a nipper. You don't want to take the chance of coming down like you used to again."

Godfrey glared. "Wally!"

Before he could take his henchman to task for revealing far too much, Miss Hinckley clasped her hands before her and firmly said, "Mr. Cavanaugh!"

When, lips tight, he glanced her way, she caught his gaze and said, "I would ask you to view this situation from our family's perspective. You came into Yorkshire at our behest—perhaps not directly but ultimately because of our approach to the National Gallery. So you and your man being caught in the snowstorm was essentially because of our need of your services."

Ellie had polished her arguments in preparation for just such a clash. Keeping her gaze level and locked with Cavanaugh's and doing her utmost not to notice the temper glinting in the distracting gold flecks in his hawklike brown eyes, she continued, "As such, the last thing the family wish is for your evaluation of our painting to be affected or in any way influenced by illness. That would definitely not be in the family's best interests."

He blinked, and she saw an awareness of what she was saying—and more, that he wasn't about to try to deny that illness might affect his judgment—and forged on with what she considered her culminating argument. "On top of that, the painting is here and not going anywhere, so there's no urgency over formulating your verdict. Indeed, even if you were well and viewed the painting this afternoon, with the snow lying so thickly, you couldn't leave or even send a report to the gallery." She paused, then still holding his gaze, stated, "There's no sense in leaving this bed until you're fully recovered and not at risk of developing any complications. For your information, by the time you reached us, you were close to frozen."

She invested the last phrase with enough force to warn him off any attempt to argue.

Judging by the frustrated look that crept into his hawk's eyes, he heard her loud and clear.

Godfrey felt about twelve years old, which was not at all how he wished to feel around Miss Hinckley. Before he could decide how he should respond, the door opened to admit a pleasant-faced motherly woman.

His angel turned to the newcomer. "Mrs. Kemp, I was just telling Mr. Cavanaugh that he should remain abed until his fever abates and he recovers fully from his ordeal." Miss Hinckley returned her gaze to him. "Mrs. Kemp is our housekeeper."

And, Godfrey suspected, a no-nonsense one at that.

Mrs. Kemp confirmed that with a brisk "Indeed, miss." To Godfrey, she said, "It will do no one any good if you push yourself into a more serious state, sir. My advice is to rest and recuperate and rise only once all signs of illness have passed." The housekeeper bustled to his side, displacing Wally, who promptly stood and moved back. Mrs. Kemp laid a palm across Godfrey's forehead and closed her eyes. A second later, she opened them and fixed him with a stern look. "Your fever's rising. You need to avoid all excitement and lie quietly. Now you're awake, I'll mix up some of my honey balsam—that should help to bring the fever down."

Godfrey cut a glance at Miss Hinckley, read the real concern in her face, and jettisoned any idea of battling the inevitable. The truth was... they were right, and he knew it. His aborted attempt to sit up had sent his head spinning; any further exertion, and he knew he would turn woozy— he was weak as a kitten and now feverish to boot!

Worse, the threat of lung fever wasn't one he could lightly dismiss; he'd suffered from the condition three times as a child and, from experience, knew that if he didn't take appropriate care, his recovery could take months. Literally months.

He hoped he'd grown out of the susceptibility, but had no idea if he actually had; since his last horrible and extended bout when he was twelve years old, he'd been careful to avoid all situations that might see the illness take hold again.

He hadn't foreseen getting caught in a Yorkshire snowstorm.

He exhaled, slumped back on the pillows, and held up his hands in a gesture of surrender. "Very well. I'll remain abed until I pass muster."

The relief that flooded all three faces turned his way was testimony as to how worried they'd been. Even—perhaps especially—the fascinating Miss Hinckley.

Godfrey seized the moment to dispatch Wally to get a report on the horses. As the bays were Wally's pride and joy, he went without argument. The housekeeper helpfully departed with a promise to be back shortly with her remedy, leaving Miss Hinckley alone with him.

Ellie was aware that their patient's gaze had come to rest on her, a rather intent expression in his distinctly hawkish eyes. That raptorlike gaze was both compelling and disconcerting; she wasn't precisely sure what she felt about him watching her when she was supposed to be watching him.

She tensed to turn away and retreat to her place by the fire, but he raised a hand to stay her.

When she looked at him inquiringly, he trapped her gaze. "My dear Miss Hinckley, I now realize that I did, in fact, wake earlier, and that contrary to my belief that I was dreaming, I wasn't."

She'd hoped he wouldn't remember—or if he did, that he would helpfully assume he had been dreaming. Apparently, she wasn't going to be that lucky. She linked her hands before her and calmly stated, "I assure you, sir, that what passed between us on that occasion is of no consequence whatsoever. It was clear at the time that you weren't in your right mind."

A curious light passed through his eyes, even as he held her gaze. After a pause of several seconds, his deep voice a touch lower, he said, "As to that, I had intended to apologize—and I should—but I make it a point not to lie, and the truth is that while I regret my deluded actions and hope you won't hold them against me, as for their outcome, I'm not sorry at all."

She remained still while her wits waltzed at his implication, and her senses skittered, unhelpfully recalling in vivid sensory detail the glide of his fingertips over her skin and the pressure of his lips against hers. One thing seemed certain: Cavanaugh's impact was going to be fatal to her peace of mind. She needed to put him in his place. She tipped up her chin. "I'm twenty-eight years old, Mr. Cavanaugh, long past the age of reading too much into such an incidental happening. Again, I assure you that I place no consequence whatever on what passed between us—you were clearly not responsible for your actions at the time." She waved dismissively and walked to the fireplace to fetch her basket; she was certainly not going to sit and mend under his disconcerting gaze. "I suggest you wipe the moments from your mind, as I already have."

He might avoid lies, but in her mind, in situations such as this, they had their place.

She hoisted the basket and made for the door. "I'll leave you in peace, sir. I daresay Mrs. Kemp will be along shortly with her balsam. Meanwhile"—she paused at the door to glance at him, unsurprised to find his gaze, harder and more raptorlike than ever, fixed on her—"I will inform my father that you have woken and, in the circumstances, have agreed to recuperate prior to viewing the painting."

Godfrey compressed his lips against a retort along the lines of not having all that much choice.

The annoying Miss Hinckley regarded him for a moment, then coolly inclined her head in farewell, opened the door, and swept out.

He watched the panel close behind her, then relaxed into the pillows and pondered what had just occurred. He was prepared to take an oath that, despite her attempt at depressing his pretensions, the intriguing Miss Hinckley was every bit as aware of him as he was of her.

If she hadn't been quite so vehement in her insistence that he hadn't known what he was doing, if she hadn't made that last, patently fallacious claim of having already forgotten what had occurred, he might have been inclined to play the gentleman and let the matter, along with his attraction to her, slide.

But now?

If she'd thought to deflect his attention from her, she'd miscalculated on a fairly major scale.

Ellie held to her stated intention and, over the luncheon table, informed her father that Cavanaugh had woken, but was showing signs of developing a fever and, after some discussion, had been persuaded to remain in bed until he had properly recovered from his recent ordeal.

Her father, Harry, and Maggie accepted that news with ready understanding and, on her father's part, a wish for Cavanaugh's speedy
recovery.

Morris, Pyne, and Masterton frowned.

Before they could quibble, Ellie continued, "Given Cavanaugh's
purpose here, we deemed it preferable he be fully recovered before he
views the painting, as illness might affect his ability to conduct the necessary examinations. There's also the issue that it was solely our wish to
sell the Albertinelli that brought Cavanaugh here, to be caught in the
storm and fall ill in the first place."

Her father nodded. "Indeed—we bear some degree of responsibility. I
quite take your point, my dear."

Ellie returned her father's gentle smile, then glanced at their three
visitors. "Besides, what with being snowed in, there's no way of notifying
the gallery that the painting has been authenticated—not until the snow
clears and the roads are open again."

"Just so," her father said. "No reason to rush the man when it looks as
if we'll be immured for a week."

"A week?" Pyne frowned. "Is that what your stableman is saying?"

Her father nodded. "A week at least. Johnson thinks there's more
snow on the way, so the situation is likely to get worse before it gets
better."

Masterton smiled easily at her father and Ellie. "Getting worse before
improving—that sounds rather like your patient."

Ellie inclined her head. "Mrs. Kemp suspects so."

"Still," Masterton went on, "as Matthew says, there's no need to rush.
Plenty of time for Cavanaugh to throw off his chill and authenticate the
painting in time to send the word south once that's possible."

Ellie was relieved when Morris and Pyne, apparently taking their cue
from Masterton, allowed the matter of Cavanaugh's illness and the consequent delay in his assessment of the Albertinelli to pass without further
discussion.

While neither Morris nor Pyne had any real say in her father's decisions, their arguments had been known to sway him. Masterton, being
able to claim a family connection and, she suspected, still having an eye
on her, occasionally stuck in his oar on family decisions, but in this case,
he was, apparently, prepared to be sensible.

"Half your luck, Matthew," Pyne said. "I wouldn't mind an old master or two hanging on my walls and being able to sell them off when need arises."

Morris humphed. "I just wish my ancestors had been half as farsighted as yours."

From what Ellie had heard from her father and also on the local grapevine, despite their earlier offers of financial assistance, both Morris and Pyne might be in significantly worse financial straits than the Hinckleys. Morris's farm outside Galphay hadn't done well over the past decade, and while Pyne's business was said to be sound, it seemed his wife was intent on running him aground.

Ellie wasn't surprised to hear the pair voice a degree of envy over the Hinckleys selling a painting they no longer even looked at and, through that simple singular act, reviving the family's fortunes.

"Nevertheless, I suspect we should hold back from making any assumptions." Masterton looked at her father. "After all, the sale of the painting is conditional on Cavanaugh's authentication."

Her father smiled. "True, but there's really no question about the painting's bona fides. It's been here, in this house, since my long-ago ancestor brought it back from his Grand Tour. He knew the artist's family and purchased it directly from them. I have no doubt as to Cavanaugh's verdict. His opinion is more in the nature of a necessary approval prior to the sale."

"I see." Masterton glanced at Ellie. "In that case, given that Cavanaugh is now here, any delay due to illness is neither here nor there. By the time the thaw sets in, you'll have your verdict, and the sale will proceed as quickly as it would have regardless."

"Precisely." For good measure, Ellie added, "Indeed, I believe we owe Cavanaugh some consideration on that score. Rather than brave the storm, he could have stopped in Ripon, in which case, his viewing of the painting wouldn't occur until several days after the thaw. Instead, as matters now stand, regardless of his illness and recovery, we'll be moving forward as rapidly as Mother Nature allows."

"Well said, my dear." Her father nodded benignly.

While Morris and Pyne remained rather grudging in their acceptance, Masterton smiled in relaxed agreement, leaving Ellie more in charity with him than she usually was.

CHAPTER 3

*B*y the following morning, Godfrey was already feeling the effects of his enforced sojourn in what, he had to admit, was an otherwise comfortable bed. His liking for idleness had never been great, and being stuck between the sheets steadily eroded what patience he had, along with his hold on his temper, resulting in an increasing querulousness that even he found trying.

Worse, that morning, he'd started coughing.

From experience, he knew that was a bad sign and tried to suppress the instinct as much as he could.

When his distracting principal jailer entered the room some minutes after the clocks had struck ten, he quickly sat up to make his case. "I need to be up and about. Nothing strenuous, but I'm sure walking a trifle and being dressed will make me feel—"

He broke off on a hacking cough, then wheezed and coughed some more.

She rushed to the side of the bed as he bent forward, sounding and feeling as if his lungs were full of gravel and mud. She set aside the basket of mending she'd brought in, but then hovered, clearly unsure what to do.

Luckily, the coughing subsided, but by the time he'd regained his breath, straightened, and raised his gaze to her face, her features had hardened and her jaw had set.

"No." Her tone brooked no argument. "As you've just demonstrated, you're in no case at all to be wandering about out of bed."

He held her gaze, then sighed and slumped on the pillows at his back. With his gaze trained on the ceiling, he sighed again, in even more heartfelt vein. He knew he was being melodramatic. He'd thought his sister, Stacie, was the family's drama queen, but apparently, he had his own talents in that sphere. Fretfully, he picked at the sheet. "Perhaps some fresh air..."

"It's currently below freezing outside."

"I was speaking metaphorically." He raised his head to look at her—and promptly started coughing again.

This time, when the coughing fit passed and, somewhat sheepishly, he met her gaze, concern had seeped into her expression.

"You really must do everything possible to get well." Ellie managed not to glare at him, but he made her feel anxious and exasperated—and just a touch helpless, which she liked even less. "Given we're definitely snowed in and will be for some time, there's no reason—no justifiable argument—for you to rush your recovery and risk developing lung fever."

From his man's comments and her own assessment, he was normally active and vital; just the thought of him brought even lower than he already was made her mind seize.

Rather than plead, she kept her tone brisk—businesslike. "Please think of this from my family's point of view. Having you collapse and sink deeper into illness will not only delay the sale of the Albertinelli, we would view such an outcome as a...well, a stain on our honor. You are our guest, under our roof, essentially at our behest." She hoped an appeal based on such grounds might sway him; judging by his clothes and horses, he hailed from a haut ton family, and she'd always understood that honor weighed heavily with them.

His eyes—mid-to-light brown with gold striations and a steadiness of gaze that forcibly reminded her of an eagle's or a hawk's imperious stare—rested on her for several moments, then he faintly grimaced and settled back on the pillows. "My apologies—I'm being tiresome. But I'm unused to being idle—I get bored rather easily."

She wasn't sure whether she was being led, but felt compelled to suggest, "Perhaps, then, we should work on distracting you."

For a second, his eyes gleamed, and she fought down a blush at the thought of the opening she'd given him. But then his lashes veiled his eyes, and he murmured, "Will it bother you to talk while you sew?"

"No—not at all."

"Then perhaps you might sit not so far away"—his gaze went to the wing chair by the fireplace—"and we can find topics to fill the silence."

"That sounds an excellent idea." Determined to remain in charge of any discussion, she walked to the chair and pushed and maneuvered it into position a yard from the bed, angled toward him.

Godfrey smiled encouragingly. He waited until she sat, ferreted about in the basket, lifted a length of fabric into her lap, and started to ply her needle, then said, "You've mentioned your family several times, and obviously, once I'm well, I'll meet them. How many members are there?"

Her sewing gave her an excuse to keep her eyes down, and that, he hoped, would loosen any reins on her tongue.

"There's my father and me—I'm the eldest. Then there's Harry—he's twenty and back home from Oxford—and the youngest is Maggie, who's eighteen." She paused to examine her stitches, then added, "Our mother died shortly after Maggie was born."

"How old were you at that time?"

"Nine. Harry was two."

"Hmm. I imagine you became something of a mother figure to your younger siblings."

She lifted a shoulder in a slight shrug; ducking his head, he glimpsed a fond smile flirting about her lips. "When they were younger, to some degree, but they're both grown now."

He settled his head on the pillow. "I have a similar situation with my half brother. He's eleven years older than me, and after our father died—I was thirteen at the time—Ryder became not so much a stand-in father but a very real presence as my big brother."

She glanced up, and the smile in her eyes and on her lips was bright with understanding. "I can imagine." After a second of studying him, she looked down again. "You're fond of him."

He nodded. "I am. I have two other older brothers and an older sister —I'm the youngest—but Ryder's the eldest by several years, and despite being our half sibling, he stands in a special place for us all."

With her looking down, he could indulge himself by staring at her— examining the way the soft winter light falling through the window shimmered on the rich gold of her hair.

Although he couldn't presently see her face, he'd realized she was blessed—or was it cursed?—with a remarkably open expression. Her features and most of all her eyes reflected her thoughts and feelings.

When she'd appealed to his understanding of honor to persuade him to remain abed, he'd seen—clearly, free of guile, and without the slightest veil—that his recovery truly mattered to her, that her insistence he get well was driven by emotion and not by any cool calculation over having her family's painting favorably assessed.

He'd felt compelled to set aside his grumpiness and, instead, search for some way to learn more about her—the subject he found most distracting.

He cast about for avenues that might prove revealing. "Has your family always lived here?"

Without looking up, she nodded. "Since at least the time of Richard the Second. The list in the family Bible goes back that far."

"So there were Hinckleys at Hinckley Hall since before the Wars of the Roses."

"Our roots in the district run deep." She glanced at him. "Obviously, you're an expert in old paintings. Is it just paintings, or does your expertise extend to other types of artwork?"

"Paintings and sculptures are my primary interest, but I'm fascinated by art of all types—even tapestries and embroideries." He caught her eye and smiled. "Most have a tale to tell. I imagine there would be all sorts of old embroideries and the like tucked away in a house such as this."

She arched her brows. "I hadn't thought of them as…bearing witness, if you like. I know where some of my grandmother's and great-grandmother's efforts hang—I must take a closer look."

"As it seems I'll be here for some time, even after I examine the Albertinelli, I wouldn't mind taking a look at such works myself."

"Once you're better, we can hunt them out."

Next topic. "Is there any village closer than Ripon?"

"Galphay is the nearest village, about a mile farther on along the lane, but it's much smaller than Ripon, more like a hamlet. Another mile or so beyond Galphay is Kirkby Malzeard. That's a decent-sized village with an inn and the usual shops." She shot him a swift glance. "Are you a Londoner born and bred?"

"I've lived most of my life in London, but I was born in Wiltshire, and I frequently visit there and also at my brothers' and sister's houses, which are scattered about the country, so I'm not unaccustomed to country life, if that was what you were really asking."

She smiled and looked back at her sewing. "It was. It helps to know you won't have unrealistic expectations of life here, at the Hall."

As to his expectations…

Even with a generous yard between them, he was conscious of the visceral tug drawing his senses in her direction. His focus was wholly on her, his attention transfixed in a way that was strange to him. While physical desire was there, it was only a part—and possibly not even the major part—of the attraction. The compulsion fixating him on her was novel, unique to her, leaving him curious and intent on further exploration. She was like a new form of artwork to him, fascinating and intriguing. "I promise not to be too demanding."

He'd intended his tone to be light, even flippant, but his underlying thoughts crept in, and the words emerged too intent, too deep.

She glanced swiftly at him, her greeny-hazel eyes a touch wider than they had been. He was fairly certain nothing of his covetous thoughts showed in his face, yet after scanning his features, she looked down again, then after a moment's hesitation, she bent and rummaged in the basket at her feet.

She gave an irritated huff. "I've left my shears in the parlor. I'll have to fetch them." She bundled up the linen she'd been working on, dropped it into the basket, rose, and only then met his eyes. "I won't be long."

Impulse prodded. Struggling up on one elbow, he waved her nearer. "Before you go, could you plump these pillows, please? It's better for my lungs if I sit up."

She hesitated for only a second, then briskly came to his side.

Warily, he sat up, grateful when no more coughing ensued. She steadied him with a hand on his linen-clad shoulder—and that light, impersonal touch sent heat streaking through him.

He froze, and she quickly removed her hand, pulled the pillows from behind him, shook them, then piled them high.

"There." She lightly patted the mound.

When he hesitated, then gingerly started to lean back, as he'd hoped, she once again laid a hand on his shoulder to steady him.

He smiled and relaxed against the mounded softness and, before she could remove her hand, raised his and closed his fingers about hers. Once again, her fingers fluttered at the contact, then stilled. He turned his head, met her eyes, and smiled his most charming smile. "Thank you." His eyes locked with hers, he raised her hand and brushed a kiss across the backs of her fingers. "You are, indeed, a ministering angel."

Her eyes had widened; for an instant, as they searched his, her expression stated that she didn't know how she wanted to react. Then she firmed her lips, straightened, and drew her fingers away; he released them only because he knew there was no point trying to hold on to them—not yet.

She hesitated for a second, her eyes scanning his face as if puzzled she couldn't see past his façade, then she stepped back, reiterated, "I'll be back shortly," and made for the door.

Ellie stepped into the corridor and shut the door on the Hall's best guest bedchamber. She released the knob and straightened. Standing in the dimness, she blinked—and blinked—trying to get her mind working again, to drag her wits and senses from dwelling on the feel of his fingers about hers and the even more disconcerting brush of his cool lips over what had proved to be unaccountably sensitive skin.

She realized she was brushing the backs of her fingers—where his lips had touched—with the fingers of her other hand.

Really? Anyone would imagine I'd never had my fingers kissed before.

She had, many times, yet those other instances had never resulted in her feeling flushed all over. She shouldn't, she supposed, be surprised that he'd done such a thing; quite aside from his rambling when he'd thought he was dreaming, ever since he'd woken, whenever she'd been in his presence, she'd been aware of his attention—not just his gaze—locked on her.

While she couldn't label him a rake, not on such short acquaintance and with no actual evidence of such a propensity, his style—clothes, manner, horses, and carriage—made him being a rake a distinct possibility.

He might think her physically perfect, and she would admit to feeling a compulsion like no other to draw nearer and explore what the strangely intense attraction flaring between them portended, but sating her burning curiosity wasn't sufficient reason to allow him to lure her any closer.

As her aunt, Lady Camberford, had frequently warned her, succumbing to a handsome stranger's practiced wiles rarely ended well.

Regardless of the snippets of information he'd shared, he was still very much a stranger to her, and his handsomeness should be neither here nor there.

In her mind, she saw him as she'd left him, propped against the pillows, his dark hair falling across his forehead, his hawk's eyes fixed on her. After several seconds of dwelling on the vision, she dragged her wits away.

Clearly, she was going to have to work at holding herself to an acceptable line. She tipped her head, consulting her instincts; she felt fairly certain that he—no matter a handsome rake or not—wouldn't step over that acceptable line, not unless she beckoned. While they were under her family's roof, his honor—and again, she felt sure he had an abundance of that—would stand firmly in his way.

"Good." All she had to do was adhere to proper behavior herself, and all would be well.

Reassured, she set out for the back parlor, where she last remembered using her shears.

Harry and Maggie would likely be there, whiling away the hours. They'd want to know about Cavanaugh, about anything she'd learned. A few minutes in their company, away from Cavanaugh, wouldn't hurt.

Godfrey waited for his ministering angel to return.

How large was the house? How far away was the back parlor?

As the minutes ticked by, his fretfulness over simply lying there grew.

He realized he hadn't coughed for some time; perhaps he was getting better.

Eventually, restlessness drove him to sit upright. Although his chest felt heavy, his breathing remained unobstructed, and no sense of giddiness assailed him.

Encouraged, he slowly swiveled until he was sitting on the edge of the bed with his legs hanging over the side. He looked at his clothes, folded and neatly piled on the dresser farther along the wall. The chair his angel had occupied sat to his right; there was no obstacle between him and his clothes—just several yards of polished board, partially covered by a rug.

He noticed the rug was, in fact, a Turkish kilim and rather fine. The thought of what else he might find in such an old house, just lying around, taken for granted by those who lived there, flitted through his brain.

He raised his head and fixed his gaze on his clothes; he would definitely feel more the thing if he got dressed.

He drew in a deeper breath, slid his feet to the floor, and slowly straightened.

The nightshirt draped about his legs, covering them to midcalf. He paused to draw in another breath and took one step.

The door opened, and he looked that way. He had an instant in which to take in Miss Hinckley's shock at seeing him out of bed before the room swam.

His senses whirled; his head reeled. He made some garbled sound, closed his eyes, and groped behind him for the bed, but he must have turned...

Where is it?

He felt himself teetering...then small hands gripped him firmly about the waist.

"Stop."

The word was a command, one he instinctively obeyed.

"Just stand still until it passes."

A minute crawled by, and sure enough, the world stopped waltzing. He wondered how much of his returning steadiness had to do with the distraction she offered—her supple strength, the gripping of her fingers, the warmth of her palms striking through the fine linen, the subtle perfume that reached him as she stood so close beside him; her nearness bombarded his senses in myriad ways, dragging his awareness from everything else.

"Don't move yet, but see if you can open your eyes."

Again, he obeyed, easing his lids up, grateful when nothing swayed. The bed lay two steps to his right. He felt her gaze on his face, but when he glanced at her, she'd looked at the bed. He noticed her lips were set in a rather grim line.

She had a hand clamped to either side of his waist, with her arm banding his back; her palms felt like warm irons through the fine linen of his nightshirt, and regardless of all else, there was comfort in her touch. "Come on. Let's get you settled again."

She sounded like his childhood nurse. He supposed he deserved that. Regardless, he was far too heavy for her to steady if he actually fell; he raised his left arm and looped it around her, but mindful of the proprieties, he settled his hand on her shoulder rather than, as he would have preferred, at her waist.

Under his arm, she shuffled a touch closer, rendering the pair of them a fraction more stable. "Now..." Using the pressure of her hands and arm, she urged him toward the bed.

Two shambling steps got him to the bed's side, and there they paused.

He looked down at her—just as she looked up at him.

Their gazes collided and locked. Time froze.

So did they, both captured by the moment.

The urge to kiss her—to taste her lips again—surged.

But her widening eyes, the comprehension and resistance he saw spiking there, had him reining back the impulse.

He rocked slightly with the effort, and she blinked and looked down, then eased away.

"Turn around." Using her hands at his waist, she helped him shuffle around until he could sink onto the edge of the bed. As he did, she released him. Setting her palms to his shoulders, she pushed.

Obliging her, he fell and landed on his back on the sheet.

She stooped and slid an arm beneath his knees and, raising the covers, helped him swing his legs onto the bed.

He closed his eyes and shifted until he was lying straight. As she lowered and straightened the covers, he groaned. "I'm sorry. I didn't imagine I would be that weak."

She made a scoffing sound, but when he peeked through his lashes, he saw she was frowning, her expression declaring she was seriously concerned.

Sure enough, after resettling the covers, lips tight, she stepped to his side and slapped a hand to his forehead. After a second, she huffed. "Your fever's rising. I should have checked earlier."

She removed her hand, planted both hands on her hips, and bent an exasperated look on him. "I need to tell Mrs. Kemp so she can have Cook prepare you the right sort of broth." She held his gaze, and there was not so much as a hint of encouragement in hers—just worry. "If I leave, will you remain in bed this time?"

Chastened, he simply said, "I promise."

She gave vent to another huff, then lowered her arms and headed for the door. "I'll be back in just a few minutes." Before the door, she bent and picked up what he realized were the shears she'd gone to fetch. She set them on a nearby dresser, then opened the door and left.

Godfrey stared at the closed door for several minutes while their recent actions and reactions replayed in his mind. She was as attracted to him as he was to her—of that, he felt sure—yet for some reason, she was intent on holding him at arm's length, metaphorically at least.

Why?

When all was said and done, he was not accustomed to such summary rejection from ladies of any age or station.

She returned within a few minutes. Judging by the tight set of her features, her temper had hardened.

So had his.

He opened his mouth, but before he could speak, she halted beside the wing chair and, having retrieved her shears along the way, fixed him with a stern look. "Mr. Cavanaugh—"

"My given name is Godfrey." The tone in which she'd spoken had been his last straw. "If you're going to insist on pushing me into bed, then I believe it's appropriate that we move to first name terms."

He watched her intently—challengingly.

She returned his look through narrowing eyes, but then her features eased, and she stepped across the chair and sat down. "Very well. Godfrey. My given name is Eleanor, but everyone calls me Ellie."

"Ellie." It suited her, with her honey-colored hair and, he judged, usually cheerful and positive demeanor.

From the basket, she retrieved the garment she'd been mending and shook it out. "I hope when Cook sends up the broth, you'll consent to drink it. Mrs. Kemp will have added a concoction of herbs that we hope will help reduce your fever. Because of the snow, there's no chance of having the doctor visit, so the old remedies are the best we can offer."

Now, he felt about five years old. He cleared his throat. "Of course. I'll be grateful for any assistance that will get me out of this bed more quickly."

He dipped his head and caught the upward twitch of her lips, but she schooled her expression to seriousness before glancing up.

"Good. That would be wise."

He tried a smile of his own. From the easing of her expression, they'd got past their mutual spurt of temper and were on an even keel again. Seeking to further that state, he asked, "Tell me about the house and the household—given the storm, when I arrived, I didn't get any view of the house. I have no idea of its size."

"Well..." Her gaze once more on her stitching, she enumerated the denizens of Hinckley Hall, then went on to describe the building. "It was extensively remodeled in Elizabeth's time into the classical three wings giving off a central spine. Because of the sheer number of rooms, one wing has been closed for...well, probably generations. Certainly for all of my life and, I believe, my father's as well."

It occurred to Godfrey that it was strange her father hadn't come to see him, but questioning his host's daughter about her father's behavior seemed bordering on the impertinent. Instead, he listened, mentally creating a picture in his mind as she described the house's attributes and outbuildings and included an outline of the estate as well. To him, the lands attached to the house seemed rather limited, but then the only estates with which he was familiar were those of the marquessates of Raventhorne and Albury—hardly comparable.

Still, from the sound of it, the estate's farms should have been sufficient to meet the family's needs; admittedly, he'd seen little beyond this room, but he would be surprised to discover the family lived extravagantly.

He wanted—very much—to learn what had prompted them to offer the Albertinelli to the gallery. Not that it would make any difference to his assessment, but he was forever curious about what led to the movement of artworks from one hand to another.

Still industriously stitching, she ended her recitation of the local amenities with the information that the family normally attended St. Andrew's Church at Kirkby Malzeard for Sunday service. Pausing, she raised her head and, frowning slightly, stared across the room, then grimaced and looked down again. "I must remind Kemp that we'll need to use the house's chapel tomorrow."

"The house has its own chapel?"

At his much-struck tone, she glanced at him, amused. "Yes. The Hall was one of the major houses in the area in Elizabeth's day."

He made a mental note to ensure he got a good look at the chapel. Who knew what treasures it might hold?

She'd been studying his face. When he refocused on her, she quirked a brow. "What else would you like to know?"

Why you're intent on pretending what's building between us isn't there.

He smiled easily. "You said your brother was at Oxford. Which college, and what did he read?"

Returning to her stitching, she answered readily.

When they'd exhausted that safe subject, daringly, he ventured, "You mentioned your advanced age—I take it you had at least one Season." He couldn't for the life of him understand why she was still unwed.

She took her time responding, but eventually said, "Actually, no. I was scheduled to have a London Season when I was nineteen, under the wing of my aunt, Lady Camberford, but a situation arose here that made my absence impossible, and subsequently, I discovered, much to my aunt's dismay, that I didn't really miss going to London."

Clearly, the situation had been something major, but whatever it had been, Godfrey could only be grateful that she hadn't arrived in the capital; not all his peers were blind.

But if she hadn't been to London, her resistance to their attraction couldn't be due to some adverse experience among the ton.

At that moment, Wally arrived with a tray on which resided a bowl of steaming broth.

Miss Hinckley—Ellie—smiled at Wally and, setting aside her mending, rose and waved him to the bed. To Godfrey, she said, "I'm going down for morning tea. I'll leave you to your meal."

"But you'll come back?" Godfrey wanted to pursue his questions, but a little time to hone his approach would be helpful.

She smiled. "I'll return in an hour. If, after the broth, you find yourself sleepy, getting some rest would be wise. The more subdued we can keep your fever, the faster you'll recover."

He summoned an appropriately grateful and reassuring smile and watched her leave and close the door. Then he looked at Wally and, after a second, lowered his gaze to the steaming bowl. "I take it there's something in that that will make me nod off."

"Very likely." Wally set the tray across Godfrey's lap. "I saw what went into it, and I'm sure it'll be good for you. So like the lady said, if you want to get better, eat up."

Godfrey picked up the spoon, wrinkled his nose, and reluctantly complied.

As he'd expected, the soup made his lids heavy. Surrendering, he let them fall.

When he raised them again, Ellie was back in the chair, stitching something else.

He stirred, and she looked up, then smiled and set aside her sewing. "You're awake." She rose and crossed to the bed. She laid a cool palm over his forehead, then her lashes flickered, and she frowned and removed her hand. "Your fever is still increasing, but at least it's not so high as to be alarming."

He wasn't quick enough to catch her hand and keep her by the bed.

She returned to her chair, sat, and informed him, "Cook will send up another bowl of broth and perhaps some bread for luncheon."

He tried to make his smile appreciative. "I'll look forward to it."

She met his gaze and arched a brow, but made no further comment.

"So where were we?" Before he'd succumbed to the soporific soup, he'd realized that, with her, his best approach to gaining enlightenment as to what hurdle stood in the way of further mutual exploration of their very definitely mutual attraction might well be to simply ask. "You told me you didn't go to London, but you must have attended local assemblies and the like." A young lady of her station wouldn't have been allowed to hide herself away, not even in North Yorkshire.

She inclined her head. "Under the wings of the local grandes dames, I attended the assemblies in Harrogate for several years."

"Well, then—you must have met and been wooed by countless local gentlemen." So why wasn't she married?

She glanced up, her gaze sharp, yet amused. "I did, and I was."

Ah—now we're getting to it. Boldly, he ventured, "I take it none of them came up to scratch."

She looked down at her stitching. "If by that you mean to ask if any gentleman made me an offer, then several did. However, none of those smitten by my beaux yeux possessed much to recommend them to me."

He debated, then asked, "Am I wrong in thinking that, out of those experiences, you've formed some view regarding eligible gentlemen— meaning those you would consider accepting?"

Her smile—what he glimpsed of it—held a sharper edge. "Indeed. Above all else, I learned to place no faith in a gentleman's protestations, and that the more handsome and sophisticated a gentleman is, the less likely it will be that he deserves my trust."

"Ah." He waited, but she didn't look up. "I see."

He was no coxcomb, yet he was aware that he was lauded as one of the more handsome, as-yet-unmarried-and-exceedingly-eligible gentlemen in the ton.

He'd wanted to know what hurdle he—they—faced. Now, he knew.

He smiled with entirely genuine equanimity.

She glanced up, searched his face, and frowned.

Nothing loath, he asked, "Your sister's eighteen. Will she be attending the assemblies this year? I would be interested in learning how you plan to counsel her regarding gentlemen suitors."

But at that, she laughed. "You've yet to meet Maggie. Once you do, you'll realize that, for her, no counseling will be required."

He allowed his puzzlement to show, but she merely smiled, still amused, and offered nothing more.

Eventually, he asked, "Are you close, you and your siblings?"

Once again engrossed in her stitchery, she nodded. "My father, Harry, Maggie, and me—after Mama died, we grew closer." She paused, then more quietly went on, "She was the center—the lynchpin—of our family, and when she was gone, we…learned to lean on each other."

He strongly suspected that what she meant was that she had stepped into the central role, holding the others together. From what he'd learned from her, not just from her words but also from her tone—the clear affection she felt for father, brother, and sister—he owned himself eager to meet the others and confirm if their family truly was as he was imagining.

She glanced at him, curiosity in her eyes. "You lost your father. Didn't you and your siblings and your mother grow closer after that?"

He grimaced and, for once, let his gaze drift from her face. "It wasn't like that—didn't happen like that—in my family. My mother was our father's second wife, and she resented Ryder—our elder half brother, whom I mentioned before. While Mama was alive…in many ways, we were forced to go our separate ways. It was…" He hadn't really thought of it before but… "Lonely."

"Oh, I see."

He looked up to see real compassion in her eyes, far more complex and soothing than mere pity. Regardless, he wouldn't have accepted even that from anyone else, yet from her…

"Is your mother still alive?"

He shook his head. "After she died, Ryder and his wife—he was married by then—stepped in and drew us all together. As siblings, over recent years, we've been closer than we've ever been, thanks to Ryder and Mary."

She smiled encouragingly. "So all's well now."

He inclined his head, but in truth, it wasn't that simple.

Courtesy of his mother's machinations, her attempts to control her children's lives, he and his siblings had missed being in any sense a real family; they'd lacked the experience of family throughout their formative years. He was the youngest, and he'd been nineteen when their mother had died; none of them had known what family life could, let alone should, be like.

Over recent years, he'd watched his siblings follow in Ryder and Mary's footsteps and, through marriage to the right person, set about creating their own families. Although they all included him at every celebration and holiday and welcomed him with open arms to their homes, he still felt like an outsider looking in on what he had come to regard as life's most precious and rewarding experience.

Family—being a true part of one—was something he now craved to the depths of his soul. But like his siblings, he didn't know how to create the necessary relationships; like them, he needed to find the right person and marry her.

Ellie had returned to her stitching. As he watched her hemming a flounce, he felt, beneath their outward calmness, the powerful tug that made him want to draw closer to her.

And he had to wonder, as the morning light faded, giving way to a dull day, whether he was, in that very moment, looking at his right person.

After another minute's silence, she asked about his schooling, ultimately leading to an inquiry as to how he had come to be an authenticator acting for the National Gallery.

That was a topic he could easily expound on, and he set himself to entertain her, which, in turn, pleased him.

Ellie owned to being fascinated by Godfrey Cavanaugh. In her experience, very few gentlemen would have so openly asked what he had. Given the attraction that lay simmering between them, his interest was unsurprising, and she'd deemed it wise to state the truth so he would understand and accept her stance.

Instead of annoying her, she viewed his straightforwardness as a point in his favor.

Then had come the vulnerability she'd sensed in him when their discussion had shifted to his family. That had touched her in a way she couldn't recall experiencing before. To divert him from what seemed to be a lingering pain, she'd suggested he tell her of his interest in art, but he'd taken her invitation and run, and she'd lowered her needle and forgotten her mending the better to watch the emotions play across his face as he painted vivid word pictures of a succession of humorous incidents from his travels through the world of art.

She was laughing without reserve—they both were—when a tap on the door heralded the entrance of his manservant bearing a covered dish on a tray.

She glanced at the clock. Over an hour had passed; it was already twelve-thirty. Catching her breath, she met Godfrey's eyes, noted he looked rather smug, and realized she'd relaxed with him to an extent that was remarkable—almost shocking. She thrust her work into her basket, grasped the handle, and rose.

His eyes tracked her movements, then he raised his gaze to her face. "I promise I'll consume everything on the tray." There was an element of hope in his eyes when he asked, "Will you be able to return after luncheon?"

And keep me company was said with his not-usually-so-expressive eyes.

Belatedly, caution raised its head; he was both handsome and sophisticated after all. "We have others stranded by the storm—I'm not sure if I'll be able to get away." She wouldn't be needed once the others rose from the table, but returning here would, she felt, be unwise. "Perhaps you would care for a book to read? My father's library is extensive."

His eyes hardened, and the glint of hope vanished, but after a second of regarding her, he inclined his head. "Any tome on the history of the house or the area would interest me."

"I'll see what I can find."

He held out his hand, and against her better judgment, she found herself gliding to the side of the bed and surrendering her hand.

His eyes trapped hers, and he raised her fingers to his lips and pressed a mercifully brief kiss to their backs. "Thank you for bearing me company—and for bearing with me." His lips quirked, and those dimples she'd speculated upon came into play. "And yes, I'm being deliberately charming, but that doesn't mean I'm not entirely sincere." He held her gaze. "Thank you for making my day pass faster. Thank you for your concern on my behalf, and please convey my thanks to your staff as well."

She nodded and drew her fingers from his; that had been very prettily said.

With a nod to him and another to his manservant, she walked to the door.

She'd enjoyed the past hours far more than she would have believed possible, and that was rather alarming.

Godfrey watched her go. When the door clicked shut, he looked at Wally, who had been standing with the tray to one side. Resigned, he beckoned. "What have they sent me?"

"More of that broth and some bread and cheese." Wally set down the tray, lifted the silver dome, and stepped back. "The harridan who runs the kitchen—she's a right dragon, but her cooking's better than fine—said you need to strike the right balance between feeding any cold and starving your fever, and that seems to mean she's put you on this broth and short rations."

Godfrey grimaced and picked up the soupspoon. "She might well be right." He swallowed a mouthful. "I just want this wretched illness to be gone."

Wally drew up a straight-backed chair, sat, folded his arms across his chest, and settled in to be patient.

"You've eaten?" Godfrey asked.

Wally nodded. "Good grub here—the staff eats well."

Godfrey drank his soup and allowed his mind to range over his morning. From Ellie's remarks, to make any headway with her, he needed to show—to demonstrate—his trustworthiness; he needed to convince her that despite his innate handsomeness and inherent sophistication, she would be safe in placing her trust in him.

Despite a few rocky moments, he felt he'd made a start, even while being confined to the bed.

He'd almost finished the soup when a tap on the door sent Wally to open it. He spoke to someone, then closed the door, and carrying a book, returned to the bed. "Footman brought this up."

Godfrey set down the soupspoon and took the inches-thick tome. He opened the front cover and read: *The History of Hinckley Hall*. He smiled and laid the book aside, then picked up the cheese knife and attacked the slab of cheese.

After swallowing the first slice, he looked at Wally. "Miss Hinckley mentioned some local gentlemen—friends of her father's—who are also stranded here courtesy of the storm."

Once more sitting with his arms folded across his chest, Wally nodded. "That'll be Mr. Edward Morris and Mr. Walter Pyne. Haven't seen either, nor heard much about them yet, other than that they go back a long ways with Mr. Hinckley, who I've also yet to set eyes on. The other gentleman—the one who helped us up the drive—is stuck here, too, but the gents are keeping to the front of the house, and I've no cause to go wandering there."

"Indeed. But what have you gathered from the staff?"

"Seems like Morris and Pyne are frequent visitors here—they come every Wednesday, which was how they came to be trapped with the rest of us. As for our rescuer, he's a Mr. Masterton—he's got some connection to the family and lives in Ripon. When the storm hit, he was on his way home from somewhere else and sought shelter here. Seems no one predicted the storm sweeping in as it did."

Godfrey slotted that information, sparse though it was, into his mental picture of Ellie Hinckley's life; he felt he was assembling the picture like a jigsaw, piece by piece. "What else can you tell me about the household?"

Wally dutifully reported all he'd seen and heard, but other than his views of the staff, who, reading between Wally's lines, seemed to be devoted to the family, Wally had gleaned little that extended Godfrey's knowledge beyond what he'd already learned from the elder daughter of the house.

As for her, with a few well-directed queries, Godfrey confirmed what he'd started to suspect, namely, that on her mother's death, Ellie Hinckley had stepped into the critical central role with respect to both her family and the household.

"She's the one who runs it all," Wally stated. "It's Miss Ellie this and Miss Ellie that—seems Mr. Hinckley leaves it all up to her."

Godfrey nodded, setting that piece of the puzzle of Ellie Hinckley in stone. For the rest…he had, he realized, a lot to learn and to confirm.

Somewhat to his surprise, he finished the bread—surprisingly tasty and gloriously fresh—as well as the lump of cheese. He let Wally remove the tray and reached for the book. "I won't need you until later."

"Right you are." Wally hefted the tray and headed for the door. "Have to say that if we were going to find ourselves stuck somewhere for days, this isn't a bad place to be holed up in."

Godfrey smiled. Despite falling ill, he wholeheartedly agreed.

He opened the book and was immediately drawn into an account of the Hall's history, written by an ancestor in the previous century.

Later, when his lids grew heavy and he let the book fall closed, his thoughts continued to revolve about the Hall and those who lived there.

He hadn't had any expectations of this excursion beyond setting eyes on the Albertinelli painting and, through verifying its authenticity, installing himself in Eastlake's and the National Gallery's good graces. Yet as sleep drew nearer and hazed his mind, he found himself wondering if at Hinckley Hall, against all the odds—because who would have predicted such a happening in an ancient country house in North York-shire?—he might have found something that would mean more to him than all the High Renaissance paintings in the world.

CHAPTER 4

*T*he following morning, after duly consuming the broth Cook sent up for him—thinner and containing different herbs—and allowing Wally to shave him, Godfrey endeavored to keep himself immersed in the story of Hinckley Hall, but no matter how hard he tried to suppress his cough, the affliction continued to worsen, becoming a near-constant distraction.

His fever hadn't abated, either; if anything, it continued to slowly build. Although he was doing his best to ignore that, there was no point pretending his recovery would occur overnight.

He'd set the book aside and was staring across the room at nothing in particular when a rap fell on the door. Rousing from his stupor, he blinked and called, "Come in."

The door opened, and an older gentleman looked in. He had a round, jowly face, and his sandy-brown hair was thinning. His coat and trousers proclaimed him to be of sound county stock, while his expression was alert and curious. "Are you up for a quick visit? We thought you might be bored."

Godfrey smiled. "I am." He noticed another man in the shadows of the corridor and waved the pair in. "Come in. There are several chairs."

The first man smiled. Hand outstretched, he advanced on the bed. "I'm Pyne. Old friend of Hinckley's. I was visiting Matthew and got trapped by the storm as well."

Godfrey gripped the proffered hand. "Cavanaugh. As I daresay you know, I'm here to examine Mr. Hinckley's painting. It's a pleasure to meet you, sir."

Pyne released Godfrey's hand and waved at the other man. "This is Masterton—you met him earlier, while trudging up the drive."

Masterton was younger than Pyne, perhaps only a few years older than Godfrey himself, and was dressed in riding clothes—tan corduroy breeches, a rather nice brown-and-black-check hacking jacket, and well-polished boots. His features were regular, even, and passingly handsome, and his reddish-brown hair was neatly styled in fashionable waves. Several inches taller than the more rotund Pyne, Masterton cut a fine figure and carried himself well.

Godfrey smiled at Masterton and held out his hand. "Godfrey Cavanaugh. I owe you considerable thanks, Mr. Masterton. If it hadn't been for your assistance, I'm not sure my man and I would have reached the house."

Smiling pleasantly, Masterton grasped Godfrey's hand. "You were on the right track. You just needed a little support over the last leg—I was happy to help."

"Regardless, I'm in your debt. Please"—Godfrey waved at the chairs—"make yourselves comfortable." He broke off to muffle a cough.

Pyne claimed the wing chair Ellie had left by the bed. Masterton looked around, then fetched the straight-backed chair Wally favored and set it alongside Pyne.

As Masterton sat, Pyne leaned forward. "Did I understand correctly that you drove all the way from London?"

Godfrey admitted he had. "I prefer my own horses, so I took care to pace them, and the journey took three days in all."

Masterton tipped his head at Godfrey. "I was out to the stable to check on my horse and noticed your pair. Their lines are superb and so perfectly matched—the stable lads are in raptures. We rarely see such prime horse-flesh around here."

Godfrey grinned. "One of my vices, I fear. I enjoy driving—and riding—and my family have a connection to the Cynsters, and through them, we have access to the best of the best." Godfrey coughed again, thankful when it proved a single cough rather than the beginning of a paroxysm; presumably, the broth was working its magic.

"Masterton's report sent me and Morris—another family friend trapped here—trudging out to the stable, too," Pyne confided. "While your horses are very fine, we were taken with your curricle. Sleek, sir—very sleek. It's a new design, isn't it?"

Godfrey nodded. "From Gillingham's in Long Acre. He was apprenticed to Hatchett, but has gone out on his own, specializing in quality and the latest designs. He's making quite a name for himself."

For the next ten minutes, the conversation meandered through the usual gentlemanly interests of riding, hunting, and shooting. After a discussion of the latest hunting rifles, Pyne seemed to recollect himself. "But enough of such mundane matters. You're here to examine the old painting. Have you seen it yet?"

"No, not yet." Resigned, Godfrey explained, "Miss Hinckley is adamant that I recover first before viewing it, on the grounds that it's in her family's best interests that my judgment isn't affected by illness when I form my first impressions."

"How, exactly, do you do that?" Masterton asked. "Form your impressions?"

Godfrey paused, then said, "It's not easy to explain to those not involved in the art world, but one's eye is educated through experience—through viewing many paintings by the various masters. One comes to know what to expect—what to look for, what ought to be there. That's the simplest way to put it."

Pyne's forehead wrinkled in thought. "So if you see the things you expect to see in this fellow Albertinelli's paintings in the painting here, that means the painting is authentic and the gallery can buy it?"

Godfrey waggled his head. "More or less."

"Assuming the painting is as expected," Pyne pressed, "what are your thoughts on its worth?"

Godfrey assumed his professional mien. "As to that, I can't say—I merely report on its authenticity, not its value. That's something the curators at the gallery will determine." His cough returned, causing him to lose his breath for a moment. His lungs were starting to feel tight.

When he lowered the hand he'd raised to his face and refocused on his visitors, he caught Pyne exchanging a weighted glance with Masterton. Then both men looked at Godfrey, and Pyne smiled. "So how did you come to be involved in this art business?"

Behind his amiable mask, Godfrey wondered why they wanted to know, because judging by the steadiness of Masterton's blue gaze, he, too, was interested. Godfrey mentally shrugged. "As a child, I became interested in art. It was something I was willing to study, and all else flowed from that." He wasn't about to mention the inspiration of the Raventhorne Abbey collection that one of his ancestors had amassed or the encouragement he'd received from his masters at Eton and Oxford. "I more or less fell into my current role—it's really all about having a good eye."

Pyne frowned. "Did you have to do an apprenticeship or something like that?"

Godfrey studied Pyne's intent expression, then glanced at Masterton, who was rather more impassive. Godfrey couldn't believe either of his visitors had any real interest in how one became an authenticator of artworks. *Are they questioning my ability to assess the Hinckley painting?*

"One is either born with a good eye or not—it's not a skill that can be taught, only refined."

"So how did the gallery come to choose you?" Masterton asked.

That, Godfrey suspected, was what they really wanted to know; at least Masterton had come out and asked directly.

"It's a matter of reputation—of museum curators and private collectors learning of your skill in detecting fraudulent works and, over many years, coming to trust your judgment. It's those curators and collectors who decide whether to enlist my services."

Increasingly irritated by the not-so-subtle inquisition, this time, when a cough threatened, Godfrey didn't fight to suppress it. The hacking in his chest had definitely got worse, and when the cough finally subsided and he raised his head and managed to draw a freer breath, he realized he felt flushed.

His fever was mounting.

The door flew open, and Ellie rushed in; from the way her gaze homed in on him, he surmised she'd heard him coughing. Then she saw Pyne and Masterton and halted. "Oh." A heartbeat later, her eyes narrowed slightly, and she rallied. "I didn't know you gentlemen were here."

Pyne and Masterton had hurriedly come to their feet. Pyne essayed a benevolent smile and gestured to Godfrey. "We were just bearing your patient company, m'dear. Boring being stuck in a bed, what?"

"Yes, I daresay it is." Her tone suggested being bored was a minor matter and not one she considered worthy of her notice. "But from the sound of his coughing, I believe Mr. Cavanaugh needs to rest quietly if he's to recover fully and be able to assess Papa's painting." She fixed both men with a severe look, doing an excellent imitation of a school ma'am. "That must be our primary goal—to ensure that Mr. Cavanaugh gets better. We're all keen to hear his opinion on the painting, and the fastest route to that end is to allow him to recover in peace and quiet."

Godfrey was unsurprised to hear both men murmur their agreement, along with assurances that they had merely been talking, but under Ellie's pointed and unforgiving gaze, they made their farewells and went to the door.

Pyne quit the room, and Ellie turned to Godfrey. Masterton made to follow the older man but, with his hand on the doorknob, paused and glanced back.

With his strength abruptly waning, Godfrey had slumped against the pillows, irritated by his weakness more than anything else.

With a disapproving humph, Ellie came to his side and set a palm to his forehead.

From beneath his lashes, Godfrey saw Masterton's gaze fix on Ellie. Although Masterton's expression remained outwardly urbane, there was a certain calculation in his gaze that Godfrey read with ease.

So Masterton had an interest in Ellie—enough of one to feel he had some rights there.

When Masterton finally turned and left the room, closing the door softly behind him, Godfrey shifted his gaze to Ellie's face. Given the perennial openness of her expression, one quick scan was sufficient to inform him that she was utterly oblivious to Masterton's regard, to his unstated claim.

There was no awareness of any understanding on her part.

Feeling distinctly reassured, Godfrey let his lids fall and smiled at the feel of Ellie's palm on his forehead.

Only to have her whisk her hand away and rather accusingly declare, "You have a much higher fever than before."

He knew she was right. "Hmm." He should have opened his eyes, caught her hand, kissed her fingers, and thanked her for deliverance. He'd missed that chance, but... "Thank you for saving me."

He wanted to think about Masterton and Pyne and her and her family...

Ellie stood by the bed and watched her patient slide into slumber. With her gaze, she traced the tight lines in his face, put there by the restlessness of fever and the pain of his congested cough; she watched the lines ease and fade as sleep claimed him.

He was remarkably handsome, even more so in repose. Without the animation of wakefulness, the angles and planes of his face were clean and sharp, blatantly aristocratic in strength and conformation.

She allowed herself to stare as his breathing, a trifle rough, slowed. She held still, waiting to see if another cough or the fever would rouse him, but he slumbered on.

Finally, she surrendered to temptation, raised a hand, and gently brushed back the lock of dark-auburn hair that had fallen across his wide brow—and wondered at the warm, soft, skittery feeling that swelled and danced inside her.

He didn't stir, and finally convinced he would remain asleep, she stepped back from the bed.

Given the curiosity in the house over their bedridden guest, she shouldn't have been surprised to find Pyne and Masterton in his room, quizzing him, yet Cavanaugh—Godfrey—wasn't just any patient. He had come very close to being frozen to death, primarily because of his exertions in hauling his man and his horses along. He'd refused to leave them to their fates, but in saving them, he'd exhausted his strength, depleted it to the point where it wasn't going to return quickly. That was no reflection on his manliness but an outcome of having pushed himself to the very extremes of endurance.

He needed time to recoup—would have needed it regardless of any complications—but with his escalating fever and worsening cough, proper rest without any irritations was truly the only way forward.

She heard a soft snore and found her lips curving.

Quietly, she walked to the door. She was tempted to lock it and bar all comers, but that would be one step too far.

After one last, lingering look, she quit the room and left him sleeping.

Of necessity, Sunday service for the household was a cobbled-together affair held in the Hall's chapel, built out from the central wing of the house.

That said, it wasn't the first time the household had been snowed in; Ellie, her father, and her siblings used the same readings, prayers, and hymns they'd used in years past to lead their little congregation.

As well as the family, all the staff attended; most of the area's families were Church of England parishioners.

Morris was there as well; he belonged to the same church and was devotedly regular in his observances. Not so Pyne, who failed to appear.

However, somewhat to Ellie's surprise, Masterton arrived in good time and made himself useful by pushing her father's chair into the chapel, then sitting with the family in the front pew and, at the appropriate time, helping her father reposition the chair so he could deliver the short sermon.

As with the readings and prayers, the sermon had been chosen to be uplifting and bolstering in the face of Nature's icy challenge. The staff duly listened and stood and raised their voices with the family; they were all in this situation together and would stand together to see it through.

At the end of the truncated service, as she had in the past, Ellie felt the normalcy of worship left the entire household reassured that all would eventually be well. As if signaling that, in the final prayer, her father mentioned their guest from London and petitioned the Almighty to lend his aid in returning their visitor to health.

Once her father uttered the benediction, the staff rose with resurgent energy and quickly filed out, keen to get back to their duties. Ellie smiled at the Kemps, then waved Harry and Maggie up the aisle.

She waited patiently until her father, with Masterton again propelling his chair, headed out into the foyer, then she set about gathering the chapel's hymnals and order of service sheets and making the place tidy once more.

She'd just finished stacking the hymnals on the shelf to one side of the small altar when Masterton returned and walked down the aisle toward her.

She straightened and faced him.

"I left Matthew in the library, bemoaning the lack of newspapers." Masterton halted before her.

"Sadly, there's not much I can do to rectify that." She didn't like the intent look in his eyes as they rested on her face; endeavoring to ignore it, she shifted to move past him and set off up the aisle.

He turned and fell into step beside her. "In a way, that's pertinent to what I wished to say. You're wasted here, Ellie, and while I applaud your devotion to caring for Matthew and the other two, you need to start thinking about your own future."

She halted. "Michael—"

"No—hear me out. My offer still stands."

"I've told you I won't be accepting it."

He met her exasperated gaze and had the effrontery to smile. "I know that's your answer—for now. But I'm a patient man."

She managed—just—not to glare. "I don't know what I can do or say to make you understand that I have no intention of marrying—you or anyone else. Not now, not in any future I foresee. I'm content with my life as it is."

He dipped his head and infuriatingly reiterated, "For now."

When she opened her mouth on a heated rebuttal, he smiled with irritating arrogance and held up a hand. "No—I don't wish to argue the point. I just wanted to remind you that my offer remains, laid at your feet."

With that, he saluted her and walked on and through the chapel's ornate archway, leaving her silently seething.

Apparently, through no fault of hers, Masterton believed that if he persevered, she would eventually weaken and accept his offer. Why he believed they would deal well together, she had no idea. Since he'd arrived in the district five years ago and introduced himself, he and she had often butted heads over what was best for the Hinckleys.

Over the past years, he'd been a constant visitor, yet in all conscience, she couldn't claim he foisted his presence on them. He usually called no more than once a week, often on Sundays, and spent his time chatting with and entertaining her father and only rarely remained overnight when the weather turned foul, as at present.

She couldn't say that he'd ever actually wooed her, either, which only made her even more determined that she would never sink so low as to accept his suit, one that, transparently, had no real affection attached to it. She didn't understand why he even wanted a wife, other than perhaps it would help with his business. She had no idea what that business was, but she could imagine that having a hostess might be expected, and that rather than going out and finding himself a wife at the Harrogate assemblies, Masterton had, instead, fixed his sights on her.

Truth be told, she suspected her refusal had only served to focus him even more determinedly on her. Some men were like that—not being able to get something only made that thing all the more avidly desirable.

His jibe "for now" lingered in her mind. Glancing back at the altar, she saw the altar cloth was still in place and went to fold and store the heavily embroidered piece.

While her hands smoothed and folded, her thoughts circled her situation, and she winced. She'd claimed she was content, and as far as the present went, that was true. But this life wasn't one she'd chosen for herself; Fate and circumstance had conspired to put hurdles in her path, blocking alternate avenues and maneuvering her into becoming the old maid she now was.

Admittedly, it had been her decision to turn aside from her London Season before it had begun and return here to care for her father and hold the household steady for her younger siblings. At the time, she'd seen no option, and even now, she did not for one minute regret her return, yet at that time, she'd believed she'd been merely putting off her Season, not permanently leaving behind the prospect of having her come-out and possibly finding a husband.

At the time, none of them had foreseen that it would take years for her father to recover, even to being able to sit in a chair. No one had imagined he would never walk more than a step or two again.

But life was life, and one did what one needed to do to care for those one loved, and looking back, even now, she saw no other path. But following that path had led to her having to lay aside her dreams—all of them. Not just of a husband and children of her own but of traveling farther than York and Harrogate, and she rarely visited even those towns anymore.

These days, the canvas of her life had reduced to the area around the Hall, from Kirkby Malzeard in the west, to Ripon in the east, and effectively marooned in such a backwater, with no reason or opportunity to venture farther, she found it difficult to see how or where she might meet an eligible gentleman who would overlook her advanced age and form a tendre for her.

That obvious circumstance undoubtedly fueled Masterton's arrogant certainty over his indefinitely available offer; he knew he faced no competitors for her hand.

She longed to puncture his swaggering self-belief, and one day, when he finally accepted she wasn't going to be a part of whatever life he planned, she would. On that, she was resolved.

After laying the altar cloth inside the cedarwood box in which it was stored, she shut the lid, then placed the box on the shelf behind the altar.

Turning toward the archway, she cast a last searching glance around. Seeing nothing out of place, she walked purposefully up the aisle and into the chapel's foyer.

"Ah—there you are, my dear."

She swung to face Morris as he rose from the window seat on which he'd been sitting and, plainly, waiting for her. Politely, she inclined her head. "Mr. Morris."

Like Pyne, Morris was the same age as her father. Of the three men, Morris had the heaviest build, yet he remained upright and active. He'd always struck Ellie as the epitome of what people meant by saying a man was a "John Bull" type; he projected the impression of having the brute strength and dogged determination to carry all before him. His dark hair was thinning, and his complexion was weathered and just a touch ruddy from the hours he spent outdoors, overseeing his acres.

He halted a yard away and smiled a touch self-consciously. "I would be honored if, when it's just the pair of us, you would call me by my given name of Edward."

Ellie managed not to blink in surprise, but she had known Morris for all of her life. Hesitantly, she said, "If you truly wish it...Edward."

He smiled as if she'd given him some gift. "Thank you." Then he sobered and met her eyes. "My dear, I realize that now might not be the best time to broach this matter, yet I feel that waiting to speak might be unwise."

Oh, dear. A trickle of presentiment dripped down Ellie's spine.

Blissfully unaware, Morris forged on, speaking earnestly and a touch forcefully. "I have long wished to make it plain to you that, if anything were to happen to Matthew or through any other happenstance you find yourself in need of a protector, out of the friendship I bear your father and, indeed, the respect I hold for you"—he broke off to bow to her—"I would be happy to marry you and act as your and your siblings' shield." He paused for a heartbeat, then, eyes hardening, added, "You have no need to fear being pressured into marriage by the likes of Michael Masterton!"

Damn it. He overheard Masterton.

Pressing her palms together, Ellie drew in a slow breath. "Mr. Morris —Edward. While I value your friendship, both with my father and through him, with me and this household, there is really no need for any such declaration."

"Permit me to be the judge of that, my dear. None of us can know the future, and having a practical alternative to any opportunist's offer cannot be a bad thing."

She opened her mouth, on what words of denial she had no idea, but Morris held up a meaty hand.

"I require no answer at this time. I have only spoken to ensure you are aware that you do, indeed, have options." Heavily, he inclined his head to her. "Now I have said my piece, I will retreat to the library and allow you to get on with your day."

She drew in a deep breath, but instead of arguing further, she compressed her lips tightly and, somewhat stiffly, inclined her head to him.

She stood in the foyer and watched Morris walk ponderously away.

His words hadn't come as a complete shock, but she had hoped they would never be spoken—at least not to her. Morris had, of course, sounded out her father about the idea Morris had taken into his head that, given his widower status, if Ellie received no suitable offers, then, ultimately, it might serve all concerned were she to become Morris's second wife. Wisely, her father had mentioned the exchange to her, assuring her he had said nothing to encourage his old friend. As Ellie understood it, Morris had proposed that, subsequent to their wedding, he would move to the Hall and manage his acres from there, effectively pooling resources with the Hinckleys, at least until Harry reached his majority and took over managing the Hall estate.

In Ellie's eyes, Morris's and Masterton's offers had at least two points in common; they were designed to improve the life of the offerer and had precious little to do with improving life for her, much less her family.

When Morris's heavy footfalls had faded, she drew in a bracing breath, then shook her head. "Men!"

Lips setting, she set out for the stairs that would take her to the kitchen, to discuss Cook's latest views on how best to bolster Cavanaugh's strength.

On reaching the back stairs, she couldn't hold back a "Faugh! Men and their notions of marriage! Hah!"

CHAPTER 5

*G*odfrey spent Sunday morning glumly languishing in bed.

He'd finally accepted Ellie's wisdom that there was no point in him attempting to evaluate the Albertinelli until he was fully recovered—in his terms, that meant being well enough to stand steady on his own feet for at least a few hours. Realistically, that was how long he would expect to have to stand and walk before and about the painting, examining it from different angles, in close inspection as well as from farther away, to adequately complete his commission for Eastlake and the gallery.

At the moment, he could barely stand long enough to use the chamber pot, and even then, Wally had to steady him.

The fever had affected his balance, and the cough had stolen his strength. Or perhaps it was the other way around.

Regardless, that morning, while thinking of the household praying in the chapel, he'd sent up a prayer of his own and made a vow that to make his wish come true, he would abide by all Ellie's strictures, down all the bitter broths the cook sent up for him, and in short, do whatever he was instructed to do in order to get better.

He hated coughing and wheezing only a touch less than he hated burning up with fever.

That morning, the fever had abated somewhat, but from experience, he knew it was likely to build as the day progressed. "So I'll possess my soul in patience and lie here in this bed."

Sadly, bearing with inactivity had never been his strong suit.

Listlessly, he picked up the book on Hinckley Hall. He was still leafing through it, but while he'd stumbled on points of interest here and there, he found it difficult to concentrate for more than ten minutes at a time.

When Ellie finally walked through his door, he was delighted to see her, but since he hadn't talked for hours, his attempt to greet her only brought on another paroxysm of coughing.

She rushed to fetch a glass of some cordial Wally had brought up earlier that morning.

He obediently sipped, then lay back on his pillows and quietly said, "Hello."

She noticed the book lying discarded on the bed. "Have you already finished it?"

"No." He paused, then confessed, "It's interesting, but I can't concentrate for long enough to make much headway."

"Ah, I see."

He heaved a sigh. "You'll be pleased to know that I've decided I should do all I can in pursuit of my own recovery, including doing precisely as you and Mrs. Kemp bid me." He met her eyes and tried to infuse resigned obedience into his gaze. "Whatever you say, I will do—even if you tell me to lie quiet for a week."

Her lips twitched. "I'm not sure an entire week will be required, but we'll see."

He frowned. "I hoped you would tell me it'll only take another day."

She laughed wryly and settled once more in the wing chair facing the bed. "It's possible that another two days abed will see you sufficiently improved to at least sit out in a chair, but listening to the wheeze in your lungs just now, I can't imagine that it will take less time than that."

She bent to the sewing basket nestled at her feet.

The constant itch of his restlessness eased at the evidence she intended to remain and keep him company. He watched her sort through garments and select one to mend. As she smoothed the fabric of a summer gown over her lap, focusing on a ripped seam, he thought of the numerous items he'd already seen her repair. "That basket of mending resembles a bottomless pit."

She smiled. "Maggie insists on flounces—they are all the rage for girls her age—but she's a hoyden and promptly rips them. And she's a terrible needlewoman, so"—she brandished her needle—"I step in."

"Hmm. I must confess that as the baby of the family, I've never been called on to step in and help, or even cover up for, my siblings."

"But have they stepped in and helped you?"

He thought about that. "I mentioned Ryder, and he's always there, my big brother, ready to step in any time I need help. Yet over the past decade, we've all, each in our own way, been pursuing what you might call our independent quests to discover our own paths in life."

She glanced briefly at him. "That sounds rather adventurous. Have your siblings found their paths?"

"Yes." He chose his words carefully. "Randolph—Rand—has become involved in the financing of inventions, while Kit builds yachts, and Stacie organizes musical performances." That might be downplaying his siblings' roles, but in essence, was the truth.

"And your path lies in examining paintings."

"Paintings, sculptures, and the like." He studied her downbent head. "So what paths are your siblings likely to take? They're old enough to have some inkling of what calls to them."

She tipped her head, plainly thinking. She set several stitches before replying, "Harry might be nearly twenty-one, but I sense he's still uncertain of what he truly wants."

When she paused, he gently probed, "But you have some idea of what would suit him, don't you?"

Although she was looking down, he caught her swift smile. "Harry's at that age where admitting that what he truly wants is exactly the life that's lying before him seems, to him, to be unambitious."

"You think he'll enjoy taking up the reins of the Hall estate?"

She nodded. "He spent all his childhood here, and he loved every minute of walking the woods, hunting, and fishing—all the typical country pursuits. His time at university gave him a broader perspective, and I think he feels he ought to be thinking about some more sophisticated occupation, but deep down, he's still the same person with the same talents and likes—he just needs to realize that."

"And that there's no shame in admitting that home is where he wants to be?"

She laughed softly. "Exactly. I see you have a sound appreciation of the way a young man's mind works."

"Indeed. I was one once." As he uttered the words, he realized how true they were, how far in his past now lay the stage of not being sure of what he wanted of life. A lot of what he wished for was already in place —with one notable exception.

He shifted in the bed. "What about your sister—Maggie?"

"Maggie, I'm not at all sure about. She keeps her own counsel." Ellie decided it was time to turn the tables before he asked about her own path in life. She looked up and caught his eye. "You have an older half brother as well as three older siblings. Are they all married?"

He nodded. "They are."

"And they have children?"

His face lit. "Lots. I have…" He was plainly counting. "Thirteen nephews and nieces." He grinned fondly. "Nine nephews and four nieces, ranging in age from a babe in arms to twelve years old."

She couldn't help but smile at his transparent enthusiasm. "You're clearly a besotted uncle."

"Of course! I'm their favorite uncle—the one who always has time to play with them."

His gaze grew distant; she studied the pleasure in his face, but then saw it fade as some other, more sobering thought took hold.

Before his mood could completely dim, she asked, "I take it you live in London?"

He hesitated, then nodded. "I have lodgings in York Street, not far from the National Gallery."

"The very hub of the capital." She set a careful stitch. "How do you spend your days? You can't be studying artworks all the time."

"Sadly, far from it." He paused, then said, "In between my trips to assess artworks, I suppose I spend most of my time with friends and family—not just in London but all about the country."

She raised her needle and swallowed a sigh. "That must be nice, seeing different parts of the country." Before he could ask if she wished she could travel, she said, "Tell me of some of the places you've visited."

After a second's hesitation, he obliged.

He was an excellent raconteur and had her laughing at several of his tales. With the eye of an artist, he painted landscapes with words, well enough for her to see them in her mind, to appreciate his liking for this place or that.

The hours slipped by. She left him to consume another bowl of broth and some bread, attended by Wally, while she joined the others for luncheon downstairs. Once the meal was concluded, she made her excuses and returned upstairs, eager to hear more of his travels.

After she'd settled in her chair—the mending basket was almost empty, but she had enough left to keep her hands busy—at her request, he moved on to describing his travels on the Continent, to cities she'd heard of but had no expectation of ever seeing.

"Dresden was surprisingly comfortable and welcoming. Quite ornate, mind you, with lots of baroque decorative touches everywhere." His eye was acute, his knowledge extensive, and his memory was capacious as well.

They whiled away the afternoon in pleasant accord. She tried to keep him occupied answering her questions, but he managed to slip in a few questions of his own, which led to a discussion of the Hall and its grounds and associated farms, and ultimately, led to a verbal excursion about the local countryside.

Eventually, Wally returned with a dinner tray, with another bowl of broth and some toast and cheese.

Godfrey sighed when he saw it and fixed her with a pleading look. "At this rate, I'll waste away before I get better." He opened his eyes wide. "I haven't been coughing as much this afternoon. Can't I graduate to real food?"

She had to admit that after spending the entire day settled in bed, he did look better. She finished folding her completed mending, then rose, approached the bed, and laid a hand over his forehead. After a moment, she lowered her hand. "Your fever has definitely reduced, but we don't want to court a relapse. However, I'll speak with Cook and report your progress and see what she and Mrs. Kemp think about you having more substantial fare."

"Thank you." His tone made the words heartfelt. His eyes met hers. "For all the hours of today. I've enjoyed your company, and that's kept me from moping—I do appreciate it."

She smiled. "I enjoyed the hours, too." She stepped away. "I must get ready for dinner. If I can get away, I'll look in later." She would make sure she did.

They exchanged nods, and she left him with Wally.

She did return later and sat beside him, and with no more mending to be done, they chatted about, of all things, the theaters in London and the Opera and musical performances he had seen and she could only dream of.

Through his eyes, that other life—the one she might have had if things had been different and her father's accident hadn't occurred—came alive.

When she finally left him to settle to sleep, she walked from his room with a far deeper appreciation of what Fate had denied her.

Monday morning dawned, and while Godfrey felt rather better, he knew he was some way from full recovery and so held to his promise to the lovely Ellie and dutifully remained abed. He was delighted to be presented with a bowl of remarkably delicious porridge drizzled with honey as well as two slices of toast and jam with which to break his fast.

Sadly, after briefly looking in on him after her own breakfast—and applauding his tack—Ellie had to leave to deal with household matters.

He made himself read more about Hinckley Hall and its history and was pleased to discover his ability to concentrate had improved. But after half an hour, his mind started to wander—flirting with the question of why Mr. Hinckley, who, curiously, he'd yet to meet, wanted to sell the Albertinelli. From all he'd thus far gleaned, the estate was—or at least should be—reasonably prosperous. Had it somehow fallen on hard times? Did the family need the money from the sale to continue to live in the style to which they were accustomed, or was there some other, non-financial reason that had prompted Mr. Hinckley to contact the National Gallery?

Godfrey's mind circled through the options, but he had no way of learning which applied. Eventually, he forced his eyes back to the book and set himself to plow on.

When a knock fell on the door, he looked up eagerly; although he'd immediately registered that the knock wasn't the same as Ellie's light tap, he was ready to welcome any distraction. "Come in," he called and waited to see who appeared.

Pyne entered, followed, this time, by another man of similar age. Gentleman farmer was Godfrey's immediate assessment, which was proved correct as Pyne clapped his hands and declared, "Good morning to you, Cavanaugh. What-ho!" Pyne gestured at the other man. "Allow me to present Mr. Edward Morris. An old friend of mine and of Matthew's. Morris has land up around Kirkby Malzeard." Pyne waved toward the west.

Morris came forward and offered his hand. "Both Walter and I were visiting here when the storm struck. We come every Wednesday to take luncheon with Matthew—with Hinckley, that is."

"I see." Godfrey shook Morris's hand, then waved his visitors to the chairs. "You come at an opportune moment, gentlemen. I find myself sorely in need of distraction."

Pyne again claimed the wing chair, leaving Morris to avail himself of the straight-backed chair Wally had left on the other side of the bed. Pyne glanced at the book Godfrey had laid down. "I see you've been reading a history, so that's hardly surprising, heh? Never could understand what I was supposed to learn by reading about people long gone. But then, I suppose you're used to dealing with all these long-dead painters."

Godfrey couldn't hide his smile. "Indeed." He recalled Pyne's Saturday inquisition, which had centered on Godfrey's peculiar occupation and his credentials to assess the Albertinelli.

He assumed that, having largely gained his answers, the man would take a different inquisitorial tack and was mildly surprised when Pyne cleared his throat and said, "Hope you don't mind me asking more about this whole art business, but I've never paid much attention to arty things —never really thought there was much value attached to paintings and the like—and now I find there is, that there's a world of business I never imagined out there, and well, I'm curious."

Perhaps because he was feeling better, Godfrey accepted that Pyne spoke sincerely, and smiled encouragingly. "No, of course not—I'm happy to tell you what I can." He settled against his pillows and gestured. "Ask away."

"Good-oh." Pyne's eyes lit. He sat straight, his hands braced on his knees. "Tell me about the old paintings like Matthew's—like the Albertinelli. Are there many of them about? Many other painters like that chap?"

"Not all that many paintings, because there aren't all that many master painters of that era—the High Renaissance, as it's known—whose works have survived to this day."

Slipping into a lecture on High Renaissance art was the definition of easy, and to his credit, Pyne appeared to lap up every word. Clearly, his interest in art truly had been piqued by the situation with his friend's Albertinelli.

While Godfrey rambled, touching on those aspects he suspected Pyne would like to hear about and responding to Pyne's questions, Morris sat more or less mum. He was listening, but remained on the periphery of the discussion. Godfrey had to wonder why he'd come.

Eventually, Pyne ran out of questions, and both he and Godfrey glanced at the clock on the mantelpiece. It was nearly ten-thirty; they'd been talking for over an hour.

"Right, then!" Pyne slapped his hands on his knees and stood. "Thank you for the information, Cavanaugh, but we'd better leave you to rest, or Ellie will be after us for tiring you out, what?"

This last was said with a jovial air, but Morris, who had also come to his feet, assumed a serious, almost severe expression. "Miss Hinckley is a caring lady. She runs this large household in exemplary fashion and has many calls on her time. She is always very busy."

The look Morris bent on Godfrey was, he suspected, meant to depress any pretensions of importance he harbored and make him feel guilty over taking up Ellie's time.

"That's true enough," Pyne allowed, "but she did say to tell you, Cavanaugh, that she expects to be up to keep you company shortly."

Morris's expression could only be described as sour—as if he'd sucked a particularly tart lemon. He shifted his gaze to Pyne, but there was nothing he could say as, with a jaunty wave, Pyne made for the door.

His gaze on Morris's face, Godfrey called, "I'll look forward to enjoying Miss Hinckley's company."

Morris shot him a dark, definitely disapproving—almost warning—look but, after hesitating for an instant, had no option but to follow Pyne out of the room.

When the door closed—firmly—behind the pair, Godfrey stared at the panels, then humphed. "Obviously, Morris harbors some interest in Ellie." He replayed the man's words and frowned. Morris had spoken of Ellie as if she were a housekeeper rather than the effective lady of the house—or as if her housekeeping skills were the only aspect of her that held value, at least to Morris. "Regardless," Godfrey muttered, "I didn't mistake his proprietary air." Morris had wanted to warn him away.

With another dismissive humph, Godfrey reached for the book on Hinckley Hall just as the door opened and Wally entered, bearing a tray that sported a teapot along with a single silver dome. Godfrey abandoned the book. "What have they sent up?" He was starving.

Wally came to the bed and, with a flourish, placed the tray across Godfrey's lap and whisked the dome away. "Proper coffee and two nice pieces of seed cake."

Godfrey grinned. "Excellent. Sustenance!"

After Wally had departed, carting away the empty cup and plate on which not a single crumb of the delicious seed cake remained, Godfrey settled to wait for Ellie to appear. Pyne had said "shortly," and surely that was now; it was after eleven o'clock.

He didn't feel like reading, and that left his mind free to wander, more or less aimlessly. He thought of his family; now, in the aftermath of Christmas, as usual spent at the abbey, they would all be at their various homes, settling back into their—in their terms—blissful family lives. Each of his siblings had their spouse and children to hold, protect, and nurture, and each had their particular interests to pursue, rolling forward through the coming year.

He considered the pictures such thoughts painted in his mind—much like a five-paneled artwork, with a panel for each Cavanaugh. The first four panels were detailed and complete, the lives they represented full and fulfilling.

Despite his closeness to his siblings, he still felt like an outsider looking in—as if he was viewing their achievements from an emotional distance. More disturbing still, even with his position as an expert authenticator of artworks well and truly established, his own painting wasn't properly filled in. It remained incomplete, with a blank section at its heart.

As if he had nothing to center him, no anchor.

After a while, he drew his mind from contemplating that intrinsic emptiness—that inner hollowness—and set it wandering again. The look Masterton had bent on Ellie resurfaced, to be followed by Morris's pseudo-warning.

His restlessness returned, a persistent, niggling insistence that he really ought to get up and…be there. For Ellie.

Both Masterton and Morris had designs on her, and Godfrey wasn't sure she knew.

He didn't consider himself an impulsive man, but when she didn't appear, the compulsion to get up, get dressed, and go and find her swelled to a level impossible to resist.

Had Morris or Masterton waylaid her?

Godfrey sat upright in the bed and considered how he felt. His head didn't swim, and his bouts of coughing seemed less frequent. He suspected he still had a fever, but it was much less than on the previous day. All in all, he was definitely getting better.

The question was, was he strong enough to stand without assistance?

There was only one way to find out.

He swung his legs out from beneath the covers and sat on the edge of the bed. His head remained steady, and he felt entirely normal. Slowly, he pushed upright.

His legs held—at least, for now. Keeping one hand on the bed, he took a cautious step away from the side—and wobbled.

He froze, locking his knees—just as a light rap fell on the door.

Aghast, he looked across the room.

The door swung inward. "It's only me," Ellie sang. "I'm sorry I—"

She broke off and stared at him.

He tried to straighten, but a cough struck, and he wheezed and started to topple.

She raced toward him as, desperate, he lunged for the bed.

Her arms came around him, locking about his lower chest.

She tried to hold him up, but his weight was greater than hers, and in a flurry of limbs, hands, and skirts, they fell in a tangle half on and half off the bed.

He collapsed on his back, and she came down on her side beside him. Her arms were still about him, one trapped beneath his back.

With her warmth seeping through the fabric of his nightshirt, with her soft curves pressed against his side and the supple length of her legs stretched alongside his, he wasn't at all sure he hadn't somehow seized a gift he didn't deserve.

"Oof!" Ellie half sat and brushed her hair, which had fallen forward, out of her face. It took her a second to remember how to breathe, then she glared at Godfrey. "You promised you would remain in bed!"

He frowned, only partly repentant. "I know, and I'm sorry. But when you didn't arrive…I felt I had to make the effort and at least see what I'm capable of."

She tried not to think about the way his deep voice reverberated through his chest, impinging on her trapped arm. Wrestling with her focus, she slapped a palm to his forehead. After a moment, she declared, "Your fever is still there, lingering."

His hawkish eyes on her face, he arched his brows. "But it's not as bad as it was, is it?"

She compressed her lips, but had to admit, "No. But it's not gone yet, and we don't want a relapse."

The closeness of their bodies had flooded her senses, and she was fighting a losing battle to concentrate on the real issue—his health—rather than on the long, hard, male body stretched alongside hers.

No matter how much her senses wanted to wallow, she had to get up and put distance between them. Setting her jaw and clinging to her determination, she wriggled her arm, trying to slide it from beneath him; he grunted and rolled away, allowing her to pull free. She tried not to notice the smooth muscles her forearm and hand skimmed across or the long lean muscles of his back, buttocks, and thighs imperfectly concealed by the fine linen of his nightshirt.

It took even greater effort to push up and back and, trying not to look flustered, scramble to her feet.

Grimly, he rose on one elbow and levered himself back and around until he could slump on the pillows again. He reached for the covers, and she hurriedly helped him pull them up and over him.

"Well, that was a failure."

She was still somewhat breathless, but at his morose tone, she observed, "You don't seem to be coughing as much today."

He thought, then arched his brows. "That's true." His eyes swung her way, and he looked at her hopefully.

But having tended Harry through various illnesses, she was immune to such wordless pleas. "You're lucky you didn't fall away from the bed —you might not have been able to get up by yourself, and lying on the cold floor until Wally or I came in and found you would almost certainly have caused a severe setback."

He arranged his features into a contrite expression.

She had to press her lips tightly together to hold back a smile. Exasperated—with herself as much as with him—she planted her hands on her hips and, when she could risk speaking, informed him, "You're worse than Harry, and Lord knows, he's a terrible patient."

"He has my very real sympathies."

"I daresay. In your case, I can only hope that knowing that your fever, lingering or not, appears to be waning and that your cough, although clearly still there, sounds to be less deep will encourage you to stay in bed until both fever and cough properly subside."

He looked at her, then sighed. "Yes, ma'am."

She bit her lip. "I sound like a shrew."

He closed his eyes and tipped his head back on the pillows. "No, you don't. This was my fault. I'm just...frustrated." Then he opened his brown-and-gold eyes, looked at her, and essayed a small smile. "I promise to behave now you're here to bear me company."

She almost snorted. "Yes, well, I can only stay until the luncheon gong sounds."

His smile lingered, flirting about his lips. "I'm grateful for whatever time you can spare me."

Lowering her arms, she walked to where she'd dropped her replenished sewing basket just inside the door. After shutting the door, she reclaimed her usual chair, bent to the basket, pulled out a piece of fabric, a thread, and a needle, and settled to hem the square.

"What are you stitching?"

"New napkins for the breakfast parlor." She glanced at him. "What would you like to talk about?"

After a moment of thinking, he replied, "Tell me about the area. Are there any local festivals peculiar to the region?"

Without the slightest effort, they filled the next hour with a comfortable discussion, with an ease that Ellie, for one, had never before experienced, not with anyone else.

～

After savoring a sustaining luncheon of soup—not broth—followed by a thick sandwich crammed with slices of roast beef with pickles and cheese, Godfrey felt considerably restored. That his ill-fated excursion of the morning hadn't dragged him down he considered a testament to his returning health.

Ellie had warned him that she would likely not be able to return until later in the afternoon, so he seized the chance to doze a little; he felt sure she would approve of that.

Wally woke him with a cup of tea and two more slices of seed cake. "Told them you liked it," he explained.

"Thank you. That was kind of you and them."

"Aye, well, we all want you to get better, and feeding you up seems to be agreeing with you."

"Mm-hmm," Godfrey mumbled around a mouthful of the sumptuous cake.

After he'd polished off both tea and cake, Wally hoisted the tray and carted it away. "I'll be back with your dinner."

Godfrey slumped against his pillows. *What now?*

The hour he'd spent chatting with Ellie before luncheon had soothed his restlessness to some degree. She was a sensible lady, and regardless of what either Masterton or Morris thought, he'd detected not the slightest hint of any real understanding existing between her and either gentleman, at least not in her mind.

Still...

Quiet voices in the corridor reached him. Wally had yet to fully close the door and was speaking to someone.

A second later, the door was pushed open, and a young man looked in. "Hello—I'm Harry. Ellie's brother."

Godfrey vaguely remembered the stripling had been present in the front hall when Godfrey had made his less-than-spectacular entrance. "Oh, yes—hello." The questioning way the lad was looking at him made him grin. "Did your sister send you up to keep me occupied?"

Sheepishly, Harry returned the grin. "In a manner of speaking. She said you were champing at the bit, but were forbidden from getting up as yet. I can sympathize, so came to see if I could be sufficiently entertaining to distract you."

Godfrey smiled and waved Harry to the wing chair. "Come, sit, and let's see how we get on."

Godfrey studied Harry as he sank into the chair, sitting upright with his hands between his knees. Ellie had mentioned he was nearly twenty-one and had recently returned from Oxford, which explained his neat but quietly fashionable coat and trousers. He was of average height, with light-brown hair and hazel eyes more brown than Ellie's gold-flecked green.

"Before I forget, Johnson—our stableman—said to tell you that your bays are no worse for wear." Harry's expression lit, bordering on reverent. "I've been out to see them—they have outstanding lines."

Godfrey smiled and volunteered that the pair came from the Cynsters, a name Harry recognized in relation to fine horseflesh, and that only deepened his reverence. From that promising start, they shifted to discussing the finer points of the horses one needed in the capital versus the horses one needed while living in the shires.

"There are some fine hunters hereabouts," Harry said. "They do better over our sort of country."

Godfrey agreed. "I grew up in Wiltshire and still visit there frequently. I do most of my riding there, so I ride hunters most of the time. I don't keep a horse in town—if I need to ride there, I hire a hack from a jobbing stable." He studied Harry's eager face. "Do you have a particular mount here?"

"Yes—a gray gelding. He's a real goer, too." Enthusiasm shone in Harry's eyes. "Mr. Morris bought him in York, but he—Captain—wasn't really up to Mr. Morris's weight, so Papa made an offer and bought him for me."

That was an opening Godfrey couldn't pass up. "Does Morris live close by?"

Harry waggled his head. "About three miles. He owns a reasonable-sized property—Malton Farm—out past Kirkby Malzeard."

"I understand he's an old friend of your father's."

"They were boys together at the local grammar school. Pyne as well." Harry paused, then matter-of-factly said, "Now Papa is confined to a chair, they visit every Wednesday, which I have to say is good of them." Harry met Godfrey's eyes. "Papa can't get out, you see."

And he'd been fretting over being confined to bed for just a few days. "I hadn't heard." Godfrey hesitated, then asked, "It was an accident, I assume."

Harry nodded. "Papa was riding with the hunt over by the dales, and he was thrown." Harry paused, then went on, "It was nearly nine years ago, now." He looked at Godfrey. "But that was why Ellie didn't have her Season—she was supposed to come out under our Aunt Camberford's wing and was already in London, but then Papa had his fall, and Ellie came home straightaway." Harry faintly grimaced. "Which was just as well, because we needed her."

That, Godfrey thought, explained a lot, including why Mr. Hinckley hadn't come to see him. "So your father can only move about on the ground floor."

Harry nodded. "He's keen to meet you, but he can't manage the stairs."

"Please convey my compliments to him, and that I regret not yet being able to come to him."

"I will. He'll be pleased to know you're improving."

The door opened. Harry glanced that way and smiled as Ellie came in. He rose. "We've been entertaining ourselves very well."

Ellie's gaze went from her brother's face to Godfrey's. Whatever she saw there made her smile. "So I see. Thank you for assisting." She caught Harry's hand, then, with open fondness, lightly pressed her shoulder to his. He grinned and leaned against her for an instant, then she released his hand, patted his arm, and drew away. "I can stay until dinnertime, so you're relieved of duty."

With their expressive faces mirroring their feelings, both Hinckleys were easy to read. The depth of the affection that flowed between them was impossible to miss and struck Godfrey as of a different caliber—more open and freely given, more powerful and less restrained—than was usually displayed, certainly within his family. They might feel the same degree of emotion, but they drew back from so openly owning to it.

For the Cavanaughs, emotion had always equated to vulnerability. Not so for the Hinckleys.

Harry looked at Godfrey. "I'll trudge out to the stable and check on the horses. I'll let you know if there's anything to report."

Godfrey smiled and saluted Harry, who waved and left, closing the door behind him.

Ellie sank into the chair her brother had vacated. "I hope he didn't badger you about horses and London life."

"Not at all, although we did discuss horses—his and mine." Godfrey wondered if there was some way to subtly inquire whether Mr. Hinckley's decision to sell the Albertinelli was due to financial necessity. It wasn't strictly something he needed to know in order to evaluate the painting, but now he'd come to know them, it was awkward feeling that the family's future might depend on his report.

That Mr. Hinckley's infirmity and his consequent inability to physically oversee his acres had extended over a significant portion of Harry's minority hadn't escaped Godfrey. An estate with an owner unable to keep an eye on things on the ground was a recipe for disaster or, at the very least, avoidable neglect.

But he could think of no acceptable way to phrase his question, and the reason Mr. Hinckley had decided on the sale might, in fact, be something else altogether.

Ellie had settled to hemming her napkins. His gaze on her, Godfrey realized her task might well be an indication of straitened circumstances. As he watched her, his impatience to get better, see the painting, and deliver the good news—not just to Eastlake but even more to the Hinckleys—swelled and grew.

Ellie glanced up at him and smiled. "So"—she nodded to the book lying by his hand—"you must have learned all about Hinckley Hall by now."

He smiled and disclaimed and seized the opportunity to steer their conversation into the safer waters of local society and the neighborhood's grandes dames.

CHAPTER 6

*G*odfrey hated—*hated*—being coddled, especially when said coddling was prompted by guilt. When, on Tuesday morning, the door to his room closed behind Ellie as she left to deal with the household, he slumped against his pillows and groaned. Feelingly.

His fever had, finally, vanished, but his cough persisted, albeit with less force and significantly lower frequency than even the day before. Regardless, when he'd advanced his arguments that he should be allowed out of bed after breakfast, he'd run into a wall of concerted opposition— from Ellie, Wally, and Mrs. Kemp. The three had presented a united front and had steadfastly refused to countenance him even sitting by the fire in his dressing gown.

During the ensuing discussion, he'd come to the appalling realization that, regarding his illness, Ellie felt guilty—*personally* guilty—on the grounds that she had been the one to write the letter to the gallery that had resulted in him being on the road to be caught in the storm; she insisted on holding herself, her father, and her family at least partly to blame for his state.

Bad enough, but Wally was also plainly eaten by guilt because it had been him Godfrey had dragged up the drive, thoroughly exhausting himself in the process, thus leading to him succumbing to his youthful malaise.

As for Mrs. Kemp, she patently saw herself as representing the collective responsibility of the household.

There was no rational reason any of them should feel guilty, much less continue to feel so, but nothing Godfrey had said had made the slightest dent in their trenchant resolution. He was to remain abed until he was well—well enough for them to no longer fear a relapse—and there was no moving them from that.

And until he was fully recovered, he was not going to be allowed to see the Albertinelli, either.

In the end, he'd bowed to their edict; he hadn't been able to bring himself to cavalierly override their concerns. He might believe there was no reason for either guilt or concern, but all three of them were convinced otherwise.

And when Wally reported that, although no more snow was falling, the drifts lay deep on the ground, and as the temperature had dropped to freezing and below, no one was able to get in or out, any immediacy over viewing the painting evaporated. There was no way to send a report to London, not until the thaw set in. Consequently, as both Ellie and Wally had been quick to point out, a few more days' convalescence would make no difference at all.

Except to him.

Could a person go insane from boredom?

A tentative tap fell on the door. Not, Godfrey concluded, someone who had visited before. Interest piqued, he called, "Come in."

The door opened, and a girl—a young lady, really—looked in. Her naturally curly, brown-blonde hair was pulled back and anchored by a band about her head. She was on the petite side in stature, her complexion more milk-and-roses than her sister's more refined tinted porcelain; given the similarity of her features to Ellie's, Godfrey had no doubt this was Maggie.

Her eyes, her expression, brightened. "Oh, good! You're awake."

Godfrey smiled. "I am, indeed. And I'm dreadfully bored. Do come in."

She smiled and came forward with a light step. Harry followed her through the door and shut it, then, with Maggie, advanced on the bed.

"If you're not up for chatter"—Harry cut a glance at his sister—"just say, and we'll leave you in peace."

"I would welcome some chatter." Godfrey smiled at them both. "So what should we chatter about?"

Her expression expectant, Maggie tugged the wing chair closer to the bed and curled up in it.

With a grin, Harry lifted the straight-backed chair from by the wall, turned it, set it down beside the wing chair, and straddled it. He folded his forearms across the chair's back and looked at Godfrey. "Incidentally, your horses are in excellent case."

"We are not going to talk about horses." Maggie sent her brother a warning look, then returned her gaze to Godfrey. "I love my mare, Daisy, and adore riding about the lanes and fields, but I've observed that when gentlemen start talking about horses, they go on and on and on."

Godfrey laughed. "Very true. So, not horses." He regarded their bright, eager faces. "You know that I'm here to examine the painting your father has offered to sell to the National Gallery?"

Both nodded, and Maggie said, "The Albertinelli one that hangs on Mama's parlor wall."

Does it? "If that's the only Albertinelli in the house, then that's the one." He looked from Maggie's brown eyes, oddly soulful in her pixielike face, to Harry's hazel ones. "Do either of you know anything about where the painting came from? Who brought it to the Hall?"

"Great-great-many-times-great-uncle Henry," Maggie said.

"He did a Grand Tour long before it became fashionable, sometime in the sixteen hundreds," Harry supplied.

"He liked art." Her gaze on Godfrey, Maggie tipped her head. "Possibly a bit like you."

Ignoring his sister's attempted digression, Harry went on, "Apparently, old Uncle Henry wanted to make a splash, so he bought paintings by famous artists of the time and brought them home."

"Artists?" Godfrey's instincts pricked. "So there were other paintings?"

"So the histories go," Maggie said. "But the only painting still here is the Albertinelli."

Harry nodded. "We think the others must have been sold at various times through the centuries."

"Just like we're selling this one." Maggie's gaze remained trained, rather disconcertingly, on Godfrey's face. "We decided that although the painting was a favorite of Mama's, it doesn't appeal to any of us, which is why it's hidden away in her old parlor where no one ever goes, and in the circumstances, she wouldn't mind if we sold it."

Harry nodded. "The harvests have been poor for the past few years, so our coffers are approaching low ebb. The money will help to keep everything running smoothly, and we believe Mama would say that was far more important than the painting, especially now she's no longer here to see it."

Their words, and even more their matter-of-fact tones and the openness of their expressions, told Godfrey that selling the painting had been a family decision rather than one made by Mr. Hinckley alone.

The Hinckleys were a truly close-knit family, bound not only by affection but also by common cause; they formed a family unit in a far more cohesive and effective way than Godfrey was accustomed to or could even remember encountering. Perhaps it was an outcome of Matthew Hinckley's accident, that he'd been forced to rely on his children in so many ways, he'd accepted their right to be involved in all major family decisions.

"I'm quite looking forward to seeing and examining the painting." An understatement; Godfrey was eaten by impatience, and the younger Hinckleys' information had only further whetted his eagerness.

Harry grinned. "I can understand the gallery sending someone like you—"

"Although you're nothing like we expected," Maggie put in.

"—but given the painting's been here since old Uncle Henry brought it home, then there's really no question it's the same one, is there? The one he bought from the artist's family."

Godfrey was intrigued. "Did he? Buy it from the artist's family?"

Harry nodded. "It's in one of his letters, and there's a declaration about the painting, too."

"Glory be," Godfrey breathed. "You have provenance."

Maggie frowned. "What's that?"

He explained, and both agreed there were letters that mentioned the painting, together with a certificate of sorts.

"I'll need to examine those as well."

"Ellie thought you would," Maggie said. "She's gathered them all together. She knows where they are."

"So, you see," Harry went on, "we're not the least anxious over what your finding will be, but we're still eager to hear it so we'll know that step is completed and the sale can go ahead."

Godfrey nodded. Their conviction regarding the authenticity of the painting—and if they had the provenance they claimed, it was a reasonable one—accounted for the lack of angst on the subject he'd encountered in everyone there. They were all keen to have him deliver his verdict, and many were curious about how he would reach it, but all were certain what that verdict would be.

To all at the Hall, him examining the painting and sending in his report were simply routine steps that needed to be taken in order for the sale to proceed.

"Even Mr. Pyne and Mr. Morris are interested," Maggie informed him, "and even Masterton seems keen to hear that your verdict's been delivered."

"But enough about the painting." Harry exchanged a swift glance with Maggie, then looked hopefully at Godfrey. "We wondered if you would tell us about your life in London. About what sort of entertainments you enjoy when there."

Somewhat to Godfrey's surprise, Maggie didn't look as enthused as her brother. She clarified, "He wants to know how you fill your days."

Harry frowned at her. "Yes, I do. *I* would find that interesting."

Godfrey had to smile at Harry's tone, which elicited a sniff from Maggie. "Well," he said, "there are the galleries, of course, and the coffeehouses—I often meet with friends there." He continued, describing the places he haunted and the more regular events he attended. Harry hung on his every word, while Maggie listened with what seemed to be her customary focus.

Some minutes later, the door opened, and Ellie came in. Given her lack of surprise on finding her siblings ensconced with him, he deduced she'd sent them to keep him amused. He was giving the pair a rundown of the favored theaters in the capital; Harry and Maggie glanced Ellie's way, but immediately returned their avid gazes to him.

When she paused, watching and transparently debating whether he needed to be rescued, he flashed her a reassuring smile.

Her lips curved. She glanced fondly at her brother and sister, then, leaving Maggie in possession of her favorite wing chair, went to claim its mate, angled by the hearth.

He was acutely—distractingly—aware that, although Ellie settled to her stitching, she was also listening as he rambled on. The inconsequentiality of his social life in the capital was suddenly not something he wished to own to. He rapidly brought his dissertation on that subject to a close.

Harry seemed satisfied, but Maggie stirred and said, "While that all sounds very *busy*, I'm not sure I would find it"—she gestured vaguely —"sufficiently fulfilling." She met his gaze. "And before you say that for me, there would be parties and balls and idle walks in the park to show off my London gowns and gaze at everyone else's, I'm not really drawn to such entertainments—I find them rather superficial."

She wasn't wrong in that. Godfrey inclined his head in acknowledgment and wondered where she was leading him.

Sure enough, she fixed him with a direct look. "What about your family? How many brothers and sisters do you have? Do you spend much time with them?"

That was a safe, even laudable topic, and one to which the Hinckley siblings would relate. He stated simply that both his parents were dead, then launched into a recitation of his half brother's, brothers', and sister's names, carefully omitting their titles, and explaining their ages with respect to him.

"Are they married, then?" Maggie asked.

He nodded and expanded his account to include their various spouses and his nephews and nieces. With a nod to Harry's interests, Godfrey added the occupations his siblings—and their spouses—had made their own.

Holding true to her direction, Maggie brought the discussion back to the people—the family. "Where did you spend Christmas? Do you all get together?"

He nodded. "We gather at Raventhorne"—he bit off the word "Abbey"—"my half brother's house."

Maggie's eyes widened. "It must be a big house." She tipped her head. "Or don't you all stay there?"

Beyond Maggie and her big eyes, Ellie slowly raised her head and stared at him.

Warily, he admitted, "It is. And yes, we all stay for several days."

Ellie set aside her stitching, rose, and walked nearer. "Raventhorne?" She halted with her hand on the back of Maggie's chair, her gaze fixed on him. "Is there a village or town by that name?"

Godfrey met her eyes. To lie or… No, he couldn't. Not to her. "No—it's an abbey. A house built within an old abbey."

Ellie's eyes widened to rival Maggie's. She drew in a long breath. "Your half brother is the Marquess of Raventhorne?"

There was a hint of panic in her tone, but "Yes" was all he could say.

"And Raventhorne Abbey is your childhood home?"

He nodded. Both Harry and Maggie were looking back and forth from Ellie—who now looked faintly horrified—to him.

"But…that means you're a lord." She made it sound like an accusation.

He wrinkled his nose. "Yes, but being Godfrey Cavanaugh and Lord Godfrey Cavanaugh… Well, there's really no difference, you know."

"But it *does* make a difference." Ellie couldn't immediately explain why, but she knew that was true. The nobility were a breed apart. To illustrate her point, she waved at Maggie and Harry. "See?"

Godfrey looked at her siblings, both of whom were now staring at him with mouths agape and amazed if not stunned expressions.

"It makes a difference to how people see you," she insisted.

He raised his gaze to her face. "Yes, I know." He let the words stand for a moment, presumably to let their meaning sink in. "That's precisely why I don't go around parading my title. People think it makes a difference to the sort of person I am, but it doesn't. I'm Godfrey Cavanaugh, either way, and there's only one of me."

"I see your point," Maggie said, and all attention deflected to her. "And I think it's commendable—making your mark without using your title to smooth your way."

Harry was frowning. "But most of those you deal with—in London, I mean—must know who you are. They'd be familiar with the nobility, so your surname would tell them."

Godfrey returned his gaze to Ellie's face. "That's another reason why, when I'm in situations such as this where my family affiliation isn't immediately recognized, I seize the chance to leave my title behind. It doesn't define who I am."

"Quite so!" Abruptly, Maggie uncurled her legs and rose. "You've been very accommodating, answering all our questions, but now Ellie is here to watch over you, Harry and I should—I'm sure she'll say—leave you to rest before luncheon."

Ellie was taken aback by the strength of Maggie's declaration, but essentially concurred. "Yes, indeed." She glanced at Godfrey and couldn't help but add, "Lord or not, you should rest."

Godfrey inwardly sighed, but smiled at Harry and Maggie and invited them to return when they had time. They grinned and waved and left him with their sister.

Before she could retreat, he sat up and tried to wrestle the pillows behind his back.

Ellie hesitated, then came to help him.

The instant she'd finished resettling the pillows, he reached up and back and caught her hand.

He used his hold to gently draw her to where he could meet her eyes, then twined his fingers with hers. "As ought to be obvious, I don't conceal my title to deceive. I avoid using it because, on hearing it, people make assumptions that simply aren't true. I'm a fourth son, and my being a lord matters not one jot to me or to my family. Other than for Ryder, our titles are accidents of birth that don't mean much—except in the eyes of those who think they do."

Shifting his hold, he slid his fingers over hers, searching her eyes and hoping she was getting his message, namely that, as far as he was concerned, socially, he and she were equals.

Before he could think of words to make that plain, she eased her fingers from his. "You really ought to rest, and I've just remembered I need to speak to Mrs. Kemp."

With a smile that could have meant anything at all, she turned and walked quickly to the door.

Godfrey watched the door close behind her, then drew in a slightly shaky breath.

Revelations were often unsettling, and the last minutes had revealed more than he'd anticipated. The compulsion to ensure she understood how he saw her, that there was no impediment to a relationship between them, rather obviously illuminated the path along which his mind—consciously or otherwise—was leading him. Had been leading him.

At some point in the past days of being marooned in bed, he—his inner self—had seen her, observed her, studied and weighed her, and made up his mind.

Ellie Hinckley was the lady he wanted as his wife.

He'd always wondered if that particular type of lightning would ever strike him. Now it had, it was clearly up to him to seize the chance Fate had dangled before him.

Godfrey settled against the refluffed pillows and started to plan.

Just a touch rattled, Ellie descended the back stairs, hoping to find Mrs. Kemp in her office off the kitchen.

Inevitably, her mind replayed Godfrey's—*Lord* Godfrey's—assertions, his assurances that his title was essentially irrelevant.

But it wasn't, was it?

Regardless of whether she believed him or not, the point in their recent exchange that had most struck her was that he'd made an effort to explain what he felt and, once they were alone, had underscored his argument. His assertion that his title was more or less meaningless to him and his family had rung true, but more than that, stressing the point to her had meant something to him.

"The question," she muttered, "is what?" She frowned. "Or should that be why?"

She had no idea. Faintly grimacing, she stepped off the last stair and went in search of Mrs. Kemp.

~

Tuesday wore on. After consuming a satisfyingly substantial three-course luncheon, Godfrey lay back and set his mind to the task of assembling all the bits and pieces of information he'd gleaned about his hosts.

One early conclusion was that he should consider his hosts to be the whole Hinckley family and not just Mr. Matthew Hinckley.

He'd yet to gain sufficient facts to form any image, much less understanding, of Matthew Hinckley himself, but his view of Ellie was sharp and clear. She was plainly the anchor for both family and household, the lynchpin about which both revolved. She carried that responsibility as both duty and right and with a confidence that spoke of long years in the role. Of the staff, he'd as yet met only Mrs. Kemp, but the respect that worthy accorded Ellie spoke volumes; the staff would follow Ellie into battle if need be.

As for Harry... Godfrey had never had a younger brother, but from his own experience, he knew young men like Harry—quiet yet sensitive to the expectations of those about them—went through a stage of not being sure of their path. Of not knowing what they wanted of life as opposed to what others thought they should want. Having returned home after his years at Oxford, Harry, Godfrey sensed, stood poised on the cusp of making that decision.

The quiet steadiness that ran beneath Harry's youthful exterior made Godfrey reasonably certain Harry would choose wisely.

Maggie, however, remained something of an enigma. On the one hand, she seemed relatively carefree, yet also willful, the sort of young lady who might require more protection than most, yet contradicting that, he'd sensed she was unusually clear-eyed and rather insightful. She understood what people didn't say as well as what they did.

So much for the family.

Now that he'd met Pyne and Morris and learned of their long friendship with Matthew Hinckley, Godfrey viewed their association with the Hinckley household as unremarkable—merely what might be expected, even to Morris's clumsy attempt to warn him away from Ellie. With respect to her and Godfrey, Morris might well see himself as acting in Matthew Hinckley's stead.

That left Masterton as the only above-stairs person Godfrey had yet to pigeonhole. He reviewed what little he'd learned from others plus what he'd observed during Masterton's visit. The man presented as a respectable country gentleman and, apparently, was some Hinckley connection.

"Connection" could mean anything. Other than Masterton living "locally"—presumably meaning somewhere within an hour or so's ride—Godfrey knew precious little about him.

Most importantly, he had no idea why Masterton had his eye on Ellie.

On arriving with Godfrey's afternoon tea, Wally promptly reported, "The snow's feet deep, and the freeze is on. Even where they've shoveled paths, the way's all icy and slippery. No going anywhere until some of it —a good deal of it—thaws."

"I see." Godfrey poured his tea, then reached for a slice of fruitcake. "How are things below stairs?"

"Very comfortable, truth be told." Wally dropped onto the straight-backed chair. "The Kemps are firm but fair, and Cook's a right wonder. The staff seem nicely settled—no sniping or anything like that."

"I gather that after his accident, Mr. Hinckley can no longer walk."

"Aye, that's right. He can only manage a few steps on his own, but 'parently, after his fall, it was feared he'd never walk again at all, so everyone's pleased he's still with them, as it were. His man's devoted, from all I've seen."

Godfrey nodded and sipped. "What about Masterton? I take it he's still here."

"Aye—he's stuck like the rest of us. All I've heard about him is he's some sort of connection of Mr. Hinckley's and came to live in the area about five years ago. He started turning up here, at the Hall, regular-like, about then, and at the start, the staff worried he was trying to ingratiate himself with Mr. Hinckley and Miss Hinckley for some nefarious purpose, but nothing ever happened, and they—the staff—say that, over the years, he's been helpful to the family." Wally shot Godfrey a searching glance. "You doing your usual trick of trying to work out how everyone fits together?"

Godfrey shrugged and set down his empty cup. "It helps to pass the time."

Wally nodded at the now-empty plate on the tray. "That fruitcake's another thing as helps pass the time—you've polished off both slices, and they were thick ones, too."

Godfrey smiled. "Tell Cook they were delicious."

"Aye, I will." Wally stood and hefted the tray. "What I won't tell her is that you're buttering her up because you like to eat and have hollow legs."

Godfrey grinned and relaxed against the pillows. "Reticence on that point might be wise."

Wally snorted and headed for the door. Before he reached it, it opened to reveal Ellie. Wally stepped back, and she entered, carrying not her sewing basket but a soft bag with beaded handles.

She smiled at Wally, glanced at the tray, then looked at Godfrey. "I see you've devoured your tea."

"Indeed. I've just dispatched my compliments to your cook."

Wally stepped outside and pulled the door shut as Ellie walked to her usual chair.

Godfrey focused on the bag. "What—no more mending?"

"No." She sat, set the bag on her lap, and drew out an embroidery hoop. "I can't remember the last time my sewing basket was empty." She studied the half-finished design stretched on the hoop. "In fact, that was so long ago I can barely remember what I'm doing with this."

Godfrey watched her work it out. Once she had her needle threaded and was pushing it through the linen, he started chatting about his sisters-in-laws' and sister's embroidery achievements, describing several memorable pieces. "Stacie has never taken to the occupation, for which she rightly blames our mother, who was not embroidery-inclined, but Mary—Ryder's marchioness—is surprisingly adept. Once fully executed, her designs are quite something to behold—they almost qualify as works of art."

Head bent, Ellie asked, "Why is that surprising? I would have thought a lady of the station to become a marchioness would be highly skilled in all the acceptable ladylike accomplishments."

"Ah, but Mary is—was—a Cynster, and as a family, they don't necessarily adhere to the usual strictures regarding a lady's education. More to the point, Mary in particular is a very *busy* sort—in the sense of organizing not just her own life but also the lives of all around her. I'm sure she would have demonstrated that propensity from an early age. It's my belief her elders thrust an embroidery hoop into her hands from the moment she was old enough to ply a needle, just to keep her busy with something other than organizing them."

Ellie laughed. "I'm sure you do your sister-in-law an injustice."

"Not at all." *Just wait until you meet her.* He didn't say the words, but the certainty that such a meeting would occur stood rocklike in his mind. "But what about you? Do you embroider because it's an acceptable ladylike occupation or because you enjoy it?"

Ellie smiled as she drew up her needle. "Because I enjoy it." She paused, then went on, "There's always a little bit of fascination in seeing a design take shape. In seeing the picture unfold." She glanced at Godfrey. "I suppose it's a bit like painting, really."

He nodded. "Just with a different medium."

She "hmmed" and continued stitching. Even though she now knew he was a lord—a scion of a noble house, no less—the ease of interaction between them, of conversation and freely exchanged views that they'd established over the past days, hadn't appreciably changed.

While she felt there should be some degree of constraint between them—between a lady of the gentry and a haut ton lord—there simply wasn't. Now that they'd grown accustomed to thinking of him and dealing with him as Mr. Godfrey Cavanaugh, and given he refused to stand on ceremony, that made it difficult for them to erect barriers of class between him and them.

She hadn't met many lords, not of his caliber, but she'd never heard of even a baron insisting on being treated as just another gentleman.

Even as the thought flitted through her mind, she realized such behavior said quite a lot about him—about the man behind the title.

The man he insisted on being.

He continued to chat about this and that—mostly about ladylike occupations—in a way that often brought a smile to her face and easy responses to her tongue. He'd clearly set himself to be entertaining, and in that endeavor, he excelled.

She hadn't yet told her father that they were housing a scion of a marquessate, but she would. However, given said scion's stated wish, she would also convey his desire not to have any fanfare made of his exalted birth.

She wondered what her father would think about that.

While she plied her needle and her design evolved, she reviewed all she'd learned about Godfrey Cavanaugh since he'd arrived at Hinckley Hall. Considering the circumstances of his arrival, considering the family's hopes for the Albertinelli painting, his illness aside, she felt rather grateful that it had been him the Keeper of the Paintings of the National Gallery had sent.

She glanced up to find him regarding her speculatively.

On seeing he had her attention, he said, "Obviously, I'm significantly improved, so perhaps tomorrow, I might escape this bed?"

She arched her brows noncommittally. "Perhaps. We'll have to see whether your cough is less chesty tomorrow."

"Assuming my cough has the good sense to subside, I might finally get a chance to interact with the others staying here. I've met Pyne and Morris, and Harry mentioned their long friendship with your father, but although I've met and spoken briefly with Masterton, I'm unclear as to his connection with the household."

She looked down lest he see in her eyes the irritation Masterton customarily provoked. "Masterton is a distant cousin—once or twice removed, something like that—on my father's side. He lives in Ripon, and as there are few other Hinckley relatives still living, Papa welcomes him here." She shrugged lightly and didn't look up. "Masterton has proved helpful over the years, especially in making Papa feel...connected with the outside world."

I tolerate Masterton because of that.

"Ah—I see." Godfrey eyed Ellie's bent head and elected not to push for more, at least not at that time.

"So tell me." She looked up from her embroidery. "What does your sister do with these musicians you say she collects?"

He smiled and swung into a description of the musical academy his sister, Stacie, and her husband, Frederick, had endowed.

But he wasn't going to forget Ellie's equivocal attitude to Masterton —that had come through quite clearly—nor the fact that she hadn't wanted to meet his eyes while discussing the man.

What, exactly, all that meant, Godfrey wasn't sure he could even guess, but the question the exchange left circling in his brain was: What was Masterton to her?

The answer came from an unexpected source.

First, however, early the following morning, his hopes of escaping the bed were dashed by the outcome of a bedside conference attended not just by Ellie, Mrs. Kemp, and Wally but also by Cook—apparently the most experienced in the treatment of chest complaints. A plump, gray-haired veteran, Cook had walked into the room in time to hear him cough as Wally had helped him to sit. She'd instantly looked askance at him, and when Ellie had asked for her thoughts on his proposal to get up and dressed and go downstairs, had shaken her head and opined, "Still too heavy on his chest. If he gets up and goes downstairs, it'll flare up again, like as not."

And that had been that.

He'd taken one look at Ellie's and Mrs. Kemp's faces—he hadn't even bothered to check Wally's—and slumped back on his pillows, defeated.

So he was languishing under the covers when, just past eleven o'clock, a tap fell on the door. At his somewhat terse "Come in," the door opened, and Maggie bounced into the room, whirled, and quickly shut the door.

Then she turned to him, grinned, and came forward to curl up in the wing chair as she'd done the previous day. "I thought you must be utterly bored, so I've come to entertain you."

He set aside the book—a second history of the house covering the years since 1700 that Ellie had found for him—that he'd slowly been leafing through, hunting for any mention of old paintings. Meeting Maggie's bright, encouraging eyes, he asked, "How are you proposing to accomplish that?"

She arched her brows and tapped her chin, then offered, "You answered a lot of our questions yesterday. Is there anything about the Hall you would like to know—anything I can tell you?"

He remembered his thought that Maggie was insightful. He suspected that also made her observant.

He wondered how to word his question so he didn't give her more ammunition regarding him than she already held. "Your sister." He felt sure Maggie had noted his interest there. "Has she any current suitors? Anyone she favors?"

Maggie's wide grin suggested he'd guessed aright; she wasn't the least surprised by the direction of his interest. "As to the second question, there's no one she encourages. But the answer to the first is that there are two."

"Two?" Who didn't he know about?

Maggie nodded in a sage way that sat oddly on her pixielike countenance. "Masterton and Mr. Morris."

"Ah. I see."

"Actually, you probably don't." Without further prompting, she elaborated, "Masterton first offered for Ellie about six months ago. She's never entertained the slightest feelings for him and declined his offer, but he seems determined to keep his offer on the table, as it were, presumably hoping she'll change her mind." Maggie shook her head. "She won't, but he doesn't seem to see that."

Maggie drew in a breath. "As for Mr. Morris—well, he's an older man with an older man's way of thinking. The notion of love doesn't enter into his thoughts about marriage, and I'm not even sure he bears any real attachment to Ellie beyond her being Papa's daughter." Maggie tipped her head. "As far as I can see, it's more a case of Mr. Morris wanting a lady to manage his household—that or simply to be able to say he has a wife, and a young wife at that. He's not really interested in Ellie herself, if you take my meaning—she could be some other lady entirely, and from Mr. Morris's point of view, that would still be satisfactory. Of course, Ellie being Papa's daughter is probably what focused Mr. Morris's interest on her in the first place. I don't think he socializes much, so Ellie's likely one of the few younger ladies he encounters."

Maggie paused to reflect, then went on, "I know Mr. Morris has spoken to Papa about his offer to 'take Ellie off his hands.'" She made a scoffing sound. "I'm not sure if Mr. Morris has spoken to Ellie herself, but Papa discussed the prospect with her, and as one would expect, she was adamant in declining."

Maggie's gaze had grown distant, and her brow furrowed slightly. After a moment, she offered, "It's not as if, over the years, Ellie hasn't had several beaux who offered for her hand—younger gentlemen who were perfectly eligible—but she never truly encouraged any of them and always politely declined their offers." Maggie paused, then went on, "I've often wondered if that was because of us—because she didn't want to leave us. And truth be told, I really don't think we would have managed without her."

As Godfrey had thought, Maggie saw more than one might expect.

Suddenly, Maggie glanced at the clock on the mantelpiece. "It's nearly time for luncheon—they'll be bringing up your tray soon." She scrambled to her feet and flashed him a mischievous look. "I'd better go." With a last smile and a wave, she whirled and made for the door.

"Thank you for coming," Godfrey called, then the door shut, and Maggie was gone.

Staring across the room, Godfrey reflected on the interlude. If he hadn't asked about Ellie's suitors, would Maggie have found some way to tell him, anyway?

He rather thought she would have.

As for what she'd told him...

Morris was no threat, certainly not a rival. Masterton, however, as far as Godfrey could tell, was a perfectly eligible suitor. He was of a reasonable age, personable, and presented well, was a distant cousin and so presumably knew and was accepted by any wider family, and he lived locally. Very likely, if Ellie married him, Masterton would be amenable to residing at Hinckley Hall so she could continue to hold the fort there, at least until Harry married.

It seemed that Matthew Hinckley had approved the offers of both men, while leaving the decision of whether to accept them entirely up to Ellie.

"Hmm." Godfrey shifted restlessly. He definitely didn't like being stuck in bed while Masterton was free to wander the house, able to trail after Ellie, spending time with her and advancing his suit.

Worse, with them all trapped in the house together, what if Ellie found herself being importuned by Morris and turned to Masterton to protect her? How would that play out?

Godfrey didn't like to think.

He needed to be out of bed and in a position to interact with Ellie—to woo her and formulate his own offer to place at her feet. He wasn't foolish enough to simply blurt out "marry me." He needed to compile a list of attributes and advantages he could offer her. He needed to act to sway her to his side.

He thought through all Maggie had said and recalled that, despite Masterton's offer still being open and before her, Ellie had steadfastly declined to accept it.

The recollection gave him a touch more confidence—enough to turn his mind to cataloguing the benefits Ellie would accrue were she to marry him. He narrowed his eyes in thought. "I need to concentrate on those aspects that matter most to her."

When it came down to it, he needed to define what Miss Eleanor Hinckley wanted in a husband.

From what Maggie had so deliberately let fall, it seemed likely Ellie had some firm stipulations on that score.

CHAPTER 7

$\mathcal{G}$odfrey bided his time until after luncheon the next day. As it happened, that was virtually a week since he and Wally had staggered over the Hinckley Hall threshold and he'd collapsed on the hall tiles.

After Maggie had left him the previous day, Wally had arrived with his luncheon on a tray and had stayed to talk about this and that. Ellie had come in later, and he and she had once again chatted about inconsequential subjects. She'd left before dinner and hadn't returned through the evening.

He'd spent the hours alone debating how best to woo her, ultimately concluding that the surest way forward required three consecutive steps. First, he needed to get better so she and her supporters would allow him out of bed, thus laying to rest any lingering guilt, however irrational.

Then he needed to view the Albertinelli painting and write and dispatch his report to the gallery.

Only once that was done would he be free to pursue Ellie.

Honor—and common sense—dictated that he hold back until he'd declared his verdict on her family's painting. Any earlier approach would run the risk of being misconstrued, and that was the last thing he wanted.

Having a clear plan—a plotted path to follow—had given him the patience to remain in bed through the morning. While his fever had vanished and he was feeling stronger and steadier, his irritating cough still lingered.

When Ellie arrived at two-thirty, embroidery bag in hand, he was primed and ready to make his case.

Before she'd even reached her chair, he stated, "Even you and Mrs. Kemp would have to agree that I'm a great deal better. My fever's entirely gone, and my cough is much improved. Surely getting dressed and coming downstairs to meet your father and perhaps have dinner with the rest of the company would not put too heavy a strain on my constitution."

He held her gaze levelly, not quite challengingly, and drew in another breath—and started coughing.

Not as deeply, not as helplessly, but...

"Gah!" he exclaimed once the paroxysm passed. "I hate this cough!"

Ellie smiled in rueful sympathy. "I know." She set her embroidery bag on the rug beside the wing chair and went to lay her palm on his forehead. "You're right in that your fever's gone and hasn't returned, but that cough is still a concern." Removing her hand, she met his eyes. "You heard what Cook said yesterday. Rush your convalescence, and you'll likely pay for it with a relapse."

He sighed and shifted restlessly, long fingers picking at the covers. "I know, but...this seems to be going on and on with no end in sight."

She truly did sympathize, but... Eyeing the disaffection in his face, she tried a different tack. "You know it's important to me—to all of us here—that you get well. Properly and completely well, and that's not simply so you can examine the painting."

He lifted his gaze to meet hers. She'd never perfected the knack of hiding what she felt, and as his gaze traveled over her features before returning to her eyes, she felt just a little exposed.

But then he sighed and relaxed on the pillows. "You're right." He held up a hand in surrender. "I acknowledge that. You don't need to fear I'll try to get up again when your back is turned."

When Ellie gifted him with a smile, Godfrey decided the capitulation had been worth it. He was annoyed with himself—with his chest and its capacity to scupper his chances of rising from the bed—but he hadn't forgotten his underlying resolve to remain in his fair head nurse's good graces.

"Good." She stepped back and turned to the chair.

As she settled with her embroidery, he reached for the book he'd been reading. He was nearly to the end, and he'd yet to find any mention of paintings—or any furnishings, come to that. The author had been more interested in architecture and landscaping.

He opened the book and continued scanning the pages. Soon, he reached the end with absolutely nothing to show for his industry. He stifled a sigh and shut the tome—and a nugget of information resurfaced, one imparted by Harry and Maggie but which had subsequently sunk beneath the clouds of boredom.

Abruptly, he switched his gaze to their sister. "Ellie." When she looked up, he went on, "Harry and Maggie spoke of letters that mentioned the painting and also some sort of declaration that proved your ancestor had bought the Albertinelli directly from the artist's family."

She nodded. "There's a sheaf of letters and papers that mention the painting. The gallery wrote that any such documents would be helpful, so I've kept them for you to see."

He could hardly contain his excitement. "They could be important— very important." Briefly, he brandished the book. "And given I've been reading for the past several days without going into a decline, could I please see those documents now?"

She blinked, then lowered her embroidery to her lap. After a moment of staring at him, a frown formed in her eyes. "Studying them won't... well, exhaust you, will it?"

He grinned and laid a hand on his chest. "I swear on my honor that examining such documents will not adversely impact my health." He paused, then arched his brows. "In fact, *not* examining them might well result in me going into an overactively frustrated state."

She threw him a look, but rose, set her embroidery on the chair, and headed for the door. "I'll fetch them, and we'll see."

Godfrey watched her go, genuinely more excited than he'd felt in weeks.

Ellie returned to the best guest bedchamber with the sheaf of documents she'd collected from the top drawer of the dresser above which the Albertinelli painting hung.

Approaching the bed, she couldn't help but note the eager excitement in Godfrey's face. He looked like a boy about to get his most-wished-for birthday present.

Smiling, she held out the papers, and he all but seized them. In doing so, his long fingers slid over hers; albeit unintentional, the caress still affected her. Still made her knees slightly weak.

"Thank you." His gaze—avid—had locked on the topmost document.

"You're welcome—I was keeping them for you." She returned to the chair and picked up her embroidery, but continued to watch him.

He flicked through the letters and documents, then sighed a happy sigh. He glanced at her. "These are far more comprehensive than I—or the gallery—expected. Far more than most people with paintings like the Albertinelli have."

She smiled. "Luckily, my ancestor—the one who bought the painting —and those who followed were rather garrulous letter-writers. And they kept everything. The family archives are extensive." She nodded at the papers. "That's where I found those."

He'd returned his gaze to the documents. Now, he shook his head. "Amazing."

She watched him sort through the letters and notes, laying them in various piles on the counterpane.

Then he started to read with utter concentration.

An hour passed, and he said not a word, just steadily worked his way through the papers, setting some aside while devouring others, then re-sorting his piles.

When a tap on the door heralded Wally with Godfrey's afternoon tea on a tray, Ellie rose. "I have to speak with Cook. I probably won't manage to return this evening."

"Mm." Godfrey hadn't looked up, leaving Wally standing with the tray poised and nowhere to set it.

Ellie softly huffed, walked to the bed, and tried to tug the letter Godfrey was perusing from his fingers; she wasn't surprised when he only clutched it tighter, but at least he looked up. "Wally is here with your afternoon tea. You need to move the papers aside."

"Oh." Godfrey looked to the side and seemed to see Wally for the first time. Then he glanced about and ended looking at the bedside table. "Put it there."

Wally sighed and did. To Ellie, he said, "It's always like this when he gets caught up in something arty. I'll see he drinks his tea, miss, and eats his dinner, come to that, although I'll probably have to wrestle those papers away to do it."

"Thank you." With an amused glance at Godfrey, she picked up her embroidery, slid it into her bag, then walked to the door. Pausing, she looked back, took in the total absorption that gripped him, then, smiling, opened the door and left him to it.

Godfrey was only vaguely aware that Ellie had gone. Wally was a hovering presence by his side, but the letter in his hand commanded his undivided attention. It wasn't from Ellie's many-times-great-uncle Henry, whose scrawl Godfrey could already identify, but was executed in a much more distinctive hand on a parchment carrying an embossed coat of arms.

A coat of arms Godfrey had seen before, many times over the years.

What he was looking at was a letter in Italian stating that the Medicis of Florence—Albertinelli's home—were unable to accept delivery of the painting one of the ladies of the house had commissioned.

Godfrey stared at the thick, yellowing parchment in his hands while his mind whirled, assembling all he knew of Florence in 1495, the year noted at the top of the letter.

Distantly, he heard Wally ask something, but he couldn't drag his mind from the black, spiky writing. "Shh," he murmured. "I have to study this."

Ellie woke the next morning to the sound of steady dripping.

She pushed back the covers, threw on her warm robe, and went to the window. Flinging back the heavy curtains, she gazed out at a sight that had her smiling. Water was slowly dripping from the eaves, and the bare branches of the trees were gradually reappearing as the snow and ice that had sheathed them melted away.

She looked up toward where the sun should be. While there was no sunshine as such, a glowing orb shone through the still-thick yet whiter clouds.

The thaw had finally arrived.

Buoyed, she continued to smile as she washed and dressed, then headed downstairs.

On reaching the front hall, she discovered the mail plus a stack of newspapers piled on the hall table.

"Just arrived, miss." Kemp came up bearing a silver salver. "The lad who brought them said the road from here to Ripon was passable by horse, but for carriages, it'll be another day or two, and he didn't think he'd be able to go much farther than the Laver. He said the drifts on the other side of the river were even deeper than here."

"Still, that we've at least got these is excellent news." Having heard the rumble of male voices from the breakfast parlor, she gathered the rolled newspapers and waved Kemp, who had stacked the letters on his salver, ahead of her. "Let's take these to the others and spread the news."

Her family had beaten her to the parlor and were already seated about the large table, along with Morris, Pyne, and Masterton. While Kemp delivered the letters to her father, Ellie set the newspapers on a side table, then slipped into her customary chair opposite her father and smiled at him when he looked inquiringly her way. "Good morning," she responded brightly. "It appears we're finally going to have a warmer day."

She exchanged greetings with the others, then helped herself to toast, and Harry passed the marmalade. The men were addressing plates of ham, eggs, and sausages and discussing the forecasts for the rest of the winter and the prospects for the local cabbage crop.

She'd poured herself a cup of tea and was taking a sip when the farming discussion reached its end, and her father looked up the table at her.

"How is Mr. Cavanaugh's convalescence progressing?"

She'd informed her father that Godfrey was a member of the aristocracy, but in light of his stated preference not to flaunt his title—a stance her father had viewed approvingly—they'd decided to honor his wishes.

She lowered her cup. "He's much improved, but Mrs. Kemp and I— and Cook as well as his man—believe a few more days are necessary to ensure a full recovery."

Her father nodded soberly. "A chill of the depth he endured is not to be taken lightly. Please offer him my compliments and assure him that him making a full recovery is important to us all."

Ellie smiled. "I will. Meanwhile, he's studying those documents from our archives—the ones that mention the painting."

Seated to her right, Masterton had been sipping his coffee. He lowered his mug and frowned. "What documents are those?"

Morris and Pyne also looked interested.

Ellie's father explained, "There were letters from when old Henry Hinckley bought the painting, and others later, after he brought it home. And various papers in Italian had been folded with the letters."

Masterton's frown deepened. "Do you read Italian?"

Her father shook his head, and Ellie said, "I just gathered everything in the archives that contained the artist's name."

"The gallery wrote that any document mentioning the painting was important and that we should show all such documents to them or, rather, to their authenticator, meaning Cavanaugh. So Ellie collected all the letters." Her father looked at her. "Now he's seen them, what did he say?"

"He said that we have far more documentation than most people with paintings like ours." She suppressed a smile at the memory of Godfrey's utter absorption, of how the papers had seized his entire awareness and not let go. "He seemed very pleased. I gather he has to study the documents carefully as part of his assessment of the painting."

"Huh," Pyne said. "Fancy that." After a moment of cogitation, he asked, "What's he think to find in the letters? Do you know?"

"I think it's that the existence of the letters and their mentions of the painting prove that Great-uncle Henry bought it and brought it here, to the Hall." Ellie shrugged. "I don't know what else he might look for or find."

"Hmm." Pyne fell silent, transparently digesting the existence of the letters.

Ellie finished her toast and drained her teacup.

As she set the cup on the saucer, Pyne glanced at Masterton, then caught her eye. "Perhaps Masterton and I might pop up and see Cavanaugh—alleviate his boredom, offer some sympathy, what?"

Remembering her last sight of Godfrey, Ellie was certain he wouldn't welcome such an interruption. "I really don't think that's a good idea." Inspiration struck. "As studying the documents is a part of his assessment of the painting, and he's already started examining them, we shouldn't unnecessarily distract him."

Pyne grimaced, but didn't argue.

Masterton merely arched his brows. After a moment, he looked at her father. "Matthew, as the road is apparently passable on horseback, I believe I'll return home." Masterton folded his napkin, laid it beside his plate, and smiled at Ellie, then swept his smile over Harry and Maggie before, ultimately, directing it at her father. "Thank you for your hospitality. I'll call in a few days to see how you're getting on."

All murmured farewells as Masterton rose. He shook hands with Pyne, Morris, and her father. Then he tipped a salute to Harry and Maggie and, at the last, caught Ellie's eye. He held her gaze for a second, then inclined his head in polite farewell. She responded with a polite yet cool nod of her own. His smile—too quietly arrogant for her liking—resurfaced, then he turned and walked from the room.

She heard Masterton speak to Kemp in the hall, asking to have his horse saddled. She returned her gaze to Morris and Pyne, wondering if they, too, would depart.

Her father read her mind, smiled, and said to his friends, "As you two came in your gigs, you'll need to wait until the roads clear further before attempting to return to your homes."

"Aye." Morris peered through the windows at the still very snowy park. "Tomorrow, perhaps—if it doesn't freeze again."

Pyne, Ellie noticed, looked rather glum at the prospect of returning to his own hearth.

Harry and Maggie excused themselves, rose, and departed.

Her father pushed back his chair and, as Morris and Pyne rose, waved them toward the door. "I told Kemp to put the newspapers in the library. We might as well adjourn there and read in comfort."

The three men made for the door, with the footman, Mike, pushing her father's chair. When they drew level with her, Ellie prepared to rise and follow them out, but her father held up his hand, signaling Mike to halt.

When Morris and Pyne paused and looked back, her father waved them on. "I'll join you in a minute."

The pair nodded and walked on. When they'd passed down the corridor leading to the front hall, her father waved again at Mike. "Leave us—I'll call when I need you."

Ellie sat back in her chair and waited.

Her father turned, met her gaze, and smiled rather ruefully. "Masterton spoke to me again. About his offer."

"Oh." Her tone effectively conveyed that she hadn't changed her mind.

Her father sighed. "I know you don't fancy him, but he seems a steady, steadfast sort, and stuck out here at the Hall as you are, your chances of meeting another eligible man aren't high." He paused, then added, "You might be hard-pressed to find a better man."

She thought of the man in the bed in the best guest bedchamber—a gentleman her father had yet to set eyes on.

Then she thought of Masterton. "I've said this before, Papa, and I suspect you shrugged it aside as a glib response, but in your heart, you must know I'm sincere when I say that I would rather die an old maid than marry a man for whom I feel not an ounce of affection."

Her father grimaced. "Aye, you did say that, and I hoped you would come around in time. Masterton even lives locally, so won't take you away from us. Indeed, he even mentioned that, when he spoke with me earlier today—that he'd be willing to live here, at least to begin with. But if you haven't changed your mind..." He held up both hands. "I've always said it's your decision, and I stand by that—I won't pressure you one way or the other."

She laid a hand on his arm. "Thank you, Papa. I appreciate that."

He blew out a breath. "Yes, well, I suppose I should tell you that Morris spoke with me again, too."

She sighed. "He found me after the service on Sunday and explained his...well, proposition."

Her father softly snorted. "He might be one of my oldest friends, but no matter how much I wish to see you wed, that's one proposal you won't hear me supporting. He's literally old enough to be your father—well, he's nearly a year older than me—and that's not what I want for you."

"It's not what I want for me, either," she assured him. She studied his face, then tightened her grip on his arm. "Please believe that I'm content to live as I am, as we do. I have a good life here, and I lack for nothing— there's nothing more I need in life."

Need, not want; prevarication rather than an outright lie.

Her father patted her hand. "You say that, my dear, but you won't know what you might have until a gentleman—the right gentleman— arrives and lays a different future at your feet." He caught her eye. "All I ask is that if that happens, you won't allow considerations of me, Harry, and Maggie, or of this household, to hold you back from seizing happiness. If it offers, take it. I did with your mother, and despite all, I have never regretted that decision."

She smiled. "Thank you, Papa. I'll remember that—just as long as you remember that I, too, have no regrets over any of my decisions to date."

Her father softly humphed and shook his head at her. "You're worse than me—always the last word."

She grinned.

"Papa? Ellie?"

They looked across to see Maggie hovering in the doorway.

"I thought I might take one or two of the newspapers up to Mr. Cavanaugh." She widened her eyes. "He must want a break from the old letters by now and might like to know what's happening in London."

Her father nodded. "An excellent idea, my dear. Ask Mike to come and push me to the library, and we'll choose a few papers for you to take upstairs."

Ellie rose. "And I had better consult with Mrs. Kemp and see what stocks we need to replenish once Johnson can drive the cart into Ripon."

Maggie summoned Mike, and together, they all quit the breakfast parlor.

Ellie paused in the front hall, watching as, with Maggie all but skipping alongside, Mike pushed her father's chair down the corridor to the library.

This was normally the time she went upstairs to check on Godfrey. The previous evening, she, Mrs. Kemp, and Cook had agreed that he should be allowed to get dressed and sit by the fire in his room today; she ought to check whether his cough had been aggravated by the change in position.

But Maggie would take the newspapers up, and that should keep him amused for at least an hour, which would allow her to finish her necessary planning with Mrs. Kemp.

Besides, while discussing Masterton's and Morris's proposals—and even more, while listening to her father's advice—her mind had insisted on bombarding her with images of Godfrey Cavanaugh.

Plainly, it would behoove her to shore up her inner defenses before she once again confronted him in the flesh.

Reasoning thus, she headed for the servants' hall.

Dressed in his striped pajamas and swathed in his dressing gown, yet groomed as befitted a gentleman—at last—and thus feeling considerably more like his fashionable self, Godfrey was sitting in one of the wing chairs, both of which were now angled before the hearth in which a cheery fire blazed, when a light tap fell on the door.

"Not Ellie" was his immediate and faintly disappointed thought. "Come in."

The door opened, and Maggie appeared. She looked around, spotted him, and smiled delightedly. "They've let you up!"

"Yes!" Lowering the magnifying glass he'd been wielding, he returned her smile. Then he saw the newspapers in her hands. "What have you brought me?"

She crossed the room and showed him. "*The Times* and the *Manchester Gazette*. There are other London newspapers downstairs, but

Mr. Morris and Mr. Pyne got to them first. Papa said he'd send them up later."

"Oh, *The Times* will do excellently to start with." He gathered the letters he'd been examining and carefully set them on a side table away from the fire. He laid the glass atop the pile, and Maggie handed him *The Times.*

She set the *Gazette* down by his chair, then crossed to the other chair and sat, curling her legs beneath her as was her wont. "Those are the letters Ellie found for you and the gallery, aren't they?"

He nodded. "They're quite remarkable—the gallery will be very pleased."

"What are you doing with them?"

He looked at her and realized she wasn't just asking to be polite; she truly wanted to know. "Believe it or not, the first thing I need to do is verify that the documents are genuine. Sometimes, in situations such as this, people have been known to write letters to make it appear that their paintings are, for instance, much older than they actually are."

She frowned. "How do you do that—prove a letter is genuine?"

"You look at the paper—parchment, usually, so it has a certain weight, texture, and color. Does it have any embossing or mark indicating the maker or the period in which it was made? Are the edges cut or raw? Then you check the ink—is it the sort of ink that comes from the time in which the letter was supposedly written? Has it faded as one might expect? Then you look at the writing itself—the style, the flourishes—and ultimately, you look at the words used. The use of some words is strongly associated with certain historical periods." He smiled. "And if everything looks right, then you can be fairly certain that all is well and the document is genuine."

"I see." Maggie looked at the documents stacked at his elbow. "Are our documents genuine?"

"Thus far, I've seen nothing that makes me think otherwise." He followed her gaze. "In fact, I'm prepared to swear that all the documents I've properly scrutinized are, indeed, genuine."

"That's good, isn't it? For the sale of our painting?"

"Yes, very good." He didn't want her asking any more probing questions; as it was, it was hard enough keeping his welling excitement suitably restrained. He shook out the paper. "I wonder whether it's snowed in London."

Maggie took the hint and rose. "I'll leave you in peace. Ellie will be up shortly—she had to have a meeting with Mrs. Kemp."

He inclined his head. "Thank you for bringing up the papers."

Maggie smiled and turned away. Then she turned back. "Oh—I meant to tell you. As riders have reached us, Masterton has left—he rode away to Ripon just as I came up the stairs."

That was good news. Godfrey raised his gaze to Maggie's face, and she promptly went on, "Mr. Morris and Mr. Pyne are still with us—they won't be able to leave until the roads clear enough to let carriages through. Ellie mentioned the letters about the painting, and Mr. Pyne immediately suggested he and Masterton should come up to see you, supposedly to save you from boredom, but it was plain he was really interested in the letters."

"Was he?"

Maggie nodded. "Ellie quashed the notion—she said they shouldn't distract you from your work for the gallery."

He studied Maggie's impish face; she'd just told him that Ellie—knowing he wouldn't appreciate the interruption—had effectively leapt to his defense. He smiled. "Thank you for telling me."

Maggie grinned and headed for the door.

Godfrey watched her go. When the door shut behind her, still smiling, he shook his head and returned his attention to *The Times*. Although his gaze settled on the page, he didn't immediately read.

His relief on hearing of Masterton's departure was not a surprise. There was nothing he could hold against the man—other than him having made an offer for Ellie's hand and, compounding that, to this point refusing to accept her rejection of his suit. No matter how personable and even likeable Masterton might be, those acts, especially the latter, were sufficient to guarantee Godfrey's animus.

Pursuing a lady after she'd refused one was not the act of a gentleman.

As matters stood, Godfrey expected to feel negatively toward any man who set his sights on Ellie. Morris, therefore, was another who had earned Godfrey's disapproval, but as long as the fellow didn't actively importune Ellie, Godfrey was willing to overlook his sins.

The fact was that while he didn't view Morris as any sort of rival—and was therefore willing to ignore him—Masterton was another kettle of fish. Until Masterton accepted Ellie's dismissal, Godfrey would remain on guard.

Much like a dog with a bone.

The analogy made him wince, but...

He prodded the protective and distinctly possessive feelings that Ellie —simply by existing—had caused to burgeon and grow. "Compulsive" didn't come close to adequately describing their power.

It occurred to him that Masterton might be similarly afflicted. If so, perhaps he should cut the fellow some slack.

Dwelling on that, he tried to see Masterton and himself through Ellie's eyes. Tried to weigh their relative pros and cons from her point of view.

He didn't know Masterton well enough to make a viable comparison, but if the opinions of London's grandes dames, hostesses, and match-makers were worth any consideration at all, then all presumptuousness and arrogance aside, he felt cautiously optimistic that, once he was free to openly woo her and give her the choice, Ellie would choose him.

That was his goal, and he was prepared to do whatever was required to achieve it.

CHAPTER 8

*A*fter taking luncheon on a tray in his room, Godfrey waited for Ellie to arrive; she usually looked in on him in the early afternoon.

Sure enough, her distinctive tap on the door sounded at two-thirty.

"Come in," he called and smiled when she appeared.

She smiled back, closed the door, and walked to where he sat before the fire.

He spoke while she was gathering her skirts to sit in the chair opposite his. "I believe I'm now well enough to view the Albertinelli."

Ellie froze, then slowly sank down. She regarded him for a moment, then shifted her gaze to the pile of documents on the side table to his right. "You've finished examining the letters and declarations?"

He nodded. "They're as remarkable as I—and the gallery—could hope for. Your ancestor was exceedingly thorough in noting everything pertaining to his purchase, and his descendants are to be commended for preserving the fruits of his endeavors."

A wave of relief flooded her. "So the painting is genuine."

He paused, then tipped his head from side to side, calculation gleaming in his hawklike eyes. "The documents certainly suggest it is, but I still need to examine the painting itself before I can declare it's an authentic Albertinelli."

She regarded him levelly, then sighed and admitted, "I'm as keen as you are—we're all as keen as you are—to have you view the painting, especially after a whole week of delay."

"I could do it—or at least commence my examination—this afternoon."

"What do you actually do when assessing a painting?"

He paused, then said, "To begin with, I need to stand before it and view it in different lights, from different angles with the light striking the surface from various directions. Then I need to see it in good strong light to closely examine the canvas, the paints themselves, the brush strokes, any drawing still visible, and also examine the composition in detail to see if it matches what's already known of the particular artist's work."

"Is much of that done while standing?"

He grimaced. "Virtually all of it. Sitting…for some reason, at least for me, doesn't work as well."

At least he'd told her the truth.

She studied his face; his color was much improved, and he'd barely coughed on both occasions she'd seen him that day, and even when he had, the sound was shallow and no longer concerning.

"Very well." She rose. "Let me summon Wally to help you dress. Until we're certain you're steady on your pins, I would prefer not to have you striding about alone."

He agreed readily enough.

She tugged the bellpull and met Wally at the door. "It's time to see if he can manage standing and walking about. If he can, I'll take him to see the painting."

"He'll want to get dressed, then." Wally nodded. "I'll see to him."

She left and went to her mother's parlor. Located at the end of the family wing, the room had essentially been shut up, its curtains drawn, since her mother had died nearly nineteen years ago. Her father's grief had been so great he hadn't been able to bring himself to allow anyone to remove her favorite things with which the room was adorned. Every knickknack and statuette remained, every painting.

The Albertinelli hung on an outer wall, in the space between two windows that looked out toward the river. Not that anyone could see the view, with the curtains so tightly drawn.

Ellie halted before the painting and, through the dimness, allowed her eyes to trace the figures she knew were there, posed before an archway. After a moment, she said, "I'm sure, Mama, that you won't mind us selling this, given we so need the funds."

She was the only one of her siblings who truly remembered their mother; she'd been nine when her mother had faded away. But her memories—of a smiling face and a soft embrace that had wrapped her in love made manifest—assured her that her mother would have been the first to urge her father to sell the painting. Although she'd had many pretty things, her mother had valued people—and the Hall and all who lived in it—more highly.

Ellie debated, but in the end, left the windows curtained. Once she and Godfrey entered, she could dramatically push aside the curtains and reveal the painting in all its glory.

Smiling at the thought, she hurried back to his room.

She tapped on the door, and at Wally's harried "Come in!" she entered to see Godfrey garbed in fashionable dark coat and trousers—and heavens! Clothed and upright, he was a great deal taller and more impressive than she remembered, with his wide shoulders, narrow hips, and long legs on elegant display. Then she noticed he was frowning.

He looked at her and tried to take a step, only to weave—causing Wally to dart in and steady him.

"Damn!" Godfrey muttered, then looked at her, simultaneously apologetic and woebegone. "Apparently, I'm not as strong as I thought."

She went to take his arm. "You've been lying abed for a week. It's hardly surprising that you need a little time to get your legs working properly again."

With Wally on one side and her on the other, he essayed another step, then, with slightly more confidence, another.

Briskly, she said, "The drifts are still blocking the roads to carriages, so you can't yet send any report. Taking the evening to exercise a little before viewing the painting isn't going to make the slightest difference to anything."

"But"—he took another step—"I *am* going to view the Albertinelli tomorrow."

"Yes. Provided you can stand without assistance, you can definitely view it then. However, I would suggest that, for today, a few short walks to help regain the use of your legs will serve everyone better."

Godfrey had to swallow the unpalatable truth that he wasn't yet up to the hours of standing that the examination of the painting would entail. But she had agreed he would see it tomorrow, so… "In that case, I believe my first short walk should be to the stairs and down them. I would like to meet your father before I view the painting."

She bit her lip. She looked adorable, and the impulse to kiss her welled. He firmly quashed it, but the temptation lingered.

She looked up and scanned his face, as if searching for signs by which to assess his strength. "I suppose we can take it in stages." She looked toward the door. "Let's see if you can make it to the gallery first, before we try the stairs."

He obediently set out, with her supporting one arm and Wally gripping the other. He had to pause a yard from the door to marshal his strength and also his balance, but by the time he stepped into the corridor, his confidence was rising. "I don't think it's really a matter of strength." He'd been eating well for the past few days. "I think it's simply remembering how to walk."

That seemed to be the case, as he conquered the long corridor with slow, regular paces. When they entered the gallery, Ellie suggested he sit for a few minutes on one of the padded benches, but he shook his head. "For the moment, I need to keep moving. Stopping will just set me back."

With an uncertain look, she acquiesced, and they continued to the head of the main stairs. There, they paused, and he looked down the first flight to the landing, above which rose a large, rectangular, lead-paned stained glass window displaying what he assumed was the Hinckley coat of arms. The work was impressive; slanting winter light struck the design and sent beams of red, blue, purple, and gold dancing over the dark wood of the landing.

The stairs were quite steep.

He drew in a bracing breath. "So far, so good." He glanced at the balustrade on his right, then drew his right arm from Wally's grip and waved Wally forward. "Go in front—if I falter, you'll be able to catch me." *And break my fall.* "I'll hold onto the balustrade."

Wally nodded and stepped onto the stairs.

"Right, then." Godfrey grasped the balustrade, glanced at Ellie, and smiled, then drew in another breath and took his first step down.

To his considerable relief, his legs behaved themselves, and their descent, although slow, passed without incident.

Ellie let out a surreptitious sigh of relief when Godfrey stepped onto the tiles of the front hall. He halted and looked around, clearly unsure which way to go.

She waved toward the corridor leading to the library. "My father—and most likely Mr. Morris and Mr. Pyne—will be in the library."

Godfrey nodded. He drew his arm free of her hold, then looped it with hers. When she looked up, he grinned at her. "That's better."

She found herself returning his infectious smile. She wasn't surprised that he wished to appear to be walking normally—without support—before the other men.

He set off again, and Wally trailed in their wake, ready to dart forward and assist if need be. But Godfrey seemed to have regained the required use of his legs, although she was pleased he kept his pace slow and steady; she got the impression he was consciously taking each step.

They reached the library door, and she opened it and sent it swinging wide.

She looked at Godfrey in time to see him fill his lungs. A subtle change swept over his face, a polite, urbane mask settling into place. That she saw the transformation so clearly brought home the fact that he hadn't been wearing any mask before—with her.

He didn't wear one with Wally, either.

Did that mean she was included among those people he didn't screen his reactions from?

She had no chance to dwell on the thought. Godfrey smiled at her, elegantly ushered her through the door, then stepped to her side once more. Arm in arm, they walked down the long room to where her father and his friends sat before the roaring fire.

"Papa, Mr. Cavanaugh is keen to meet you." She and Godfrey halted a few feet from her father's chair. She smiled at her father, then looked at Godfrey. "My father, Mr. Matthew Hinckley."

Godfrey executed an abbreviated bow. "Mr. Hinckley, it's a pleasure to finally make your acquaintance. I regret that the aftermath of the storm has kept me from meeting you until now."

Mr. Hinckley inclined his head and extended his hand, which Godfrey stepped forward and grasped. "I'm delighted to see you on your feet again, sir, and I regret that my condition"—as Godfrey released his hand, Mr. Hinckley gestured to his legs—"made it impossible for me to visit you earlier." Mr. Hinckley paused, studying Godfrey's face. "I take it you've recovered sufficiently to join us."

"Indeed. If it's no imposition?"

"Not at all, not at all." Mr. Hinckley waved to Morris and Pyne. "I believe you've already met these gentlemen."

"I have." Godfrey nodded to both men.

"Here!" Pyne leapt up from the chair closest to the fire, the one opposite Mr. Hinckley's. "Sit here. I'll fetch another."

Godfrey inclined his head in thanks, then smiled at Ellie and drew his arm from hers. "Thank you for your escort, Miss Hinckley."

Ellie felt like curtsying, but restrained the urge. She watched Godfrey cross unaided to the chair Pyne had vacated. Once seated, he leaned across and shook Morris's and Pyne's hands.

Ellie glanced at her father, a question in her eyes.

Her father smiled at her. "You may leave him with us, my dear. I'm sure we'll have plenty to chat about to pass the time."

She nodded; with a last glance at Godfrey, who was responding to some question from Pyne, she turned and left the room.

From beneath his lashes, Godfrey watched her go, then, having assured Pyne that he was, indeed, fully recovered, turned to Mr. Hinckley. "I expect to commence my assessment of the Albertinelli tomorrow."

"Excellent!" Hinckley thought, then asked, "How long will your examination take?"

"Until I've sighted the painting, I can't say. The process varies considerably, depending on the painting and on its current state. Some can be verified in a few hours, while others might take several days."

"But," Morris said, "only days, not weeks?"

Godfrey nodded. "Few paintings would require more than three or, at the most, four days of study."

Mr. Hinckley leaned forward. "How, exactly, do you go about it—your process?"

Godfrey explained his approach to examining paintings, expanding on what he'd told Ellie earlier. Pyne remained genuinely interested and asked several pertinent questions to which Godfrey readily replied.

Morris remained largely silent, but Godfrey could see he was listening intently; he seemed a man of few words.

In contrast, Pyne was garrulous, and Matthew Hinckley easily held his own as the conversation moved on from Godfrey's upcoming task for the National Gallery to the steps involved in any purchase they made—a procedure with which Godfrey had considerable experience. From there, the talk shifted to the weather and the snowstorm and its impact not only on the Hinckleys' proposed sale but also on Pyne's printing business in Ripon and, even more, the crops on both the Hinckley estate and Morris's Malton Farm.

Although Godfrey had no acres to manage, courtesy of his boyhood spent on the Raventhorne estate, he had a passing understanding of crops and the effects of unseasonable weather. The impact of the heavy snow and the freezing conditions was the one topic on which Morris grew almost eloquent. Godfrey deduced that while Matthew Hinckley wasn't overextended to the point of being dependent on his current crops, Morris was a great deal more nervous over what the ultimate effect on his income might be.

Subsequently, Matthew Hinckley swung the talk to hunting and fishing, and all three men grew enthused while describing the local amenities. Godfrey had to smile at their tales; they'd patently grown up doing all the sorts of things boys did together, and when, with a twinkle in his eye, Matthew asked if Godfrey had any similar stories of his own, he found himself enjoying sharing his recollections of some of his youthful adventures.

The hours passed surprisingly easily.

At one point, with Pyne and Morris engaged in an argument over conflicting memories of an old event, Matthew Hinckley leaned across and, lowering his voice, addressed Godfrey. "Although the snow has created an unavoidable and ongoing delay to our business, I'm nevertheless glad to see you up and about, sir." The older man paused, his eyes searching Godfrey's, then said, "I prefer to be frank and ask outright if, once you've completed your task for the gallery and all is squared away with them, it would be appropriate—and if you'd be willing—to act as an advisor to me and my family regarding the sale?"

Godfrey blinked and rapidly considered the question. Once he'd finished with his commission... He refocused on Mr. Hinckley's face. "I'm not a valuer as such, but I would be happy to advise you to the best of my ability—and yes, after I send in my report to the gallery, I see no impediment to acting as an advisor to the Hinckleys."

"Excellent." Mr. Hinckley eased back in his chair. He glanced at his friends—and Godfrey did, too, noting that Pyne and Morris were still engrossed. When he turned back to Mr. Hinckley, the older man said, "It's important to me—to the family—that we realize the best price we can." He faintly grimaced. "While our need isn't urgent, it is quite real—the harvests have been so poor these past years that in order to keep the estate in the black, I've had to draw on Ellie's and Maggie's portions. And while Ellie especially would assure me I should use all the funds her mother and I set aside for her dowry to keep the Hall afloat, that's not what I want, and I'm determined to restore the funds as soon as the painting is sold."

Godfrey hesitated, but felt compelled to say, "While I've yet to see the painting and so cannot make any definite statement as to its worth, if it is as it should be, then its sale should bring in more than enough to repair any deficit and still leave a sizeable sum to bolster and protect the estate for many years."

Stark relief showed in Hinckley's eyes. He sat back and nodded to Godfrey. "Thank you for that. It eases the burden on my shoulders."

Pyne looked across and demanded Hinckley add his recollections to the discussion at hand.

Allowing said discussion to rage across him, Godfrey reflected on the more private exchange, noting that Matthew Hinckley was as disarmingly open, straightforward, and easy to engage with as his children.

That fact was underscored when Harry and Maggie joined them, and the talk turned to politics and the latest news from London.

They were deliberating on the changes the railroads had wrought throughout the country when Kemp appeared to announce dinner. Ellie arrived on Kemp's heels. Godfrey felt a flash of pleasure when her gaze instantly sought him out.

He met her eyes and smiled, genuinely pleased on several counts, and saw her relax.

She came forward as the men all stood, and Harry moved to take the handles of his father's chair.

"Here—let me." Godfrey smiled at Mr. Hinckley as he walked across. "The chair will give me added stability should I need it."

Ellie was pleased, and Hinckley smiled and inclined his head. "If you wish, Mr. Cavanaugh."

Godfrey grasped the handles and pushed the chair toward the door. Ellie fell in alongside, and Harry and Maggie waved Pyne and Morris on, then brought up the rear.

Ellie directed Godfrey to the dining room.

As he pushed the chair through the open doorway, his gaze fell on the small statue that had been used to prop open the heavy door. He blinked and stared. *Is that a Lombardo cherub?*

Ellie touched his arm, and he faced forward and steered the chair to the head of the table.

A footman stepped in to help Godfrey position the chair.

"Thank you, Mr. Cavanaugh." Over his shoulder, Mr. Hinckley threw the footman a smile. "And you, Mike." He turned back to Godfrey and indicated the chair to his right. "Please, sit by me, sir."

Godfrey inclined his head, and Kemp appeared to draw out the chair. Godfrey acknowledged the butler with a nod.

Kemp almost smiled. "It's a pleasure to see you downstairs, sir."

Godfrey sat, and Maggie claimed the chair to his right, with Morris on her right, next to Ellie, seated at the table's foot.

Harry came to sit opposite Godfrey, with Pyne on his left, on Ellie's other side.

Resigning himself to not being able to converse with Ellie, Godfrey nevertheless was surrounded by Hinckleys.

The meal began with a hearty pheasant soup. His mind returning to the statue by the door, Godfrey asked whether the Hinckleys had many ancestors who had traveled as widely as the Henry Hinckley who had bought the Albertinelli.

He was promptly regaled with tales of Henry's three brothers. "All of them got bitten by the traveling bug and spent years roaming about, mainly on the Continent," Matthew said.

"I remember," Maggie put in, "that Aunt Tabitha—Papa's sister—told me that one of the brothers—Francis, I think—even traveled into Russia."

"I don't think any of them went as far as the Orient, though," Harry said.

"Still," Godfrey observed, "they sound as if they traveled far and wide."

Mr. Hinckley nodded. "They did, indeed. They made quite a competition of it, between them."

Godfrey had to wonder what else—what other amazing and revealing documents—he might find languishing in the Hinckley archives. He glanced down the table and saw that Ellie was successfully entertaining Morris and Pyne.

As the soup plates were removed, Harry asked whether Godfrey had traveled beyond England and, if so, to where. That resulted in a discussion that lasted through the main course and on as they tackled a sumptuous Queen of Puddings made with luscious blackcurrant jam.

When his dish was scraped clean, Godfrey laid down his spoon and sat back with a satisfied sigh. "That was delicious." To Mr. Hinckley, he said, "Your cook is a treasure."

Hinckley grinned. "Aye, she's been with us forever—born on the estate. Lucky for us, she likes it here, and nothing will tempt her away." He met Godfrey's eyes. "I hope the company lived up to the meal— you've been patient with all our questions."

"Not at all." Only then, thinking about it, did Godfrey realize how relaxed and positively *comfortable* he felt. "I've thoroughly enjoyed the evening."

Maggie trained her inquisitive gaze on his face. "You come from a rather different, much more wealthy family—what are your family dinners like?"

He blinked. "These days?" He tipped his head in thought, then offered, "Truth to tell, not being married, I don't actually attend many family dinners as such. The most similar experience would be when I and my siblings get together, and then there's so many of us—" He broke off to explain to Mr. Hinckley, "I have four siblings, and they're all married, and some of their children are now old enough to join us." He turned back to Maggie and concluded, "With everyone around a single table, it's rather noisy and riotous."

"But happy?" Maggie insisted.

He smiled and nodded. "These days, yes." Thinking of the past, however...

Sobering, he met Maggie's eyes, then looked across the table at Harry. "But when I was your age and younger...no." He recalled the distinctly chilly dinners he'd endured as a boy, when his father had been alive and they'd all lived at Raventhorne House. Then after his father had died and he and his siblings had moved to live with his mother at her London house, the atmosphere about the dining table had been distinctly tense and often fraught. "In those years," he said, "our family dinners were nothing like this—not warm at all, and we younger ones all kept quiet and hardly said a word. We kept our eyes on our plates and only spoke to answer questions an older person directed our way."

Maggie stared at him. "That sounds awful."

He nodded. "It was." He forced himself to smile, even if the gesture was a touch grim. "Which goes to show that having wealth doesn't mean"—he gestured about them—"laughter and warmth. Ease and comfort." He glanced again at Harry, then looked back at Maggie. "The family is what makes family dinners enjoyable, and in all honesty, I envy you what you have, what you experience here every day."

Maggie studied him for a moment, then said, "So money truly doesn't buy happiness."

He smiled wryly. "No, it doesn't."

At the other end of the table, Ellie rose. "Maggie? Papa, please don't dally too long."

"Oh, I don't think we'll dally at all, my dear." Mr. Hinckley exchanged a glance with Morris and Pyne, then looked at Godfrey. "What say we take our brandies in the drawing room? That way, the ladies won't sit there being bored."

Godfrey grinned and pushed back his chair. "That sounds like an excellent idea."

The company readily rose, and Godfrey pushed Mr. Hinckley's chair across the front hall to the drawing room and stationed it as directed to one side of the hearth, close to the fire and angled toward the other chairs and the sofa.

Only as he moved to take the chair Mr. Hinckley indicated, the one beside his, did Godfrey realize that he'd stood and walked without thinking. Apparently, his mobility had returned.

Pleased, relieved, and reassured, he sat.

Kemp came in bearing a tray with glasses and two decanters. While the butler supplied the gentlemen with brandies and Ellie and Maggie accepted small glasses of sherry, Mr. Hinckley leaned closer to Godfrey and, lowering his voice, murmured, "Thank you for saying what you did in there. About happiness and comfort not being guaranteed by wealth."

Godfrey met the older man's eyes. "It was only the truth."

"You and I know that. Ellie knows that. But my younger two as yet lack the experience to believe that."

Godfrey looked at Maggie and Harry, then murmured back, "If so, I'm glad to have been of service."

And, he realized, he was. Quite aside from being Ellie's brother and sister—which would have recommended the pair to Godfrey's care regardless—both were likeable and generous souls worthy of his protection in their own right.

"Has Mr. Cavanaugh mentioned his conclusions regarding the letters and documents about the painting?" Ellie asked.

Godfrey looked to where she sat on the sofa, then he smiled and, responding to the eager looks on everyone else's faces, proceeded to explain just how impressive he had found the letters and documents collected by the Hinckleys' long-ago ancestor.

Given Pyne's predictable curiosity over how he determined whether letters and declarations were genuine or not, which Godfrey saw no reason not to sate, the exposition lasted until the tea trolley was wheeled in.

While they switched their empty glasses for cups of tea, Godfrey concluded, "I can't stress sufficiently how remarkable it is to find a painting with such documentation so carefully gathered and preserved intact." He looked at Mr. Hinckley. "In truth, the documents themselves are valuable in their own right, but when offered together with the painting, they'll add significant value and prestige to the whole, at least in the gallery's estimation."

Mr. Hinckley inclined his head. "That's good to know."

Godfrey sipped his tea, then offered, "In fact, it's almost as if your ancestor, in buying the painting, always intended it ultimately to be sold."

Mr. Hinckley set down his cup with a clink. "From what you've said, I'm starting to think so as well." He looked at Ellie, Maggie, and Harry and smiled. "That painting has been gathering dust upstairs for decades. It's time it was brought into the light, and for the family to reap the benefits of old Great-uncle Henry's foresight."

Everyone smiled. Everyone agreed.

"Now all that remains," Pyne observed, "is for Cavanaugh to view the painting, then tell the gallery it's all above board."

~

After breakfast the next morning, with a sense of excitement and expectation in the air, Ellie led Godfrey up the main stairs and down a corridor into a different wing from the one in which his bedroom was situated.

"The family's rooms are along here." She gestured to right and left as she continued walking along an old but fine Turkish runner. "Mama's parlor is the room at the end."

She led him to the door at the far end of the corridor, opened it, and continued into the room.

Anticipation rising, Godfrey followed. He'd waited more than a week for this moment.

Ellie halted in the middle of the room, facing an outer wall. She turned her head, met his gaze, then gestured to the medium-sized work hanging above a small chiffonier between two curtained windows. "This is our Albertinelli painting."

Despite the room being shrouded in shadows, the painting captured and held his attention. He walked forward, his gaze locked on the canvas within the wide, heavily ornate frame. The frame looked to date from the same period as the painting and was very well preserved.

To his left, he sensed Ellie moving; she gripped the long curtains covering the window on that side and drew them wide.

Light spilled in, but the sky was overcast; the pale, gray light that permeated the room provided barely enough illumination for him to make out the figures in the composition.

It still held him spellbound.

Then Ellie walked around him and opened the curtains on his right, and the first wraith of suspicion writhed deep in his brain.

He stepped closer and peered at the painting's surface.

Surely not—it can't *be.*

His heart sank as his instincts pricked ever more strongly.

Never in his life had he been so thankful for the facility, learned at his mother's knee, to conceal all emotion behind an impassive mask.

His gaze devouring the painting, he slowly reached up and removed it from the wall.

Holding the frame, he walked to the window on his right, the one admitting the strongest light. Halting before the pane, he angled the painting first one way, then the other, but he couldn't see well enough to be certain of what he thought he was seeing.

Ensuring his features revealed nothing of his inner turmoil, he glanced at Ellie. "The light here is too poor for me to work with. Is there any room in the house with strong, even light?"

Ellie searched his face, but could read absolutely nothing in his professionally uninformative expression. "Natural light?" When he nodded, she mentally reviewed the possibilities; in this season, most rooms in the house suffered from poor light, but one might do. "How about the conservatory?"

He thought, then nodded. "That might work well."

"Of all the rooms in the house, it has the best natural light." She started for the door. "I'll take you there."

Carrying the frame, he followed. As she led him along the corridor and around to the side stairs, she noticed his gaze constantly dipping to dwell on the painting.

Poor light or not, he was being drawn into his study of the canvas, becoming absorbed with the painting, just as he had with the documents.

The bottom of the side stairs lay only a few yards from the short corridor that led to the glass-walled conservatory. She opened the door and led the way inside.

Shaped like the nave of a church, the conservatory extended outward from the end of the central wing. Hip-high redbrick walls ran away from the house, eventually angling inward to form a half-hexagonal end. Above the walls, panes of glass set in lead frames soared upward, then inward, to meet along the roof's leaded spine. Green-and-white tiles covered the floor, laid in a chequerboard pattern.

Walking down the room, she spoke over her shoulder. "My father built the conservatory for my mother—it was his wedding gift to her. During winter, the room's heated by hot water from a boiler in the cellar that circulates through pipes in the walls and floor."

"I see."

He sounded distracted, literally absentminded.

She smiled to herself and halted in the sparsely furnished area toward the end of the room. During the colder months, the ferns and palms that, in summer, were sited all around the conservatory were gathered in the room's center, away from the chilled windows.

She turned to Godfrey as he halted a yard away; predictably, his gaze remained locked on the painting. "Will you need anything more by way of furniture in addition to what's already here?"

Godfrey raised his head, stared at Ellie as he replayed her words, then glanced around. There were two round white-painted wrought iron tables and eight matching chairs, deeply cushioned, arranged around the room's perimeter. He looked past Ellie to the end of the room where strong, steady light—not just direct light from the sky but also light reflected off the snow—poured in through the glass panes. "No." He glanced around again. "In fact, this will be perfect. The fewer visual distractions, the better."

The painting claimed his attention again.

Ellie shifted. "In that case, I'll leave you to it."

He nodded, but she didn't walk away. He realized and, still holding his mask firmly in place, looked at her.

She smiled gently, as if amused. "How long do you think your examination will take?"

He looked down at the canvas. After a moment, he said, "Given what this is, I'll need to be thorough."

Exceedingly thorough.

"So." She tipped her head and waited for him to look at her again. "Does that mean hours?"

He couldn't hold back a disbelieving grunt. "Hours certainly. Possibly days."

"Oh. I see." She studied him for an instant, then said, "I'll let Papa know. I'll send Wally to summon you for meals."

He nodded noncommittally, but he wasn't going to be eating with the family until he sorted this out.

His attention once more drawn—mesmerized—by the painting in his hands, he listened as Ellie walked away. He heard the door open and click shut—waited until he was certain she wouldn't, for some reason, return.

Then and only then did he allow his rigid mask to slip. He stared, utterly nonplussed, at the painting. Despite the evidence of his eyes, he remained mired in disbelief. He shook his head. "How the devil could this have happened?"

~

The Albertinelli painting that, apparently, had hung on the wall in the upstairs parlor of Hinckley Hall, unsighted and undisturbed for decades, was a fake.

A forgery.

The following morning, having left the conservatory only to grab a few hours' sleep, Godfrey was back, pacing the green-and-white tiles from side to side before the painting, which he'd propped upright on a chair. Every now and then, he halted and stared at the canvas in sheer frustration.

How on earth had it come to be there?

A careful scrutiny of the canvas itself and the specific paints used—as attested by the relative smoothness of the dried surface—plus the distinctive brushstrokes that had first caught his educated eye had confirmed his initial fears.

What hours of subsequent cogitation had failed to elucidate was how a painting with such indisputable provenance, that had been brought into this house and had, apparently, never left it, had been replaced by a forgery by Henrik Hendall.

Godfrey knew Hendall's work. The Amsterdam-based forger produced superb copies, and in recent years, his works had started popping up all over Europe and England. Consequently, Godfrey had studied Hendall's technique extensively and was arguably the reigning expert when it came to detecting the otherwise very-difficult-to-detect forgeries. As he'd mentioned to Pyne, it was all about one's eye. Given his chosen occupation, Godfrey had ensured his eye was up to the task of picking out Hendall's work.

He was immutably certain the forgery was Hendall's.

But Hendall was relatively young and had been active only over the past five years.

And, most tellingly, the master forger worked only from the original.

As Godfrey was prepared to swear this work was a Hendall forgery, then it inescapably followed that, at some point over the past five years, the original Albertinelli had been removed from the house.

"Likely," he muttered, "it was removed from the frame, rolled up, and spirited out."

The postulation sent him back to the painting. He tipped it forward and examined the tiny nails that secured the backboard to the outer frame, confirming that the nails were relatively new.

He resettled the painting on the chair. Based on the condition of the nails, he revised his estimate of when the Albertinelli had been taken. "More like three years ago, not five."

Regardless, someone had removed the painting, and no one in the house had, apparently, noticed.

What was seriously confounding was that, instead of simply making away with the painting—highly valuable and easy to sell to unscrupulous collectors, even without the provenance—whoever stole it had arranged to have Hendall copy it, which had to have taken place either in Amsterdam or in some nearby English town like Hull, easily reached from Amsterdam by ferry. Hendall wouldn't have taken the risk of not being able to quickly flee back to the relative safety of his home base.

"And then"—Godfrey halted before the painting and glared at it —"whoever the thief was, he went to the considerable risk of smuggling the copy back into the house, replacing it in its frame, and rehanging it on the wall in that parlor."

He couldn't see any other way of explaining the presence of the Hendall copy other than via that sequence of events. "But why go to the trouble—let alone the expense—of getting the copy made?"

Another question niggled. The time Hendall would have taken to make his copy meant that the spot on the parlor wall where the Albertinelli had hung would have been empty for weeks. "At absolute minimum, three weeks."

Hendall was good, but work of that quality, forgery or not, took time.

Why had nobody noticed the painting was missing?

Godfrey thought back to the room he'd entered with Ellie. He might have become almost instantly fixated on the painting, but out of habit, he'd noticed the other furniture.

There had been no dust on the polished surfaces, and none had swirled into the air when Ellie had drawn back the curtains.

Perhaps knowing he would be shown into the room, the staff had dusted and cleaned.

But the room hadn't possessed that musty smell that permanently closed rooms inevitably developed.

"I'll have to ask how frequently the staff clean that room."

Regardless of the answer, how had the thief—presuming it was someone who didn't know the family and the house—known where the painting was hung? It hadn't been displayed in a main reception room and, as he understood it, had been hidden away in the unused upstairs lady's parlor for the past decade and more.

And how had any thief from outside known the painting wouldn't be missed—at least long enough for the copy to be made and rehung in place of the original?

He could think of numerous questions, but the most pertinent was: Where was the Albertinelli—the original—now?

He stared, frowning, at the forgery, then pulled out his fob watch and consulted the dial. It was almost eleven o'clock.

He'd breakfasted early and had only briefly crossed paths with Mr. Hinckley and Harry. He'd been cravenly glad that neither had pressed him for his verdict.

He hadn't said anything about his findings to anyone yet. Aside from all else, he didn't want to break the news—whatever he elected to say—to the Hinckleys in front of Morris and Pyne. Luckily, when he'd passed the pair in the front hall that morning, they'd been discussing leaving after luncheon; he'd waved and called that he would see them at the luncheon table.

Godfrey looked out of the conservatory windows. Although the park still slumbered under a blanket of snow, when he'd seen Wally that morning, Wally had mentioned that the roads were said to be mostly clear.

He would definitely wait until Morris and Pyne left before saying anything to the Hinckleys.

The more vexed issue was deciding what to say. What he should do, especially now that he knew why Matthew Hinckley had decided to sell the Albertinelli—that the family's need of cash was very real.

That knowledge…left him confronting a quandary unlike any he'd previously faced.

As a forgery, the Hendall was exceptional. Brilliant, in fact. There were very few other assessors—certainly none in England—who would be likely to detect the very slight differences in the brushstrokes, not unless they had a genuine Albertinelli of the same period against which to compare. The canvas Hendall had used was almost perfect to pass as one from the early sixteenth century, and the paints were a close match as well, although perfectly duplicating paints from that era was impossible.

In truth, the only reason Godfrey had detected the forgery was because he was an expert in Hendall's work and had studied a host of the man's forgeries of High Renaissance masters' paintings to the point he could identify the master forger's hand.

Yet the Hinckleys had provoked his protective instincts in an entirely novel way. He wanted—with an intensity he'd never felt before with respect to any action—to protect them from the shock and loss the forgery looked set to cause.

In the circumstances…he could say the painting was genuine and expect his authentication to pass unchallenged.

But that would be a lie, a deception of the worst sort, perpetrated on people—not just the Hinckleys but also Eastlake and the directors of the National Gallery—to whom he owed his professional honesty; he'd been commissioned specifically to deliver that.

Still…could he bring himself to do it?

Just the thought turned his stomach; he'd witnessed enough lies and deceit in his life for the notion to provoke a visceral rejection.

Despite that, he stared at the painting and wondered whether he was capable of that level of deception.

Alternatively, could he tell the Hinckleys that the painting was real, while informing Eastlake and the gallery of the forgery, and somehow, in some way, buy the forgery himself?

He could afford it, and the Hinckleys would no longer be pressed for cash.

He would still have to gird his loins and lie to them.

Jaw clenching, he started listing all the possible responses he might make, yet the inescapable question remained: Should he verify the forgery as authentic or cleave to the truth and dash the Hinckleys' hopes?

CHAPTER 9

*G*odfrey skipped luncheon, too exercised by the decision before him to settle to eat with the family while pretending nothing was wrong. With the family he was convinced beyond reason he had to help get through this situation.

In some ways, he felt as if *he* was the instigator of the problem rather than whoever had stolen the Albertinelli.

Irrational nonsense, yet…that was how he felt. Somehow, he had to make this right.

He was sitting with his back to the end wall of the conservatory with the painting propped on a chair before him, two paces away, when he heard the door open, followed by the soft pats of Ellie's slippers as she walked down the room. The skies had cleared, and the afternoon sunlight streamed in from over his shoulders, illuminating every line of the supposed Albertinelli composition.

With her gaze on Godfrey, Ellie halted level with the painting.

He didn't rise but, feeling her gaze, raised his to her face.

She smiled faintly and arched her brows. "Have you completed your assessment yet?"

He stared at her for several seconds, then said, "I grew up in a house with a collection of paintings that inspired in me a love of art. In that regard, I was blessed. But at the same time, my mother, who was definitely no pattern-card for the role, through her own actions, taught me all about deception and deceit and, most especially, the cost of those to others."

His lips twisted in a self-deprecatory grimace, and his gaze grew distant. "My mother was a truly dreadful person. She was monstrous, in fact, although we didn't comprehend just how monstrous until the very end. However"—he drew a tight breath—"courtesy of her and her teachings, I developed an eye—and an instinct, as well—for..." Tipping his head, he thought, then went on, "I suppose you could say for anything that strays from the genuine."

His voice had remained low and even. He seemed to be studying, pondering, something far away, beyond her, beyond the painting. She had to wonder if, in some strange way, it was himself he was examining in an aloof, detached fashion.

"Originally," he continued, "that instinct was focused on people, on steering me, guiding me, through the shoals of lies and fabrications and self-interested prevarications that abound in the ton. There were times when it seemed deceit and deception were all around me and only by honing and trusting in that instinct would I survive."

Her father had mentioned Godfrey's comments about the family dinners he'd endured as a boy. His statement that wealth didn't buy happiness had clearly been based on experience.

After a moment, he pulled back from whatever vista had held him and, once again, met her gaze. "I didn't hate my mother so much as truly despise the type of person she was. She was the antithesis of the mother any boy—any child—wants. As I grew older, my antipathy toward all deceits, all attempts to deceive, grew stronger. And stronger. You could say I've developed an obsession over exposing deceptions wherever I find them. Wherever my now-well-honed instinct alerts me to them. And nowhere is that more so than with works of art."

He paused, and his gaze returned to the painting. "I've become recognized as an expert authenticator of artworks not so much through being an expert in identifying the genuineness of works but because of my facility for detecting fakes, forgeries, and frauds."

Ellie's heart wavered. What was he telling her? When he said nothing more, just stared at the painting, taking her courage in both hands, she asked, "And the Albertinelli?"

His gaze returned to her face, his hawkish eyes clear and hard. "I can't yet say." He paused, then added, "I need to be sure."

She could hardly argue that, especially not now she'd gained some insight into what drove him in his authenticator role. She met his gaze and nodded. "Very well. I'll let the family know you need more time."

Godfrey held her gaze and inclined his head. "Thank you. I'll tell you and your family as soon as I'm able."

He forced himself to look back at the painting. At the edge of his vision, he saw Ellie study him for a moment, then she turned and retreated up the long room.

On hearing the soft snick of the door shutting behind her, he leaned forward, set his elbows on his thighs, steepled his fingers before his lips, and stared at the painting.

He hadn't meant to say all that he had. The words had come tumbling out—a stream of thought given voice. But he had heard himself. Restating what had shaped him and fueled the evolution of his present life and, ultimately, brought him there—to the Hinckley Hall conservatory, staring at a painting that shouldn't have existed—had thrown the challenge confronting him into stark relief.

Could he—just once—accede to this deception and allow Hendall's Albertinelli to stand as the original, backed by the unshakeable provenance?

For Ellie and the Hinckley family, could he do that?

Could he become what he abhorred more than anything else in life?

Staring fixedly at the painting, he muttered against his fingertips, "Or is there another way?"

On venturing downstairs to breakfast the next day, Godfrey was grateful and hugely relieved to have Matthew Hinckley inform him that in their household, Sunday was deemed a day of rest for all, and thus no one would press him for his decision regarding the Albertinelli.

Mr. Hinckley's statement was delivered with a pointed look at Harry and Maggie, whose innocent expressions made Godfrey's lips twitch. He did like this family—all of them.

"I appreciate that, sir," he replied. "Having a day to reflect will be welcome."

Now that Morris and Pyne had departed for their own hearths, the company was reduced to just the Hinckleys, which suited Godfrey very well. He listened to the ambling conversations between the siblings and their father regarding a book Harry had just finished reading, a new type of embroidered ribbon Maggie was sporting on her winter Sunday gown, and Ellie's report regarding a cob with a sore hoof.

Undemanding and anchoring conversations with which to start the day.

After they'd cleared their plates, Mr. Hinckley caught Godfrey's eye. "We'll be departing shortly for Sunday service at St. Andrew's in Kirkby Malzeard. You're very welcome to join us."

Godfrey smiled. "Thank you. I would like that."

He rarely attended church in London, but tended to make the effort when in the country, either at Raventhorne or at Rand's, Kit's, or Stacie's houses, wherever he happened to be.

Ellie smiled, clearly pleased by his acceptance. "We'll be leaving from the front hall at nine-thirty."

From her father's and siblings' expressions, they were equally delighted, as if his acceptance signaled he saw himself as one of them— or at least one with them.

While that hadn't been his intention, he wasn't unhappy with that outcome. In truth, with every passing day, he viewed the Hinckleys a little more certainly as his tribe—his to protect.

At the appointed time, they gathered in the front hall, and Harry and Godfrey elected to ride rather than attempt to squash into the somewhat ancient family coach. The coach arrived before the front steps, followed by the stableman, Johnson, leading a strong bay as well as Harry's gray hunter.

When Godfrey descended to take the bay's reins, Johnson tipped him a salute. "This one should suit you, sir. His name's George." Johnson gave a little sigh. "He was born here, and Miss Maggie had the naming of him."

Godfrey grinned. "I gather she was interested in royalty at the time."

Johnson bobbed his head. "Just so." He handed over the reins and ran a hand down George's nicely arched neck. "But he's a sound hack, and although the saddle's worn, it's comfy."

"Thank you." Godfrey gathered the reins, looked George in the eye, then stepped to his side and mounted. George shifted, but settled. Godfrey tipped his head to the waiting Johnson. "He'll do."

Harry was already mounted and waiting. As Godfrey nudged George to join Harry at the rear of the carriage, Kemp shut the carriage door on Maggie and waved at the coachman. The carriage rumbled off, and falling in beside Harry in the vehicle's wake, Godfrey filled his lungs and felt his mood lift.

With his declaration, Mr. Hinckley had gifted him this day to rest his mind from grappling with the challenge facing him. As he and Harry trotted down the drive, Godfrey resolved to set aside all concerns, take the day as it came, and enjoy it.

The air was cold, but fresh and clear, with the tang of snow sharpened by the scent of pines and firs. While the grooms had shoveled the drive, snow lingered in crisp drifts to either side, and in the park that surrounded the Hall, the thick blanket of white extended as far as Godfrey could see.

He was bundled up in his greatcoat, with his scarf wrapped snugly about his neck and his hands protected by fur-lined gloves. Wally had ruthlessly brushed his hat, and it was duly perched on Godfrey's head; he was grateful there was no wind to send it bowling into the nearest drift. Indeed, the country about them lay almost preternaturally still, all activity muffled by the snow; beyond the occasional birdcall, the sound of them traveling was the only disturbance, rapidly fading as they passed.

They turned out of the drive into the lane, where the snow had been worn away by passing traffic enough to expose the center of the roadway. The coachman urged his pair on, and Godfrey and Harry trotted along behind.

They crossed a river. "The Laver," Harry informed Godfrey. "It forms the western boundary of our park."

After a moment of orienting himself, Godfrey asked, "Are all the Hall's lands on the same side of the river as the house?"

Harry shook his head. "Those woods"—with his head, he indicated the woods on the western bank—"the section north of the lane, are part of the Hall estate. The lane is our southern boundary, and we have the woods to the west and north as far as they stretch, and farmland to the north and to the east."

Godfrey nodded. The Hinckley Hall lands couldn't be termed extensive, yet if well managed, would likely be sufficient to support the Hall, at least during normal times.

They reached the tiny village of Galphay shortly after and traveled past the handful of cottages. Not much farther, they reached another lane and turned north, soon meeting other carriages and riders heading to the church.

St. Andrew's Church proved to be a sizeable edifice built in medieval times. After halting their horses and the carriage in the graveled area beside the church, Godfrey helped Harry assist Mr. Hinckley into his wheeled chair. Then with Harry pushing his father ahead, Godfrey strolled between Ellie and Maggie and admired the lines of the church's tower and its mullioned windows. As they neared the door in the south face of the tall stone tower, he noted the carving decorating the door frame and gracing the stone arches of the windows.

"That's twelfth century," he murmured, impressed.

Ellie smiled. "You're right—the congregation here dates from before that time."

It was still an active and quite decently sized congregation; as he and Ellie followed Harry, Maggie, and Mr. Hinckley down the aisle to the second pew on the left, the ornately carved pews to either side were commendably filled.

Harry halted the chair alongside the second pew, and Mr. Hinckley grasped the pew's raised side, levered himself up, and shuffled to claim the first place on the bench seat.

In what was obviously an established routine, Harry pushed the chair on, and Maggie, Ellie, and Godfrey followed as Harry rounded the front pew and made for the side aisle. Harry positioned the chair in a spot against the wall, while Ellie—followed, at Maggie's urging, by Godfrey—filed into the pew from that end. Maggie followed him, and Harry brought up the rear.

With Ellie next to her father, they sat, and Godfrey noted the smiles, nods, and quiet greetings Mr. Hinckley and Ellie, and Maggie and Harry, too, exchanged with many of those in the surrounding pews.

Judging by the tenor of those exchanges, the Hinckleys were not only well-known but also well-liked and respected.

While they waited for the minister to enter, Godfrey studied the interior of the church—the nave, the chancel with its ornate arches, and the chapel to one side. It was not only beautiful but also eminently functional. As he gazed at stonework he knew had stood there for centuries, the aura of permanence, of a place of worship anchored in this soil with roots buried deep, reached him clearly.

Sensing rising expectation that the minister would soon arrive, he glanced around again, admiringly tracing the line of the nave's roof back to the foyer inside the south-facing door and saw Morris stepping into the central aisle. Morris continued to the pew opposite the one the Hinckleys occupied.

Godfrey recalled Morris lived nearby. He hadn't seen either Pyne or

Masterton, but both lived in Ripon, which boasted a cathedral; Godfrey imagined that if either man was so inclined, they would attend services there.

Morris sank into the space at the end of the pew—clearly his accustomed place. The pew was otherwise empty; locals probably regarded it as the Malton Farm pew. He exchanged nods with Mr. Hinckley, then directed half bows to Ellie and Godfrey.

Godfrey returned a nod as another gentleman, closer in age to Godfrey and well-dressed in neat and plain style, entered Morris's pew from the other end. Oblivious to the newcomer, Morris was exchanging a whispered comment with Mr. Hinckley. The unknown gentleman's gaze rested on Morris in an assessing way as the man walked closer.

Then the man bent, and when he straightened, he held a scrap of a paper in his hand.

Morris finally noticed the man. The gentleman held out the paper. "I believe this is yours, sir."

Morris took the paper, stared at it, then fleetingly looked at the man and mumbled a thank-you. Morris stuffed the paper into his pocket and pointedly stared straight ahead.

The well-dressed man smiled faintly and sat a little way from Morris.

Puzzled, Godfrey studied Morris's now-ruddy face. From his pinched lips, Morris would have liked to put more distance between himself and the stranger, but couldn't without drawing attention to that fact.

Before Godfrey could make anything of that observation, a stir at the back of the church heralded the arrival of the minister. Godfrey rose with the rest of the congregation and, curious to see what sort of cleric inspired such an enthusiastic flock, gave his attention to the robed forty-something clergyman who took up his position on the steps before the altar, smiled on his congregation, then raised his hands.

"Let us pray."

Godfrey was only too ready to do so. As the service rolled on, through familiar hymns, lessons, and an engaging sermon, a sense of peacefulness stole over him.

A sense of belonging, of being in the right place and no longer needing to search to find that.

As he rose for the final hymn and, standing beside Ellie and sharing her hymnal, raised his voice to twine with hers, simple pleasure infused him. When the hymn ended, and they sat again, he stole a look at Ellie's face.

Serene, assured, she was looking at the minister, but she felt Godfrey's gaze, glanced his way, met his eyes, studied them for a second, then smiled softly and returned her attention to the minister.

Godfrey followed her gaze, yet his awareness had shifted; he looked inward, fascinated by the reality that had taken root within him. He liked it there, sitting beside Ellie as if he were a part of the Hinckley tribe. The family, the Hall, and its household had slipped into his soul and filled a yawning emptiness the existence of which he hadn't previously understood. He'd always felt that inner emptiness, but until now, he hadn't appreciated what the feeling stemmed from—a lack of belonging, of not being a vital part of something larger than himself.

If he surrendered to the compulsion that was urging him to pursue Ellie and succeeded in claiming her hand, he could secure and embrace all he'd recently found and permanently eradicate that deep-seated emptiness. That fundamental loneliness.

Yet to have a chance with Ellie, he first needed to successfully negotiate the challenge the Albertinelli represented.

What to do?

As he sat and listened to the minister introduce the final prayer, Godfrey finally grasped the entirety of what hinged on his decision, yet he could still not see the right path forward.

For a moment, his confidence faltered. His gaze came to rest on the minister as he called for bowed heads. Godfrey complied and decided he could do worse than ask for divine guidance.

He emptied his mind and let the words of the prayer flood in. Let the sentiments evoked well and flow through him.

When the prayer ended and the minister raised his hands and spoke the benediction, Godfrey blinked and looked inward again.

He didn't find any answer waiting, yet despite that, he felt more settled, more certain.

Right and wrong weren't nebulous concepts but active choices, and he knew which was which.

The service ended, and he rose with the Hinckleys, swapping places with Ellie so he could assist Mr. Hinckley back into the chair that Harry wheeled around.

At Mr. Hinckley's insistence, Ellie, Godfrey, and Maggie went ahead up the aisle, falling in with the rest of the congregation, leaving Mr. Hinckley, attended by Harry, to talk with Morris and several others who paused to chat.

Feeling significantly more assured, Godfrey smiled charmingly when Ellie introduced him to the minister, Reverend Pearson. After shaking the man's hand and complimenting him on his sermon, Godfrey offered Ellie his arm. Smiling, she took it, and together with Maggie, they stepped off the porch to mingle with the rest of the congregation on the snow-dappled lawn.

At Ellie's direction, they strolled to where several couples were exchanging news. She was plainly well-known and was greeted with warmth and with interested and curious glances directed at Godfrey. She introduced him as a gentleman from London come to assist with a business decision of her father's. Godfrey smiled and played to that role.

Glancing back at the church door, he saw Morris exit and stride purposefully away.

Godfrey bent and whispered in Ellie's ear, "Morris just left. Should I go and help with your father?" There was a single step down from the porch to the lawn.

Ellie shook her head. "No need. Harry's with him—they'll manage."

Godfrey inclined his head in acceptance and returned to the fray, answering a local lady's question regarding what plays were currently exciting attention in the capital.

A moment later, he glanced back at the church—to see Harry wrestling with his father's chair. The rear wheels had gone over the edge of the porch easily enough, but had bogged in the slushy snow.

Before Godfrey could move, the gentleman who had sat beside Morris strode out of the church, checked when he saw Harry, Mr. Hinckley, and the chair, and after a fractional hesitation, went to assist.

Between them, the man and Harry got the chair unstuck and rolled it onto the lawn.

Harry smiled at the gentleman and offered his hand, which the gentleman shook.

Mr. Hinckley added his thanks, and the trio paused to chat.

Godfrey returned his gaze to Ellie and, at her questioning look, murmured, "All's well."

Ellie met his eyes and let her smile speak for her. She'd realized there'd been a problem because the muscles in his arm, beneath her hand, had tensed; he'd been about to go to her father's aid when the stranger had stepped in.

If the stranger hadn't assisted, Godfrey would have. Without anyone requesting it or prompting his attention, he would have gone to help, simply because her father and brother had needed assistance.

She'd had other suitors, and in her experience, in such a situation, not even Masterton, had he been beside her, would have felt moved to assist without her suggesting it.

Godfrey, on the other hand, often spontaneously stepped in to help—not only with her but also with her family—and he did so without considering whether the action would gain points with her or anyone else.

Godfrey Cavanaugh was, quite simply, a *nice* man—the epitome of a true gentleman. That he was a lord born and bred only made that more remarkable and made the constant battle not to fall under his spell all the more fraught. Indeed, she doubted he even knew he was casting a spell, which only made the attraction drawing her to him even more potent.

She knew she should resist. Her problem was that, for the first time in her life, she didn't want to.

From the corner of her eye, she saw her father in his chair, with Harry pushing and the unknown gentleman pacing alongside, nearing. She excused herself from the ongoing conversation and turned with a smile.

Maggie and Godfrey followed her lead; they flanked her as her father introduced them to the newcomer.

"My elder daughter, Eleanor—Ellie to everyone hereabouts—my younger daughter, Maggie, and Mr. Cavanaugh, a visitor from London." Her father gestured to the gentleman. "This is Mr. Jeffers, based in York and currently visiting the area."

They all shook hands. Ellie judged Jeffers to be in his mid-thirties. He was well-dressed with dark hair, neatly styled, although not as fashionably so as Godfrey's. The quality of his clothes was good, neither notably expensive nor cheap, and their cut suggested Jeffers favored a decent provincial tailor.

Jeffers readily responded to a comment on the weather from Godfrey, engaging them all with a self-deprecating tale of some of the more amusing effects of the recent storm in York.

From there, the conversation rolled on surprisingly easily. Jeffers was unstintingly polite, much in the same way Godfrey was; he made personable, easygoing, and entertaining company.

Ellie finally asked him, "Is there any particular local spot you've come to visit, sir?"

Jeffers's easy smile lightened his blue eyes. "Not specifically. You could say that this excursion has been more about sating my curiosity and getting an idea of the lay of the land. My partner and I recently took over an enterprise in York, and as winter is generally slow business-wise, the weather aside, this was an opportune time to take a look around the district."

She smiled. "I see." Him being part owner of a business fitted the image he presented.

"If I might ask, Jeffers," her father said, "where are you staying?"

"I'm at the Queen's Head." Jeffers nodded down the street. "Only a short stroll away."

Her father squinted up at him. "Bill Wood taking good care of you?"

Jeffers smiled. "He is, thank you."

"Nevertheless, it's Sunday," her father persisted, "and the roast Bill serves is always overdone. More like old boots. Instead of wrestling with it, why don't you join us? Nothing extravagant, but our Cook is generally regarded as a local wonder."

"I can attest to that," Godfrey put in. "I've yet to meet a dish she's prepared that is less than mouthwatering, and thanks to the snow, I've been at Hinckley Hall for the past ten days."

Jeffers arched his brows at Godfrey. "That's a recommendation difficult to pass up." He smiled at Ellie, then at Harry and Maggie, before looking at their father. "I have to admit to growing bored with my own company." Jeffers gracefully inclined his head. "I would be honored to accept your kind invitation."

"Right, then, that's settled." Mr. Hinckley clapped his gloved hands and looked around, noting the dispersing crowd. "Everyone's leaving, so we may as well, too."

Harry explained, "Our carriage is in the forecourt with the others, and Mr. Cavanaugh and I are riding."

Jeffers nodded. "I'll hie back to the Queen's Head, get my horse saddled, and meet you in the street."

With that agreed, they parted.

As he escorted Ellie and Maggie to the carriage, Godfrey pondered Jeffers. Beneath the man's urbanity, there lurked a certain edge, yet Godfrey had no sense that Jeffers was anything other than he claimed to be—a businessman recently arrived in York taking a look around the nearby countryside.

Indeed, Jeffers's accent didn't hail from the north. In fact, if Godfrey had to guess, the man was grammar-school educated, and given his looks, it was perfectly possible he was some aristocrat's illegitimate son. Not that that told them all that much about Jeffers, the man, but it would explain his polished manners and ready conversation.

After helping Mr. Hinckley up the carriage steps, then handing Ellie and Maggie up and shutting the door, Godfrey mounted George and joined Harry in ambling after the carriage as the coachman steered it down the street.

Mounted on a nice-looking roan, Jeffers was waiting outside the Queen's Head. He fell in beside Harry, and as they continued riding along, Godfrey found himself grinning at Jeffers's observations about things he'd seen on his recent foray, having gone as far west as the edge of the dales; the man had a distinctly dry sense of humor.

They reached the Hall in good time, and on being returned to his wheeled chair in his own front hall, Mr. Hinckley led the way into the drawing room.

At Mr. Hinckley's wave and his recommendation to Jeffers not to stand on ceremony, they spread themselves in the available chairs. Godfrey sat alongside Ellie on the sofa, while Jeffers claimed the armchair on her other side, the one opposite Mr. Hinckley's position. As Harry and Maggie sat in chairs facing the sofa, Kemp arrived bearing a tray hosting the sherry decanter and glasses.

Mr. Hinckley looked at Godfrey. "I hope the excursion hasn't over-tired you, sir."

Godfrey smiled. "No, indeed. Rather, I found the fresh air invigorating." In reply to Jeffers's puzzled look, Godfrey explained, "I was caught out in the snowstorm and, subsequently, confined to bed for a week."

"Ah, I see." Jeffers grimaced. "Quite aside from the snow, the wind was quite vicious, even in York."

Kemp had just finished distributing glasses of the fine Jerez sherry when the sound of an arrival reached them. A moment later, a footman opened the door to admit Masterton.

He walked in with his usual confident stride—which hitched and slowed when he saw Jeffers. After a second of staring at Jeffers, Masterton dragged his gaze to Mr. Hinckley. "Good day, Matthew." Halting, Masterton nodded to Mr. Hinckley, then glanced again at Jeffers. "I didn't know you would be entertaining company." Recollecting himself, Masterton sent a faint smile Godfrey's way. "Other than Cavanaugh, of course."

Mr. Hinckley waved that aside. "You know you're always welcome to join us, Michael. This is Mr. Jeffers from York—he's visiting the area."

Godfrey watched as Masterton and Jeffers exchanged nods, on Jeffers's part with relaxed ease, while Masterton seemed a trifle stiff. Godfrey wasn't sure whether Masterton had recognized Jeffers and disapproved of his presence, or whether Masterton was miffed simply over finding an outsider sitting down with the family he appeared to consider in some way his concern.

With what seemed his customary facility, Jeffers commented to Mr. Hinckley about the house, and the pair fell into an undemanding exchange.

Kemp approached and offered Masterton a glass of sherry. Masterton picked up the glass, surveyed the available seats, then moved to sit in the chair beside the sofa, beyond Godfrey.

Invited by his father to explain the house's history to Jeffers, Harry complied. It was evident the younger Hinckley had made a study of the house's past. From his perusal of the books Ellie had lent him, Godfrey recalled several colorful snippets, which he volunteered as embellishments to Harry's accounting.

Allowing Harry to reclaim center stage, Godfrey sat back, amused. After a moment, he glanced at Masterton and found the man watching Jeffers, who was leaning back in his chair, to all appearances happy to be entertained.

Kemp returned to announce luncheon, and they all rose. Godfrey gave Ellie his arm, which she took, and they followed Harry, pushing his father's chair, with Jeffers pacing alongside. Masterton had fallen in on Harry's other side, while Maggie came up beside Godfrey. He smiled and offered her his other arm, and with an impish grin, she looped her arm in his.

In the dining room, they arranged themselves around the table, with Mr. Hinckley at its head and Ellie at its foot. Godfrey claimed the chair on her right, while Masterton, not to be outdone, took the chair on her left.

Maggie sat on Godfrey's other side, with Harry beside her, and as befitted an invited guest, Jeffers sat on Mr. Hinckley's right, opposite Harry.

The meal began with a warming soup and continued through four substantial courses. Having finished describing the house to Jeffers, Harry asked Jeffers's opinion of York.

Although it transpired that Jeffers had moved from Doncaster to York only three months before, nevertheless, he had stories to tell that confirmed he'd spent those months exploring the city.

Deftly, he asked Godfrey about various similarities with London, and between them, they kept the conversation rolling effortlessly and the company well entertained.

Ellie noted that Masterton listened, but said nothing; then again, he customarily volunteered little about his private life or personal views. While at the Hall, he tended to talk primarily of Hall matters; today, with that topic very much in abeyance, he made no attempt to introduce it into the conversation, for which Ellie was grateful. Jeffers didn't need to know her family's business.

When they adjourned to the drawing room for tea and cakes, she was quietly pleased by how well the day had gone; Jeffers had more than repaid their invitation by making her father laugh countless times and engaging with Harry and Godfrey as well. She was impressed that Jeffers had made no especial effort to attract and hold Maggie's attention or hers; personable and handsome he might be, yet he was transparently not on the hunt for female company.

Was he married? She realized they hadn't asked. Jeffers had mentioned a partner, but through all his tales, he hadn't mentioned a wife, although there'd been no reason for him to do so; none of his tales had impinged on his private life.

The tea trolley arrived, and she poured, and Godfrey and Maggie helped distribute the cups and hand around the platter of petits fours. Ably assisted by Harry's and Maggie's insatiable curiosity, Godfrey and Jeffers between them steered the conversation on in pleasant and relaxed vein.

Eventually, with the tea and cakes consumed and the cups and saucers set aside, Ellie was congratulating herself on having overseen an unrelievedly pleasant afternoon when, with her father, Jeffers, Harry, and Maggie absorbed in a discussion of the theatres in York, Masterton leaned toward Godfrey and said, "As you're up and about socializing, Cavanaugh, I assume you've completed your assessment of the Albertinelli. So what's your verdict?"

Ellie leapt in. "As you know, Michael, Papa holds strong views on the observance of the Sabbath. In addition, Mr. Cavanaugh has explained that assessments such as his take time to complete, and in this case, as it is the National Gallery involved, he wishes to be especially thorough."

Masterton searched Godfrey's face. From the corner of her eye, she

saw that Godfrey had adopted his charming—and utterly uninformative
—mask.

"Miss Hinckley is correct," Godfrey quietly stated. "While it might
seem odd to the uninitiated, it does take time to cross every t and dot
every i."

Masterton looked like he wished to argue, but in the face of Godfrey's
unruffled assertion, he was forced to back down. "I see."

At that moment, Jeffers straightened and said to her father, "I most
sincerely thank you for your hospitality, Mr. Hinckley." Smiling, he
inclined his head to Ellie. "Miss Hinckley. I've truly enjoyed my day at
the Hall, but I should be on my way before the light starts to fade."

Jeffers rose, as did Godfrey and Harry and, rather more reluctantly,
Masterton. The men shook hands, then Jeffers bowed over Ellie's and
thanked her prettily before nodding to Maggie and, at the last, turning to
exchange a more specific farewell with his host.

Watching Jeffers take his leave of Mr. Hinckley, Godfrey could not
fault the man's manners, demeanor, or behavior. On the subject of Jeffers,
his instincts remained entirely quiescent; he felt confident Jeffers posed
no threat to the Hinckleys, even though Godfrey was perfectly certain that
Jeffers was nowhere near as harmless as he seemed.

Regardless, Godfrey's well-honed talent informed him that Jeffers
hadn't lied, not once. He might be concealing things, but nothing of what
he'd revealed had been false.

Harry had rung for Jeffers's horse to be saddled and brought to the
door. Kemp appeared to say the horse was waiting, and with final good
wishes all around, Jeffers departed.

The family, Godfrey, and Masterton resettled, but the conversation
soon flagged.

Given the hour was sliding toward three o'clock, no one was
surprised when Masterton rose and announced that he, too, should leave.
To Mr. Hinckley, he said, "I know you would put me up, Matthew, but I
need to get back to Ripon tonight."

"Of course, Michael." Mr. Hinckley shook Masterton's hand. "Safe
journey."

With nods for the rest of them, Masterton left. In the front hall, he
called for his horse. Minutes later, they heard the front door shut, then
rapid hoofbeats faded down the drive.

Godfrey swiveled and looked out of the window. The afternoon light,
while not strong, hadn't yet started to wane. He looked at Ellie, then at

Maggie and Harry. "I haven't seen much of your park, although from the history books, I understand it's quite extensive. I gathered there are stone pathways wending through it." He arched his brows at Harry and Maggie. "Can I tempt you to show me the best views?"

"Of course! I'll show you." Maggie bounced to her feet.

"Capital idea." Harry beamed. "I'll come, too."

Ellie shot Godfrey a laughing smile. "I'll come as well." She, too, swiveled to look out of the window at the sky. "There's no sign of rain, and after days of being cooped up inside, we could all do with some exercise."

Smiling benignly, Mr. Hinckley waved them away. "I'll be in the library when you get back." Harry rose and summoned a footman to assist his father. To Godfrey, Mr. Hinckley said, "I'll be interested in hearing your opinion of the park, even half buried by snow."

Godfrey tipped him a salute and followed the three younger Hinckleys into the front hall. After donning coats, scarves, gloves, and in Maggie's and Ellie's cases, muffs and galoshes, they left the house through a garden hall, the door of which, Maggie informed Godfrey, gave directly onto the major path that would take them all the way through the park, eventually returning them to the terrace on the other side of the house. "We can then get in through the morning room door," she said.

Godfrey looked up at the still-clear blue sky. "How long will it take?"

"About half an hour or so," Ellie replied.

He smiled at her and offered his arm. She looped her arm in his, and they set off, pacing along the path in Maggie and Harry's wake.

The path proved to be solid stone, about a yard wide and firm and stable beneath a crust of lingering snow.

Maggie skipped ahead, pausing to point at a robin flitting through the trees. Harry thrust his hands into his pockets and plowed along, halting here and there to direct Godfrey's attention to some ornamental feature— a statue standing in a grove, an urn spilling snow-crusted ivy to wreathe about the base of its pedestal.

Godfrey looked, then glanced around. "I take it the grounds were landscaped at some point."

"In our grandparents' time," Ellie confirmed. "A man from Scotland came down and laid out the paths and built the bridges."

"Bridges? More than one?"

Harry pointed. "If you peer through the trees over there, you can just make out the bridge that leads over the river and into the woods."

Godfrey peered and spotted the dull gray of twin stone posts sitting up amid the snow, anchoring graceful stone arches that spanned the width of the river.

Harry went on, "And a little way along, we'll come to a tributary that runs through the grounds. This path cuts across it, and the second bridge is there."

It was as plain as the proverbial pikestaff that Harry was proud of his home; the look on his face as he trudged through the snow said it all.

As well as the expected firs and spruces, the park contained many different trees; oaks, beeches, aspens, and many more were artfully scattered in clumps and stands and strategically planted on what, in summer, would be expansive lawns. At one point, Godfrey paused and looked back at the house. "This must be very pretty in summer."

Ellie smiled. "It's wonderful—green and cool and restful."

They shared smiles of appreciative understanding and walked on.

Maggie had sped around the next bend, and as Harry followed, she ambushed him with a snowball.

Harry gasped and shook the snow from his head and shoulders, then whooped and gave chase. Laughing and shrieking, the pair rushed on, over the bridge across the tributary and along the next section of path that curved through stands of winter-bare trees to eventually take them back toward the house.

Watching her siblings, Ellie chuckled. "They've been very restrained over the past week of being trapped inside." She glanced at Godfrey. "Thank you for suggesting this walk—we all needed it."

Closing his hand over hers where it rested on his sleeve, he lightly squeezed. "Thank you for consenting to come—for me, this interlude is truly a pleasure."

Her gaze lingered on his face, as if confirming what he'd implied but hadn't said: that the walk would not have been such a pleasure without her company.

He met her gaze readily, willing her to see that and more.

After a second, her lashes veiled her eyes, and she looked forward.

They neared the smaller stone bridge that spanned the narrow dip at the bottom of which a small stream tinkled with bell-like clarity, still running beneath a deep covering of snow.

The snow lay thicker on the bridge than on the path, with a solid layer of ice beneath. They started across, treading in Maggie's and Harry's footsteps. Godfrey looked ahead, but the younger pair had disappeared around the curve in the path.

"Oh!" Ellie clutched his arm.

He snapped his gaze to her as she dragged on his arm, struggling to stay upright as her galoshes slid on the underlying ice.

He planted his feet and hauled her to him; she landed breast to chest, hip to thigh, against him.

She stilled.

Gently, he freed his sleeve from her grip, wrapped his arms around her, and steadied her against him. "I've got you."

Her thick coat and his greatcoat cushioned the contact, yet he still felt her warm softness filling his arms, a very welcome sensation in the prevailing cold.

After several seconds during which he didn't think she breathed, she looked up. Her eyes met his, her gaze open and direct, and he saw in the medley of woodland greens and golds an awareness and something more than curiosity.

"Yes, you do," she replied, her voice low and husky, and it was his turn to search for hidden meanings.

Attraction—transparently mutual, potent, and shockingly powerful—all but throbbed between them.

The tug was palpable, a visceral tightening that compelled.

He felt as if he was falling into her eyes, into her soul.

Uncertain yet driven, he slowly lowered his head.

She made a small sound, reached up and cupped his nape with her gloved hand, and stretched upward on her toes.

That was agreement enough; he swooped, and his lips found hers.

He kissed her—gently, carefully, as if she were as fragile as spun glass. His lips moved on hers in a kiss as delicate as a falling snowflake—temptation and fascination combined.

Sparks of sensation danced along his nerves, teasing, taunting, luring.

Then her lips firmed, their lush softness an unimaginable delight, and she kissed him back, her lips cruising his in a sweet, evocative savoring that sent tingles of expectation down his spine.

Then warmth flared into heat, and the kiss turned seeking, searching; she wanted more, and he met her quest with his own burgeoning need.

"Where are they?" Maggie's piping voice rang across the snow.

Ellie and Godfrey broke from the kiss. They stared at each other and heard Harry reply, "I don't know, but they'll be along in a moment. Come on! It's getting colder."

Ellie drew in a tight breath and tensed to step back.

Godfrey set her on her feet and held her until he was sure she was steady.

Her hands resting on his sleeves, she cleared her throat. "The day's closing in. We should get on."

He didn't trust his voice, or what he might say, so simply nodded.

He lowered his arms, feeling the loss as her hands fell away, then he offered her an arm, and after a fractional hesitation, she took it.

They walked off the bridge and on along the path.

Thoughts, hopes, and errant impulses flitted through his brain.

They rounded the curve and, in the distance, saw the Hall, solid and enduring in gray stone, with its pitched lead roofs, garlanded with snow, stark against the pale-blue sky. Side by side, Harry and Maggie were walking toward the house, apparently joking and laughing, and the vista was framed by winter-bare trees, their branches still thinly coated with snow.

Godfrey drank in the sight, then surreptitiously glanced at Ellie, scanning her features. Her expression was as serene as before, but there was a touch more color in her cheeks, and her eyes... He rather thought they were shining.

He looked ahead. He felt good. Not just happy but settled. And although she was the source of his fascination and attraction, that anchored feeling wasn't solely due to her but owed much to the totality of what he had stumbled upon there, at Hinckley Hall.

A family, a household, living in peace and long-established harmony.

It was no wonder he felt so compelled to protect them.

The weight of that responsibility was quite real; he felt it keenly—the need to see them safely through the coming storm, one he'd brought with him, the vagaries of which he was far more familiar with than they.

He couldn't see any end to that feeling; it had taken root so deeply inside him. He wanted to be their shield into the future—if they would allow it, if they would accept such protection from him.

If Ellie would have him.

He glanced at her again. Through the past days, they'd drawn steadily closer—as witnessed by that tantalizing kiss—but with the issue of the painting hanging between them...

No. He faced forward. It would be wrong to speak now—not yet.

They'd been walking steadily toward the house. Ahead of them, Harry and Maggie reached the terrace, went up the steps, opened a glass-paned door, and slipped inside.

As they neared the steps, Ellie murmured, "Just so you know, I don't regret so much as one second of what transpired on the bridge."

He looked at her, waited until she glanced his way, then trapped her gaze. "That's good to know, because I don't, either."

Speculation shone in her eyes, just as much as it flared in his mind.

Not yet.

He forced himself to look ahead. He guided her up the steps, then she drew her arm from his and led him into the house.

They parted in the gallery; the household kept country hours, and it would soon be time to get ready for dinner.

Godfrey let himself into his room and closed the door. Wally would be up soon to fuss over his wet boots and the damp greatcoat Godfrey shrugged off and laid over a chair.

He walked to the window and looked out at the park, slowly being swallowed by deepening shadows.

Courtesy of this day of rest, what he had to do stood clear in his mind. His present conundrum was: Which way of doing that would best serve the Hinckleys?

He wished he could consult Ryder—or even Rand or Kit—but they were too far away. He couldn't lean on their wise counsel. This time, he had to rely solely on his own judgment.

The longer he stood and stared at nothing, the clearer in his mind his way forward grew. He needed to formulate a plan that would fulfill his duty to his patrons and himself, while shielding the Hinckleys and guiding them along the path that held the greatest hope for them.

On leaving the Hall, Masterton rode hard toward Ripon. He was halfway there when he recalled that Jeffers had met the Hinckleys at the church in Kirkby Malzeard.

Hauling his hunter to a plunging halt, Masterton swore. "The bastard must be staying somewhere near there."

After a second of rapid calculation, he set his jaw, dragged his horse's head around, and raced back the way he'd come. He continued past the Hall at a reckless pace, hoping to catch Jeffers on the road.

Luck was with him; Jeffers hadn't been hurrying. Masterton caught up with him on the other side of Galphay.

Jeffers heard the pounding hooves and slowed to look behind him, then continued trotting slowly along.

Biting back another curse, Masterton drew alongside. It took him a moment to settle his mount to the slower pace. Then he looked at Jeffers and, eyes narrowed, demanded, "What the devil do you think you're doing, cozying up to the Hinckleys?"

Jeffers turned his head and regarded Masterton with a steady, level gaze. Nothing in Jeffers's expression suggested he was in any way perturbed by Masterton's challenge. "As you're already aware, I'm in the area casting my eye over our firm's business interests."

Masterton snorted derisively.

Jeffers faintly smiled and looked ahead. "I find it always pays to have a solid understanding of the realities of any undertaking."

Masterton scowled. "As regards the Hinckleys, what undertaking would that be?"

"What, indeed?" Jeffers replied. "I've been asking myself that for the past half hour."

Masterton bridled. "Look here, Jeffers. I don't know what your game is, but you can steer clear of the Hinckleys. You and your master might have got your claws into Morris and Pyne, but Hinckley's a different kettle of fish. There's no reason for him to fall into your clutches, so no reason for you to ingratiate yourself there."

Masterton's tone was openly aggressive, but Jeffers remained unmoved.

"Do you think so?" He arched his brows as if contemplating the question.

When, goaded, Masterton snapped, "Yes, I damn well do!" Jeffers looked at Masterton.

Jeffers's features hardened, as did his gaze, and in a voice as unforgiving as granite, he said, "I'm protecting my interests, Masterton. I suggest you focus on your own."

Jeffers held Masterton's gaze for several seconds, then looked ahead and urged his horse into a canter.

His face mottling with impotent rage, Masterton reined in his mount. He glared after Jeffers, then swore and, jaw clenching, wheeled his horse for Ripon.

CHAPTER 10

*W*ith his way forward clear in his mind, Godfrey rose early and beat all the Hinckleys to the breakfast table. After more than adequately breaking his fast, before any of the family appeared, he escaped the breakfast parlor and set out to pace the path through the park, the better to prepare his approach—his presentation.

The pervasive stillness of the snowy landscape was conducive to thinking and planning. By the time he returned to the house, he felt ready for what lay before him.

By then, the dining room was empty. The others had all breakfasted and were off about their usual morning occupations. Godfrey knew he would find Mr. Hinckley in the library, but Ellie's father wasn't first on his list to be made privy to his news. By dint of asking Kemp, Godfrey tracked Ellie down in the housekeeper's room.

Judging by the pleased expression on her face and the papers she'd gathered and held in her hands, she'd finished her meeting with Mrs. Kemp and was on the cusp of leaving. She glanced up when he halted in the open doorway.

The smile that lit her face warmed him through and through. She looked at him questioningly. "Did you need me for something?"

Godfrey nodded and found his tongue. "If you have a few minutes?"

Her smile deepened. "Of course." She walked toward him. "Just let me put these in the morning room."

He stepped back and waved her on, then trailed her to the front hall and across the tiles to the narrow reception room opposite the drawing room. Entering in her wake, he realized this was her domain.

She crossed to an elegant lady's desk angled before one window, set down the papers, then, smiling, turned to him. "The menus for the next week. It's nice to have them done and out of the way."

He managed a smile in reply, but it felt a trifle strained.

She walked up, halted before him, searched his eyes, then arched her brows. "What do you need?"

He cleared his throat and said, "There's something I'd like to show you. If you'll come with me?"

She looked at him curiously. He stepped back and ushered her before him, out of the room, across the hall, and into the corridor leading to the conservatory.

"Oh." She threw him a glance over her shoulder—one of rising expectation. "The painting?"

Fighting to keep his expression unreadable, he nodded.

He followed her into the huge glassed room, then stepped past her and led the way to where he'd set the painting on a chair, facing the far end of the room. He took her hand and drew her to stand directly before the painting, at the perfect distance for viewing the canvas, bathed as it was in soft, diffused light falling through the glass above and behind them.

He positioned her there, then shifted to stand behind her and placed his hands on her shoulders.

She twisted her head to look searchingly at him. "Have you completed your assessment?"

He nodded. "I wanted you to be the first to hear it."

She looked at the painting. "Very well."

He drew in a slow, unhelpfully tight breath. "I'm going to tell you all I've learned about this painting, and I would like you to listen to the whole and, if you can, wait until the end before you react."

She glanced at him, a touch of uncertainty creeping into her gaze. "All right."

He looked over her shoulder at the painting. When she followed his gaze, he hauled in a deeper breath. "The provenance your family holds—all the documents—prove unequivocally that the painting that was hanging in your mother's parlor when she died was an original Albertinelli, exactly as described in your ancestor's letters."

"That's good, isn't it?" From her tone, she'd sensed that all was not well.

"It was, yes. But the painting you're looking at—the one that's been hanging in your mother's parlor for the past three years—isn't the original Albertinelli your ancestor brought home. This painting is a forgery—albeit a very good forgery—by an artist named Hendrik Hendall."

It took her a second to absorb that. *"What?"* She tried to swing around, but he held her in place. Over her shoulder, she demanded, "How can that be?"

"Wait. There's more to tell." She quieted, and he continued, "I know beyond question that the work is Hendall's, and I also know that this copy was created in only the last five years, because Hendall has only been painting forgeries over that time. The nails used to resecure the painting in the frame suggest the copy was put into the frame about three years ago. On top of that, Hendall only creates forgeries with the original before him—he's a copyist. He needs the original to copy directly from."

He leaned forward and looked at her face. She was frowning, trying to make sense of what he was telling her.

"So"—he looked once again at the painting—"the situation we're facing is that you *did* have the original Albertinelli, but about three years ago, someone entered the house and spirited the Albertinelli away. Hendall would have needed at least three weeks, most likely more, to create this copy, so the frame would have hung empty—or there would have been an empty space on the parlor wall—for at least four weeks, possibly longer."

He paused, then slowly turned her to face him. He met her eyes; they were full of confusion and burgeoning anxiety. "The first question I have is this: Would it have been possible for the painting to vanish like that, for four or more weeks, without anyone noticing?"

When she blinked at him, he went on, "This house is so large, I can imagine that if a thief took the painting out of the frame, rolled it up, and carried it under his jacket, he might have been able to take the painting out of the house without anyone noticing. But the space on the wall would have been there for weeks."

Ellie stared into Godfrey's face. She could barely breathe. After several dizzying moments, she managed to get out, "A *forgery!*"

Her knees quaked.

Godfrey caught her about her waist and guided her back to the chair she'd last seen him sitting in; it was placed to afford an excellent view of the canvas. She sank down and, utterly baffled, stared at the painting—

one she would have sworn was the same one she'd known from birth. Slowly, she shook her head. "I just can't…take this in."

He would never have told her it was a forgery if it wasn't.

That meant it was a forgery, and she couldn't understand…

He crouched before her and took her hands in his. Concern showed clearly in his usually impassive face. "Ellie?" He chafed her hands. "Darling, this is not the end of the world. Trust me—there are things we can do, steps we can take, to make things right."

She blinked and focused on his face. Far better than on the wretched painting which was not the painting she and all her family thought it was. After a moment, her inner panic subsided enough for his words to register when he repeated, "Could the painting have vanished for weeks?"

She sat back and thought, then reluctantly nodded. "Mrs. Kemp dusts in there occasionally, but only every few months or so. With no one going in there, there really is no need."

He trapped her gaze. "So there would have been periods during which the painting could have been gone from the wall."

"Yes." She looked past his shoulder at the canvas propped on the chair. "And if whoever it was replaced the Albertinelli with that…" She shook her head. "Even I wouldn't have noticed."

He remained hunkered in front of her, his gaze on her face. "I want you to think carefully—who else besides the family and staff currently here would have known of the painting? Not just glimpsed it but have known it for what it was—an old master's work and, even more specifically, an Albertinelli?"

She thought back. "Dr. Hatchett—he spent a lot of time with Mama in that room. And her nurse and the local midwife, and my governess and Maggie's as well, and Harry's tutors, and the minister and the deacon—all would have been in that room fairly frequently. Mama held court there, and she was terribly fond of that painting." She focused on his eyes and grimaced. "And that's not counting Mama's close friends. She had a circle of lady friends, and when she fell ill, their husbands often visited, too. Plus, of course, Pyne and his wife and the Morrises as well."

Godfrey grimaced. "That's far too many people to imagine investigating."

She blinked. "Investigating?"

He met her eyes. "The person who took the painting had to be someone who knew it was there and who knew the house well enough to get in and out without being seen."

She frowned. "The house is so large, anyone could have broken in and just looked around and found it."

But he was shaking his head. "No." He swung half around and pointed at the painting. "No itinerant or burglar would have bothered with that. It's hardly attractive to the general viewer. Only someone who knew what it was and what it was worth would have given it a second glance."

She had to admit that was true. The painting was simple and relatively plain, just three figures—women in richly hued gowns with long shawls over their heads—meeting on stone steps before an ornate archway with the sky and the hint of a hill behind. The precision of the lines of the archway and gowns, the colors—even dimmed by the patina of centuries —and the soft expressions on the women's faces were what had drawn her mother to the piece and prompted her to have it hung in pride of place in her private parlor. But speaking generally, it wasn't an eye-catching work.

Frowning, she stared at the painting. "What aren't you saying?"

He sighed and swiveled to sit on the floor by her feet. He drew up his long legs, looped his arms about his knees, and stared at the painting, too. "The critical question is, as this is a forgery, where is the original Albertinelli? It has to be somewhere. I had hoped only a few outsiders would know of the painting, and a little quiet investigating might have told us who took it, and we could follow the trail from there. But clearly, it's not going to be that simple."

"How do you think it was done—stolen and taken from the house?"

Godfrey explained about the painting being removed from the frame. "I'm certain that was what happened because the nails securing the frame are, at the most, three years old. The surface of nails changes with time." He glanced at her. "I'm assuming you're not going to tell me that the painting was reframed three years ago?"

She shook her head. "As far as I know, that frame is the one my ancestor brought home or had the painting put into before he hung it, and it hasn't been touched since—at least not in my lifetime."

He nodded. "That's what I thought. And judging by the way the nails have been put in, whoever did so wasn't a professional framer, so there's no sense asking around the local artist's shops. Whoever took the painting returned with the copy weeks later, put it back in the frame, and rehung the picture on the wall."

She frowned. "But why? Why go to the bother of having a copy made and putting it back?"

"Indeed. And that's another very telling point." He paused, then said, "This isn't any run-of-the-mill theft. Usually, the only reason a copy would be switched for an original, as has happened here, is if it was in the best interests of either the thief or the eventual new owner for there to be no hue and cry raised over the missing painting." He paused, then admitted, "In this case, either could be possible."

She seemed to ponder that, then sighed. "I have to say that I'm cravenly glad we aren't going to be asking questions of all the people who knew of the painting. I've known most of them for all of my life, and while it seems one must be a thief, all the others aren't. Any suggestion we harbor suspicions... It would be hellishly tricky not to hurt people simply by asking the most basic questions." She met his eyes. "That's not a path my father or I would wish to take."

He raked a hand through his hair, then lowered his arm. "Given the number of possibilities, I doubt we would get far by that route, anyway."

She sighed again, this time in defeat. "So we're left with a worthless forgery and no way to find the original." Her tone was dull.

"No." He pushed to his feet. "We have another way forward."

She blinked at him. "We do?"

He nodded. "The forger, Hendall. He lives in Amsterdam. I know where to find him. Once we speak with your father, if he agrees, I propose to visit Hendall and ask him who commissioned this work." He gestured to the painting.

"Will he remember, do you think?"

"Oh yes. He won't have forgotten an Albertinelli."

She looked into his face. "But will he tell you?"

He couldn't hold back a small, entirely unhumorous smile. "Given I'll be acting for your family and you hold irrefutable evidence that the original is yours..." He tipped his head. "I can think of several types of pressure that might be brought to bear on Hendall. Enough that he will find it much easier to simply tell me who brought him the painting to be copied and, if he knows, who now holds the original."

She frowned. "Could they be the same man?"

"In this case, that's unlikely. Whoever stole the painting is almost certainly known to the household—to you and your family. Unless you know any avid collectors of High Renaissance art?"

She shook her head.

"Then the most likely scenario of what happened to the Albertinelli is that whoever stole it sold it to an avid and unscrupulous collector."

"But why would such a person give us back our painting? Presumably, they'll have paid the thief and consider the painting theirs."

He nodded. "But you hold provenance that is undeniable. The painting was yours, and unless whoever holds it now can produce a legitimate bill of sale that transfers the painting from your hands to theirs... legally, they will have to hand it over." His smile growing more edged, he met her gaze. "And trust me—having a title and the connections that go with it can be extremely useful in certain situations."

She tipped her head as if studying him through newly opened eyes. "So you're proposing to act as our family's agent and travel to Amsterdam to confront this forger?"

He nodded. "If your father agrees."

Her face darkened. "You're not going now—this week? At this time of year, the crossing will be dangerous, and you'll risk having a relapse regardless." She rose. "Papa might agree to the plan, but I'll make sure he understands that you can't go—at least not until the weather and your chest improve."

Godfrey frowned and was about to protest when he caught her eye, and the notion bloomed in his brain that her obsession with his health was remarkably similar to his obsession with her well-being. With his eyes locked with hers, he hesitated, then conceded, "I'm sure if I asked, my brother Kit would be happy to sail one of his yachts to Amsterdam and ask Hendall a few pointed questions." The thought made him grin.

"Good." She seemed relieved. She looked again at the painting—the forgery—then, with an almost puzzled expression, returned her gaze to him. "You agreed to that too readily—what are you planning?"

Despite all, he nearly laughed. Then again, she wasn't wrong. "I keep mentally tripping over the fact *that*"—he waved at the forgery—"is here. That it exists at all. Given the isolation of Hinckley Hall and that this particular Albertinelli wasn't even known to exist, then the risk of a major hue and cry—one that reached farther than the immediate vicinity—was all but nonexistent. If the painting had vanished, you and the local authorities would simply have concluded that someone had stolen it, and that would have been that. Instead"—he gestured again at the forgery—"we have this. Why the...well, deception?"

That was why the forgery's existence kept niggling so insistently; why perpetrate such a deception on the innocent and unthreatening Hinckleys? "I honestly can't see why our thief went to the considerable effort and expense of replacing the painting with such a high-class forgery, sufficient for everyone here to think the painting was still at the Hall, where it belonged." He paused, then grimaced. "As for what I'm planning...I really don't know, but pursuing an answer to the why of the forgery strikes me as one possible way forward."

After a moment, he looked at Ellie. "When your father let it be known that he'd decided to contact the National Gallery about selling the Albertinelli, did any of your acquaintance, when they heard of it, display any odd reaction?"

She thought, then slowly shook her head. "Not that I'm aware of, but Papa might know more."

Godfrey nodded and met her eyes. "In that case, unless you would advise otherwise, I think it's time we spoke with your father."

Godfrey opened the library door and held it for Ellie, then followed her into the room.

It was heading toward noon, and Mr. Hinckley was seated in his chair beside the fire, reading the newspapers that had been delivered that morning.

At the sounds of their footsteps, he lowered the sheet and smiled at them. "Good morning." He nodded to Godfrey. "I missed you at breakfast —I heard you were up early."

"I was." Godfrey waited until Ellie gathered her skirts and sat on the sofa, opposite her father, then sat beside her. "I completed my assessment of your painting and took a long walk to order my thoughts."

"Ah." Mr. Hinckley folded the newspaper and set it on the side table by his elbow. Then he set his hands in his lap and, his expression one of pleasant expectation, looked at Godfrey.

This is going to be harder than I thought.

Before he could speak, Ellie leaned forward, drawing her father's gaze. "Papa, Godfrey is certain the painting we have is a forgery."

Mr. Hinckley blinked, and all color drained from his face. "What?" He looked from Ellie to Godfrey, then back again, clearly reading the truth in their faces. "But..." Mr. Hinckley's face creased with confusion. "How?"

"Indeed." Reclaiming the reins, Godfrey succinctly outlined what he was now convinced had occurred. After answering Mr. Hinckley's questions, Godfrey concluded by stating that it might be possible to reclaim the painting, so all might not be lost.

Unsurprisingly, Mr. Hinckley wished to know how.

After explaining his plan to demand the name of who had commissioned the forgery from the forger himself, with a glance at Ellie, Godfrey said, "I had thought that, with the weather as it is, I might ask one of my brothers who has his own yacht to go in my stead, but on reflection, I doubt that will work." He sat straighter. "It will have to be me, because Hendall will know who I am—what I do—and so know there's no point in trying to obfuscate and deny his involvement." He paused, then added, "I anticipate a certain amount of persuasion will be needed to convince Hendall to cooperate, but ultimately, given you hold the provenance and I can testify to the forgery being his, I believe he'll cut his losses and reveal who paid him to copy the Albertinelli."

Ellie frowned. "If it has to be you who speaks with this Hendall person, that will have to wait until later in the year, once the seas are safe to cross."

Mr. Hinckley regarded his daughter for a moment, no doubt taking in the militant look in her eye, then humphed and didn't argue. Instead, he looked at Godfrey and asked, "Once you know who commissioned the forgery, what then?"

"Then we speak with that person and make it clear that the only way they'll escape retribution is by assisting in reclaiming the original painting from whomever they've sold it to and restoring it to the rightful owners—namely, the Hinckleys."

Mr. Hinckley's expression turned thoughtful, then he nodded. "I like the way you think." He glanced sidelong at Ellie, then returned his gaze to Godfrey. "As I mentioned to you before, the family can manage, at least well enough for now, without the extra funds from the sale of the painting."

From the older man's expression, Godfrey understood that he wasn't supposed to tell Ellie just how concerned her father was over the family's financial position; knowing that he himself would bail them out if the need arose, he nodded his agreement to Mr. Hinckley's unstated request.

Mr. Hinckley glanced again at Ellie, then drew breath and addressed Godfrey. "One question I feel I must ask, Mr. Cavanaugh, is why you're willing to go to such lengths for us. We can't afford to pay for your time—"

Godfrey waved the notion aside. "I don't seek payment, sir." He looked at Ellie and smiled a touch ruefully. "And truth be told, I don't need money—that's not what's driving me in this." He held Ellie's gaze for a moment, willing her to see his principal reason, then looked at her father. "Those who know me and my interest in artworks would say I'm obsessed with detecting and exposing forgeries. It's something of a personal crusade, which has its genesis in my experiences at the hands of a close family member who was a past master at deception and deceit. What I do now—what I am now—is a reaction to my past. In the field of authenticating artworks, I'm now regarded as an expert in detecting fraudulent works..."

He paused as a novel thought struck. After a moment, he went on, "I was going to say that my reputation is why Eastlake and the directors of the gallery called me in, which is the bald truth. Knowing what I now do about your painting, I have to wonder if Eastlake, who is very well connected in the world of art, which isn't all that huge, had heard some rumor about the Albertinelli that prompted him to tap me on the shoulder."

Ellie shifted. "You mean he—Eastlake—already suspected that our painting might be a forgery?"

Godfrey nodded. "It's possible. He wouldn't have said anything to me —he would have wanted me to form my own opinion." If so, that testified as to how highly Eastlake valued his expertise. "But," he went on, following the thread to its logical conclusion, "that also means it's possible that Eastlake himself has some inkling as to who has the Albertinelli now."

Mr. Hinckley had been watching them. When they both fell silent, he asked, "Is that good? Eastlake knowing?"

With rising enthusiasm taking hold, Godfrey met the older man's eyes. "It might very well be. As soon as I get back to town, I'll call on him and see what he can tell us. He hasn't seen your provenance yet. Once I lay it before him, I can guarantee he'll be hot to help you reclaim the Albertinelli"—he grinned—"if for no other reason than ultimately to acquire it for the gallery. The gallery's collection is Eastlake's passion."

Just as detecting forgeries was his. Ellie looked at her father and saw that he, too, had seen the passion and commitment Godfrey devoted to his avowed obsession; it showed in his focus, in the intensity he brought to the question of righting the wrong of the forgery. In his unwavering determination to help them reclaim what was theirs.

Her father nodded to her, then transferred his gaze to Godfrey. "Right, then, Mr. Cavanaugh. If you're willing, I hope you'll guide us in this matter."

Godfrey's eyes lit. "I would, quite literally, be honored to do so, sir. And please—call me Godfrey."

Her father smiled. "Well, then, Godfrey. What's your advice as to our next step?"

Godfrey tipped his head in thought, then offered, "I believe the next step is for me to write my report for Eastlake, stating that the painting the family currently holds is a Hendall forgery, switched for the original approximately three years ago, but that the family holds conclusive provenance that the original Albertinelli belongs to the family, and I believe a concerted effort should be made to reclaim the Albertinelli from whomever holds it now."

He looked up, a grin dawning as he glanced from her father to her. "I'll include a description of the various documents your family holds. I believe I can guarantee that will elicit Eastlake's support and his full cooperation."

Her father nodded. "Very well, my boy. You have my blessing to pursue our painting to the top of your bent."

Godfrey's smile was transparently genuine. "Thank you, sir. You won't regret it."

CHAPTER 11

*L*ate that night, with the house quiet about her, Ellie stood at the window in her bedroom and stared out at the starlit sky.

How many women had stood as she was, pondering the same topic—men?

In large measure, life had passed her by—or she had passed life by, consciously, because of the decisions forced upon her.

When her mother had died, she'd stepped into the role of pseudo-mother to her siblings and, soon after, had also assumed responsibility for the tasks that fell to the lady of the house. Those hadn't been decisions taken after discussion and consideration, yet the effect—the impact on her life—had been the same. In most respects, her childhood had ended with her mother's death.

The second time she'd turned aside from life—from living the life she should have had—had been her own decision, one she'd taken without hesitation and over which she still felt no regret. When her father had fallen and damaged his spine, Harry and Maggie had needed her, and so had her father. He'd been in dire straits for months; it had been over a year before he'd progressed to sitting in his chair for most of the day.

If she hadn't turned her back on her London Season and come home, the family, the household, and the estate would have fallen apart. At no time had she—or anyone else—doubted that. Her return had been critical to everyone's survival over those long, distressing, chaotic weeks.

So, no regrets. Yet...

She was still a woman. Beneath her capable, pragmatic, and assured outer shell, her heart still harbored the dreams she'd set aside, the ones she'd never had a chance to reach for. Children of her own, a family—a home. Given how deeply her roots ran at the Hall, it might be said that she'd achieved the last aspect at least, yet although she loved the place, it lacked the one thing necessary to anchor her dreams.

It lacked him—the man she'd never had a chance to meet and marry.

Over the years, she'd had local suitors aplenty, yet although they'd wooed her, their eyes had been on her supposed inheritance and the status an alliance with her family would bring. In the area, the Hinckleys had always been considered well-to-do, a financial and social step up from most of the surrounding gentry. Although they held no title, their very longevity in the area lent a certain cachet, and the size and age of the house and the assumed prosperity of their lands only further consolidated their position.

That position hadn't been a help; for her, all it had done was attract gentlemen she was then forced to discourage.

Yet for once, here and now, that wasn't the case. Godfrey Cavanaugh was a lord, a nobleman, and a wealthy one to boot. While he appreciated the Hall for what it was, he had absolutely no designs on the place.

He did have designs on her—they were attracted in a way she'd never encountered before. Mutually drawn to each other by a complexity of feelings and urges that constantly demanded her attention.

Her consideration.

She was considering now.

Considering the likelihood that tomorrow, after he wrote his report on the painting, with the roads clear again, he might well opt to take that report to Eastlake personally and leave for London.

Tomorrow.

She—they—might only have tonight. This night, if they wanted to see what might be. If they wished to explore what the magic of that kiss on the snowy bridge portended—where the sensations that had stirred might lead them.

She didn't need to think to know he wouldn't come to her; he wasn't that sort of man. The sort a woman needed to discourage.

He was the sort of man who waited for a lady to make up her mind.

Arms crossed, she stared at the myriad stars twinkling, bright and brilliant, against the backdrop of the night-black sky.

Like those previous decisions, this one, too, would be hers.

~

Godfrey was pacing before the fire in his room, debating the best order in which to lay out the facts of the situation for Eastlake, when a tap fell on the door.

He halted and blinked. He recognized that tap.

His feet had him at the door before he'd even thought. Grasping the knob, he opened the door—and stared as his eyes confirmed who was on the other side.

He blinked again. "Yes?"

To his increasing surprise, Ellie raised her hand, pressed her palm to his chest, and pushed, urging him backward.

His senses leaping at the pressure of her palm over his heart, he obliged and took two steps back.

Keeping her hand where it was, locking her eyes with his, she stepped into the room. With her other hand, she reached behind her, caught the door, and pushed it closed.

Hopes rising even while he told himself this would be about something else, he arched his brows at her.

She held his gaze. "I'm here to explain something."

She was in his room alone with him, and the rest of the household was already abed. He raised his brows even higher. "What?"

Her gaze remained rock-steady. "This."

She stepped close, raised both hands, framed his face, and drew it down as she stretched on her toes, tipped up her face, and pressed her lips to his.

He was...*captured*. In that instant, he was caught by her, snared by her directness, her boldness, for her kiss was no mere brush of the lips. This kiss burned.

His response was instantaneous. His own heat and passions flared, surging in accord with hers, and that immediate attunement only deepened the wonder, the irresistibly potent lure that the pressure of her lips had become.

He wanted more. Much more. His arms locked about her—then seized her, held her, pressed her to him. His lips fought hers for dominance, and on a sigh, she melted into his embrace and surrendered.

Her lips parted in welcome, and he surged into the sweet haven of her mouth and laid claim.

The caress and press of her hands at his nape urged him on.

He angled his head, deepened the kiss, and obliged.

Ellie thrilled at his mastery, at the understated assurance with which he made her senses sing. His lips and tongue branded and seduced, tempted and tantalized. She couldn't get enough; splaying her fingers, she sent them raking through his thick hair, glorying in the silky texture, then she clutched and held him to her and wrestled once more to take as well as give.

The kiss settled into a rhythm, almost a dance, one taking the lead then ceding to the other, each devouring, then savoring, a back-and-forth that consumed her senses and, given his absorption, his, too.

Heat welled and grew, and desire spiraled and gushed within her.

The need for *more* thudded, a slow, escalating beat in her veins. She pressed closer and felt his arms tighten about her, accepting, welcoming, locking them together. His arms were steel bands, while the press of his hands on her back signaled his desire. As did the hard ridge of his erection impinging on the soft curve of her stomach.

For a split second, she wondered if missishness would intrude. Instead, her senses leapt ever more greedily, hungrily, and need of a sort she'd never felt before—primal and compulsive—flowered and filled her.

This, with him, was what she wanted. What she needed to fulfill her inner yearning.

She'd been right to come, to knock on his door and engage with him. With renewed determination, she plunged into the moment. With renewed purpose, she gave herself up to exploring this—all that was and all that might be between them.

Godfrey didn't want to surface from the hedonistic wave of passion that had engulfed him, that had swept him from his mental moorings and left him a slave to desire—his and hers.

He was aware she and the sheer power of what had flared between them had overwhelmed his reasoning, shoving all aside to let passion erupt and rule, to let desire lead the way.

He didn't want to find his mental feet, yet some deep-seated worm of worry, a niggling fear, insisted he had to be sure, that he had to know one vital thing.

It took effort—more effort than he would have credited—to draw back from the kiss. Reining in his craving for more of her was almost beyond him, but finally, he managed to ease back from the building conflagration. The instant their lips parted, he hauled in a breath, raised his head, opened his eyes, and looked into her face.

Her lips were kiss-bruised, rosy and swollen. Her lashes flickered, then rose, and she looked at him—looked directly into his eyes.

Her desire, her wants, her needs were there, clearly etched in the vibrant green-and-gold-flecked brown.

That she wanted him rocked him to his core.

But he had to know.

He moistened his lips and asked, "Why?"

She blinked, but didn't request clarification. After a second, she tipped her head and replied, "Because I'm drawn to you—more than I've ever been to any other man. And I know that you're drawn to me. I had to know what that meant. What we might discover if we follow the path our senses, our feelings, are urging us down."

Her eyes confirmed all that was true. Still... "So you're not here out of any sense of gratitude?"

Her smile was spontaneous. "No." That smile warmed her eyes and, as usual, warmed him—caressed him in some intangible way. She set her hands on his shoulders and held his gaze. "Yes, I'm grateful for what you've done—for the way you've handled a difficult situation—and also for the help you've offered into the future, whatever that might entail. But no. Gratitude in no way figured in my thoughts, in my decision to come and knock on your door."

Relief flooded him, swiftly followed by resurgent desire.

His hands, at her waist, instinctively—compulsively—tightened, but her eyes informed him she wasn't yet finished, that she had more she wished to say.

Still holding his gaze, she evenly, if huskily, stated, "What brought me here, to you, tonight, was...a need to take my courage in my hands and, for once, reach for something I want. Something I actively desire. Something I want for me and me alone. To act in a way I know I must to make myself more than I currently am." Her voice lowered. "That's what pushed me to do something I never have before—that's what had me knocking on your door."

She'd managed to make his wits reel again. Her words had unleashed such a torrent of hopes and clamoring needs that he felt stunned anew, barely able to hold against the pummeling tide.

But her eyes, what he saw there... "You've never been with a man before?"

"No."

He had to clear his throat to get out the words "So I'm your first?"

She nodded. "Yes. And no, I don't imagine I'll be the first lady with whom you've lain."

He cleared his throat enough to mutter, "Just as well."

Her answering smile held echoes of Maggie's impishness, but then she sobered.

Ellie looked into his eyes and decided he deserved to know the rest. "You are the only man who has ever sparked even an iota of desire in me. Until I met you, I didn't know what physical desire was—I'd never experienced it. You gave me that—the shivery sensations, the thrills that crimp one's lungs. As for physical passion, that was even more unknown to me, yet between us"—she waved between them—"this has to be that, this heat and longing. This wanting."

"It is." His voice, deep and low, reverberated inside her.

"What I feel for you," she went on, "the fascination, the curiosity, the irresistible lure—must be akin to what you feel for a fabulous work of art." She tipped her head. "In some ways, you are that—you inspire so much in me."

He held her gaze and shook his head. "I might experience those feelings for inanimate works of art, but they are nothing but pale wraiths compared to what I feel for you—the feelings you evoke in me."

She allowed her lips to lightly curve. "It seems we're a matched pair. I hoped that was so, and put simply, I couldn't let tonight slip by. I have to know where desire and passion can lead me—even if for only one night."

The comment jerked Godfrey back to earth. He stared at her while an immediate rejection of her words rose in a turbulent wave from the deepest part of him. Yes, she'd made her feelings clear, and he appreciated how much courage that must have taken, for a lady of her station to come to his room and so clearly state why. To so unequivocally admit and honor her own feelings, her desires and wants.

He drew her to him again and, bending his head, took the lips she offered in a kiss that, within seconds, transformed into a ravenous melding of their lips, a heated duel of their tongues.

Passion ignited, powerful and pure.

No, he wasn't going to resist.

With them both clinging to the kiss, he backed her toward the bed, and she readily fell in with his direction.

Yet...she'd given him her truth. Didn't she deserve his in return?

By the time the backs of her legs met the edge of the mattress, they were both hot and heated, and the passion the kiss had called forth was just this side of searing. He pulled back and raised his head.

He looked into her eyes, large, wide, bright with desire. "Obviously"—his voice was a gravelly growl—"our feelings—our wants and needs—are entirely compatible." He dragged in a breath and locked his eyes with hers. "But I've been down this road before. I know what my feelings usually are." He shook his head. "What I feel for you, when I'm with you... That—*this*—is something else. Something extraordinary."

Holding her gaze, he struggled to find the right words. "You are the only woman I've ever imagined a future with—something that lasts for far longer than one night. Even before we've enjoyed this night, explored where our mutual passions lead us, I know—to the depths of my soul know—that I will want to remain with you, to stand beside you, not just for tomorrow but for however long I can."

Suddenly, the words were there, pouring over his tongue. "I *want* to be by your side to protect you and your family against whatever might come, not just next week but through the coming decades. I *want* to live with you, to make a life with you." He paused, then said, "I've never wanted that with anyone else."

Her eyes couldn't get any wider; he wondered if it was his imagination that stars now shone in their depths.

The sight compelled him to admit, "To me, you are unique. Uniquely wonderful in that you are the key that opens the door to my most-desired future. A future I hadn't even sighted before I came here and met you."

"Oh." A wealth of wonder shivered through that single syllable. Her hand rose to lightly touch his cheek, almost as if to convince herself he was real.

He hauled in a breath and forced himself to go on, to say what he had to say. "So, dearest Ellie, you need to know, to understand, before we take any irrevocable step, that if we do go on, if we take that step, then I will strive to make all those things I want come true." His voice lowered. "That I will move heaven and earth to seize that future I didn't know existed before I saw you."

Ellie blinked and blinked again. Joy of a type she had never felt was geysering through her. This man, something in her chanted. *This* man.

His chest swelled against her breasts as he drew in another, this time shaky breath and, his eyes locked with hers, asked, "Is that what you want?"

She didn't have to think. She pushed her hands over his shoulders, wound her arms about his neck, stretched up, and kissed him again—this time with all the pent-up longing in her soul. "Yes," she breathed when she drew back. She raised her eyes to meet his. "*Yes*," she affirmed, "I want you. For tonight and for however many nights you and Fate allow me."

The tension that had held him eased as uncertainty fled; for once, she could read that clearly in his face. His eyes hawk bright, he returned, "Fate will no doubt have her say, but for me, that means forever."

"Forever," she agreed.

He smiled, the edge passion had lent his features still evident. "For us, forever starts tonight."

She felt her lips irrepressibly lift and pressed closer as he bent his head.

Their next kiss sent flames dancing across her skin as their passions, unleashed, roared to unrestrained life.

Despite that, he was, indeed, the master she'd imagined him to be; he refused to rush, even when, driven by an urgency she could barely comprehend, she tugged and insisted.

He soothed and treated her to another caress, then another even more evocative, until her head spun and her wits careened so wildly she lost touch with them entirely, even while her senses danced.

Waltzed to a tune he orchestrated.

Passion rose and fell, wave after wave, building and steadily rising higher and higher in a tide that swept all modesty and hesitations aside.

Desire swelled to a tumult in her blood, compelling and insistent.

Between them, they stripped off her clothes, then his.

And no matter what he thought, he was an artwork in her eyes; the long, sculpted muscles of his back, buttocks, and thighs formed a line she could gaze at for hours.

Not that she caught more than a glimpse, and when he turned back to her, all capacity for thought fled.

Then he lay beside her, and she couldn't resist setting her hands to the naked planes of his chest and exploring.

He allowed it, but that was only the first minor act in a glory of mutual adventuring as they learned and explored each other's bodies, each other's reactions, and she discovered another level of sensation and feeling—uncovered another plane of tenderness, devotion, and reverence to this, to the moment, to the togetherness it wrought.

And through it all, her need only swelled.

By the time he moved over her, she was aching with that need, so empty and yearning she could barely wait for him to join with her and complete her.

Complete them; when he thrust in and pain briefly flared and she froze, with his muscles unforgivingly locked, he held steady above her.

Until she exhaled, then tentatively moved. The sensations were so much more than she'd imagined, so evocative, so truly *intimate*. From beneath her lashes, she met his eyes, then she smiled, tightened her arms around him, and whispered, "Come on."

He exhaled in a rush, then filled his lungs and complied and taught her what she'd never thought she would learn. He showed her the pathways of pleasure.

The end, when it rolled over them, shattered their senses and filled their minds with the blinding brilliance of searingly intense sensation. To her, it felt as if the power released was so great, it fundamentally altered the bedrock of her being.

The sensation crested and broke, leaving glory spreading through them, warmth and lingering pleasure diffusing beneath their skins, and in her mind, it was as if a bell tolled.

In recognition of a new state—a new life?

Exhausted, he slumped upon her; she rather liked feeling his weight draped protectively over her. But then he lifted and disengaged and rolled to lie on his back by her side. Unable to stop smiling, she turned, snuggled closer, and settled her head on his shoulder. He softly grunted and draped an arm around her, and she slid her leg over his.

Wrapped in each other, they surrendered to oblivion.

Ellie came to consciousness slowly, waking with a languidness that was simply delicious.

Then she realized where she was, that the firmness beneath her cheek was no pillow and the weight across her shoulder far heavier than the covers, and that, she decided, with a contented smile, was even more delectable.

As she lay there, no longer quite so boneless yet unwilling to stir, thoughts looped lazily through her mind.

This man.

He was the one she'd been waiting for, even if she hadn't realized she was.

Somehow, in just over a week, he'd carved out a niche in her heart and taken up residence.

Abruptly, her thoughts ceased their whirling as one truth—a new truth —took center stage.

This was surely what love felt like—this warmth that suffused one from the inside out at the mere thought of the other person.

She loved him.

She poked at the notion, but it was resilient and strong, immutable and undeniable.

She'd expected such a revelation to have emotional fireworks attached, but no—it simply was.

Was it that, as yet unrecognized by her, that had driven her to his room and his bed?

She hadn't thought so, but then, at the time, she hadn't known it was there. And perhaps love was the source of the compulsion she'd felt to knock on his door and see what might be; she'd never been an emotional coward.

Having only just recognized the correct term for what she felt, she hadn't told him she loved him, but that was all right, wasn't it? He'd said they would have forever to explore what was between them.

He hadn't said the word, either, but she'd heard that gentlemen, especially those of his station, tended to avoid it.

Clever of them, she'd always thought. While such avoidance might smack of emotional cowardice, it also indicated a healthy respect for the power wielded by that emotion, and respect for love was no bad thing.

Indeed, if he'd readily professed to feeling that particular emotion, she would have questioned whether he truly did.

But he had spoken of forever…

She frowned. She'd assumed he'd meant marriage, but on replaying his words, she realized that was another word he hadn't uttered.

He'd spoken of having a life together, of protecting her and hers…

Her thoughts seized. Men of his ilk were often referred to as "protectors" with regard to their mistresses.

He'd specifically offered protection. Was that what he was thinking—that she would be his mistress?

Her thoughts churned. Had she misunderstood?

Uncertainty swamped her, along with a vulnerability that had her eyeing the door. She needed to get away and regroup before she faced him again. If he didn't want or appreciate her love...she would need to hide it, to screen it from his eyes.

And then she would need to figure out a way to politely decline his forever.

Carefully, she tensed and tried to ease away from him, to lift her leg free of his.

Immediately, the arm about her shoulders tightened, and a large warm palm landed on her thigh, holding that leg where it was, nestled between his.

"Oh no," he murmured. "You don't get to slip away in the night, not after that."

She blinked. He was an experienced lover—that had been obvious; what had been so special about their engagement? Curiosity got the better of her. "That what?"

He turned toward her, his arms settling loosely around her. "You are everything I've ever wanted—ever dreamed of—in a lady. You're passionate and intense and so honest and open. So genuine in all you feel and share—so much more than any other lady I've met."

She lifted her head and looked into his face. His lashes still brushed his cheekbones. His voice was deep and rumbly, as if he was half asleep.

As she stared, his lips curved. "And now I've got you in my bed, I'm not about to let you go. You're mine—now and forever."

Frustration bloomed, but if he was speaking without thinking... "What does that mean?" Her heart started to thud. "What do you intend me being yours 'now and forever' to mean?"

That got his eyes open.

Godfrey looked at her and consciously allowed all he felt for her to illuminate his expression until he felt certain his love shone in his eyes. "When I arrived at the Hall, I had no thoughts of marriage. In fact, getting married didn't figure in my calculations at all—I had no interest in the institution, no need to embrace it. And I had never met a female who even remotely brought the thought to mind." He paused, then said, "And then I saw you, and everything changed."

His smile deepened, and remembering, he let his lashes fall. "So what I mean by those words…"

Suddenly, he realized why she'd asked; he hadn't actually said. He opened his eyes, fixed them on hers, and clearly enunciated, "I want you to marry me. I want you for my wife. I want to put my ring on your finger and change your name to Lady Godfrey Cavanaugh." He paused, then amended, "Eleanor, Lady Cavanaugh." He smiled and, once again, knew his feelings were on show. "That sounds absolutely perfect."

He looked at her, studied her face—as usual, her reactions flowed openly across the canvas. She didn't, transparently didn't, understand how precious she was; he would have to keep telling her in myriad ways. When she didn't speak but just looked at him uncertainly, he arched his brows.

She pressed her lips together for an instant, then asked, "Are you sure you're awake?"

He laughed and hugged her closer. "I'm fully awake." Tipping his chin to his chest, he caught her eyes and added, "This is me reaching for my dream."

Barely breathing, Ellie stared into his eyes, hardly daring to believe. He was a nobleman, and she was the daughter of ancient but minor gentry. On one level she hoped, while on another, she had to wonder if he was serious.

His eyes searched hers, and as if sensing her thoughts, he sobered. His expression grew intent, then he caught her hand, raised it to his lips, and brushed a kiss across her knuckles. "I know we haven't discussed the details, but we can figure those out as we go along. For now, all I ask is this: Please, Ellie, agree to be mine."

And for once, his expression was totally unscreened; there was no barrier to her seeing—reading—what was in his heart. He might not have said the word, but he felt the same power she did. She swallowed, then forced herself to drag in a tight breath. She freed her fingers from his grasp, raised both hands and framed his face, and allowed herself to drown in his eyes. "Beneath your unconscious arrogance, behind your unflagging, sophisticated assurance, even deeper than your invincible honor, you are a dear, dear man."

She let all she felt color those simple words. He searched her eyes and saw her feelings there.

He grunted softly, then turned his head and pressed a warm kiss to her palm. "The only person's 'dear man' I will admit to being is yours." His eyes sought hers again. "Yours and only yours, darling Ellie." He tipped his head fractionally. "So will you accept me, Ellie dearest? Please say yes."

She smiled.

Godfrey saw her answer in her wonderfully expressive eyes and cherished the sight even as he heard the "Yes" that fell from her lips. He smiled, feeling as if the last of his worldly cares had sloughed from his shoulders, obliterated by the certainty that that small, simple word had come direct from her heart.

She seemed to feel as he did, that this was a moment to celebrate. She pressed closer, raising her lips again to his.

He tried to do the gentlemanly thing and point out that she was new to the activity and they didn't need to rush—but she was adamant. And persuasive.

So much so that, in the end, he lay back and let her have her way.

As a gray dawn lightened the sky, Godfrey lay comfortably, cradling the warm bundle of Ellie—his wife-to-be—in his arms.

He'd woken ten minutes before and had lain still, luxuriating in the sensations and even more in the knowledge of the step they'd taken. Neither of them was the sort to commit to something they didn't believe in.

That they were, now, committed to each other was beyond question.

Ellie had woken a bare minute ago; he'd felt the tension returning to her limbs.

He waited, watching, until her lashes fluttered, then rose. He smiled into her eyes. "Good morning."

She colored delightfully even as she returned his smile. "Good morning."

After several seconds of studying his face, she patted his arm. "I really should get back to my room."

Reluctantly, he raised his arm and let her go. He lay back and watched as, with no overt show of modesty, she collected her clothes and started to get dressed. He sighed and rose and went to help her with her stays.

As he did up the tiny hooks, he asked, "When should we break the news to your father? I should speak with him first."

"I hadn't actually thought that far."

"I'll do whatever you think best, but I can't help but feel we'll do better to keep our engagement to ourselves until I send off my report to London and, possibly, until I've looked into recovering the Albertinelli—just so your father doesn't misconstrue and suspect my offer and your acceptance is in any way connected to that. For instance"—with the last hook in place, he straightened—"that your acceptance is an attempt on your part to soften the blow of the forgery, to distract your family from it—"

"Or an attempt to repair the family's coffers by marrying well?" She turned and arched a brow at him.

Undeterred, he continued, "Or worse, that I've insisted on your agreement as 'payment' for my services in reclaiming the painting."

Ellie would have liked to dismiss all those suggestions as nonsensical, only they weren't. Planting her hands on her hips, she frowned.

Godfrey ducked his head to look into her face. "You know my motivations are in no way linked to the situation with the Albertinelli, don't you?"

She had to smile at his uncertain look; she was beginning to realize that when he said he'd never felt this way about anyone else, he was speaking literally. "Yes." She raised a hand and touched his cheek. "Of course I know that." She sighed. "And I would like to say that my father would never think such a thing…but the timing is unfortunate, and I have to acknowledge it's a possibility."

And it was just like Godfrey to see that possibility and attempt to steer them—her father included—clear of it. Whether he knew it or not, he tended to think of others before himself; she strongly suspected that if it hadn't been for the forged painting, he would be pushing to send an announcement to the *Gazette* that very morning.

But misunderstandings were not the way to commence their life together. She nodded. "You're right. We should wait until you've sent off your report, and we can see how the matter plays out."

"Well," he temporized, "at least until we've determined what steps we need to take to reclaim the original."

She tipped her head, considering. "A few months should see that much resolved, don't you think?"

He paused, calculating, then nodded. "I'll write my report today. With luck, it'll be in the post by this evening."

She smiled, then tossed her gown over her head and wriggled the garment down. "Can you do up the back?"

She heard him chuckle, then he twitched the gaping sides together and started deftly sliding the tiny buttons into their holes. After a moment, he leaned forward and breathed in her ear, "Aren't you glad I'm an experienced man?"

She shivered and nodded. "Indeed. The benefits are manifold."

Surprised, he laughed. Five minutes later, after dragging herself away from a scorching kiss, she left his room and all but skipped to hers.

CHAPTER 12

*D*espite Godfrey's best intentions, he didn't finish his report until the following morning. Compiling, organizing, and describing every detail of the provenance the Hinckleys held, laying out his reasons for deeming the painting currently at Hinckley Hall a forgery, and outlining his suggestions for reclaiming the original had taken much longer than he'd anticipated. He'd lost count of how many attempts he'd discarded, but on Wednesday morning, as the clocks throughout the house whirred, then bonged and chimed for eleven o'clock, almost two full weeks since he'd arrived, he finally signed his covering letter to Eastlake with a definitive flourish.

"Done!" He set down the pen, waved the page to dry it, then blotted his signature.

He looked down the length of the library to where Ellie sat opposite her father before the fireplace. The cheery blaze in the hearth gilded her features as she looked Godfrey's way; his gaze lingered on her face, a smile he suspected was slightly besotted on his lips.

"Completely finished?" she asked.

"I just need to get it ready for the post." He set the covering letter on top of the stack of sheets detailing the provenance and the forgery, then carefully folded the pages and enclosed them in an envelope sheet. The library desk was supplied with sealing wax and candle; after securing the envelope's flaps with a blob of red wax, he removed his signet etched with the Cavanaugh family crest and used it to mark the seal.

Once the wax was dry, he picked up the pen and inscribed the front of the packet with Eastlake's direction.

"There!" He picked up the packet and pushed back the chair.

He was about to rise and cross to the bellpull when a tap fell on the door. It opened, and Kemp came in. "Mr. Masterton, Mr. Morris, and Mr. Pyne."

Kemp glanced Godfrey's way, and he waved the letter. The butler diverted toward the desk, while behind him, the three gentlemen filed in.

Putting aside the newspaper he'd been reading, Mr. Hinckley smiled at his visitors. "Good morning to you all."

Masterton, Morris, and Pyne moved toward the fireplace. Ellie tucked away her embroidery and rose, and greetings were exchanged all around.

Kemp reached the desk and accepted the letter with a short bow. "I'll ask one of the grooms to take this into Ripon immediately, sir."

"Thank you, Kemp." Godfrey rose and, as Kemp made for the door, ambled down the room to join the group before the fire.

Masterton turned to greet him with a swift smile and noticed Kemp departing with the letter. "Cavanaugh. I was going to inquire if you were still studying the painting, but is that what I think it is?"

Pyne and Morris had also noticed Kemp and the letter. They, too, turned inquiring gazes on Godfrey.

He greeted the three men, then admitted, "Yes, that's my report on its way to the directors of the gallery."

"Well, then." Pyne looked from Godfrey to Mr. Hinckley. "What's the verdict? I take it it's good news?"

All three men looked from Mr. Hinckley, to Godfrey, then back again.

Godfrey inclined his head to Mr. Hinckley, indicating that it was the older man's decision as to what was revealed.

"As a matter of fact," Mr. Hinckley said, "the answer is no. Sadly, our painting has proved to be a forgery."

"What?" Morris looked dumbfounded.

"Really?" came from Pyne.

Masterton frowned. "But...how could that be?"

"How, indeed?" Godfrey murmured. All three men looked genuinely shocked.

"Sit"—Mr. Hinckley waved to the various chairs—"and between us, we'll try to explain."

Ellie resumed her seat. Once Godfrey, Masterton, Morris, and Pyne had settled in armchairs pulled into a circle, her father commenced the story of what they believed had happened to the painting old Henry Hinckley had brought home from Italy centuries ago.

Ellie studied Masterton, Morris, and Pyne. Given that whoever stole the painting would know the one now at the Hall was a forgery, she watched to see if any of their reactions seemed strange or strained or too studied. Despite seeing nothing but surprise and shock, she couldn't help wondering if one of the three was their thief. Morris and Pyne had arrived for their customary Wednesday visit; they'd been regular visitors over the period during which the painting had been stolen and replaced, as had Masterton, who tended to call in whenever he was passing.

It could have been one of the three, but as she and Godfrey had concluded, there were simply too many people who had known of the painting to suspect everyone it might have been.

Godfrey had remained silent, sitting outwardly relaxed in the armchair beside hers while her father explained how they believed the thief had made away with the original Albertinelli, then returned with the forged copy and replaced it in the frame in her mother's parlor.

"So, you see, we had no idea the original had been stolen." Her father raised his hands in a gesture of resignation. "But it has been, so sadly, we no longer have it to sell."

Morris and Pyne looked perturbed and unsettled, while Masterton appeared to be pondering deeply.

After several seconds of silence, Pyne's gaze flicked to Godfrey, then he cleared his throat and ventured, "Perhaps a second opinion…?"

Ellie glanced at her father as he waved that aside and stated, "I have complete faith in Lord Godfrey's abilities."

It was the first the three had heard of Godfrey's title. The change in Pyne's expression was almost comical, while Morris's jaw fell. Ellie fought down a grin. It was time that tidbit came out, and her father had chosen the perfect time to reveal it.

Seated on Godfrey's other side, Masterton had swung his gaze to Godfrey. He stared, then muttered in a stunned, almost horrified tone, "*Lord* Godfrey?"

Godfrey merely arched his brows. "I prefer not to use my title when acting in my professional capacity."

Masterton's expression turned decidedly sour.

Ellie compressed her lips into a determinedly straight line; now was not the time to smile. Given Masterton's seemingly never-fading hopes of her, he wouldn't like seeing her consorting with a handsome lord and possibly getting ideas.

If only he knew...

Her composure nearly broke when Masterton said to Godfrey, "Now you've completed your assignment here, my lord, and the roads are clear, I assume you'll be leaving shortly. When do you expect to be on your way?" Masterton managed to make the question passably polite.

His expression studiously mild, Godfrey glanced at Ellie, then met Masterton's gaze. "That's yet to be decided."

Predictably, Masterton frowned. He shot a searching look at Ellie; she met it with her customary unperturbed assurance, although, inside, she was dancing with happiness that there was now no chance whatsoever that Masterton would ever succeed in pressuring her to marry him.

Airily, she switched her gaze to the other men.

Pyne had recovered from the compounding shocks of the successive revelations. "I say, Matthew, that's rotten luck. But what will you do now?"

Morris, too, looked at her father. "Now you won't have the funds from selling the painting."

Her father's expression remained relaxed. "As it happens, the situation with the painting might not be a complete loss."

"Oh?" came from Pyne.

Morris looked equally interested, and even Masterton looked up.

"Apparently," her father said, "the forgery is an exceptionally good one. Lord Godfrey recognized the artist's work and knows who the forger is. Given we have the documents that prove beyond question that the original Albertinelli is ours..." Her father broke off and appealed to Godfrey. "I have that right, don't I, my lord?"

Godfrey nodded. "Indeed. There is no question that legally, that particular painting belongs to the Hinckleys."

"Yes, well," Mr. Hinckley went on, "as that's the case, there might be a way to reclaim the painting and, thereafter, complete the sale to the gallery. It's possible this business with the forgery might turn out to be simply a delay. Luckily, we have sufficient funds to see us through—we can wait to see what transpires."

All three visitors were now frowning.

Eventually, Masterton said, "I confess I don't quite understand. If the original painting has vanished, how will you reclaim it?"

Mr. Hinckley looked at Godfrey. "If you would, my lord?"

Pyne's, Morris's, and Masterton's gazes swung to Godfrey, and he explained, "I intend to visit the forger and, from him, learn the name of whoever commissioned the copy of the Albertinelli and follow the trail from there."

Throughout their revelations, Godfrey had been watching the newcomers' faces. Pyne continued to look intrigued, and Morris's curiosity appeared appeased, while Masterton's expression had turned impassive, and his tone was faintly aggressive when he asked, "And then what?"

Evenly, Godfrey replied, "Once we've determined who now holds the original painting, we can use the provenance to reclaim it under law." He paused, then added, "It might take some time, but there are various levers that can be pulled to make the attempt more likely to succeed."

Masterton's frown had rematerialized. He nodded, but distantly, as if he was now pondering something else. "I see."

Ellie viewed Masterton's expression and inwardly shook her head. She would wager he was in the throes of realizing that she and her family were, even now, not at the point of being forced to turn to him for assistance. He'd first discussed the notion with her father prior to them deciding to sell the painting. She and her father both regarded accepting financial assistance from Masterton—who, when all was said and done, was a very distant connection—as a last resort; neither had considered it wise to place themselves in Masterton's debt, thus giving him a weapon to hold over her head to force her to marry him.

Cynically, she wondered what steps his latest calculations would prompt him to; that seemed to be the way he lived his life, with every action calculated to be of most benefit to him.

Meanwhile, Pyne had asked Godfrey when he intended to set out to confront the forger, and with a glance her way, Godfrey had replied that given he would have to travel to the Continent, the timing of his journey would depend on the weather.

For his part, Morris had clearly thought things through and was now making approving noises, while Pyne was transparently encouraging.

Ellie glanced at the clock on the mantelpiece and saw that it was already noon. She looked at Masterton. "Will you stay for luncheon?"

He met her eyes, glanced briefly at Godfrey, then returned his gaze to her. "Thank you. I will."

His tone remained distant, almost absentminded, but his intention to

keep an eye on any interaction between her and Godfrey could not have
been plainer.

Once again mentally shaking her head while holding back a satisfied
smile, Ellie rose and, waving the men back when they started to come to
their feet, left to inform Kemp and Cook that they had not two but three
guests for luncheon.

Godfrey was aware of the suspicious, dog-in-the-manger glances
Masterton was directing his way. Too bad; he was not in the mood to
pander to the other man's apparent but mistaken belief that he had some
proprietary interest in Ellie.

Indeed, as the company adjourned to the dining room and Godfrey
strolled beside Ellie with Masterton, rigidly impassive, pacing on her
other side, Godfrey was hard-pressed to keep his smile to himself and his
expression suitably unrevealing.

She'd come to his room last night, and they'd indulged in another
interlude of passion and increasingly unrestrained loving. It was, he knew,
the latter that left him with a knot of warmth in his chest and the besotted
look he had to work to keep from his face.

Every now and then, his mask slipped, and sheer happiness edged his
smile.

Harry and Maggie joined the company for luncheon; somewhat to
Godfrey's surprise, the pair were noticeably subdued.

Then again, with the subject of the forgery exhausted, at least for now,
Mr. Hinckley had turned the conversational spotlight from the affairs of
Hinckley Hall to Morris and Pyne and their situations, subjects that held
little interest for Harry and Maggie, or even Ellie, Godfrey, and Masterton. Yet from the way the trio of old friends spoke openly of their
concerns, including alluding to their financial states, it was clear that,
among the three, sharing such hopes and fears was a lifelong habit.

As all three seemed to lack family members with whom they might
have discussed such matters, Godfrey could see that having close and
trusted friends to fill the void was no bad thing.

Meanwhile, he, Ellie, Masterton, and the two younger Hinckleys
made inroads into the tasty golden pies Cook had provided and largely let
the conversation roll over them.

At one point, Masterton asked Ellie about the local Easter fair. He shot a look at Godfrey as she replied, as if to underscore that he was a local, a man who would be there when Godfrey left.

Godfrey merely smiled and paid attention to Ellie's information.

From the ongoing discussions about the head of the table, where Morris and Pyne sat flanking Matthew Hinckley, Godfrey gathered that, while the Hinckleys might be financially under pressure, circumstances had already pushed the other two to the point of requiring additional funds—Pyne to keep his printing business afloat and Morris to keep Malton Farm running.

Given the current state of the economy, Godfrey wondered if the pair had fallen into the clutches of moneylenders, especially when Pyne quipped that he wished he had an Albertinelli he could sell. Subsequently, however, both Pyne and Morris reported that they'd recently met with a gentleman from the concern that had advanced them the necessary funds and had been pleasantly surprised to discover said gentleman to be a reasonable man. Apparently, the man had met with Morris and Pyne separately and had gone over their accounts, then had reassured them that they would be allowed a reasonable time over which to repay the money.

Although the debts were still hanging over their heads, the pair were clearly relieved, and as Matthew Hinckley bracingly remarked, that was surely good news.

Morris nodded. "So once his lordship gets back your painting, we'll all be on an even keel again."

Godfrey's already-firm determination to recover the painting hardened a touch more.

Eventually, with the platters all but cleared, Kemp entered, went to Ellie's side, and whispered that Mrs. Kemp would appreciate a word.

Ellie nodded and eased back her chair. "Papa?" When her father looked her way, she waved at the table. "As it seems we're all finished, perhaps you should return to the library where you'll be more comfortable?"

Everyone took the hint and rose. While Ellie went off to speak with the housekeeper, Godfrey grasped the handles of Mr. Hinckley's chair and, with Morris and Pyne pacing on either side and continuing their conversation, pushed his host across the front hall and down the corridor to the library.

After installing Mr. Hinckley in his usual spot and receiving a smile and a nod in thanks, Godfrey retreated to the armchair he'd earlier occupied and relaxed in an elegant sprawl.

After following their little procession into the front hall, Harry and Maggie had excused themselves and gone off to another parlor. Watching the pair go, Pyne had humphed in benevolent fashion. "Can't blame them not wanting to sit and listen to us old men talk."

Masterton, who had left the dining room with everyone else, had slipped away somewhere; Godfrey assumed he'd gone off to use the necessary.

Relieved of any immediate need to converse with the man, Godfrey let the voices of the three older men, once again gathered about the fireplace, wash over him while he contemplated his next steps—both with respect to reclaiming the Albertinelli and also in securing Ellie as his wife.

Inevitably, the pathways to both goals would intertwine; he was going to have to put some thought into the order of his actions and Ellie's, too.

After several minutes of attempted cogitation, he realized there was no need for him to sit there and have to consciously block out the other men's words. He rose and, when the three older men looked his way, smiled and half bowed. "If you'll excuse me, gentlemen, there are a number of matters I should look into."

The three smiled, and Mr. Hinckley waved him away with an "Of course."

Still smiling, Godfrey turned to the door just as Masterton walked in.

Masterton saw him on his feet and halted.

Godfrey strolled toward the door and saw Masterton hesitate, wavering as if unsure what he wished to do.

Masking his rising curiosity, drawing level, Godfrey politely inclined his head and kept walking.

As he reached the door and stepped into the corridor, he heard Masterton turn and come after him.

He walked on and obligingly halted in the middle of the front hall. He swung to face the library corridor and waited.

Having quit the library, Masterton followed him up the short corridor and into the hall. He halted a few feet away. For a moment, Masterton stared at Godfrey, then Masterton's features firmed, and he said, "I suspect you and I wouldn't see eye to eye on a number of subjects, but I do have the Hinckleys' best interests at heart."

Godfrey had no reason to argue that; as far as he knew, Masterton had been supportive of the Hinckleys at every turn. Allowing the comment to stand unchallenged, he waited.

Masterton nodded as if accepting Godfrey's silence as an indication of some sort of detente. After a moment during which he plainly gathered his thoughts, he went on, "Both you and I know there's a good chance the Hinckleys won't be able to reclaim the Albertinelli. That whether they—and you—will succeed is very much up in the air."

Again, Godfrey said nothing; the man was right.

Masterton thrust his hands into his trouser pockets and looked down, then he shifted closer and, lowering his voice, said, "When I was a boy, I was occasionally brought here to visit. I used to run free through the house—all over, as a boy left alone to explore will do. From that time, so many years ago, I remember seeing old paintings—more than one—left on the floor, set to one side in the attic of the disused wing."

Godfrey frowned slightly. "I've heard mention of a disused wing. Do you know for how long it's been closed up?"

"Multiple decades at the very least. The wing had been shut up long before I ventured in." Masterton paused to search Godfrey's face. "Look—I have no idea if the paintings are still there, much less whether they're valuable or just old Auntie Someone's daubs. They might even be more forgeries." His earnest tone held a touch of urgency. "But I thought… well, I know Matthew's need of funds is greater than he lets on, and as you're here and haven't yet departed, I wondered whether you might take a quick look-see." He glanced toward the library. "I don't want to get anyone's hopes up, and for all I know, the paintings might not even be there anymore."

Masterton looked back at Godfrey. "Regardless, I thought I would go and find out and wondered if you would be interested in coming along, too."

The annals of history were peppered with instances of long-lost masterpieces discovered in the most unlikely places. Godfrey was well aware that many great finds had been made in just this way—by someone thinking to go poking in an old attic or cellar. Quite aside from the compulsion to help the Hinckleys—which Masterton patently shared—Godfrey couldn't have turned his back and walked away from the prospect of unearthing some unexpected find if his life had depended on it.

Endeavoring to hide his eagerness, he nodded. "All right." He glanced around. "How do we get into the disused wing?"

Masterton turned toward the stairs. "The only door that still opens is on the first floor."

Godfrey followed Masterton up the stairs and to the right along the gallery, in the opposite direction from Godfrey's room and also the family wing. Masterton strode straight to a door set in a wider, taller panel in the side wall toward the end of the gallery; to Godfrey's educated eye, the panel was set into the rectangular archway framing the entrance of another corridor, presumably the one leading into the now-disused wing.

Without hesitation, Masterton reached for the door's knob, turned it, and pushed the door open. The hinges creaked faintly, but the door didn't stick and swung open readily. "Huh." Masterton seemed as surprised by that as Godfrey. "It's never been locked," Masterton said, "but…" He shrugged. "Perhaps Kemp occasionally sends the maids through to dust."

Masterton stepped through the doorway and held the door as Godfrey followed.

A quick glance around suggested that no maid had been past the door, to dust or do anything else, for a very long time. A thick layer of dust coated the bare, no-longer-polished boards, and cobwebs draped every corner.

Given they were hoping to discover old paintings, the sight of the webs was heartening. Spiders rarely congregated in damp places; their presence suggested the roof of the old wing was sound.

Masterton shut the door and started walking along the corridor. "If I remember correctly, the stairs to the attic are near the center."

Following in Masterton's wake, Godfrey breathed in, testing the air. While it was musty and stale, he detected no hint of mold or mildew. He looked around. "Do you know why the family closed this off?"

"As I understand it, it was purely to reduce the size of the place—the number of rooms they needed to keep up."

That certainly seemed to be the case; Godfrey detected no sign of structural damage or deficiencies in door frames, walls, architraves, or ceiling.

As he'd walked along, Masterton had been scrutinizing the left-hand wall. Abruptly, he stopped and splayed his fingers over the faded paper, then lightly pushed, and a concealed door popped open. "Here they are." He threw Godfrey a glance as he drew the door wide. "The stairs are rather rough."

Thus warned, when he followed Masterton into the relative gloom of the stairwell and halted on a narrow landing, Godfrey wasn't surprised to find bare, unfinished timbers and a railing that looked likely to harbor splinters. He moved forward, and the door to the corridor swung shut behind him, leaving the stairs lit only by faint light filtering down from a skylight far above.

Already climbing the steep upward flight toward the next landing, Masterton said, "Luckily, the steps seem sound enough."

Masterton was heavier than Godfrey; seeing the other man reach the landing and turn and continue up the next flight, Godfrey followed without further hesitation.

Four longish flights took them to the level of the attic. Godfrey reached the end of the fourth flight to find Masterton waiting to one side of the upper landing. As Godfrey joined him, Masterton reached for the latch that secured the attic door. "Right—let's see."

He opened the door, and Godfrey, standing directly in front of it, found himself looking into a large, reasonably well-lit space. He stepped over the threshold, then went farther, allowing Masterton to enter behind him. Godfrey looked up and down the long room, which ran uninterrupted from gable to gable. "It seems they never partitioned this."

"At least that gives us light enough to see."

Dormer windows set into the roof allowed daylight to stream in, revealing old trunks, ancient bandboxes, and pieces of long-outdated furniture scattered haphazardly across the floor.

Masterton looked around, then huffed and, in a rather odd tone, said, "Lucky." He paused, then pointed at the far end of the room. "Over there."

Godfrey looked and spotted several medium-size picture frames leaning against the wall beneath the farthest dormer window. He headed that way, sidestepping the clumps of household detritus in his path.

Masterton followed.

The closer Godfrey got to the stacked paintings, the harder it got to breathe.

He halted directly before them, with two yards of empty space between, and stared, barely able to believe his eyes.

Three of the canvases had been turned to the wall; only the nearest faced the room.

With his every faculty and all his senses locked on the dark and murky painting, his eyes tracing the lines beneath the dust and accumulated grime, he felt literally giddy. He crouched—to get a different angle and also to ensure he didn't sway in shock.

He was dimly aware that Masterton had halted beside and a little behind him.

In a tone that held something of Godfrey's stunned awe, Masterton murmured, "Lord above. There really are old paintings here."

It took several seconds for the oddness of the words to penetrate the haze filling Godfrey's mind. He frowned. "What?"

He started to rise, to turn and face Masterton.

The back of his skull exploded with pain.

He fell, and blackness swallowed him.

Consciousness dripped into Godfrey's brain, not steadily but in fits and starts.

His head pounded, but instinct held him still. He kept his eyes closed and, as the fog shrouding his senses thinned, tried to get his bearings—tried to recall where he was and what had happened.

Then he remembered. Everything.

He sent his senses searching. He was lying on his back, presumably on the attic floor.

He heard a sound, then heavy footsteps approached. Remaining limp and unmoving was surprisingly easy; none of his muscles seemed to be working. He couldn't even raise his lids enough to squint through his lashes.

Someone, some man—Masterton?—crouched beside him, and he felt large hands roughly seize his, pulling his arms across his chest, then some silky material was wound tightly about his wrists, lashing them together.

"There," the man said, and yes, it was Masterton. He dropped Godfrey's bound wrists onto his chest, but remained crouched alongside.

Godfrey felt Masterton's gaze on his face, then Masterton muttered, "You brought down this fate on your own head." Accusation rang in his tone as he went on, "You're too damned clever by half. Bad enough you recognized Hendall's work, but to go and ask the blighter who commissioned the Albertinelli copy—"

Even in his present state, Godfrey made the logical deduction.

"—obviously, I couldn't allow that!"

Equally obviously, I no longer need to visit Amsterdam.

Surreptitiously, Godfrey tried to tense his fingers, but couldn't manage even that much.

Abruptly, Masterton stood. "Ever since you came, everything's gone wrong."

Godfrey continued to lie unmoving as Masterton stalked away, then he turned and came raging back. The veneer the man had adopted earlier had cracked and fallen apart; barely suppressed panic rang in his voice as he all but hissed, "It's getting too complicated, and obviously, I can't have you poaching on my patch. I can't let you give Ellie ideas. She's *my* pawn —she'll marry me eventually, once she loses all hope of anything more to her taste. I can't have you jeopardizing that!"

Godfrey almost frowned but, just in time, froze his features. Was the motivation behind Masterton's attack Ellie or the forgery?

Or was it both?

He would have sworn Masterton felt nothing for Ellie, yet he'd offered for her hand and, now, seemed in a genuine state over Godfrey stealing her away or even swaying her to look farther afield for a husband. And what did Masterton mean by referring to Ellie as his pawn?

Godfrey couldn't see how any of that connected with the forgery, but Masterton was still raving, so he forced himself to focus and listen.

"And as for you helping Matthew get the original painting back so he can sell it to the gallery and repair his finances, that would completely scupper my plan!"

Godfrey wished he could open his eyes and demand to be told exactly what Masterton's overly complicated plan actually was.

"*Obviously*, Matthew and Ellie need to turn to me! *Me*—their cousin —not some poncy wealthy lord!"

Could he manage to speak and ask why?

"*Damn it!*"

Godfrey finally managed to ease his lids up enough to view a sliver of room through the fringe of his lashes. At first, he saw nothing more than distant rafters, but then Masterton paced into sight.

The man appeared at his wits' end, as if wrestling with some irreconcilable dilemma; he'd buried both hands in his hair and was clenching them. "God knows, I've been patient. Four and more years of buttering up Matthew. Four and more years of waiting for Ellie to see the light, swallow her damned pride, and agree to marry me. That's all I ask—all I need! But with that bastard Cawley selling out, I'm going to need the funds from selling Hinckley Hall sooner rather than later." Masterton released his hair, swung around, and his face contorting with fury, came striding back to Godfrey. He drew back his booted foot and kicked Godfrey in the calf. Eyes closing, Godfrey only just managed not to react, but he needn't have worried—Masterton was already striding away again, declaring in a voice that sounded as if he was appealing to the heavens, "And I absolutely cannot afford to have some puffed-up lord get in the way of that!"

All Masterton's disparate utterances whirled one last time in Godfrey's mind, then tumbled into place,—into a pattern—and finally, he saw the full picture of Masterton's scheme. Chill fingers clamped about Godfrey's nape as he studied the whole.

It was Masterton who had taken the Albertinelli—presumably because, for whatever reason, he'd needed the money. He'd had it copied so the Hinckleys wouldn't raise a hue and cry—presumably because if the authorities had got involved, Masterton might have fallen under suspicion and, ultimately, been caught.

But whatever cash Masterton had got from the sale hadn't been enough. He was in debt, presumably to a moneylender, and having ingratiated himself with the Hinckleys and noting the family's relative isolation, he'd seen an opportunity. Harry wasn't of age and wouldn't be for another five years. If Masterton succeeded in marrying Ellie, then if anything subsequently happened to Matthew Hinckley, the most obvious hands into which the reins of the estate would fall would be Masterton's —Matthew's cousin and, in legal terms more importantly, his son-in-law.

Masterton's push to marry Ellie—and to ensure she didn't marry anyone else—was purely a step in that wider scheme, albeit a crucial one.

Godfrey almost laughed. He'd already scuppered Masterton's plan, did the blighter but know it.

Of course, to actually scupper Masterton's plan, Godfrey had to remain alive.

The thought instantly sobered him; he tried again to tense his fingers and, this time, managed to curl them. Relief crept through him; he'd started to worry that the blow to his head might have done permanent damage. He tested his toes and found he could curl them more or less normally. Next, he tried to lift his ankle and managed an inch before the weight of his foot became too much for his weakened leg to bear.

Masterton had been pacing at some distance, but now he came striding back.

Godfrey lay still and fought not to show any sign of consciousness.

Masterton halted beside him and nudged Godfrey's arm with his booted toe, clearly testing if he was still unconscious.

Godfrey remained limp, his features lax.

Masterton humphed, crouched, grabbed the material wrapped about

Godfrey's wrists, and pulled the knot even tighter. "There." He released the material and patted the knot. "That should hold you, even if you wake up—at least until I get back." Masterton paused, then went on, "And if you do manage to get to your feet and attempt to get down those stairs, with your hands tied—"

Although unable to see it, Godfrey heard the smile in Masterton's voice.

"—you'll fall and break your neck, and I won't have to do anything more drastic to remove you from my path."

Masterton rose and, again, stood looking down at Godfrey. "You, my lord, have left me no choice. I have to get my plan back on track, and the only way to do that is to remove you entirely. That will solve everything."

Godfrey doubted it, but clung to his façade of unconsciousness as Masterton swung on his heel and stalked away.

Halfway across the room, Masterton muttered, "Luckily, I know just the man to take care of you, one who has as much at stake in this as me, and thank the Lord, he's close by. I'm sure he'll happily do the deed, then when your powerful family comes asking questions, I can put my hand on my heart and swear that I had nothing to do with your death." Again, Godfrey heard a smug smile color Masterton's voice. "And there won't be any way they'll be able to prove otherwise."

Masterton's footsteps continued, then Godfrey heard the fading patter as Masterton went down the stairs.

Your death.

That, Godfrey decided, was clear enough. But who was the man Masterton had gone to fetch—his chosen executioner?

Godfrey lay unmoving. He was still too weak to sit up, even to hold up his hands and examine whatever was binding his wrists.

He didn't know how much time he would have before Masterton came back, but until control over his limbs returned, he simply had to wait...

He might have slipped into unconsciousness again; when he blinked and realized he could fully open his eyes, he thought the gray light seeping in from outside had dimmed.

Time had passed, but he had no way of telling how much.

Gritting his teeth against the pain in his head, he tried to sit up. When that proved beyond him, after regaining his breath, he closed his eyes and, with an effort that left him groaning, rolled onto his left side.

When the throbbing in his skull eased, he opened his eyes—and found himself staring at the painting that had so distracted him earlier.

His new angle, virtually level with the canvas, had him staring directly at it from only a few feet away.

He drank in every line, all he could make out through the layers of dust and grime, then drew in a long, slow breath.

Today is not a day on which I want to die.

CHAPTER 13

a fter a lengthy discussion with Mrs. Kemp over the state of the household linen, Ellie returned to the library where she found her father still chatting with Morris and Pyne, but no sign of Godfrey—or Masterton, for that matter.

She waited for a break in the men's conversation, then asked, "Do any of you have any idea where Lord Godfrey went?"

The three looked around, as if confirming that Godfrey wasn't elsewhere in the library.

"Thought he would have come back by now," Pyne said.

Her father offered, "He said he had some matters to take care of."

"He left not long after we got here," Morris added.

"Actually," Pyne said, "Masterton came in just as Lord Godfrey left. I remember Masterton turning and following his lordship out, and"—Pyne waved at the open library door—"I heard them talking in the hall. Couldn't tell what they were saying, but I think they went on together."

"Perhaps they went out for a stroll," Morris said.

"Perhaps." Ellie looked out of the window; the light outside was already fading. She flashed a quick smile at her father and his friends. "I'll look around."

She left the library and returned to the front hall. She couldn't imagine why Godfrey and Masterton would go strolling in the park, but regardless, the wind had come up, and the air outside was icy; they would have come in by now. So where would her lover have gone?

Smiling at being able to use that word for him, she headed for the back parlor. But when she opened the door, she found Harry and Maggie curled up on either side of the fire, reading books, and no sign of anyone else. She suppressed a frown. "Have either of you seen Lord Godfrey?"

They shook their heads.

"Do we have to call him a lord from now on?" Maggie asked. "I thought he didn't want us to."

"Not to his face," Ellie replied, "but in public or when there are others around, you should."

"Oh."

With a wave, Ellie left her siblings and proceeded to methodically check the reception rooms currently in use, to no avail.

After a moment's thought, she climbed the stairs to Godfrey's room. He wasn't there, but his greatcoat, hat, scarf, and gloves were. She stared at them. "So he's not outside."

Increasingly puzzled, she descended the stairs and found Kemp in the front hall, instructing Jimmy, their fresh-faced lad-of-all-work. She stepped onto the tiles. "Kemp, do you know where Lord Godfrey and Mr. Masterton are?"

A slight frown marred Kemp's brow. "No, miss. I haven't seen either of them since luncheon."

Jimmy jigged, his eyes growing wide and fixing on Kemp's face.

Kemp noticed. "What is it, Jimmy?"

"I seen 'em, sir—the gents."

Relief winging through her, Ellie smiled. "Where was that, Jimmy?"

The boy—he was all of ten years old—transferred his bright gaze to her face. "It was while I was taking up the kindling for the fires in the bedrooms, miss. I was coming back for my next load, and I'm havin' to use the main stairs on account of Cook's girl slopped a pitcher of water on the back stairs, you see, and I saw both gents going down the gallery"—Jimmy pointed toward the disused wing—"that way. They didn't see me, and I didn't 'xactly see where they went. I reached the stairs and started on down, and then I heard a door squeak. I was just telling Mr. Kemp about it, miss—I know he doesn't like any doors to squeak."

"That would be the door to the disused wing, miss." Kemp looked faintly self-conscious. "I haven't tended its hinges for some time."

"That's quite all right, Kemp. We don't use that door."

Jimmy screwed up his face. "I can't rightly say that the gents went into the old wing, miss. When I came back up on my way to tend the rest of the rooms, I looked down the gallery, and all the doors along there were closed." He looked up at Ellie. "P'raps they just looked and didn't go through."

Presentiment tickled Ellie's nape, but she held onto her smile. "Very likely, but thank you for telling me. I'll look along the gallery and see where they went."

She parted from Kemp and Jimmy and reclimbed the stairs.

Masterton knew the house well; he'd visited on and off since childhood. He would know about the disused wing, but why take Godfrey there? Admittedly, Godfrey might have been curious, but she doubted he would have asked Masterton to be his guide rather than herself or Harry or Maggie.

She turned right along the gallery and checked each room as she went, but found no trace of either man. Eventually, she reached the door set in the panel blocking off the corridor that ran down the old wing. She halted before it. "Well, let's see." She opened the door and heard the telltale creak. She pushed the door wide and gazed down the corridor. It stretched away into the gloom of the old wing and, as she'd expected, was devoid of life. She strained her ears for any hint of movement or voices, but heard nothing. The light outside was fading, but enough remained to be certain there was no one in the corridor.

She humphed, unsure whether she was disappointed or reassured. Already wondering where next to look, she started to turn away, and her gaze swept over the bare floor—and the boot prints left in the dust.

She let go of the door and walked forward, studying the impressions. Two sets of men's boot prints led down the corridor.

Increasingly quickly, she followed the trail. The earlier tickle of presentiment swelled to an icy sensation that intensified and urged her on.

The trail led to the door to the attic stairs. She pushed it open. She had to squint in the dimness, but as her eyes adjusted, she spotted the boot prints—both sets—continuing up the stairs.

She hurried up. On the first landing, she spotted a sight that made her blood run cold. Two pairs of boots had gone up the stairs, but only one had come down.

Yet she hadn't seen the returning boot prints in the corridor... "He went down to the ground floor." She stared blankly as realization bloomed. "He's using a door downstairs to come and go."

And she knew which "he" that would be.

She drew in a quick breath and rushed up the remaining flights. The door at the top giving access to the attic stood ajar. Her heart in her mouth, she pushed it open.

With no idea of what she might find, she walked in and, through the gloom, barely daring to breathe, looked searchingly around.

She spotted Godfrey slumped against the side wall to her right. With a gasp, she ran toward him, dodging the clumps of old boxes and discarded furniture that littered the floor between them.

As she neared, she saw that his hands, bound together, lay motionless in his lap. Worse, he remained unmoving, his head turned to the side, as if he was staring at something.

Horrified, she spotted a trickle of what could only be blood running from his hairline down the side of his cheek.

Most terrible of all, he hadn't yet glanced her way.

She was nearly upon him when, finally, he lifted his head as if it weighed a ton and looked at her, then smiled—a weak travesty of his usual charming, dimpled smile.

"Oh—hello." His eyes closed, and his lips pinched as he struggled to sit straighter.

Hello? She swooped down to crouch by his side and immediately fell to tugging at the knot in the cloth wound about his wrists. "What happened? Who did this to you?"

And yes, that was blood on his cheek, presumably seeping from a wound hidden beneath his dark-auburn hair.

Somewhat frantic, she glanced around. "And where's Masterton?"

She looked at Godfrey, who was now frowning.

"Actually," he said, speaking rather carefully, "it was he who knocked me out and tied me up. I wasn't completely conscious at the time, but I could hear well enough, and he was the only one about." As she tugged to loosen the knot, his eyes cleared, and his features hardened. "He led me up here, showed me those paintings"—he tipped his head toward where he'd been staring and winced—"and while I was distracted, he struck me down."

"Good Lord!" She glanced to the side and noted the four frames stacked against the wall beneath the nearest window. Returning to her desperate task, she finally got the knot undone and fell to unwinding the strip of cloth. "What on earth does he think he's about?"

"He wants to marry you, for a start."

She humphed. "I've known that for years, but I won't have him."

"He doesn't know about us, and he thinks you'll eventually weaken, especially if he gets rid of me. And then once he's your husband, he plans to somehow take control of the Hall and sell it."

Startled, she looked into Godfrey's face, and he nodded grimly. "He's in debt and needs the money."

She blinked, then pulled the cloth free of his wrists and flung it aside. "He's the one who took the Albertinelli."

Godfrey nodded again. "So he couldn't have me visiting Hendall and asking who commissioned the forgery."

"The...the bastard!" Still crouched, she glanced around again. "Where did he go? Do you know?"

"Not specifically."

She turned back to find Godfrey pushing against the wall in an attempt to stand, and she quickly rose to help him.

He struggled to get his feet under him. "He muttered something about going to fetch someone to kill me so he could later swear he didn't do it."

She gave vent to a strangled sound and managed to get him upright to the point of leaning against the wall. She eyed him doubtfully. "Can you walk?"

He gave her a small smile. "Not yet—and if you try to help me, I'll just fall on you." Propping his shoulders against the wall, he caught her hands in both of his and locked his eyes on hers. "Ellie, you have to go and get help."

"No." She didn't have to think; every instinct she possessed insisted she stay with him. She glanced at the door. "I'm not leaving you to face that blackguard alone."

A stubbornness almost equal to hers filled his face. "But—"

"If I go"—she gripped his hands back—"and he returns with whomever he's gone to fetch, what's to stop him—"

She broke off, and they both looked toward the door as the sound of heavy footsteps mounting the stairs—not one pair but two—reached them.

"Too late," Godfrey murmured.

Ellie slipped her fingers from his, then gripped his hand tightly and turned to stand beside him, facing the door. It was the only way into or out of the attic.

Masterton appeared beyond the doorway, but he was glancing back and waving at someone else to precede him.

"Come on." He sounded harried and impatient. "All you have to do is finish him off."

A man in a greatcoat loomed in the doorway, then Jeffers stepped into the attic.

Frowning, he immediately turned to face Masterton. "What?" Jeffers hadn't seen Ellie and Godfrey, who were gaping at him from the end of the room. Instead, with an expression of utter bewilderment, he stared at Masterton. "What are you talking about?"

"It's simple." Masterton walked in and waved toward Godfrey, then he glanced that way and saw Ellie. Masterton's jaw dropped. For a full five seconds, he goggled at her, then choleric color rushed into his face. "Damn you!" Fists clenching, he came striding down the room, pausing only to kick a box out of his way. "Damn it, woman! *What the devil are you doing here?*"

His voice had risen to a roar.

Ellie stared—as did Godfrey and Jeffers—as midway down the room, Masterton paused, hauled in a huge breath, then fell to pacing, ranting and raving incoherently. "Damned female! What now? I'll have to—no, I can't. She'll never keep her mouth shut. But what then? What if—no, that won't do. But if she's gone…that might work. The others will fall apart. They'll be ripe for the plucking. Yes, that's the way forward."

Abruptly, he halted and swung to face Ellie. Eyes narrowing to slits, he stabbed an accusing finger at her and strode closer, stopping a mere three paces away to jab that finger toward her face. "It's your own damned fault! There's nothing else for it. We'll have to kill you, too."

Ellie's breath hitched.

"Wait." Jeffers had followed Masterton and caught his sleeve. "We who?" Jeffers hauled Masterton around to face him.

His gaze on the two men, Godfrey took advantage of the distraction to test his balance. It was improving—not perfect, but it would have to do.

Masterton scowled at Jeffers. "Here." He thrust his hand into his coat pocket and pulled out a pistol—an American revolver. He caught Jeffers's hand and slapped the gun into his palm. "All you have to do," Masterton continued in the tone of a frustrated adult instructing a recalcitrant child, "is to shoot them." He glanced at Godfrey and Ellie. "Luckily, I loaded two bullets. I assumed you wouldn't need more."

The expression on Jeffers's face was one of dawning, incredulous, and horrified comprehension.

Godfrey noted it; as Jeffers gripped the gun and stepped back from Masterton, Godfrey returned his attention to Masterton.

"Just hold on a minute." Jeffers plainly gathered himself, then spoke quietly and distinctly. "You told me that if I came with you, you would be able to repay the money you owe the firm. So where is it?" Jeffers glanced at the gun in his hand as if he'd never seen one, much less held one, in his life. "And what the deuce has shooting them with this gun, two bullets or not, got to do with anything?"

Godfrey braced against the wall and shifted his feet, confirming his control over his limbs had returned.

Masterton's jaw clenched, and he gritted out, "I keep telling you—it's simple. For me to get the money I owe your master, Cavanaugh has to die." His narrowed eyes flashed briefly to Ellie. "And now that Ellie has stupidly made her choice, she'll have to be dispatched as well. I brought Cavanaugh here because no one will think to look for him—and now her, too—up here. And no one will hear the shots, either—we're too far away from the rest of the house, and the walls are feet thick." He drew a tense breath and went on, in the same rigidly even tone, as if what he was suggesting was entirely unremarkable, "All you need to do is put a bullet in his brain—or his heart, if you prefer. And then in hers, too."

Godfrey released Ellie's hand and stepped to his right—away from her.

She shot him a glance. Without taking his eyes from Masterton and Jeffers, Godfrey gestured at her to go the other way, creating an ever-widening gap between them.

Regardless of Jeffers's resistance, Godfrey assumed that, if the gun was pointed at anyone, it would be pointed first at him.

Knowing Godfrey as she now did, Ellie had no difficulty under-standing his plan; she just didn't agree with it.

She could see the sense in separating, yet her instincts were clamoring at her to stay as close to him as possible.

For several moments, she dithered and remained where she was.

Before them, Jeffers, holding the gun at his side, scowled at Masterton and belligerently stated, "What I don't understand is why you imagine I'm going to help you kill them." Jeffers raked his free hand through his thick hair. "For God's sake—*kill them?* What on earth made you think I would?"

Ellie stopped thinking and, following her instincts, edged toward

Godfrey, who was stealthily moving around the wall so that a stack of boxes would lie between him and the other men.

Masterton's choler returned in full force. He stepped closer to Jeffers and sneered in Jeffers's face. "Isn't that what men like you do? You're cold-blooded killers, all of you! And now you're here, so if your master wants his money, *you* do the deed." Masterton glared at Jeffers, apparently waiting, then Masterton flung up his hands. "Just get on with it, man!"

Masterton swung toward Ellie and Godfrey—to where they had been. "What...?" He looked wildly around and spotted them, just as Godfrey bent and picked up an old walking stick.

Masterton yelped and spun toward Jeffers. "Quick! Shoot them!"

When Jeffers, turning to look at Godfrey and Ellie, didn't raise the gun, Masterton lunged and grappled for the weapon.

Jeffers fought to fend him off, but Masterton was larger and heavier and utterly desperate. With no time to break Jeffers's grip, Masterton clamped his hand around the other man's, wrenched the gun up, and pointed it at Godfrey.

"No!" Ellie screamed. She flung herself at Godfrey, intending to push him aside. Instead, she tripped over a box and lurched across in front of him.

Just as Masterton squeezed Jeffers's fingers, and the gun discharged.

Searing pain lanced across Ellie's upper arm, and she staggered backward, then her legs gave way, and she crumpled.

Godfrey caught her.

She would have smiled, but couldn't. As he eased her to the floor, she hauled in a breath, gritted her teeth against the pain, and bit off, "It's just a graze."

Godfrey barely heard. All he could see was that she was hurt and bleeding. The bastard had shot her—his Ellie.

Inside, something dark and violent rose and gripped him.

Then the fading roar of the shot was overridden by yells and running footsteps.

Godfrey raised his head and, over the pile of boxes, saw Harry and Maggie racing down the room.

He snapped his gaze to Masterton as, in a flat panic, Masterton beat off Jeffers and swung the gun toward Ellie's siblings.

He still had one bullet left.

Godfrey gripped the old walking stick, surged up, and launched himself through the boxes, scattering them. Wielding the heavy stick like a club, he whacked Masterton's hand and the gun skyward.

A sharp crack sounded, and the gun discharged—harmlessly into the rafters.

Maggie shrieked and ducked to the side, but as Godfrey's momentum carried him into Masterton, Harry, grim-faced, lowered his head and came barreling on.

He, Godfrey, and Jeffers piled on Masterton, but the man had near-manic strength. He fought like one demented—like one having an unrestrained temper tantrum at being denied what he wanted—kicking, punching, flinging his limbs and body about.

Glimpsing an opening, Godfrey clenched his jaw, drew back his arm, and with every ounce of strength he could muster, plowed his fist into Masterton's face.

Bone crunched, not Godfrey's.

The blow rocked Masterton back on his heels. He blinked once, then his eyes rolled up, and in a series of thuds, he collapsed on the floor.

For several seconds, with his chest heaving while he nursed his bruised knuckles, Godfrey stood over Masterton, but the man was well and truly unconscious.

Godfrey glanced at Jeffers, who was bent over with his hands on his knees, hauling in air even harder than Godfrey was. He caught Jeffers's eye and gave him a nod.

Wearily, Jeffers nodded back. Then he bent and, rather gingerly, picked up the gun Masterton had dropped and held it out to Godfrey. Jeffers met Godfrey's eyes. "Not my line of work."

That had become apparent, yet Godfrey had to wonder why Masterton had been so convinced matters were otherwise. But solving the riddle of Jeffers could wait. Godfrey took the gun, checked the chambers were empty, then slid it into his pocket. "Thank you for your help."

Jeffers straightened and looked at Masterton with disgust etched in his face. "Frankly, it was entirely my pleasure."

Yes, there was definitely a tale there.

Jeffers glanced around, then walked over to fetch the length of cloth Masterton had used to tie up Godfrey. Twisting the cloth between his hands, Jeffers nodded at Harry. "Let's tie him up before he wakes."

Harry, who had managed to catch his breath while listening to the exchanges, nodded and bent to help Jeffers manhandle Masterton onto his front so they could lash his hands behind his back.

"I found this." Maggie came forward brandishing a length of rope. "Perhaps we should hobble him as well."

Jeffers looked up, found a smile, and reached for the rope. "Good idea."

Everyone was safe. All was under control. On that realization, Godfrey's mind, his entire awareness, shifted. Leaving the others to deal with Masterton, he clambered over the scattered boxes to where Ellie waited, pale but alive, sitting propped against the wall.

She met his worried gaze with a faint and rueful smile. "I missed all the excitement."

"Excitement?" Godfrey dropped down to sit beside her, then avoiding her wound, which she was clutching, he put his arms around her and slowly, feelingly, hugged her. He buried his face in her hair and let out the shaky breath that felt as if it had been lodged in his chest from the moment she'd been shot. When she leaned into him, he tightened his hold. "I thought I'd lost you, you crazy woman."

He raised his head and pressed a long, hard kiss to her temple. He felt as if he was holding himself together—bottling up a maelstrom of turbulent, violent, powerful feelings—by the skin of his teeth. He'd never known he could feel so viscerally, so profoundly—not about anything.

She drew in a slow, deep breath, awkwardly raised the hand of her injured arm, and patted his encircling arm. "You're not going to lose me so easily, for the simple reason that I'm not about to let you go."

He softly snorted. "I gathered that—you were supposed to have gone the other way."

"And then the devil would have shot you, and that wouldn't have suited me at all."

After a moment of simply soaking in her warmth, the reality of her presence, he sat up and gently drew his arms from her. "Let me see."

She eased away the hand she'd clamped over the wound and allowed him to check it. "See?" She peered at it, too. "It's not that bad."

He frowned at the raw gash marring her delicate flesh. "It might be a graze, but it's a deep one. You're going to have a scar." He wasn't sure what offended him more—that she'd been hurt or that she would carry a permanent reminder of Masterton.

She ducked her head, captured his gaze, and gently smiled. "I really don't care. You're alive. I'm alive." She glanced to where her siblings and Jeffers were discussing what to do with Masterton, who was apparently still unconscious. "And thanks to you, Harry and Maggie are also alive, and Jeffers as well, and that's really all that matters."

He couldn't disagree. He wondered whether he could trust his legs to hold them both up and realized the shock of her being shot and the ensuing action had apparently galvanized his limbs and brain into cooperating again.

"How's your head?" She looked at him anxiously.

He arched his brows. "Surprisingly better. Still throbbing a bit where he hit me." He gently probed beneath his hair. "A goose egg that's sensitive, but nowhere near as bad as before."

He pushed off the floor and got to his feet, confirmed his balance wasn't about to desert him, then reached down and helped her up. He put an arm around her, and she leaned against him, just a little, as they sidestepped the tumbled boxes and joined the others, still standing over Masterton, who hadn't yet stirred.

After assuring the others that her wound was minor and she was otherwise perfectly well, Ellie looked down at Masterton, her expression severe and full of banked anger. "Leave him here." She cut across the ongoing discussion of what to do with him. "We'll send Kemp and the footmen to fetch him."

There was something in her tone that had everyone else nodding.

They turned and headed for the door, with Ellie, still clutching her wound, walking within the circle of Godfrey's arm. Jeffers went ahead and held the door wide for Godfrey and Ellie to pass through.

Poised to step over the threshold, Godfrey halted, then blinked. He could barely believe he'd forgotten...

He looked at Harry and Maggie. "There are four framed paintings resting against the wall beneath the last window." He pointed. "Can you fetch them, please, and bring them downstairs?"

Harry and Maggie readily turned and went back to collect the paintings.

Godfrey returned his attention to Ellie, smiled reassuringly into her eyes, and guided down the steep stairs what was, to his mind, the most precious object the attic contained.

$\mathcal{W}$ith Godfrey hovering, Ellie paused in the front hall to tell Kemp of the happenings in the old wing—which almost succeeded in throwing the butler into a fluster, something she'd never seen and, even now, failed to accomplish. She concluded by asking Kemp to arrange to have Masterton fetched from the attic.

"He'll probably have revived," Godfrey warned. "Best send at least three burly footmen."

Kemp's spine stiffened. "Indeed, sir. I'll go myself and supervise."

"We should put him in some small room—one he can't get out of." Despite having his arms wrapped about two paintings, Harry managed to look belligerently combative.

When Kemp glanced at Ellie, she confirmed, "We need to keep Mr. Masterton under lock and key while we speak with Papa about what to do."

Kemp nodded. "Very good, miss. There's a room off the scullery that will suffice. We'll hold him there until we receive further orders."

"Thank you, Kemp." Ellie was about to set out for the library when Jeffers cleared his throat.

When everyone looked at him, he colored faintly and said, "You might want to have your staff seal the door through which Masterton brought me into the house. I gather it's been left unlocked for some time. Anyone could get in that way and"—Jeffers glanced upward in the direction of the door through which they'd entered the gallery, which had no lock—"gain entry to this part of the house."

"Good gracious," Ellie said. "I hadn't realized you didn't come through the front door. Which door was it?"

Jeffers described what she and Kemp recognized as the outside door from what was known as the summer parlor.

Grimly, Kemp nodded to her. "I'll see to it immediately, miss—as soon as we have Mr. Masterton secured."

"That," Godfrey said as they turned toward the corridor to the library, "coming in through the summer parlor and through the disused wing, was the route Masterton used to spirit the Albertinelli out of the house."

Ellie nodded. "And to bring in the forgery to put in its place."

They walked into the library to discover that Morris and Pyne had been about to depart but, having heard the exclamations and voices in the front hall, had waited to support her father if such support proved necessary.

Ellie smiled reassuringly at all three men as Godfrey solicitously steered her to one of the armchairs, but her father's, Morris's, and Pyne's gazes had dropped to her arm, and from their shocked expressions, she realized the blood staining her sleeve and bodice wasn't reassuring at all. "It's just a scratch," she assured them as she sank down.

Godfrey stepped back and looked at her father. "With your permission, sir, I believe I should summon Mrs. Kemp and Cook to tend to Ellie's arm."

She tried to insist the injury wasn't serious—just a graze, albeit a nasty one—but Godfrey was adamant it be treated immediately, a notion supported by everyone else in the room.

Resigning herself to losing that battle, she tried to suggest that, instead, she go upstairs and tend the wound herself, but was unanimously overruled. Within minutes, she was being fussed over by Mrs. Kemp and Cook, neither of whom would listen to a word from her as they cut off her damaged sleeve, bathed the gash, and dried it.

While waiting for her wound to properly dry, Mrs. Kemp glanced at Godfrey and spotted the blood on his cheek. It seemed he'd completely forgotten about his injured head. But he was promptly set upon by Mrs. Kemp and Cook and made to sit while they sponged the blood from his face and examined the gash on his head. The discussion over whether to make him wear a bandage like a turban proved entertaining, at least for everyone else. In the end, Cook pronounced the wound sufficiently healed to be left as it was.

The relief on Godfrey's face was almost comical.

Then Cook and Mrs. Kemp returned to Ellie, exclaimed in low voices over her graze, then salved and bandaged it and left her with a thick shawl under which to huddle until she went upstairs and changed her gown.

Her father cleared his throat and offered to delay the pending discussion if she wished to go up and change, but aware of the pent-up impatience in the room, she staunchly replied, "You need to be told of the latest developments as soon as possible, and we've already lost nearly half an hour."

She was also curious about the four paintings Godfrey had had Harry and Maggie carry down; he'd directed they be stacked by the door. In her most authoritative tone, she stated, "Later will be time enough to change my gown." She looked up and arched a brow at Godfrey, still hovering by her chair.

He met her gaze, hesitated, but finally, gave way, stood down, and settled in the armchair beside her.

Despite feeling rather cross at all the fuss, she couldn't hold his smothering concern against him, not after what she'd experienced on finding him barely conscious in the attic.

Her fingers itched to reach out, grasp, and twine with his, but they hadn't yet announced their betrothal, and such an action would raise eyebrows along with questions best left for later.

Until after they'd dealt with Masterton.

She met Godfrey's eyes. "Perhaps you could open proceedings by explaining how you came to be in the attic with Masterton."

Godfrey duly related the story Masterton had spun him about there possibly being other paintings in the attic of the disused wing. "As it happened, there were four paintings there, but from what Masterton let fall, I suspect that was purely serendipitous—he hadn't known any paintings were actually there but had concocted the tale to lure me to the attic." Godfrey paused, then added, "Then he knocked me unconscious."

"Good heavens!" Morris exclaimed. Together with Pyne and her father, and Jeffers, too, Morris was avidly following the unfolding drama.

Godfrey continued, recounting what he'd heard while lying incapacitated on the attic floor. His descriptions of Masterton's revelations fell into shocked silence. "It seems"—Godfrey shot a glance at Ellie—"that Masterton's current plan isn't merely to marry Ellie but to use his position as her husband to—somehow—take control of the Hinckley estate and sell it." He looked at Mr. Hinckley. "He said he needed the funds. And as he had also been the one to steal and sell the Albertinelli, me saying I intended to travel to Amsterdam and get the name of the person who had commissioned the forgery drove him to take drastic action."

He paused, then concluded, "After tying me up, Masterton left, saying he was going to fetch someone who would 'do the deed,' so that later, he could swear he hadn't been the one who killed me."

Shaken and stunned though she was at the full gamut of what might have been, Ellie determinedly took up the story, explaining how she'd hunted high and low for Godfrey and Masterton. "If it hadn't been for Jimmy, our lad-of-all-work, and his sharp eyes and ears, I wouldn't have known to look in the old wing." She described the boot prints in the dust and how she'd followed them and found Godfrey. "Then Masterton returned, with Mr. Jeffers."

All eyes swung to Jeffers.

To give the man his due, he merely nodded in acceptance, cleared his throat, and said, "I suspect I had better begin by explaining how I came to know Masterton." He paused, then went on, "My partner, Thornton, and I have long had a dream of setting up a bank. Not a big institution, just a small, provincial one. Thornton and I were at grammar school together and, subsequently, worked as bank clerks in Doncaster, learning the ins and outs of the system. We realized that having a decent loan book— lending money to businesses and the like at a reasonable rather than extortionate rate—was the key to becoming a successful small bank. About the same time, a bit more than a year ago, both of us inherited similar sums from our fathers. Neither of us has any dependents, so we pooled our funds and looked around for a suitable loan book to buy."

He paused, then went on, "We found what appeared to be a suitable venture—an old moneylender in York wanted to retire and was offering his book of loans for sale. After examining the viability of the loans— that's Thornton's strong suit—we purchased the book. We knew there were a few personal loans—loans not secured against a property or a business—that would need to be wound up. That's my role—I visit the clients and explain that the owner of their loans has changed and outline our new rates and schedule of payments. With most of our loans, that hasn't been difficult. In most cases, we've extended the time of the loan and reduced the rate of interest to a more reasonable level. That's pleased and reassured our clients. Both Thornton and I believe that a bank should not involve itself in usury." Jeffers nodded to Pyne and Morris. "Mr. Pyne and Mr. Morris can confirm much of what I've said."

Both men colored a touch, but when the others looked their way, nodded, and Pyne stated, "Mr. Jeffers came to see me a few weeks ago, before the storm. I was very happy to find I'm now dealing with Jeffers and Thornton and not old Cawley. He *was* a usurer, no doubt about that!"

Morris nodded earnestly. "Indeed." He tipped his head to Jeffers. "And I second Walter's comments about dealing with Jeffers and Thornton—a big improvement over the past."

Pleased by the praise, Jeffers inclined his head in acknowledgment, then returned his gaze to Godfrey, Ellie, and her father. "As you will have guessed, Masterton was also a client of Cawley's—a long-term client whom Cawley had been bleeding for more than a decade. Masterton is the sort who fritters away any money he gets his hands on—and he was always wanting more. From our point of view, he had no assets, no prospects, and in short, wasn't a client we wished to keep on our books. I met with him in Ripon last Friday and explained that we were calling in his loans and would not be advancing him any further funds and that he had two months to make other arrangements."

Ellie's father humphed. "How did he take that?"

Jeffers lightly shrugged. "At first, not well, but ultimately, he realized we were not to be moved and, I believe, expected to borrow from one of the other York moneylenders, or so he gave me to understand, although he saw that as only a temporary measure." Jeffers hesitated, then went on, "Masterton stated that Jeffers and Thornton were fools to reject him—that his financial future was essentially guaranteed. When I questioned that, he turned cagey, but hinted that his future prosperity was somehow linked to Hinckley Hall." Jeffers met Godfrey's, then Ellie's eyes. "That accords with what you believe to be his current plan."

Ellie quelled a shudder and managed a nod.

Jeffers faintly winced and looked at her father. "I'm afraid that, in accepting your hospitality last Sunday, I did have something of an ulterior motive. I was curious about the Hinckleys and the relationship between you and Masterton. I had no idea he would turn up as well." His tone turned apologetic. "It's possible my presence further spooked him—when I left, he came racing after me to warn me away from Hinckley Hall."

Godfrey grunted. "You being in the vicinity and calling in his loans might have undermined his confidence to some degree, but it was me confirming the painting he'd switched was a fake and saying I intended to speak with the forger that was the ultimate trigger for today's events."

Ellie's father stirred. "Regardless, you both were behaving in good faith and as circumstances required. Neither of you are in any way to blame for Masterton's actions."

"He's an adult," Harry all but growled. "No one pushed him to steal the Albertinelli or to try to marry Ellie and plot God only knows what else. He made his own decisions—he bears the responsibility for them."

"Hear, hear," Pyne said.

Everyone else nodded.

"If I might ask," her father inquired of Jeffers, "how much does Masterton owe your firm?"

"Just over one thousand pounds." Jeffers paused, then continued, "Having studied Mr. Masterton's borrowing habits over the past ten and more years, Thornton and I fully expected to write off the debt. We didn't believe Masterton would ever pay it—I seriously doubt that, these days, any other moneylender would accept him as a client."

After a second plainly gathering his thoughts, Jeffers went on, "So that's how I came to know Masterton, and he, me. Today, he came and found me—he'd guessed I was staying at the inn at Kirkby Malzeard while visiting clients in the area. He told me that all I had to do was go with him, and he would be able to repay the money he owed the firm." A cynical smile played across Jeffers's face. "Given what occurred, it seems fairly clear that, despite all I had told him of our firm, Masterton believed I was…I suppose one might say the bully boy for another moneylender like Cawley, and as such, that I would be amenable to using violence to achieve my supposed master's ends."

"That," Ellie said, "is why he kept referring to 'your master.'"

Jeffers nodded.

Godfrey stirred. "If you *had* been a bully boy from another money-lender, today might not have gone our way."

"No." Jeffers met Godfrey's gaze. "But luckily, Masterton made a mistake." Jeffers looked at the others. "So that's how I came to walk into the attic with Masterton. To everyone's shock, he then produced a gun and insisted I shoot dead both Lord Godfrey and Miss Hinckley."

Morris's, Pyne's, and her father's jaws sagged. Eventually, Pyne remarked, "'Great heavens' and 'Good Lord' really aren't exclamation enough."

Ellie's father's expression turned thunderous. "That *bounder*! To shoot people—take their lives—just for money?" He drew in a deep breath and, lips pinched, shook his head. "I always wondered from where he got his funds, but I never imagined—"

"That those funds were actually ours? Got by selling Mama's painting? By borrowing against—essentially mortgaging—the Hall itself?" Harry looked disgusted. "Bounder is *far* too weak a word."

No one disagreed.

Kemp appeared in the open doorway; when Ellie's father looked his way, the butler announced, "We have secured Mr. Masterton in the room off the scullery, sir. We have also boarded up the external door in the old summer parlor—we discovered the lock had been forced. Mr. Masterton has regained consciousness and is demanding to be set free and, if not that, then allowed to see you, sir."

"Thank you, Kemp." Ellie's father glanced around the circle of faces, then returned his gaze to Kemp. "You may tell Mr. Masterton that we are presently discussing his future. He will be informed of the outcome of our deliberations in due course."

Kemp very nearly smiled. He bowed deeply. "Indeed, sir." With that, he turned and strode off, plainly relishing his role.

Ellie glanced at her father. His chair was too far away for her to reach over and squeeze his hand, but from his tone, she knew Masterton's betrayal had cut him deeply; he was always one to think the best of every man, and Masterton had wormed his way into his affections by playing on their kinship.

Discovering that Masterton had stolen the Albertinelli and had deceived them in so many ways was, for a man as open, honest, and true as Matthew Hinckley, a bitter and distressing pill to swallow.

"We haven't yet heard what happened after Masterton pulled out a gun," Morris prompted.

Ellie might have viewed such blatant curiosity unkindly, but she caught the glance Morris—and Pyne, too—threw her father. They knew how he was feeling and sought to distract him and everyone else.

Friends—the three were very old friends.

She looked at Godfrey. He'd seen the silent exchange as well and smoothly said, "Masterton tried, unsuccessfully, to get Jeffers to shoot us. While they argued, assuming the gun would be pointed at me first, I tried to edge away from Ellie, around the wall toward some boxes, but then Masterton saw that I'd moved. He grabbed the gun and shot in my direction, but Ellie"—he flicked her a glance laden with suppressed emotion—"flung herself in the bullet's path. That's how she came to be shot."

"I had intended to push Godfrey *out* of the bullet's path, but I tripped and ended in the way myself." She quickly continued, "Then Harry and Maggie burst into the room." She frowned at the pair. "How did you even come to be there?"

Harry glanced at Maggie, then said, "You came and asked if we'd seen Lord Godfrey or Masterton, and we hadn't. We thought it odd they'd both vanished, and after you left, we talked about where they might have gone."

"I was sitting in the window seat." Maggie took over. "I went back to reading my book, but then I saw Masterton and Mr. Jeffers walking through the park."

"We couldn't think where they were going," Harry said. "We watched and—"

"We saw them going into the old wing." Remembered excitement filled Maggie's voice.

Harry threw her a disapproving look. "We couldn't imagine what they were doing."

Undeterred, Maggie blurted, "So we rushed around, into the old wing."

"We were in time to hear them going up the attic stairs," Harry said.

"We crept along behind." Maggie paused, her expression sobering. "When we got to the attic door, we heard Masterton ordering Mr. Jeffers to shoot Ellie and Godfrey. We huddled on the landing and tried to think what to do."

"But then everything happened at once—a shot rang out, and we ran in to see what was happening and stop it." Harry faintly grimaced. "Masterton pointed the gun at us." Harry looked at Maggie, then at his father. "Masterton would have shot us, but Godfrey knocked the gun up, and the shot went into the roof."

Harry blew out a breath and looked at Godfrey. "And then we all set-to with Masterton."

Pyne was nodding. "We thought we heard a shot—two, in fact—but we couldn't imagine from where."

Ellie's father humphed. "Old houses like this have very thick walls. We thought it might be hunters in the woods."

Kemp entered the room, circled to Ellie's side, and bent to quietly inquire, "What would you like to do about dinner, miss?"

She looked at the clock and realized it was already past six. A glance at the windows confirmed that night had fallen long since.

She turned to the others. "Papa, as we've yet to decide what to do about Masterton, might I suggest that Mr. Morris, Mr. Pyne, and Mr. Jeffers join us at table and we continue our deliberations over dinner?"

Her suggestion was approved by all.

When appealed to, Kemp confirmed that the first course could be served immediately. As everyone rose, Ellie murmured to Godfrey, "I'm going upstairs to change my gown."

He met her eyes. "Are you sure you're all right?"

What she saw in his golden-brown gaze warmed her, banishing the last of her lingering chill. "Yes." She squeezed his arm. "Don't worry. I'll be back before anyone misses me."

He grunted. "I already miss you."

She so wanted to kiss him, but contented herself with patting his chest. "Just hold the fort."

"Always."

She slipped out of the library ahead of everyone else and rushed for the stairs.

Godfrey watched her depart, then claimed the right to push Mr. Hinckley into the dining room.

Ellie returned as Kemp and a footman were circling the table, placing a bowl of thick oyster soup before each guest. Once she, now a vision in a plum-silk gown, sat, Mr. Hinckley said grace, and everyone set about appeasing their appetites, which, given the excitement of the last hours, were considerable.

The soup was delicious and warming, yet as he sat on Ellie's right and supped, Godfrey felt warmth of a different kind sinking all the way to his bones.

Masterton had been exposed, and Ellie, Harry, Maggie, Mr. Hinckley, and Jeffers, too, were safe. As was Godfrey.

Today had been a triumph for them all; they'd won through, and now all that remained was to tie up the loose ends.

For him, however, he would argue the triumph was even greater. Through solving the mystery of the Albertinelli and the consequent action of the past days, he'd found the place in which he could be...all he could be.

Here, with Ellie, with her family, he could reach for his most precious dream and have a real chance of achieving it.

Here, with Ellie, he could and would live a full and satisfying life.

The prospect filled him with such eagerness, such impatient joy, that just thinking about it left him giddy. As he laid aside his soupspoon, he couldn't stop smiling.

From the head of the table, Mr. Hinckley looked at Jeffers, seated opposite Godfrey. "It seems that Masterton sold a painting of our family's that"—Mr. Hinckley glanced at Godfrey—"I assume would have raised a considerable sum."

Godfrey nodded. "Anything up to three thousand pounds or even more."

Mr. Hinckley returned his gaze to Jeffers. "We believe that was about three years ago. Yet Masterton is still in debt and apparently needs more cash. Do you have any idea what he did with such a sum?"

"Not as such," Jeffers replied. "But what I can tell you is that Cawley's records show that Masterton paid two and a half thousand off his slate..." Jeffers squinted, clearly trying to remember. "And yes, that was nearly three years ago."

"What the devil does he do with the money?" Harry spread his hands. "He lives in lodgings in Ripon. This isn't London with extravagant prices for everything."

Jeffers smiled faintly. "No, but there are plenty of opportunities to gamble in York—the races, the dens—and both are as bad as anything you'll find farther south." He paused, then looked at Mr. Hinckley. "Cawley's notes on Masterton say he—Masterton—gambles heavily, and he likes to play the part of a well-heeled gentleman, which also runs through money. Cawley's assessment was that Masterton's funds went on the tables, the nags, and on wine, women, and song."

Mr. Hinckley grimaced.

Kemp approached, and Mr. Hinckley waved the butler to present the main course.

Once they'd all been served and had swallowed their first mouthfuls, Mr. Hinckley said, "Looking back, I can see that Masterton was always careful to hide such propensities from me." He glanced at Ellie and her siblings. "From everyone here. As we don't get out much, that wouldn't have been difficult."

"We never met him anywhere but here," Ellie pointed out. "We had no reason to suspect that his true character was different from what we saw."

Godfrey felt protectiveness surge; the Hinckleys—all of them—were so honest and straightforward, it hadn't occurred to them that Masterton wasn't. On a flash of insight, he realized that he didn't want the family—any of them—to change, to lose their faith in transparency, in openness; instead, in the future, he would act as their shield.

He who knew all about deception and deceit; it was as if Fate—not Eastlake—had sent him to Hinckley Hall.

Harry swallowed and frowned. "Speaking of the Albertinelli, one point I don't understand is that Masterton himself was the one to suggest we think of selling it." He appealed to his sisters. "Do you remember?"

Maggie nodded. "He didn't tell us to sell that particular painting, but he suggested that if there was an old one we thought might be valuable and we didn't actually like..." She glanced at her father. "Do you remember, Papa?"

Frowning, clearly racking his memories, Mr. Hinckley slowly nodded. "Yes. You're right. I hadn't thought of selling the Albertinelli until Masterton suggested it."

"How long ago was that?" Jeffers asked.

Harry replied, "About six months ago."

Jeffers nodded. "That coincides with Cawley's attempts to get his debtors to pay back as much as possible before he sold his loan book."

"But," Ellie said, clearly puzzled, "Masterton knew the painting then hanging in Mama's parlor was a forgery. Why on earth draw attention to it?"

Godfrey allowed the footman to remove his empty plate, then glanced up the table. "I can probably answer that. Through stealing and selling the original Albertinelli, Masterton learned how much the painting was worth—which was likely far more than he'd initially imagined. The forgery by Hendall is exceptional—there was a good, even excellent chance that it would pass as the original. Very few in this country would have recognized it as a forgery. If it had sold, then given the amount the family would have gained, I suspect Masterton had hopes of laying hands on at least some of it as a loan. Regardless, if he was already working on his long-term plan of marrying Ellie and gaining control of and subsequently selling the Hall, then from his point of view, your attempt to sell the painting would benefit him either way. If it sold to the gallery, the Hinckley estate would be in much better shape when he eventually got his hands on it—he would just have to find some way other than financial hardship to pressure Ellie to marry him. On the other hand, if the painting was identified as a forgery and the sale didn't go ahead, that would leave the family more financially stretched—in his eyes, more vulnerable—and he would have redoubled his efforts to convince Ellie to marry him with promises of financial rescue."

Harry snorted. "He couldn't have financially rescued a cow barn."

Godfrey tipped his head. "But no one here knew that, and he would have taken great care that you never found out—not until you discovered he'd sold the Hall and, I daresay, vanished."

Jeffers nodded. "That sounds about right. Cawley had a note on file that he believed Masterton had returned to York and Ripon because London got too dangerous for him."

Silence fell. Kemp and the footman reappeared and set out dessert plates, a bowl of rhubarb trifle, a platter of meringues, an apple pie, and a jug of cream. At Ellie's urging, everyone helped themselves, then settled to consume their selections.

The moment of gustatory reflection was broken by Mr. Hinckley. "I suppose," he said, his tone resigned and harsh, "that one doesn't need to ask how the blackguard thought to take control of the estate long enough to sell it." He patted the arm of his chair. "So easy for a man confined to a chair to have an accident."

No one contradicted the statement; the sense of betrayal hung heavy in the air.

Maggie had paled. "Papa, when are we going to decide what to do with Masterton? I don't think any of us"—her gaze swept over those seated at the table and also over Kemp and the footman, standing mum against the wall, silent witnesses to the revelations—"want him in the house."

The forthright assertion—with which no one disagreed—refocused everyone on their next step.

Ellie glanced around the table; everyone was laying down their spoons and napkins. "Perhaps we should continue our discussion in the drawing room."

Her father nodded and pushed back from the table.

Everyone rose. Godfrey once again claimed the handles of her father's chair, and in a group, they quit the dining room.

In the hall, Morris and Pyne exchanged looks, then halted. Obligingly, Godfrey halted her father's chair, and when Ellie stopped alongside, Morris said, "Matthew, you and your family know that Walter and I will support you in whatever you decide to do about Masterton."

"And," Pyne put in, "you don't need to ask if we'll hold our tongues about this—of course we will."

"Indeed. However," Morris continued, "it's late, and as the night is clear, we should both be off home. There's also the fact that Masterton is family, and it might be better for all concerned if Walter and I weren't present—there may be aspects of your deliberations you would prefer to keep strictly within the family."

Her father grimaced. "Sadly, that's true." He held out his hand. "Thank you both. I appreciate your consideration."

Morris, then Pyne, shook her father's hand, then Godfrey's when he offered it. As Kemp came up bearing their coats, Pyne grinned at her father. "You can tell us whatever you wish us to know when we call next week."

With nods to Ellie, the pair donned their coats, wound their scarves about their necks, set their hats on their heads, and when Mike arrived with the news that their carriages were outside, waved and departed.

As Kemp shut the front door, her father huffed and glanced at her. "As I suspect we all agree with Maggie, we'd better get on with it."

They turned toward the drawing room to discover that Jeffers, who had gone ahead with Harry and Maggie, had returned to stand in the doorway.

He tipped his head toward the front door. "I heard what they said, and they're right. It might be best if I took my leave of you as well."

"Actually, Jeffers," her father replied, "if we might impose, I would like you to stay. You have experience of men like Masterton, and while I have no right to ask it, I would appreciate your advice."

Jeffers hesitated, then gracefully half bowed. "I would be happy to provide whatever assistance I may. I admit to feeling somehow complicit in what occurred—my firm does, after all, hold Masterton's IOUs, and it was his need to pay them off that precipitated all this."

"You, sir, are no more to blame than I am," her father declared. He waved Jeffers back into the drawing room. "Now let's sit and discuss what to do with our blackguard."

Godfrey propelled her father's chair into the room and positioned it in his accustomed place, close by the hearth.

Ellie had followed. Harry and Maggie had claimed two of the armchairs and encouraged Jeffers to sit in the one between.

Stepping away from her father's chair, Godfrey joined her. With a slight smile on his lips and a gently challenging look in his hawklike eyes, he appropriated her hand and guided her to sit on the sofa, then sat beside her, openly retaining possession of her hand.

She looked at him, considered drawing her fingers free, then inwardly shrugged and left her hand in his, savoring the reassurance and comfort that flowed from the simple contact.

Thinking of comfort… She looked at Jeffers. "Mr. Jeffers, I assume your horse is presently in our stable?"

He nodded. "I rode over with Masterton. His horse is there, too."

"This house is large, and the road to Kirkby Malzeard will be cold and dark, especially on horseback." She smiled at Jeffers. "I hope, sir, that in the circumstances, we can persuade you to accept our hospitality and remain overnight."

Appreciation flickered in Jeffers's eyes, but he looked at her father.

"My daughter is lady of the house," her father said, "and she's right. And as Lord Godfrey said, had you been another sort of man, today would have ended very differently for our family. You must allow us to show our appreciation and provide whatever comfort we may."

After the barest hesitation, Jeffers inclined his head. "Thank you. You're all very kind. I would be glad to remain overnight."

"Good—that's settled." Her father thumped the arms of his chair. "Now"—both his tone and features hardened—"let's decide what to do about Masterton."

As Godfrey had suspected, Hinckley family decisions—those that affected the entire family—involved the active participation of all four members. From Maggie's extreme view that Masterton should be sent straight to the gallows, to Harry's determination that Masterton should be incarcerated for decades at the very least, to Mr. Hinckley's suggestion of appealing to the local magistrate for advice, each proposal was explored —and all were rejected on the undeniable grounds that Masterton was known to be a cousin of sorts.

Eventually, Jeffers, who, like Godfrey, had listened without comment to the debate, glanced at Maggie and stated the problem clearly. "If the punishment you settle on is likely to become public knowledge, there will inevitably be a scandal—a large one, given this is North Yorkshire and not London—and society being what it is, deserved or not, that scandal will adversely impact the whole family." With his gaze, Jeffers included Mr. Hinckley, Ellie, and Harry, too.

"Sadly," Godfrey said, "Jeffers's point is incontrovertible. Any besmirching of Masterton's character will extend to all of you."

Maggie flung herself back in her chair. "Then what are we to do?"

Harry protested, "We can't just let him go!"

"Not, at least, without some degree of assurance and also retribution." Godfrey looked at Mr. Hinckley. "You are by no means the first family to discover you have a bad apple in your midst. You are not the first to have faced the conundrum of how to punish the guilty party while protecting the innocent from collateral harm. I've been involved in such deliberations before and, if you wish, can make a suggestion."

Mr. Hinckley waved him on. "Please do. There must be some way to resolve this to everyone's satisfaction."

Godfrey wasn't so sure his suggestion would meet with Maggie's or Harry's enthusiastic approval, but as he laid out what he thought was the family's best way forward, he saw consideration flare in Ellie's siblings' eyes.

When he reached the end of his dissertation, everyone remained silent, turning over the prospect in their minds, then Harry said, "My one question is why would he go along with that?"

"One facet of Masterton's character that has struck me," Godfrey said, "is that when faced with a reverse or a hurdle, he immediately makes new plans. He constantly shifts and adjusts, and the only thing one can be sure of is that he's always focused on advancing some plan to lay his hands on money that isn't his."

Jeffers nodded. "I agree—that's how I read his character, both from Cawley's notes and my own observations."

Mr. Hinckley slapped his hands on his knees. "Well, then, I can't see any reason not to put Lord Godfrey's suggestion to the test. Let's have the blackguard in and put our proposal to him, shall we? Are we agreed?"

Ellie nodded, and rather more reluctantly, Harry and Maggie did as well.

"Allow me." Jeffers rose and tugged the bellpull.

Kemp arrived and was dispatched to fetch Masterton.

Mr. Hinckley stroked his chin, then looked at Godfrey. "My lord, would you be willing to lay out our position? I fear that if any of us were to speak, our tempers might get the better of us."

Godfrey felt Ellie's fingers press his in supplication; he stroked her hand with his thumb and inclined his head to her father. "Given the circumstances, I would be honored to act as your mouthpiece, sir."

Harry and Maggie busied themselves seeking out the hardest, most uncomfortable straight-backed chair they could find and set it with its back to the drawing room door, facing the hearth and the horseshoe formed by the chairs occupied by them and the others.

Masterton was duly escorted in, attended by Kemp and two footmen. A bruise was blooming on Masterton's cheekbone, and his clothing was disheveled; clearly, the footmen who had brought him down from the attic had not been inclined to be gentle.

The instant Masterton set eyes on Matthew Hinckley, his face lit, and he hurried forward as fast as his hobbled ankles allowed. "Matthew! There's been some terrible mistake—a misunderstanding—"

"*Silence!*"

Even Godfrey jumped. Glancing at Ellie's, Harry's, and Maggie's wide eyes, he surmised that Matthew Hinckley rarely roared.

Masterton reacted as if he'd been struck. His face blanked and paled, and he halted.

Mr. Hinckley continued in a more restrained but equally awful tone, "To me, sir, you are lower than the low—less than nothing. You forfeited my regard—every last scrap—when you ordered Jeffers to shoot my daughter and Lord Godfrey. You will sit"—Mr. Hinckley jabbed a finger at the hard chair—"and hold your forked tongue and listen to what we have to say to you. You will not speak unless invited to. Is that clear?"

Masterton hesitated, then mutely nodded and, when Mr. Hinckley pointed again at the chair, moved to it and sat. Masterton's wide-eyed gaze stated clearly that he'd never before encountered or even imagined this side of Mr. Hinckley.

Mr. Hinckley signaled to Kemp and the footmen to remain, and they took up positions near the door.

Satisfied, Mr. Hinckley glanced at Godfrey. "Lord Godfrey, if you would?"

Deeming his hopefully soon-to-be father-in-law's tack an excellent one, Godfrey remained seated and turned fractionally, transparently remaining at his elegant ease as he caught Masterton's eyes. "The Hinckleys have concluded that there is no place for you within their family or wider British society." Godfrey glanced at Jeffers, then returned his gaze to Masterton. "You have burned every bridge you ever had. You owe substantial debts you are unable to pay to Jeffers and Thornton, and even more to the Hinckleys themselves. If the firm and the family wished, they could have you clapped in Newgate, quickly and without any fuss, and left there to rot, for as we all now know, you have no capacity whatever to pay the debts you have already incurred."

Godfrey paused to let the threat of Newgate sink in, then went on, "You should be under no illusion that isn't an option strongly favored, and it will be the family's fallback should you fail to agree to their alternative proposal."

Slowly, Masterton blinked, then his gaze focused more intently on Godfrey. "What proposal?"

And there it was; Masterton was already revising his plan.

"The alternative the family have agreed to offer you is banishment."

Masterton blinked again. "But—"

"Under this proposal," Godfrey continued, "you will be taken to Hull, provided with a ticket to Rotterdam, and seen onto the ferry. From Rotterdam, you may go wherever you please with the single proviso that you are never to set foot on British soil again. Should you attempt to do so, you will be taken up by the authorities and conveyed directly to Newgate." He held Masterton's gaze and smiled coldly. "My family are more than powerful enough to ensure that outcome, and once in Newgate, for you, there will be no escape."

Masterton's face was a study of a man thinking rapidly; calculation invested every line.

No one was surprised when he raised his head, looked at Mr. Hinckley, then transferred his gaze to Godfrey and said, "You'll need to provide me with some funds. You can't just"—he gestured with his hands, still bound by the cloth—"toss me penniless onto the Rotterdam docks."

Godfrey smiled even more chillingly. "I assure you we can. There will be no funds, not from the Hinckleys or anyone else. More, you will have only the clothes on your back. You will not be allowed to stop by your lodgings, nor will you be allowed to take your horse or tack on board. You will leave England with nothing but the clothes you stand in and your wits."

Masterton's face had gradually blanked as the reality of what he was being offered sank in.

"Should you agree to these terms," Godfrey continued imperturbably, "you will spend the night in your current quarters beside the scullery. Tomorrow at first light, you will be escorted under guard to Hull, a ticket will be purchased for you, and you will be seen onto the ferry."

Godfrey paused. Until that moment, he hadn't remembered the one element of Masterton's plan that they hadn't been able to deduce. Godfrey glanced at Mr. Hinckley, then at Harry and Maggie, and hoped they would remain as silent yet disapprovingly accusative as they had thus far.

"However," he went on, returning his gaze to Masterton and infusing as much of Ryder's brand of aloof intimidation into his tone as he could, "even that much consideration—banishment rather than Newgate—is conditional on you explaining to the family's satisfaction what you did with the Albertinelli."

Masterton had been gazing at his bound hands; now, he glanced up, his expression distant. He blinked; it seemed likely he'd already been working on his next plan. "What I did..." He humphed. "Cawley was pressing me for money—I had to give him something. He knew I haunted this house, worming my way into Matthew's good graces, so Cawley suggested I look around here and see what was lying about. I remembered the painting was supposed to be by some famous artist, so I checked the signature and went back to Cawley and asked what it might be worth. Cawley arranged all the rest—he got in touch with someone who knew a nobleman who was willing to pay thousands for that particular painting, but he—the nobleman—insisted there be no hue and cry, which suited me, given I had hopes of more from Hinckley Hall. The buyer directed me to Hendall. We arranged for Hendall to come and work in Hull, so when he was ready, I took the painting out through the disused wing and took it to him." Masterton shrugged. "You can guess the rest."

Godfrey asked, "Who was the buyer?"

"A Count Wurtzberg. I never met him. The transaction—the exchange of the original painting for the money—was handled by Hendall."

Godfrey knew of Wurtzberg, more than enough to know Masterton had spoken the truth. His heart sank as all prospect of reclaiming the Albertinelli vanished.

He hid his disappointment and, after a second of reviewing all that had been said, went on, "I believe you owe the Hinckleys the truth of what you had planned for them and Hinckley Hall. We understand your offer to marry Ellie was merely the first step in your plan."

He'd expected some resistance, but it seemed that, in moving on to concoct a new plan, Masterton grew dismissive of his previous failed efforts. The devil shrugged. "It was a fairly obvious ploy. If I could get Ellie to agree to marry me—and she would have if the family's straits grew dire enough that she felt compelled to marry to save the Hall—I would have been in a position to influence Harry and his thinking. Matthew"—Masterton glanced briefly at his cousin, who had believed in his inherent goodness for so long—"is older than he looks. He would have died soon enough. It didn't really matter when, because once I'd married Ellie, any moneylender worth his salt would have understood my plan and waited, knowing they'd eventually get paid."

Before Harry could erupt, Godfrey asked, "How did you think to persuade Harry to sell the Hall?"

Masterton sniffed. "That would have been the easy part—he's not even twenty-one. If I'd married Ellie in the next few years, I would have had years to work on Harry, to make him trust me and believe all I told him. Then, whenever Harry inherited, I would have worked on him to sell the place." Masterton glanced up at the ornate ceiling. "It would have worked, too."

"Sadly, as to that"—Godfrey leveled a stern look at Harry, who appeared to be barely succeeding in keeping his mouth shut—"we will never know."

Still gazing at the ceiling and transparently oblivious to anyone's feelings but his own, Masterton continued, "Once Harry sold up, I would have taken the money and not looked back. I would have been set for life."

His tone suggested that in his imagination, he was viewing a gilded future that had unfortunately slipped from his grasp.

His overweening self-centeredness silenced them all.

Godfrey had followed his instincts in asking Masterton for explanations regarding the Albertinelli and his more recent larger plan. Glancing at the Hinckleys' faces, and at Jeffers's, Godfrey realized Masterton's answers had been important. The family had—each of them—extended a degree of trust to the man, and he had comprehensively betrayed them. None of the Hinckleys, and certainly not Jeffers or Godfrey himself, would feel a shred of regret over Masterton's banishment.

Godfrey refocused on Masterton. "That, I believe, is all we need to know, except for our final question—do you agree to leave England and never return? Or would you rather we convey you directly to Newgate?" When Masterton brought his gaze to Godfrey's face, he arched his brows. "Your choice."

Masterton huffed out a strangled laugh and spat, "Some choice." As if realizing his future wasn't yet settled, he quickly added, "I'll go to Rotterdam."

Godfrey hadn't expected anything else. He signaled to Kemp. "Please return him to the room beside the scullery."

CHAPTER 15

*T*he instant the door shut behind Masterton, Jeffers cleared his throat and said, "As I'll be leaving in the morning myself, I would like to offer to join your men in escorting Masterton to Hull. I know the docks there and will happily purchase his ticket and watch until the ferry is well out to sea with him on it." Jeffers shook his head. "Meeting Masterton has been an education—one that will stand me in good stead in assessing future debtors."

Godfrey smiled appreciatively, as did Ellie.

Mr. Hinckley inclined his head. "Thank you, Mr. Jeffers. If it won't inconvenience you overmuch, I would be relieved to know there was someone with my men who understood the depths of Masterton's duplicity."

"Indeed. I doubt he'll even attempt to cozen me." Jeffers glanced at the Hinckleys—Harry and Maggie as well. "I would also like to assure you that my partner and I will not be pursuing Masterton's debt. We were prepared to deem it a write-off from the first, and so we shall. We wouldn't have pursued him in the first place if we'd had any inkling he would resort to criminal acts to get the funds." Jeffers looked at Godfrey. "I gather you intend to retrieve the painting from that count?"

Godfrey hesitated, but he couldn't not speak. "Sadly, that was a piece of bad news." He met Mr. Hinckley's eyes. "Count Wurtzberg is something of an infamous figure in the art world—he's an avid, avaricious collector with no conscience whatsoever. As he also has strong ties to the

Austrian royal family, it's proved difficult to pursue the many works that are suspected to have vanished into his private collection. Essentially, within Austria, the count is above the law."

Ellie's fingers gripped his, and she swiveled to face him. "So we won't be able to reclaim the Albertinelli?"

He faintly grimaced and squeezed her fingers back. "I'll certainly look into it and see what can be done, but"—he glanced at the other Hinckleys, all now distinctly sober—"I don't want to get your hopes up."

Mr. Hinckley sighed. "What will be, will be." He glanced at his children. "Let's see what tomorrow brings."

With a nod to himself, Mr. Hinckley returned his attention to Jeffers. "Mr. Jeffers, I and my family are indebted to you for your assistance throughout this sorry business, and I regret that you and your partner, through no fault of yours, have become embroiled in my cousin's schemes. While I appreciate your offer to waive Masterton's debt, I'm afraid we cannot accept it—for good or ill, Masterton was a member of this family, and leaving such a debt unpaid would be a stain on the family's honor. I believe you said the sum involved was just over one thousand pounds. I will hold myself responsible for repaying it, if you and Mr. Thornton will let me know the full sum."

Jeffers opened his mouth, then closed it. He glanced at Ellie, Harry, and Maggie, but their serious expressions gave him no encouragement to argue. Nevertheless, he ventured, "That's very kind of you, sir, but it's really not necessary."

Mr. Hinckley widened his eyes. "But surely your firm requires capital to continue to operate as a legitimate and respectable bank?"

Jeffers shifted. "Well, yes, obviously we would prefer to get the funds in, but in this particular instance, we'll manage."

Godfrey decided he quite liked Jeffers.

Mr. Hinckley shook his head. "Young man, you must see that I cannot countenance leaving such a debt unpaid."

Godfrey wasn't surprised by Mr. Hinckley's stance; indeed, he'd expected it. "If I might make another suggestion?"

When Jeffers and the Hinckleys looked his way, he directed his query to all four Hinckleys. "Do you value the ugly cherub you use as a doorstop in the dining room?" When they all blinked, he clarified, "Are you fond of it? Do you have any sentimental attachment to it? Does it mean anything or represent anything important to you?"

Harry frowned. "No. As you say, it's ugly."

Mr. Hinckley humphed. "We use it as a doorstop because it's ugly and we have no other use for it."

Ellie and Maggie nodded.

"In that case"—Godfrey looked at Harry—"perhaps you might fetch it?"

Harry gave him an odd look, but stood and left the room. He was back in less than a minute, carrying the cherub.

Just over a foot tall, on a base of perhaps five inches square, the marble cherub stood with one hand resting on a short column. Its round bald head, exaggeratedly rounded features, and cupid-bow lips, instead of giving it a benevolent air, made it look faintly menacing.

Harry halted before Godfrey and held out the statue. "Ghastly thing."

Godfrey took it in his hands. He turned it this way and that, examining the lines and searching out the tiny etching he knew would be there, confirming it was, indeed, what he'd suspected. Reassured on that point, he smiled, then he looked at the Hinckleys before turning his gaze on Jeffers.

"This"—Godfrey hefted the statue—"is a sculpture by Pietro Lombardo, created sometime around 1500." He looked at Mr. Hinckley. "If you and your family have no use for it, I suggest you give it to Jeffers." He looked at Jeffers. "And I will give you a formal declaration as to its authenticity, along with a letter of introduction to a gentleman in London, who will happily give you at least twelve hundred pounds for it, and if I were you, I'd haggle for more." Godfrey looked at the cherub. "Indeed, at auction, this piece could fetch as much as two thousand pounds."

Jeffers stared, then looked at Mr. Hinckley. "Are you sure? The debt is only just over a thousand."

Mr. Hinckley looked at his children, then returned his gaze to Jeffers. "If you're willing to take the statue as payment of Masterton's debt, then we would be very pleased to settle in this way."

Godfrey grinned, rose, and held out the statue.

Jeffers rose, too, and took the cherub from Godfrey's hands. Jeffers raised the statue, studying it, then looked at the Hinckleys and grinned. "It is ugly, isn't it?"

Everyone laughed—the first laugh any of them had uttered since going up to the old attic.

Jeffers settled the statue in the crook of his arm and turned to Mr.

Hinckley. "With your permission, sir, I'll retire. We'll need to start early tomorrow if we're to get Masterton on the evening ferry."

"Indeed, sir." Mr. Hinckley held out a hand, and Jeffers shook it. "The Hinckleys are in your debt."

Jeffers smiled. "Actually"—he juggled the statue—"I believe the shoe is on the other foot." He looked around at them all. "Thank you—all of you."

Godfrey offered his hand. "It's been interesting, Jeffers."

Jeffers grinned and shook his hand. "A good way to put it." Proving he was an observant man, Jeffers glanced at Ellie, then arched a brow at Godfrey. "I take it I might see you around these parts in the future."

Godfrey tried to school his features to impassivity, but his smile refused to fade. "Very likely." He clapped Jeffers on the shoulder. "I'll leave the declaration of authenticity and the letter of introduction on the table in the front hall."

Jeffers made his farewells to the Hinckley siblings, and Ellie summoned Kemp to show him to his room.

Once the door closed behind Jeffers, Ellie sighed with relief and rising happiness. She turned to Godfrey, but her father beat her to it.

"Thank you, Lord Godfrey." As Ellie and her siblings and Godfrey resumed their seats, her father continued, "Your help throughout this trying time has been invaluable. Indeed, had you not been here, I don't know how we would have managed—if we would have avoided Masterton's snares. As for the Albertinelli..."

Ellie watched her father's gaze grow distant, then he sighed. "It was my Henrietta's favorite, and I'm sad to know it's gone, but I suppose we have the forgery to remind us of it—as you say, it's a very good replica." Her father returned his gaze to Godfrey, who had once again taken Ellie's hand, but from where her father was positioned, he couldn't see that. Her father went on, "From your comments earlier, I take it you hold out little hope of reclaiming the painting."

Godfrey dipped his head. "I'm happy to make the attempt, but the count is not known for bowing to pressure from other countries to return stolen artworks."

Her father grunted. "In that case, I see no point in asking you to further waste your time. Now the roads are clear and our painting has proved to be a forgery and we've learned that the original is out of reach, I daresay you'll be keen to head back to London."

"As to that, sir..."

Alerted by the suppressed excitement in Godfrey's voice, Ellie glanced at him.

He flashed her a smile, then looked at her father. "You might have lost the Albertinelli—although with your permission, I will see what can be done about that—yet rather ironically thanks to Masterton luring me up to your old attic, I've discovered you own four other canvases that I suspect are of equal and possibly even greater value."

Ellie blinked.

Godfrey looked at Harry and Maggie. "Those four paintings we left in the library. Could you fetch them, please?"

Faces lighting, Harry and Maggie leapt to their feet and hurried out.

Godfrey looked at Ellie, then at her father. "I've only seen one of the four. The other three were turned to the wall, but judging by the frames, I'm hopeful they will all be of similar ilk."

Harry shouldered open the door and came in, carrying two of the paintings; he paused to hold open the door, allowing Maggie to enter with the other two.

Godfrey rose and lifted and lined up two side tables before the chair Masterton had previously occupied. "Let's lean them along here."

Ellie watched, intrigued, as Godfrey took each painting and briefly studied it before setting it on the floor in front of the tables, facing them all as Harry and Maggie resumed their seats.

Godfrey remained standing to one side of the line of frames. He pointed to the first. "This is the one that was facing outward, so I've had a little time to study it." His gaze on the painting, he drew in a deep breath —as if he was holding in welling, geysering excitement. When he spoke, his voice sounded slightly strained. "I can't be certain, not without examining it in better light and verifying all the necessary criteria, but I feel..." His tone lowered to one approaching reverence. "I'm almost certain it's a Titian. Not just from Titian's studio—there are quite a few paintings by his students—but from the hand of the master himself."

With the rest of her family, Ellie stared at the canvas. It depicted two rather voluptuous women, partially unclothed, in what she took to be a garden setting.

"That one, alone, is close to priceless." Godfrey pointed to the next painting. "And then there's this one, which is almost certainly a Botticelli. His work is relatively easy to recognize. And this one, I think, is a Correggio, while this"—he pointed to the last of the four paintings—"is, I believe, by del Sarto."

The supposed Titian and the Botticelli both featured scantily clad females, while the Correggio and the del Sarto were portraits of men and rather dark and dreary. The frames of all four paintings were richly ornate and, even after all these years, obviously originally gilt. Given that Ellie's grandparents and her great-grandparents before them had been staunch Calvinists, it wasn't hard to see why the paintings had been relegated to the attic.

Godfrey had remained standing, staring at the paintings. "In all honesty, finding four paintings of that time moldering in an attic isn't that surprising. Our ancestors—especially those of the older families—collected paintings when on their Grand Tours. It was almost an expected part of that rite of passage throughout the seventeen hundreds. But subsequent generations didn't appreciate the style of such artworks, so consigned them to attics or got rid of them." He glanced at her father, then at Harry, Maggie, and finally Ellie herself, and smiled. "You are all inestimably lucky that your more-recent ancestors had an attic to which to dispatch these and that the attic is still in decent state, with no damp or rodents or rot." He looked back at the paintings, and Ellie could hear the awe as well as the excitement in his tone as he said, "But most of all, you are unbelievably lucky that your old Uncle Henry had such excellent taste!"

They'd all heard and been infected by Godfrey's rising enthusiasm. Harry leaned forward on the edge of his seat to better study the paintings. "So you're saying that these are...what? More valuable than the Albertinelli?"

Godfrey nodded. "Any one would be worth at least as much as the Albertinelli, and the Titian and the Botticelli—assuming my judgment is sound and that's what they truly are—are worth much, much more."

The next ten minutes went in excited chatter as they peered at the paintings and asked questions, and Godfrey answered in scholarly style.

Eventually, they sat back and, still stunned by their good fortune, stared at each other.

"Well!" Maggie grinned widely. "What an amazing end to an exciting day."

Smiling, Ellie nodded.

Her father tapped his fingers on the arm of his chair. "Lord Godfrey." When Godfrey, still standing, swung around and, smiling as much as any of them, looked at her father, he went on, "I'm not au fait with how such matters are arranged, but would you be willing to act for the family in selling one or possibly two of these?"

Godfrey hesitated, then glanced at Ellie, a question in his eyes.

She felt her smile deepen and nodded. It was time.

Godfrey straightened and faced her father. "Sir, I would be honored to act for your family, but you need to know that…" He paused and held out his hand to Ellie. She took it and rose to stand by his side. Together, they faced her father as Godfrey continued, "I've asked Ellie to do me the honor of becoming my wife, and—"

"And," she cut in, unable to hold back a beaming smile, "I've agreed."

Her father sat back in his chair. His gaze scanned her face.

Ellie beamed and hoped he could see what was in her heart.

Her father's lips slowly lifted, his expression lightening as he took in her happiness.

Godfrey tightened his grip on her hand. "Ellie and I hope you will give us your blessing, sir."

Beaming now, her father studied them. "My daughter has finally made her choice, and I'm delighted—nay, thrilled—that she has found a gentleman such as you in which to place her trust." He inclined his head to them. "You most definitely have my blessing."

"Thank you, Papa." Before Ellie could move to her father, Maggie squealed and flung herself into Ellie's arms.

"I say! That's great news." Harry seized Godfrey's hand and pumped it. He met Godfrey's eyes and earnestly stated, "I know you'll take good care of Ellie."

"I intend to," Godfrey replied. *Of Ellie and all the Hinckleys.*

He moved to Mr. Hinckley and grasped the hand the older man offered. "Your daughter is a pearl beyond price, sir. I will always treasure her."

Mr. Hinckley nodded. "See that you do—but in truth, I have no doubt about that. For all you appreciate paintings, you're one who understands that beauty reaches much deeper than the skin."

Godfrey dipped his head in acknowledgment as his gaze returned to his bride-to-be.

Ellie finally managed to disengage from Maggie and Harry and bent to hug her father. "Thank you again, Papa. You won't regret it."

"Of course I won't!" He patted her shoulder. "You're obviously happy, and that's all I ask."

Beaming radiantly, Ellie straightened and looked at Godfrey—and he couldn't help but beam back.

As he reclaimed her hand, Mr. Hinckley harrumphed. "Now then, what are your plans?"

They all sat again and, with the fabulous paintings quite forgotten, excitedly discussed the when and where of Godfrey and Ellie's wedding.

At Mr. Hinckley's suggestion, Harry rang for Kemp, and Mr. Hinckley informed that worthy of the family's glad tidings and dispatched him to unearth a bottle of champagne from the cellar.

Kemp duly returned bearing the staff's good wishes as well as a bottle and glasses. Soon, the others were toasting Godfrey and Ellie, then Godfrey made everyone laugh by proposing a toast to old Uncle Henry. "Because, when all is said and done, it was his eye for a good painting all those years ago that led to me coming to Hinckley Hall."

They all raised their glasses, cheered, and drank.

Godfrey caught Ellie's eye and raised his glass to her in a silent toast. Then he relaxed beside her and looked at the others—at their smiling, now-slightly-flushed faces and their transparent happiness and joy. Clasping Ellie's hand, he raised it to his lips and kissed her fingers. "Thank you, my love, for bringing me this—for giving me this family." He met her eyes and quietly stated, "This is what life's truly about."

That night, Godfrey and Ellie were the last to head upstairs.

Earlier, he had written the promised documents for Jeffers and left them as arranged on the hall table, then with Ellie pacing alongside, had pushed her father to his rooms on the ground floor, where his manservant had been waiting to assist him.

Now as, hand in hand, he and Ellie left the darkened front hall and, guided by the single lamp left burning on the landing, climbed the stairs, Godfrey looked within himself and found nothing but peace and contentment.

I'm happy—truly happy.

At the head of the stairs, when he would have turned toward his room, Ellie tugged, and when he halted and arched his brows at her, she smiled and led him in a different direction.

Curious, eager, he let her tow him through the gallery and down a corridor, let her draw him into a room that was redolent with the subtle perfume he associated with her.

The curtains had been drawn against the chilly night. A lamp stood softly glowing on a table by the wall and, together with the small fire burning in the grate, endeavored to cast a golden light over the room.

It was into that light that she led him—into that welcoming warmth. Then she turned and drew him into her arms, and he finally knew what it felt like to come home.

Stepping into her embrace, he bent his head as she stretched up, and they kissed—unhurriedly sinking into the moment and savoring it. Savoring the sense of embarking together on a voyage to a destination both familiar and desired.

Metaphorically hand in hand with her, he reached for that, along the way acknowledging the slow but steady escalation of their hunger, the welling expectation of fulfillment, and the turbulent stirring of their passions. Yet tonight, he sensed a change—a sharper edge to passion, an extra bite to need, both his and hers.

Compelled, he angled his head and deepened the kiss, and she framed his face, met his questing tongue with hers, and urged him on.

Then her hands were pushing his coat off his shoulders.

His fingers found the buttons closing the back of her gown and deftly undid them.

In a flurry of increasingly heated kisses and frantic, grasping hands, they stripped the layers from each other until only skin remained.

Wrapped in each other's arms, they tumbled onto her bed, rumpling the covers, then urgently, blindly, pushing them aside. And suddenly, going fast wasn't enough. Didn't promise satiation enough.

Drawing on every ounce of expertise he possessed, he caught their flapping reins and hauled. He rolled her onto her back, wrenched away from the all-consuming mating of their mouths, bent his head, and set his lips to her breast.

She stilled, panting. Waiting.

He closed his lips about one turgid peak and suckled, and she arched beneath him.

Ellie's eyes were wide, yet she was blind—oblivious to everything but the sensations that welled and washed through her, evoked by his touch, sure and true, and by the scorchingly hot caresses of his lips and tongue. Scintillating, exhilarating, galvanizing—the thrills streaked down her veins to stoke the fluid heat welling at her core.

He paid due homage to her breasts, and all she could do was wallow in the moment, in the glorious realm of passion and desire to which he had taken her.

Then he skated lower, savoring her silken skin, tracing the indentation of her waist; her whirling awareness tracked his touch as he explored each dip and hollow with lips and tongue. Meanwhile, his hands boldly sculpted her curves, until, driven beyond passivity, she shifted restlessly, moaned, and sank her nails into his shoulders.

He hummed in wordless response, then set about methodically working his way farther down her body. She wasn't sure whether to sigh in delight or gasp in expectation when he parted her thighs, wedged his shoulders between, and set his mouth to her slick softness.

At the first lick, she writhed. When he suckled, she panted and sank her fingers into his hair.

Godfrey gave no quarter. Pleasure flooded him at the taste of her nectar on his tongue, and her responses, wordless, incoherent, yet clear in their demand, impelled him to push her on—to make her writhe and gasp and clutch at his hair, before he sent her flying on her first foray into paradise.

As the last of her tremors faded, with her fractured breathing filling his ears, he raised his head and looked up the length of her body, then rose still farther to drink in the full sight of her with the aftermath of ecstasy still stamped on her features.

His gaze locked on her face, pleasure-ravaged beauty personified, and something moved inside him, like a seed unfurling under the sun. That she was his sun came as no surprise, but as that new growth thrust up— powerful, resilient, enduring—the façade the years had sealed over his heart cracked and fell away.

And emotion erupted, pure and powerful.

Struck by the force of it, with his wits and senses reeling, he couldn't breathe. He closed his eyes and tried to contain the maelstrom, tried to push down the raging tide of *feelings* swirling, unrestrained, through him, but the emotions he'd earlier corralled and locked away had broken loose and now demanded, commanded...

He opened his eyes and found her watching him, as if she could sense the turmoil inside him.

Then she sat up and reached for him, and he seized her and clung.

He drew her close, then shifted so he could clutch her still tighter and buried his face in her hair. "I thought I'd lost you." His voice was gruff and guttural, the words dragged from his depths. "In that instant, when you dashed across and the shot rang out... It felt as if my world was *just about to end.*"

Trapped against him, she huffed, her breath a heated gust across his chest. "So you understand how I felt." She pulled back enough to look into his eyes. "You know why I had to try—why I had to save you."

Some part of him raged *No, you didn't!* Yet looking into her eyes, he saw the same power that gripped him and couldn't look away. He couldn't deny his truth or hers.

He released her so he could raise his hands and frame her face—so he could look into her eyes, into her soul, and see all he felt mirrored there. "I knew I loved you—that I had fallen in love with you—but until that moment, I didn't realize... I had no clue what being in love really meant. Until that moment, I didn't understand what love truly was—what a force it was, how powerful and compelling, how undeniable and irresistible it could be." He paused, then acknowledged, "That it could—and would—control me."

She searched his eyes. "And now?"

"And now, I know." He looked inside and saw the whole truth. "And I wouldn't have it any other way."

Her smile lit the room. It was all he could see.

Ellie freed her arms and, dislodging his grip on her face, reached for his—so she could anchor herself and her giddy, whirling wits. "I love you. I fell in love with you..." She bit her lip, then confessed, "Virtually at first sight."

He blinked. "When I staggered into the front hall and swooned at your feet?"

Her smile couldn't get any wider. "Yes, then. I tried to tell myself my feelings were purely due to your survival and recovery being so important to the family, but my concern owed little to that. And through all that followed, you steadily gained in my estimation—you gained my respect, my trust, as well as my senses' admiration."

He smiled, but while his lovely hawklike eyes were clear, his gaze remained intent. After a second, it switched to the bandage on her arm, which he'd been careful not to jar. He raised a hand and oh-so-lightly skimmed his palm over the linen band. "When I saw you shot—wounded while protecting me—while a large part of me raged and reacted, another part recognized what your actions meant." His gaze returned to her eyes.

"That you loved me with the same depth and breadth—the same intensity—with which I had come to love you."

He held her gaze and drew in a tight breath. "You are my heart, my sun—my life. Without you, I will shrivel and die. I will happily—joyously—spend the rest of my days loving, protecting, and caring for you." He faintly smiled and shook his head—more, she sensed, at himself than at her. "It's impossible, now, for me to even contemplate any other life."

Unwaveringly, she held his gaze and let her smile reflect every last iota of her feelings. "I had never felt love—the type of love a woman feels for a man—until I met you. Know that, whatever you feel, I feel the same, too."

A slow grin softened his face. He caught one of her hands and carried it to his lips. "We're a matched pair. Just as well we're getting married."

She laughed, wrapped her arms about his neck, and tipped backward. He allowed her to topple them onto the bed. Back into an engagement informed by their desires and fueled by their passions, yet now, with the power that bound them acknowledged and embraced, that earlier sharp edge, that extra bite, had transformed into an irresistible heat that sent exhilaration and anticipation swirling higher and lent an extra dimension to every physical thrill, making each more exquisite.

She gasped and clung and tipped back her head, trying to find air to assuage her tight lungs as their combined passions, unrestrained, rolled through her, through him, and rendered them both mindless.

Mindless with hunger, each for the other.

Desperately seeking the sharpest thrill, the pinnacle of pleasure each could gift the other.

They rolled across the sheets, heated and wanting.

Desire turned ravenous and raked them with claws honed by need.

Until they joined and the power surged and filled them, and the sense of togetherness drew in as intimacy—true intimacy with no screens, no reservations, no barriers of any sort—unfurled, gripped, and in the inferno of their passions, forged them into one.

One in thought, one in deed, one in their drive to reach the beckoning peak and seize their due.

One in every way that counted, linked by so much more than passion and desire.

They strove for completion, to reach and claim the ultimate prize.

Then, abruptly, they were there, caught all but simultaneously in that rapturous instant of scintillating sensation and expanded awareness as her climax called on his.

Hearts pounding, eyes open, gazes locked, they clung suspended for a single heartbeat.

Then they shattered.

Fractured into shards of light and heat and all-encompassing incandescent glory.

As one, they rode the wave until it faded and left them adrift, clinging to each other on oblivion's sea.

Together, as they were meant to be.

EPILOGUE

$\mathcal{T}$hey were married on the twenty-third of March, when daffodils and jonquils nodded in brilliant yellow-and-white drifts beneath the greening trees of the park at Hinckley Hall.

Godfrey and Ellie had originally thought to hold the ceremony in the old chapel of the Hall, but the number of locals who had known the Hinckleys for generations and Ellie all her life and would therefore wish to attend rendered the chapel impractical. They'd happily settled for the even more ancient St. Andrew's in Kirkby Malzeard to the delight of all the villagers and surrounding farm families, who, on the day, had turned out to cheer the bride on her way and stare wide-eyed and take note of and whisper about all the latest fashions displayed by the London nobs who rolled past in their elegant carriages.

That one of their own was marrying into a noble family was seen by all as a cause for celebration.

The ceremony passed off without a hitch, which was no surprise to Godfrey given that Mary, Felicia, Sylvia, and Stacie, and their respective spouses and children, had arrived at the Hall over a week before, and together with Ellie, the ladies had taken the entire enterprise in hand.

As Ellie had remarked to Godfrey, "By marrying you, it seems I've gained the older sisters I never had."

Godfrey had grinned. "You've given me your family—it's only fair I return the favor."

Shortly after they'd announced their engagement, Ryder's wife, Mary, had convened a family gathering at Raventhorne Abbey to welcome Ellie to the Cavanaugh clan. Godfrey had taken Ellie to meet his brothers and their wives and children. Ellie's initial trepidation had lasted all of a minute. That was how long it had taken before Sylvia had unceremoniously thrust her youngest, Gilly, into Ellie's arms so Sylvia could separate her sparring sons, Manfred and Jordan, who had reached the stage of rolling around on the hall tiles in the otherwise august foyer of the abbey. With thirteen children in residence, most under ten years of age, the abbey had rung with shouts, shrieks, and laughter, making all the adults, the staff included, smile indulgently. With chubby little Gilly in her arms, the not-yet-one-year-old girl-child tugging at Ellie's hair, Ellie had caught Godfrey's eyes, grinned, and relaxed.

In short order, she'd been embraced by the group; by dinnertime, she'd been entirely at ease.

Godfrey suspected his sister, Stacie, had conspired with Mary over Ellie's wedding gown. A stylish confection in soft ivory satin and Brussels lace, the gown set off Ellie's neat figure, delicate complexion, and golden-brown hair to perfection; in the gown, to Godfrey's eyes, she glowed like the pearl she was—priceless. The sight of her as she'd walked down the aisle toward him would forever remain seared in his memory.

In all honesty, he couldn't remember all that much of the actual ceremony; he'd been too busy riding the wave of happiness that having Ellie beside him—with her hand in his and with the knowledge that they were together and soon would be man and wife, acknowledged before God and all their world—sent surging through him.

What had followed after they'd each said "I do" had passed in a haze of joy.

Now, at the wedding breakfast in the Hall's ballroom, resplendent with decorations of spring-green leaves and yellow and white flowers, echoing the palette outside, with the meal devoured and the speeches done, Godfrey paraded with Ellie on his arm, trying to keep his pride within bounds while introducing her to the surprisingly large contingent of Cavanaugh relatives and connections who had happily made the trek to North Yorkshire. Given that number included many of the haut ton and several grandes dames, such as Mary's mother, Lady Louise Cynster, and Stacie's mother-in-law, the Dowager Marchioness of Albury, he remained alert, uncertain how Ellie would cope with such personages or, indeed, they her. As they paused to chat with each knot of guests, the protectiveness that had awakened at his first sight of Ellie and that subsequently had become an intrinsic part of him remained vigilant, ready to step in and defend her if need be, but everyone was as delighted to meet her and warmly congratulate them as he could wish. It seemed their marriage was universally welcomed.

From various comments he overheard, he suspected he had Mary and Stacie to thank for that unanimous benediction; it sounded as if his powerful sister-in-law and his sister had put it about that they'd been hugely relieved at the news of his engagement as they'd started to fear he would never wed.

As far as Godfrey knew, such an assertion was a huge exaggeration, but there was no doubt that Mary's and Stacie's transparently genuine embracing of Ellie as his bride had effectively silenced any tempted to be mean-spirited about a mature lady from a provincial gentry family snaring one of the haut ton's most-eligible partis.

He and Ellie had just excused themselves from another group of elders and turned to move on when a line of laughing, cheering children came snaking through the milling crowd. Led by Godfrey's oldest nephew, Ryder and Mary's eldest son, Lord Robert, Viscount Linton, a strapping twelve-year-old, the line circled Godfrey and Ellie, then many gentle but insistent small hands and bodies urged them toward the area opening up on the dance floor.

Laughing themselves, Godfrey and Ellie consented to be herded along.

"Here they are, Mama!" Robert called, then the children melted into the crowd, leaving Godfrey and Ellie at the edge of an expanse surrounded by their loved ones and friends.

The musicians set bow to string.

Godfrey smiled at Ellie, bowed, and held out a hand. "Might I have this dance, Lady Cavanaugh?"

Ellie laughed, sank into a curtsy, and set her hand in his. "Indeed, my lord, you may."

He grasped her fingers. Their eyes met and held as she rose and stepped close, and he slid his arm about her waist, raised her hand, and drew her to him, into the dance.

They whirled, and the rest of the world fell away. Lost in each other's eyes, for those few moments, for him and for her, only the other existed.

Just the two of them, wrapped in a cocoon of contentment, of peace and quiet joy.

This was their new reality, and they grasped that instant to savor all it was and all it would be.

Sounds and movement as the others in the bridal party joined them drew them from their absorption, then other guests thronged the floor, and laughter and conversation abounded.

At the end of the wedding waltz, with Ellie, Godfrey escaped to the side of the room where long windows looked out over a section of the park. He lifted two glasses of champagne from the tray Mike, the footman —beaming fit to split his face—offered. Thanking Mike with a smile, Godfrey handed one glass to Ellie and sampled the other.

Ellie sipped and sighed, then surveyed the guests. "This has been"— she glanced mischievously at him—"the best wedding I've ever attended."

He grinned. "It's the best wedding I've ever attended as well, and I suspect I've been to many more than you."

She huffed, but smiling, didn't disagree.

Godfrey found his gaze drawn to the vista outside. "I'm dying to explore the park thoroughly." When the snows had finally melted, he'd found a large sculpture he thought was by an Italian master. He'd since learned that the park was extensive and "all sorts of bits and pieces" were scattered through it. "The Hall is an intriguing place."

One they'd agreed to live in, at least until Harry gained his majority; after that, they would see.

Thinking of Ellie's brother, who Godfrey had insisted be one of his groomsmen along with Ryder, Rand, and Kit, Godfrey turned back to the crowd in the ballroom and scanned the heads. He spotted Harry chatting with Carter Cynster, a cousin of Mary's and a budding artist whose path Godfrey frequently crossed. Carter was only a year or two older than Harry, but possessed infinitely more worldly experience. Despite that, the two had clearly found common ground.

"What do you imagine they're talking about so avidly?"

Godfrey glanced at Ellie and saw her staring in the same direction. He looked again at the two young men, at the gestures both were making. "At a guess, I'd say hunting or shooting. Carter's home is in the Scottish Lowlands, so there's likely similar game there."

He looked again at the park—at the transformation spring had wrought—then glanced around the room, at Harry, at Mr. Hinckley in his chair, part of a large circle of friends and connections that included Godfrey's brothers. Looking farther, Godfrey noted Kemp and the staff, all beaming as they ferried around trays of tea and cakes. At the last, he found Maggie chatting with a group of local young ladies while sliding surreptitious glances at Carter Cynster.

Godfrey hid a faintly cynical smile; Maggie might be dreaming, but at least she had good taste.

She was also thoroughly happy, almost as radiant as Ellie. Being Ellie's principal bridesmaid and shouldering the duties Mary, Stacie, Felicia, and Sylvia had coached Maggie in had transformed Maggie, too. She was no longer so wildly coltish—or at least that side of her had been tempered by a newfound appreciation of the world beyond the Hall. Maggie was now looking forward to spending the upcoming Season with her aunt, Lady Camberford; with Mary and Stacie insisting on acting as pseudo-aunts as well, Godfrey felt certain Maggie would have an amazing Season.

"What are you thinking?"

Godfrey glanced at Ellie and found himself the focus of a faintly intrigued gaze. He glanced once more around the room. "I was just thinking that your family—your father, Harry, and Maggie—and the staff here as well, seem to have…" Not quite sure of what he wished to say, he gestured.

"Turned some sort of corner?"

He nodded. "Yes—as if our wedding has signaled a new dawn, somewhat like spring after winter." He met her eyes. "Is it fanciful or vain to think that our marriage has, at least in part, been a catalyst for that?"

She studied his eyes, then gently smiling, shook her head. "I would say that our marriage is the much-desired culmination stemming from the critical incident that enabled everyone here to change—to embrace a fresh outlook on life." Her smile deepened, and on his arm, she leaned closer. "In case you're wondering, that critical incident was you arriving at the Hall."

When he opened his mouth to gainsay that, she pressed her fingers to his lips. "When I was waiting for you to arrive, I had a vision of you as a knight on a white charger, and so you proved to be. You swept in and protected us and steered us through a difficult time to this"—she glanced fleetingly around—"this happiness, this splendor. And I'm not the only one to think so. I heard Papa say that he owed the National Gallery and your Mr. Eastlake his heartfelt thanks for sending you to us."

A warm glow swelled in Godfrey's chest. His eyes on hers, he mouthed against her fingers, "Thank you. There is nothing so wonderful as feeling needed and appreciated as well."

When she smiled and lowered her hand, he went on, "But as to thanks, perhaps we all owe our ultimate thanks to your old Uncle Henry. Without his farsightedness, none of this would have occurred."

Ellie laughed and raised her glass, and Godfrey raised his, and they clinked the rims. "To old Uncle Henry," they chorused and drank.

Surveying the joyful crowd gathered to celebrate their nuptials, Ellie was struck—again—by the sense of inclusion, of being embraced into a large, noisy, rambunctious, supportive, and protective family. She hadn't spoken lightly when she'd named Mary, Felicia, Sylvia, and Stacie—her new sisters-in-law—as the sisters she'd never had. There'd been an instant bonding, an immediate recognition of having the same values, the same fundamental aspirations and aims. And out of that, faster than she would have imagined possible, had grown trust of the sort she'd previously thought took years of shared experience to forge.

She had that now, a strong and stalwart group of ladies at her back. With their support, she felt she could face the world—even the haut ton— and weather any and all challenges the future might hold.

She looked across the room—at the painting that Mary and the others had insisted be given pride of place above the mantel of the large fireplace halfway down the long room. Carter Cynster was presently standing before it; judging by his gestures, he was lecturing a trio of older ladies on the painting's finer points.

"I still find it difficult to take in that Ryder and Mary managed to persuade Count Wurtzberg to return the Albertinelli."

Godfrey chuckled. "While I'm sure Ryder was appropriately intimidating, it was undoubtedly Mary who carried the day. Once she learned that the count doted on his daughter and was exercised about her chances of making a good match, she knew exactly on what front to mount her campaign."

Mary had induced the count to do the right thing and return the Albertinelli to the Hinckleys in return for seeing his daughter make her come-out next year in the heart of London's haut ton, under the Marchioness of Raventhorne's wing. Apparently, for an Austrian count, that was a coup of no mean standing.

Ellie grinned. "If I hadn't met Mary, I would wonder why you use military terms to describe how she thinks."

Godfrey huffed. "She's a Cynster by birth. There's a certain streak of ruthlessness that runs through them all. But don't think I'm complaining. With the return of the Albertinelli and your father and Eastlake confirming its sale to the gallery, along with the del Sarto, not only are the directors in alt, but so is Eastlake." Godfrey grinned at the memory of his recent meeting with that august gentleman. "Frankly, finding all those paintings at Hinckley Hall has made my name."

"*Confirmed* your name," Ellie insisted. "Eastlake already knew enough to trust you."

The crowd before them parted, and Sylvia walked through, arm in arm with her husband, Kit, the Cavanaugh brother closest in age to Godfrey. The couple were followed by Rand and Felicia—Godfrey's elder brother and his wife. Mary and Stacie—languidly trailed by their husbands, Ryder and Frederick—were flitting about, sharing the hostess's duties; Ellie had been sternly informed that it was not acceptable for a bride to act as hostess at her own wedding breakfast.

"We wondered," Kit said, as the three couples formed a loose circle, "whether you had any plans for a wedding trip?"

Ellie glanced at Godfrey. They'd discussed the prospect at length. She smiled and nodded.

After setting their empty glasses on a passing footman's tray, Godfrey caught her hand and twined her arm with his. "We thought," he said, "to wait until after the Season, then sail to Italy. It's been a few years since I visited the galleries there, and I want to show them to Ellie."

"Damn!" Kit lightly punched Rand's arm. "Why is it you always win?"

Rand chuckled. "I know how to calculate the odds." To the others, all of whom looked mystified, he explained, "We had a wager going—I plumped for Italy, while Kit insisted you'd choose France, Stacie said Spain, and Ryder thought Germany."

Godfrey laughed. "We might well visit all those places"—he met Ellie's eyes—"eventually. But spending summer in a villa overlooking the Mediterranean sounded just perfect for now."

Smiling back, Ellie lightly squeezed his arm. They'd agreed on that with no real argument.

"Hmm." Felicia slid a look at Rand. "That does sound appealing. You'll have to tell us all about it when you get back."

Rand frowned. "Italy is a long way from London."

"That," Felicia tartly informed him, "is entirely my point."

The others all laughed, and Godfrey and Kit proceeded to rib Rand over his habit of growing overly engrossed in the latest inventions and investment opportunities arising therefrom.

Other guests came to join them, and gradually, the group broke up.

When a few minutes later, Ellie and Godfrey moved on, she was still marveling at how very much at ease she felt with everyone there—not just the neighbors she'd known all her life but also the members of the haut ton, many of whom she hadn't previously met.

She glanced at Godfrey, and when he caught her eyes and arched an interrogatory brow, she smiled and confessed, "I never expected to feel like this—to be the woman, the lady, you've made me." She sobered a fraction, then went on, "I never expected to find myself walking arm in arm with...a man who understands me. With a gentleman—a noble lord, no less—a partner who completes me and whom I, in turn, complete."

Godfrey felt his inner glow swell as her words resonated with his own feelings. Lowering his shields, he looked into her eyes and let her see his unwavering agreement as he lifted her hand and carried her fingers to his lips. "Yes." He brushed a kiss to her fingers. "That's precisely it. You and I were meant to be a couple. We complement each other so that, together, we are more, much more, than either of us could ever be alone."

Holding her gaze, he pressed another kiss to her fingers. "We are who we are, and you're mine, and I'm yours."

The smile that lit her face was one of radiant joy.

Making a mental note to do whatever was required to see that smile as often as possible throughout the rest of his life, he lightly squeezed her fingers and, lowering her hand, laid it on his sleeve as, together, they turned to face the room. For her ears alone, he murmured, "And our future is *ours* to shape."

Ellie laughed, and they walked on, more than ready to embrace their new life, more than content to embrace the love they'd found and, together, hearts, minds, and souls as one, set out on life's greatest adventure.

She looked about—saw her family, friends, neighbors, saw her newly acquired family and all their connections. She swept her gaze around, taking in the ballroom, so festive and bright after being shut up for decades. She noted the staff, all bright-eyed and brimming with enthusiasm and an underlying hope.

The hope for a future they felt confident would come.

She glanced at Godfrey, let her gaze linger briefly—lovingly—on his chiseled profile.

This man.

He'd saved her family and her home, had given both a sound and stable future filled with possibilities. He'd opened doors for her siblings and opened their eyes to wider horizons as well.

He was selfless in giving to her and to them.

Yet she didn't feel indebted to him. Throughout the past weeks, through talking with her new sisters-in-law and his brothers, she'd come to understand that she and her family and even Hinckley Hall itself had given him something he'd truly craved. The basis for a real family. His own family. Not just those already here but all who might yet come.

Between them, the scales were balanced.

As, with a smile on her lips, she moved with him into the crowd of guests still wishing to fête them and their union, she couldn't find better words than those he'd used months earlier to sum up the entirety of what they both, in their hearts, believed.

Family is what life is truly about.

That sentiment said it all, and she was as eager as he to see where it led them.

Dear Reader,

As the youngest of the Cavanaugh siblings, Godfrey's tale was always going to be a bit different. With his half brother, two older two brothers, and his sister now all wed and happily engaged with their own growing families, it seemed clear that Godfrey would approach the issue of marriage for himself in a rather more relaxed way. I couldn't see him being all that concerned with marriage one way or the other. In contrast, he would, I felt sure, feel a certain pressure to make his own mark in the world, to carve out his own niche. I had a lovely time researching the National Gallery and its interests in those times, and also delving into the world of the High Renaissance painters and their artworks – until I could understand Godfrey's obsession with the field!

Devising the reason behind Godfrey's visit to Hinckley Hall in deepest Yorkshire, and all that came next, Godfrey falling into Ellie Hinckley's life and finding his connection to a family of his own, and the rising of his protective instincts in defending the Hinckleys against an unknown villain and the consequences, skullduggery and all, was great fun.

I hope you enjoyed reading of Godfrey and Ellie's journey into love, marriage, and happiness.

And so, we've reached the final chapter in The Cavanaughs. From the time Ryder Cavanaugh walked onto my page in the opening scene of *The Taming of Ryder Cavanaugh*, and brought his siblings in his wake, I knew I would have to write about them, too. The chance to craft the stories of a group of siblings holding together to survive a dreadful family situation and coming about to each find love and happiness and a real purpose in life was simply too compelling to resist.

To round out my releases for this year, the fourth volume of Lady Osbaldestone's Christmas Chronicles, *Lady Osbaldestone's Christmas Intrigue*, will be released on October 15, 2020 for you to enjoy in the lead-up to Christmas.

As ever, I wish you continued happy reading!

Stephanie.

For alerts as new books are released, plus information on upcoming books, exclusive sweepstakes and sneak peeks into upcoming novels, sign up for Stephanie's Private Email Newsletter http://www.stephanielaurens. com/newsletter-signup/

Or if you don't have time to chat and want a quick email alert, sign up and follow me at BookBub https://www.bookbub.com/authors/stephanie-laurens

The ultimate source for detailed information on all Stephanie's published books, including covers, descriptions, and excerpts, is Stephanie's Website www.stephanielaurens.com

You can also follow Stephanie via her Amazon Author Page at http://tinyurl.com/zc3e9mp

Goodreads members can follow Stephanie via her author page https://www.goodreads.com/author/show/9241.Stephanie_Laurens

You can email Stephanie at stephanie@stephanielaurens.com

COMING NEXT:

**The fourth instalment in LADY OSBALDESTONE'S CHRISTMAS CHRONICLES
LADY OSBALDESTONE'S CHRISTMAS INTRIGUE
To be released on October 15, 2020.**

#1 New York Times *bestselling author Stephanie Laurens immerses you in the simple joys of a long-ago country-village Christmas, featuring a grandmother, her grandchildren, her unwed son, a determined not-so-young lady, foreign diplomats, undercover guards, and agents of Napoleon!*

At Hartington Manor in the village of Little Moseley, Therese, Lady Osbaldestone, and her household are once again enjoying the company of her intrepid grandchildren, Jamie, George, and Lottie, when they are unexpectedly joined by her ladyship's youngest and still-unwed son, also the children's favorite uncle, Christopher.

As the Foreign Office's master intelligencer, Christopher's been ordered into hiding until the department can appropriately deal with the French agent spotted following him in London. Christopher chose to seek refuge in Little Moseley because it's such a tiny village that anyone without a reason to be there stands out. Neither he nor his office-appointed bodyguard expect to encounter any dramas.

Then Christopher spots a lady from London he believes has been hunting him with matrimonial intent. He can't understand how she tracked him to the village, but determined to avoid her, he enlists the children's help. The children discover their information-gathering skills are in high demand, and while engaging with the villagers as they usually do and taking part in the village's traditional events, they do their best to learn what Miss Marion Sewell is up to.

But upon reflection, Christopher realizes it's unlikely the Marion he was so attracted to years before has changed all that much, and he starts to wonder if what she wants to tell him is actually something he might want to hear. Unfortunately, he has set wheels in motion that are not easy to redirect. Although Marion tries to approach him several times, he and she fail to make contact.

Then just when it seems they will finally connect, a dangerous stranger lures Marion away. Fearing the worst, Christopher gives chase— followed by his bodyguard, the children, and a small troop of helpful younger gentlemen.

What they discover at nearby Parteger Hall is not at all what anyone expected, and as the action unfolds, the assembled company band together to protect a secret vital to the resolution of the war against Napoleon.

Fourth in series. A novel of 81,000 words. A Christmas tale of intrigue, personal evolution, and love.

Preorders available by August, 2020

RECENTLY RELEASED:

THE INEVITABLE FALL OF CHRISTOPHER CYNSTER
Cynster Next Generation Novel #8

#1 New York Times *bestselling author Stephanie Laurens returns to the Cynsters' next generation with a rollicking tale of smugglers, counterfeit banknotes, and two people falling in love.*

A gentleman hoping to avoid falling in love and a lady who believes love has passed her by are flung together in a race to unravel a plot that threatens to undermine the realm.

Christopher Cynster has finally accepted that to have the life he wants, he needs a wife, but before he can even think of searching for the right lady, he's drawn into an investigation into the distribution of counterfeit banknotes.

London born and bred, Ellen Martingale is battling to preserve the fiction that her much-loved uncle, Christopher's neighbor, still has his wits about him, but Christopher's questions regarding nearby Goffard Hall trigger her suspicions. As her younger brother attends card parties at the Hall, she feels compelled to investigate.

While Ellen appears to be the sort of frippery female Christopher abhors, he quickly learns that, in her case, appearances are deceiving. And through the twists and turns in an investigation that grows ever more serious and urgent, he discovers how easy it is to fall in love, while Ellen learns that love hasn't, after all, passed her by.

But then the villain steps from the shadows, and love's strengths and vulnerabilities are put to the test—just as Christopher has always feared. Will he pass muster? Can they triumph? Or will they lose all they've so recently found?

A historical romance with a dash of intrigue, set in rural Kent. A Cynster Next Generation novel—a full-length historical romance of 124,000 words.

And if you haven't already indulged:
PREVIOUS VOLUMES IN THE CAVANAUGHS

The first volume in THE CAVANAUGHS
THE DESIGNS OF LORD RANDOLPH CAVANAUGH

#1 New York Times bestselling author Stephanie Laurens returns with a new series that captures the simmering desires and intrigues of early Victorians as only she can. Ryder Cavanaugh's step-siblings are determined to make their own marks in London society. Seeking fortune and passion, THE CAVANAUGHS will delight readers with their bold exploits.

An independent nobleman
Lord Randolph Cavanaugh is loyal and devoted—but only to family. To the rest of the world he's aloof and untouchable, a respected and driven entrepreneur. But Rand yearns for more in life, and when he travels to Buckinghamshire to review a recent investment, he discovers a passionate woman who will challenge his rigid self-control...

A determined lady
Felicia Throgmorton intends to keep her family afloat. For decades, her father was consumed by his inventions and now, months after his death, with their finances in ruins, her brother insists on continuing their father's tinkering. Felicia is desperate to hold together what's left of the estate.

Then she discovers she must help persuade their latest investor that her father's follies are a risk worth taking...

Together—the perfect team
Rand arrives at Throgmorton Hall to discover the invention on which he's staked his reputation has exploded, the inventor is not who he expected, and a fiercely intelligent woman now holds the key to his future success. But unflinching courage in the face of dismaying hurdles is a trait they share, and Rand and Felicia are forced to act together against ruthless foes to protect everything they hold dear.

The second volume in THE CAVANAUGHS
THE PURSUITS OF LORD KIT CAVANAUGH

Bold and clever, THE CAVANAUGHS are unlike any other family in early Victorian England. #1 New York Times bestselling author Stephanie Laurens continues to explore the enthralling world of these dynamic siblings in the eagerly anticipated second volume in her captivating series.

A gentleman of means
One of the most eligible bachelors in London, Lord Christopher "Kit" Cavanaugh has discovered his true path and it doesn't include the expected society marriage. Kit is all business and has chosen the bustling port of Bristol to launch his passion--Cavanaugh Yachts.

A woman of character
Miss Sylvia Buckleberry's passion is her school for impoverished children. When a new business venture forces the school out of its building, she must act quickly. But confronting Kit Cavanaugh is a daunting task made even more difficult by their first and only previous meeting, when, believing she'd never see him again, she'd treated him dismissively. Still, Sylvia is determined to be persuasive.

An unstoppable duo
But it quickly becomes clear there are others who want the school--and Cavanaugh Yachts--closed. Working side by side, Kit and Sylvia fight to secure her school and to expose the blackguard trying to sabotage his

business. Yet an even more dastardly villain lurks, one who threatens the future both discover they now hold dear.

The third volume in THE CAVANAUGHS
THE BEGUILEMENT OF LADY EUSTACIA CAVANAUGH

#1 New York Times *bestselling author Stephanie Laurens continues the bold tales of the Cavanaugh siblings as the sole Cavanaugh sister discovers that love truly does conquer all.*

A lady with a passion for music and the maestro she challenges in pursuit of a worthy cause find themselves battling villains both past and present as they fight to secure life's greatest rewards—love, marriage, and family.

Stacie—Lady Eustacia Cavanaugh—is adamant marriage is not for her. Haunted by her parents' unhappy union, Stacie believes that, for her, marriage is an unacceptable risk. Wealthy and well-born, she needs for nothing, and with marriage off the table, to give her life purpose, she embarks on a plan to further the careers of emerging local musicians by introducing them to the ton via a series of musical evenings.

Yet despite her noble status, Stacie requires a musical lure to tempt the haut ton to her events, and in the elevated circles she inhabits, only one musician commands sufficient cachet—the reclusive and notoriously reluctant Marquess of Albury.

Frederick, Marquess of Albury, has fashioned a life for himself as a musical scholar, one he pursues largely out of sight of the ton. He might be renowned as a virtuoso on the pianoforte, yet he sees no reason to endure the smothering over-attentiveness of society. Then his mother inveigles him into meeting Stacie, and the challenge she lays before him is...tempting. On a number of fronts. Enough for him not to immediately refuse her.

A dance of subtle persuasion ensues, and step by step, Frederick finds himself convinced that Stacie's plan has real merit and that it behooves him to support her. At least for one event.

Stacie's first musical evening, featuring Frederick as the principal performer, is a massive success—until Fate takes a hand and lands them in a situation that forces them both to reassess.

Does Frederick want more than the sterile, academic life he'd thought was for him?

Can Stacie overcome her deepest fears and own to and reach for her girlhood dreams?

Impulsive, arrogant, and used to getting his own way, Frederick finds his answer easily enough, but his new direction puts him on a collision course with Stacie's fears. Luckily, he thrives on challenges—which is just as well, because in addition to convincing Stacie that love can, indeed, conquer all, he and she must unravel the mystery of who is behind a spate of murderous attacks before the villain succeeds in eliminating all hope of a happy ending.

A classical historical romance set in London and Surrey, in the heart of the ton. Third novel in The Cavanaughs—a full-length historical romance of 122,000 words.

ALSO AVAILABLE:

The first volume in Lady Osbaldestone's Christmas Chronicles
LADY OSBALDESTONE'S CHRISTMAS GOOSE

#1 New York Times *bestselling author Stephanie Laurens brings you a lighthearted tale of Christmas long ago with a grandmother and three of her grandchildren, one lost soul, a lady driven to distraction, a recalcitrant donkey, and a flock of determined geese.*

Three years after being widowed, Therese, Lady Osbaldestone finally settles into her dower property of Hartington Manor in the village of Little Moseley in Hampshire. She is in two minds as to whether life in the small village will generate sufficient interest to keep her amused over the months when she is not in London or visiting friends around the country. But she will see.

It's December, 1810, and Therese is looking forward to her usual Christmas with her family at Winslow Abbey, her youngest daughter, Celia's home. But then a carriage rolls up and disgorges Celia's three oldest children. Their father has contracted mumps, and their mother has sent the three—Jamie, George, and Lottie—to spend this Christmas with their grandmama in Little Moseley.

Therese has never had to manage small children, not even her own. She assumes the children will keep themselves amused, but quickly learns that what amuses three inquisitive, curious, and confident youngsters isn't compatible with village peace. Just when it seems she will have to set her mind to inventing something, she and the children learn that with only twelve days to go before Christmas, the village flock of geese has vanished.

Every household in the village is now missing the centerpiece of their Christmas feast. But how could an entire flock go missing without the slightest trace? The children are as mystified and as curious as Therese—and she seizes on the mystery as the perfect distraction for the three children as well as herself.

But while searching for the geese, she and her three helpers stumble on two locals who, it is clear, are in dire need of assistance in sorting out their lives. Never one to shy from a little matchmaking, Therese undertakes to guide Miss Eugenia Fitzgibbon into the arms of the determinedly reclusive Lord Longfellow. To her considerable surprise, she discovers that her grandchildren have inherited skills and talents from both her late husband as well as herself. And with all the customary village events held in the lead up to Christmas, she and her three helpers have opportunities galore in which to subtly nudge and steer.

Yet while their matchmaking appears to be succeeding, neither they nor anyone else have found so much as a feather from the village's geese. Larceny is ruled out; a flock of that size could not have been taken from the area without someone noticing. So where could the birds be? And with the days passing and Christmas inexorably approaching, will they find the blasted birds in time?

First in series. A novel of 60,000 words. A Christmas tale of romance and geese.

The second volume in Lady Osbaldestone's Christmas Chronicles
LADY OSBALDESTONE AND THE MISSING CHRISTMAS CAROLS

#1 New York Times *bestselling author Stephanie Laurens brings you a heart-warming tale of a long-ago country-village Christmas, a grandmother, three eager grandchildren, one moody teenage granddaughter, an earnest young lady, a gentleman in hiding, and an elusive book of Christmas carols.*

Therese, Lady Osbaldestone, and her household are quietly delighted when her younger daughter's three children, Jamie, George, and Lottie, insist on returning to Therese's house, Hartington Manor in the village Little Moseley, to spend the three weeks leading up to Christmas participating in the village's traditional events.

Then out of the blue, one of Therese's older granddaughters, Melissa, arrives on the doorstep. Her mother, Therese's older daughter, begs Therese to take Melissa in until the family gathering at Christmas—otherwise, Melissa has nowhere else to go.

Despite having no experience dealing with moody, reticent teenagers like Melissa, Therese welcomes Melissa warmly. The younger children are happy to include their cousin in their plans—and despite her initial aloofness, Melissa discovers she's not too old to enjoy the simple delights of a village Christmas.

The previous year, Therese learned the trick to keeping her unexpected guests out of mischief. She casts around and discovers that the new organist, who plays superbly, has a strange failing. He requires the written music in front of him before he can play a piece, and the church's book of Christmas carols has gone missing.

Therese immediately volunteers the services of her grandchildren, who are only too happy to fling themselves into the search to find the missing book of carols. Its disappearance threatens one of the village's most-valued Christmas traditions—the Carol Service—yet as the book has always been freely loaned within the village, no one imagines that it won't be found with a little application.

But as Therese's intrepid four follow the trail of the book from house to house, the mystery of where the book has vanished to only deepens. Then the organist hears the children singing and invites them to form a special guest choir. The children love singing, and provided they find the book in time, they'll be able to put on an extra-special service for the village.

While the urgency and their desire to finding the missing book escalates, the children—being Therese's grandchildren—get distracted by the potential for romance that buds, burgeons, and blooms before them.

Yet as Christmas nears, the questions remain: Will the four unravel the twisted trail of the missing book in time to save the village's Carol Service? And will they succeed in nudging the organist and the harpist they've found to play alongside him into seizing the happy-ever-after that hovers before the pair's noses?

Second in series. A novel of 62,000 words. A Christmas tale full of music and romance.

The third volume in LADY OSBALDESTONE'S CHRISTMAS CHRONICLES
LADY OSBALDESTONE'S PLUM PUDDINGS

#1 New York Times bestselling author Stephanie Laurens brings you the delights of a long-ago country-village Christmas, featuring a grandmother, her grandchildren, an artifact hunter, the lady who catches his eye, and three ancient coins that draw them all together in a Christmas treasure hunt.

Therese, Lady Osbaldestone, and her household again welcome her younger daughter's children, Jamie, George, and Lottie, plus their cousins Melissa and Mandy, all of whom have insisted on spending the three weeks prior to Christmas at Therese's house, Hartington Manor, in the village of Little Moseley.

The children are looking forward to the village's traditional events, and this year, Therese has arranged a new distraction—the plum puddings she and her staff are making for the entire village. But while cleaning the coins donated as the puddings' good-luck tokens, the children discover that three aren't coins of the realm. When consulted, Reverend Colebatch summons a friend, an archeological scholar from Oxford, who confirms the coins are Roman, raising the possibility of a Roman treasure buried somewhere near. Unfortunately, Professor Webster is facing a deadline and cannot assist in the search, but along with his niece Honor, he will stay in the village, writing, remaining available for consultation should the children and their helpers uncover more treasure.

It soon becomes clear that discovering the source of the coins—or even which villager donated them—isn't a straightforward matter. Then the children come across a personable gentleman who knows a great deal about Roman antiquities. He introduces himself as Callum Harris, and they agree to allow him to help, and he gets their search back on track.

But while the manor five, assisted by the gentlemen from Fulsom Hall, scour the village for who had the coins and search the countryside for signs of excavation and Harris combs through the village's country-house libraries, amassing evidence of a Roman compound somewhere near, the site from which the coins actually came remains a frustrating mystery.

Then Therese recognizes Harris, who is more than he's pretending to be. She also notes the romance burgeoning between Harris and Honor Webster, and given the girl doesn't know Harris's full name, let alone his fraught relationship with her uncle, Therese steps in. But while she can engineer a successful resolution to one romance-of-the-season, as well a reconciliation long overdue, another romance that strikes much closer to home is beyond her ability to manipulate.

Meanwhile, the search for the source of the coins goes on, but time is running out. Will Therese's grandchildren and their Fulsom Hall helpers locate the Roman merchant's villa Harris is sure lies near before they all must leave the village for Christmas with their families?

Third in series. A novel of 70,000 words. A Christmas tale of antiquities, reconciliation, romance, and requited love.

ABOUT THE AUTHOR

#1 *New York Times* bestselling author Stephanie Laurens began writing romances as an escape from the dry world of professional science. Her hobby quickly became a career when her first novel was accepted for publication, and with entirely becoming alacrity, she gave up writing about facts in favor of writing fiction.

All Laurens's works to date are historical romances, ranging from medieval times to the mid-1800s, and her settings range from Scotland to India. The majority of her works are set in the period of the British Regency. Laurens has published over 75 works of historical romance, including 40 *New York Times* bestsellers. Laurens has sold more than 20 million print, audio, and e-books globally. All her works are continuously available in print and e-book formats in English worldwide, and have been translated into many other languages. An international bestseller, among other accolades, Laurens has received the Romance Writers of America® prestigious RITA® Award for Best Romance Novella 2008 for *The Fall of Rogue Gerrard.*

Laurens's continuing novels featuring the Cynster family are widely regarded as classics of the historical romance genre. Other series include the *Bastion Club Novels*, the *Black Cobra Quartet*, the *Adventurers Quartet,* and the *Casebook of Barnaby Adair Novels.*

For information on all published novels and on upcoming releases and updates on novels yet to come, visit Stephanie's website: www.stephanielaurens.com

To sign up for Stephanie's Email Newsletter (a private list) for heads-up alerts as new books are released, exclusive sneak peeks into upcoming books, and exclusive sweepstakes contests, follow the prompts at http://www.stephanielaurens.com/newsletter-signup/

To follow Stephanie on BookBub, head to her BookBub Author Page: https://www.bookbub.com/authors/stephanie-laurens

Stephanie lives with her husband and a goofy black labradoodle in the hills outside Melbourne, Australia. When she isn't writing, she's reading, and if she isn't reading, she'll be tending her garden.

www.stephanielaurens.com
stephanie@stephanielaurens.com

CPSIA information can be obtained
at www.ICGtesting.com
Printed in the USA
LVHW021948190720
661082LV00013B/2224

9 781925 559255